THE END OF IT ALL

And Other Stories

AN ED GORMAN BIBLIOGRAPHY

Jack Dwyer series:
New Improved Murder (1985)
Murder Straight Up (1986)
Murder in the Wings (1986)
The Autumn Dead (1987)
A Cry of Shadows (1990)

Tobin Series:
Murder in the Aisle (1987)
Several Deaths Later (1988)

Jack Walsh Series:
The Night Remembers (1991)

Robert Payne Series:
Blood Moon (1994;
as Blood Red Moon, UK (1994)
Hawk Moon (1995)
Harlot's Moon (1998)
Voodoo Moon (2000)

Sam McCain Series:
The Day the Music Died (1999)
Will You Still Love Me Tomorrow (2000)
Wake Up Little Susie (2001)
Save the Last Dance for Me (2002)
Everybody's Somebody's Fool (2004)

Non-Series:
Rough Cut 1985
Grave's Retreat (1989)
What the Dead Men Say (1990)
Cage of Night (1992)
Daughter of Darkness (1997)
Rituals (1998)

Short Story Collections:
Prisoners and Other Stories (1992)
Dark Whispers (1993)
Cages (1995)
Moonchasers (1996)
Famous Blue Raincoat (1999)
Such a Good Girl (2001)
The Dark Fantastic (2001)
The Long Silence After (2001)
Different Kinds of Dead (2006)
Out There In the Darkness (2007)
The Moving Coffin (2007)
The End of It All (2009)

As E.J. Gorman:
The Marilyn Tapes (1993)
The First Lady (1995)
Senatorial Privilege (1997)

THE END
OF IT ALL

And Other Stories

by

Ed Gorman

RAMBLE HOUSE

ISBN 13: 978-1-60543-354-7

ISBN 10: 1-60543-354-3

Ramble House Edition: 2009
Cover Art: Gavin L. O'Keefe
Preparation: Fender Tucker

To Marty Greenberg
the world's number one anthologist
and all-around great guy

THE END OF IT ALL
and Other Stories

THE END OF IT ALL

And Other Stories

OUT THERE IN THE DARKNESS

1

The night it all started, the whole strange spiral, we were having our usual midweek poker game—four fortyish men who work in the financial business getting together for beer and bawdy jokes and straight poker. No wild card games. We hate them.

This was summer, and vacation time, and so it happened that the game was held two weeks in a row at my house. Jan had taken the kids to see her Aunt Wendy and Uncle Verne at their fishing cabin, and so I offered to have the game at my house this week, too. With nobody there to supervise, the beer could be laced with a little bourbon, and the jokes could get even bawdier. With the wife and kids in the house, you're always at least a little bit intimidated.

Mike and Bob came together, bearing gifts, which in this case meant the kind of sexy magazines our wives did not want in the house in case the kids might stumble across them. At least that's what they say. I think they sense, and rightly, that the magazines might give their spouses bad ideas about taking the secretary out for a few after-work drinks, or stopping by a singles bar some night.

We got the chips and cards set up at the table, we got the first beers open (Mike chasing a shot of bourbon with his beer), and we started passing the dirty magazines around with tenth-grade glee. The magazines compensated, I suppose, for the balding head, the bloating belly, the stooping shoulders. Deep in the heart of every hundred-year-old man is a horny fourteen-year-old boy.

All this, by the way, took place up in the attic. The four of us got to know each other when we all moved into what city planners called a "transitional neighborhood." There were some grand old houses that could be renovated with enough money and real care. The city designated a ten-square-block area as one it wanted to restore to shiny new luster. Jan and I chose a crumbling Victorian. You wouldn't recognize it today. And that includes the attic, which I've turned into a very nice den.

"Pisses me off," Mike O'Brien said. "He's always late."

And that was true. Neil Solomon *was* always late. Never by that much but always late nonetheless.

"At least tonight he has a good excuse," Bob Genter said.

"He does?" Mike said. "He's probably swimming in his pool." Neil recently got a bonus that made him the first owner of a full-size outdoor pool in our neighborhood.

"No, he's got Patrol. But he's stopping at nine. He's got somebody trading with him for next week."

"Oh, hell," Mike said, obviously sorry that he'd complained. "I didn't know that."

Bob Genter's handsome black head nodded solemnly.

Patrol is something we all take very seriously in this newly restored "transitional neighborhood." Eight months ago, the burglaries started, and they'd gotten pretty bad. My house had been burglarized once and vandalized once. Bob and Mike had had curb-sitting cars stolen. Neil's wife, Sheila, was surprised in her own kitchen by a burglar. And then there was the killing four months ago, man and wife who'd just moved into the neighborhood, savagely stabbed to death in their own bed. The police caught the guy a few days later trying to cash some of the traveler's checks he'd stolen after killing his prey. He was typical of the kind of man who infested this neighborhood after sundown: a twentyish junkie stoned to the point of psychosis on various street drugs, and not at all averse to murdering people he envied and despised. He also knew a whole hell of a lot about fooling burglar alarms.

After the murders there was a neighborhood meeting and that's when we came up with the Patrol, something somebody'd read about being popular back East. People think that a nice middle-sized Midwestern city like ours doesn't have major crime problems. I invite them to walk many of these streets after dark. They'll quickly be disabused of that notion. Anyway, the Patrol worked this way: each night, two neighborhood people got in the family van and patrolled the ten-block area that had been restored. If they saw anything suspicious, they used their cellular phones and called the police. We jokingly called it the Baby Boomer Brigade. The Patrol had one strict rule: you were never to take direct action unless somebody's life was at stake. Always, always use the cellular phone and call the police.

Neil had Patrol tonight. He'd be rolling in here in another half hour. The Patrol had two shifts: early, 8:00-10:00; late, 10:00-12:00.

Bob said, "You hear what Evans suggested?"

"About guns?" I said.

"Yeah."

"Makes me a little nervous," I said.

"Me, too," Bob said. For somebody who'd grown up in the worst area of the city, Bob Genter was a very polished guy. Whenever he joked that he was the token black, Neil always countered with the fact that he was the token Jew, just as Mike was the token Catholic, and I was the token Methodist. We were friends of convenience, I suppose, but we all really did like each other, something that was demonstrated when Neil had a cancer scare a few years back. Bob, Mike and I were in his hospital room twice a day, all eight days running.

"I think it's time," Mike said. "The bad guys have guns, so the good guys should have guns."

"The good guys are the cops," I said. "Not us."

"People start bringing guns on Patrol," Bob said, "somebody innocent is going to get shot."

"So some night one of us here is on Patrol and we see a bad guy and he sees us and before the cops get there, the bad guy shoots us? You don't think that's going to happen?"

"It *could* happen, Mike," I said. "But I just don't think that justifies carrying guns."

The argument gave us something to do while we waited for Neil.

~ ~ ~ ~ ~

"Sorry I'm late," Neil Solomon said after he followed me up to the attic and came inside.

"We already drank all the beer," Mike O'Brien said loudly.

Neil smiled. "That gut you're carrying lately, I can believe that *you* drank all the beer."

Mike always enjoyed being put down by Neil, possibly because most people were a bit intimidated by him—he had that angry Irish edge—and he seemed to enjoy Neil's skilled and fearless handling of him. He laughed with real pleasure.

Neil sat down, I got him a beer from the tiny fridge I keep up here, cards were dealt, seven card stud was played.

Bob said, "How'd Patrol go tonight?"

Neil shrugged. "No problems."

"I still say we should carry guns," Mike said.

"You're not going to believe this but I agree with you," Neil said.

"Seriously?" Mike said.

"Oh, great," I said to Bob Genter, "another beer-commercial cowboy."

Bob smiled. "Where I come from we didn't have cowboys, we had 'mothas.'" He laughed. "Mean mothas, let me tell you. And practically *all* of them carried guns."

"That mean you're siding with them?" I said.

Bob looked at his cards again then shrugged. "Haven't decided yet, I guess."

I didn't think the antigun people were going to lose this round. But I worried about the round after it, a few months down the line when the subject of carrying guns came up again. All the TV coverage violence gets in this city, people are more and more developing a siege mentality.

"Play cards," Mike said, "and leave the debate society crap till later."

Good idea.

We played cards.

In forty-five minutes, I lost $63.82. Mike and Neil always played as if their lives were at stake. All you had to do was watch their faces. Gunfighters couldn't have looked more serious or determined.

The first pit stop came just after ten o'clock and Neil took it. There was a john on the second floor between the bedrooms, and another john on the first floor.

Neil said, "The good Doctor Gottesfeld had to give me a fingerwave this afternoon, gents, so this may take a while."

"You should trade that prostate of yours in for a new one," Mike said.

"Believe me, I'd like to."

While Neil was gone, the three of us started talking about the Patrol again, and whether we should go armed.

We made the same old arguments. The passion was gone. We were just marking time waiting for Neil and we knew it.

Finally, Mike said, "Let me see some of those magazines again."

"You got some identification?" I said.

"I'll show you some identification," Mike said.

"Spare me," I said, "I'll just give you the magazines."

"You mind if I use the john on the first floor?" Bob said.

"Yeah, it would really piss me off," I said.

"Really?"

That was one thing about Bob. He always fell for deadpan humor.

"No, not 'really,'" I said. "Why would I care if you used the john on the first floor?"

He grinned. "Thought maybe they were segregated facilities or something."

He left.

Mike said, "We're lucky, you know that?"

"You mean me and you?"

"Yeah."

"Lucky how?"

"Those two guys. They're great guys. I wish I had them at work." He shook his head. "Treacherous bastards. That's all I'm around all day long."

"No offense, but I'll bet you can be pretty treacherous yourself."

He smiled. "Look who's talking."

The first time I heard it, I thought it was some kind of animal noise from outside, a dog or a cat in some kind of discomfort maybe. Mike, who was dealing himself a hand of solitaire, didn't even look up from his cards.

But the second time I heard the sound, Mike and I both looked up. And then we heard the exploding sound of breaking glass.

"What the hell is that?" Mike said.

"Let's go find out."

Just about the time we reached the bottom of the attic steps, we saw Neil coming out of the second-floor john. "You hear that?"

"Sure as hell did," I said.

We reached the staircase leading to the first floor. Everything was dark. Mike reached for the light switch but I brushed his hand away.

I put a *ssshing* finger to my lips and then showed him that Louisville Slugger I'd grabbed from Tim's room. He's my nine-year-old and his most devout wish is to be a good baseball player. His mother has convinced him that just because I went to college on a baseball scholarship, I was a good player. I wasn't. I was a lucky player.

I led the way downstairs, keeping the bat ready at all times.

"You sonofabitch!"

The voice belonged to Bob.

More smashing glass.

I listened to the passage of the sound. Kitchen. Had to be the kitchen.

In the shadowy light from the street, I saw their faces, Mike and Neil's. They looked scared.

I hefted the bat some more and then started moving fast to the kitchen.

Just as we passed through the dining room, I heard something heavy hit the kitchen floor. Something human and heavy.

I got the kitchen light on.

He was at the back door. White. Tall. Blond shoulder-length hair. Filthy tan T-shirt. Greasy jeans. He had grabbed one of Jan's carving knives from the huge iron rack that sits atop the butcher-block island. The one curious thing about him was the eyes: there was a malevolent iridescence to the blue pupils, an angry but somehow alien intelligence, a silver glow.

Bob was sprawled facedown on the tile floor. His arms were spread wide on either side of him. He didn't seem to be moving. Chunks and fragments of glass were strewn everywhere across the floor. My uninvited guest had smashed two or three of the colorful pitchers we'd bought the winter before in Mexico.

"Run!" the burglar cried to somebody on the back porch.

He turned, waving the butcher knife back and forth to keep us at bay.

Footsteps out the back door.

The burglar held us off a few more moments but then I gave him a little bit of tempered Louisville Slugger wood right across the wrist. The knife went clattering.

By this time, Mike and Neil were pretty crazed. They jumped him, hurled him back against the door, and then started putting in punches wherever they'd fit.

"Hey!" I said, and tossed Neil the bat. "Just hold this. If he makes a move, open up his head. Otherwise leave him alone."

They really were crazed, like pit bulls who'd been pulled back just as a fight was starting to get good.

"Mike, call the cops and tell them to send a car."

I got Bob up and walking. I took him into the bathroom and sat him down on the toilet lid. I found a lump the size of an egg on the back of his head. I soaked a clean washcloth with cold water and pressed it against the lump. Bob took it from there.

"You want an ambulance?" I said.

"An ambulance? Are you kidding? You must think I'm a ballet dancer or something."

I shook my head. "No, I know better than that. I've got a male cousin who's a ballet dancer and he's one tough sonofabitch, believe me. You—" I smiled. "You aren't that tough, Bob."

"I don't need an ambulance. I'm fine."

He winced and tamped the rag tighter against his head. "Just a little headache is all." He looked young suddenly, the aftershock of fear in his brown eyes. "Scared the hell out of me. Heard something when I was leaving the john. Went out to the kitchen to check it out. He jumped me."

"What'd he hit you with?"

"No idea."

"I'll go get you some whiskey. Just sit tight."

"I love sitting in bathrooms, man."

I laughed. "I don't blame you."

When I got back to the kitchen, they were gone. All three of them. Then I saw the basement door. It stood open a few inches. I could see dusty light in the space between door and frame. The basement was our wilderness. We hadn't had the time or money to really fix it up yet. We were counting on this year's Christmas bonus from the Windsor Financial Group to help us set it right.

I went down the stairs. The basement is one big, mostly unused room except for the washer and drier in the corner. All the boxes and odds and ends that should have gone to the attic instead went down here. It smells damp most of the time. The idea is to turn it into a family room for when the boys are older. These days it's mostly inhabited by stray waterbugs.

When I reached the bottom step, I saw them. There are four metal support poles in the basement, near each corner. They had him lashed to a pole in the east quadrant, lashed his wrists behind him with rope found in the tool room. They also had him gagged with what looked like a pillowcase. His eyes were big and wide. He looked scared and I didn't blame him. I was scared, too.

"What the hell are you guys doing?"

"Just calm down, Papa Bear," Mike said. That's his name for me whenever he wants to convey to people that I'm kind of this old fuddy-duddy. It so happens that Mike is two years older than I am and it also happens that I'm not a fuddy-duddy. Jan has assured me of that, and she's completely impartial.

"Knock off the Papa Bear bullshit. Did you call the cops?"

"Not yet," Neil said. "Just calm down a little, all right?"

"You haven't called the cops. You've got some guy tied up and gagged in my basement. You haven't even asked how Bob is. And you want me to calm down."

Mike came up to me, then. He still had that air of pit-bull craziness about him, frantic, uncontrollable, alien.

"We're going to do what the cops *can't* do, man," he said. "We're going to sweat this son of a bitch. We're going to make him tell us who he was with tonight, and then we're going to make him give us every single name of every single bad guy who works this neighborhood. And then we'll turn all the names over to the cops."

"It's just an extension of the Patrol," Neil said. "Just keeping our neighborhood safe is all."

"You guys are nuts," I said, and turned back toward the steps. "I'm going up and calling the cops."

That's when I realized just how crazed Mike was. "You aren't going anywhere, man. You're going to stay here and help us break this bastard down. You're going to do your goddamned neighborhood *duty*."

He'd grabbed my sleeve so hard that he'd torn it at the shoulder. We both discovered this at the same time.

I expected him to look sorry. He didn't. In fact, he was smirking at me. "Don't be such a wimp, Aaron," he said.

2

Mike led the charge getting the kitchen cleaned up. I think he was feeling guilty about calling me a wimp with such angry exuberance. Now I understood how lynch mobs got formed. One guy like Mike stirring people up by alternately insulting them and urging them on.

After the kitchen was put back in order, and after I'd taken inventory to find that nothing had been stolen, I went to the refrigerator and got beers for everybody. Bob had drifted back to the kitchen, too.

"All right," I said, "now that we've all calmed down, I want to walk over to that yellow kitchen wall phone there and call the police. Any objections?"

"I think blue would look better in here than yellow," Neil said.

"Funny," I said.

They looked themselves now, no feral madness on the faces of Mike or Neil, no winces on Bob's.

I started across the floor to the phone.

Neil grabbed my arm. Not with the same insulting force Mike had used on me. But enough to get the job done.

"I think Mike's right," Neil said. "I think we should grill that bastard a little bit."

I shook my head, politely removed his hand from my forearm, and proceeded to the phone.

"This isn't just your decision alone," Mike said.

He'd finally had his way. He'd succeeded in making me angry. I turned around and looked at him. "This is my house, Mike. If you don't like my decisions, then I'd suggest you leave."

We both took steps toward each other. Mike would no doubt win any battle we had but I'd at least be able to inflict a little damage and right now that's all I was thinking about.

Neil got between us.

"Hey," he said. "For God's sake you two, c'mon. We're friends, remember?"

"This is my house," I said, my words childish in my ears.

"Yeah, but we live in the same neighborhood, Aaron," Mike said, "which makes this 'our' problem."

"He's right, Aaron," Bob said from the breakfast nook. There's a window there where I sometimes sit to watch all the animals on sunny days. I saw a mother raccoon and four baby raccoons one day, marching single file across the grass. My grandparents were the last generation to live on the farm. My father came to town here and ended up working at a ball bearing company. Raccoons are a lot more pleasant to gaze upon than people.

"He's not right," I said to Bob. "He's wrong. We're not cops, we're not bounty hunters, we're not trackers. We're a bunch of god-damned guys who peddle stocks and bonds. Mike and Neil shouldn't have tied him up downstairs—that happens to be illegal, at least the way they went about it—and now I'm going to call the cops."

"Yes, that poor thing," Mike said, "aren't we just picking on him, though? Tell you what, why don't we make him something to eat?"

"Just make sure we have the right wine to go with it," Neil said. "Properly chilled, of course."

"Maybe we could get him a chick," Bob said.

"With bombers out to here," Mike said, indicating with his hands where "here" was.

I couldn't help it. I smiled. They were all being ridiculous. A kind of fever had caught them.

"You really want to go down there and question him?" I said to Neil.

"Yes. We can ask him things the cops can't."

"Scare the bastard a little," Mike said. "So he'll tell us who was with him tonight, and who else works this neighborhood." He came over and put his hand out. "God, man, you're one of my best friends. I don't want you mad at me."

Then he hugged me, which is something I've never been comfortable with men doing, but to the extent I could, I hugged him back.

"Friends?" he said.

"Friends," I said. "But I still want to call the cops."

"And spoil our fun?" Neil said.

"And spoil your fun."

"I say we take it to a vote," Bob said.

"This isn't a democracy," I said. "It's my house and I'm the king, I don't want to have a vote."

"Can we ask him one question?" Bob said.

I sighed. They weren't going to let go. "One question?"

"The name of the guy he was with tonight."

"And that's it?"

"That's it. That way we get him and one other guy off the street."

"And then I call the cops?"

"Then," Mike said, "you call the cops."

"One question," Neil said.

While we finished our beers, we argued a little more, but they had a lot more spirit left than I did. I was tired now and missing Jan and the kids and feeling lonely. These three guys had become strangers to me tonight. Very old boys eager to play at boy games once again.

"One question," I said. "Then I call the cops."

I led the way down, sneezing as I did so.

There's always enough dust floating around in the basement to play hell with my sinuses.

The guy was his same sullen self, glaring at us as we descended the stairs and then walked over to him. He smelled of heat and sweat and city grime. The long bare arms sticking out of his filthy T-shirt told tattoo tales of writhing snakes and leaping panthers. The arms were joined in the back with rope. His jaw still flexed, trying to accommodate the intrusion of the gag.

"Maybe we should castrate him," Mike said, walking up close to the guy. "You like that, scumbag? If we castrated you?"

If the guy felt any fear, it wasn't evident in his eyes. All you could see there was the usual contempt.

"I'll bet this is the jerk who broke into the Donaldsons' house a couple weeks ago," Neil said.

Now he walked up to the guy. But he was more ambitious than Mike had been. Neil spat in the guy's face.

"Hey," I said, "cool it."

Neil glared at me. "Yeah, I wouldn't want to hurt his feelings, would I?"

Then he suddenly turned back on the guy, raised his fist and started to swing. All I could do was shove him. That sent his punch angling off to the right, missing our burglar by about half a foot.

"You asshole," Neil said, turning back on me now.

But Mike was there, between us.

"You know what we're doing? We're making this jerk happy.

He's gonna have some nice stories to tell all his criminal friends."

He was right. The burglar was the one who got to look all cool and composed. We looked like squabbling brats. As if to confirm this, a hint of amusement played in the burglar's blue eyes.

"Oh, hell, Aaron, I'm sorry," Neil said, putting his hand out. This was like a political convention, all the handshaking going on.

"So am I, Neil," I said. "That's why I want to call the cops and get this over with."

And that's when he chose to make his move, the burglar. As soon as I mentioned the cops, he probably realized that this was going to be his last opportunity.

He waited until we were just finishing up with the handshake, when we were all focused on each other. Then he took off running. We could see that he'd slipped the rope. He went straight for the stairs, angling out around us like a running back seeing daylight. He even stuck his long, tattooed arm out as if he was trying to repel a tackle.

"Hey," Bob shouted. "He's getting away."

He was at the stairs by the time we could gather ourselves enough to go after him. But when we moved, we moved fast, and in virtual unison.

By the time I got my hand on the cuff of his left jean, he was close enough to the basement door to open it.

I yanked hard and ducked out of the way of his kicking foot. By now I was as crazy as Mike and Neil had been earlier. There was adrenaline and great anger. He wasn't just a burglar, he was all burglars, intent not merely on stealing things from me, but hurting my family, too. He hadn't had time to take the gag from his mouth.

This time, I grabbed booted foot and leg and started hauling him back down the stairs. At first he was able to hold on to the door but when I wrenched his foot rightward, he tried to scream behind the gag. He let go of the doorknob.

The next half minute is still unclear in my mind. I started running down the stairs, dragging him with me. All I wanted to do was get him on the basement floor again, turn him over to the others to watch, and then go call the cops.

But somewhere in those few seconds when I was hauling him back down the steps, I heard edge of stair meeting back of skull. The others heard it, too, because their shouts and curses died in their throats.

When I turned around, I saw the blood running fast and red from his nose. The blue eyes no longer held contempt. They were starting to roll up white in the back of his head.

"God," I said. "He's hurt."

"I think he's a lot more than hurt," Mike said.

"Help me carry him upstairs."

We got him on the kitchen floor. Mike and Neil rushed around soaking paper towels. We tried to revive him. Bob, who kept wincing from his headache, tried the guy's wrist, ankle and throat for a pulse. None. His nose and mouth were bloody. Very bloody.

"No way you could *die* from hitting your head like that," Neil said.

"Sure you could," Mike said. "You hit it just the right way."

"He can't be dead," Neil said. "I'm going to try his pulse again."

Bob, who obviously took Neil's second opinion personally, frowned and rolled his eyes. "He's dead, man. He really is."

"Bullshit."

"You a doctor or something?" Bob said.

Neil smiled nervously. "No, but I play one on TV."

So Neil tried the pulse points. His reading was exactly what Bob's reading had been.

"See," Bob said.

I guess none of us were destined to ever quite be adults.

"Man," Neil said, looking down at the long, cold unmoving form of the burglar. "He's really dead."

"What the hell're we gonna do?" Mike said.

"We're going to call the police," I said, and started for the phone.

"The hell we are," Mike said. "The hell we are."

3

Maybe half an hour after we laid him on the kitchen floor, he started to smell. We'd looked for identification and found none. He was just the Burglar.

We sat at the kitchen table, sharing a fifth of Old Grandad and innumerable beers.

We'd taken two votes and they'd come up ties. Two for calling the police, Bob and I; two for not calling the police, Mike and Neil.

"All we have to tell them," I said, "is that we tied him up so he wouldn't get away."

"And then they say," Mike said, "so why didn't you call us before now?"

"We just lie about the time a little," I said. "Tell them we called them within twenty minutes."

"Won't work," Neil said.

"Why not?" Bob said.

"Medical examiner can fix the time of death," Neil said.

"Not that close."

"Close enough so that the cops might question our story," Neil said. "By the time they get here, he'll have been dead at least an hour, hour and a half."

"And then we get our names in the paper for not reporting the burglary or the death right away," Mike said. "Brokerages just love publicity like that."

"I'm calling the cops right now," I said, and started up from the table.

"Think about Tomlinson a minute," Neil said.

Tomlinson was my boss at the brokerage. "What about him?"

"Remember how he canned Dennis Bryce when Bryce's ex-wife took out a restraining order on him?"

"This is different," I said.

"The hell it is," Mike said. "Neil's right, none of our bosses will like publicity like this. We'll all sound a little—crazy—you know, keeping him tied up in the basement. And then killing him when he tried to get away."

They all looked at me.

"You bastards," I said. "I was the one who wanted to call the police in the first place. And I sure as hell didn't try to kill him on purpose."

"Looking back on it," Neil said, "I guess you were right, Aaron. We should've called the cops right away."

"Now's a great time to realize that," I said.

"Maybe they've got a point," Bob said softly, glancing at me, then glancing nervously away.

"Oh, great. You, too?" I said.

"They just might kick my black ass out of there if I had any publicity that involved somebody getting killed," Bob said.

"He was a frigging burglar," I said.

"But he's dead," Neil said.

"And we killed him," Mike said.

"I appreciate you saying 'we'," I said.

"I know a good place," Bob said.

I looked at him carefully, afraid of what he was going to say next.

"Forget it," I said.

"A good place for what?" Neil said.

"Dumping the body," Bob said.

"No way," I said.

This time when I got up, nobody tried to stop me. I walked over to the yellow wall telephone.

I wondered if the cozy kitchen would ever feel the same to me now that a dead body had been laid upon its floor.

I had to step over him to reach the phone. The smell was even more sour now.

"You know how many bodies get dumped in the river that never wash up?" Bob said.

"No," I said, "and you don't, either."

"Lots," he said.

"There's a scientific appraisal for you. 'Lots.'"

"Lots and lots, probably," Neil said, taking up Bob's argument.

Mike grinned. "Lots and lots and *lots*."

"Thank you, Professor," I said.

I lifted the receiver and dialed 0.

"Operator."

"The police department, please."

"Is this an emergency?" asked the young woman. Usually I would have spent more time wondering if the sweetness of her voice was matched by the sweetness of her face and body. I'm still a face man. I suppose it's my romantic side. "Is this an emergency?" she repeated.

"No; no, it isn't."

"I'll connect you," she said.

"You think your kids'll be able to handle it?" Neil said.

"No mind games," I said.

"No mind games at all," he said. "I'm asking you a very realistic question. The police have some doubts about our story and then the press gets ahold of it and bam. We're the lead story on all three channels. 'Did four middle-class men murder the burglar they captured?' The press even goes after the kids these days. 'Do *you* think your daddy murdered that burglar, son?' "

"Good evening. Police Department."

I started to speak but I couldn't somehow. My voice wouldn't work. That's the only way I can explain it.

"The six o'clock news five nights running," Neil said softly behind me. "And the DA can't endorse any kind of vigilante activity so he nails us on involuntary manslaughter."

"Hello? This is the Police Department," said the black female voice on the phone.

Neil was there then, reaching me as if by magic.

He took the receiver gently from my hand and hung it back up on the phone again.

"Let's go have another drink and see what Bob's got in mind, all right?"

He led me, as if I were a hospital patient, slowly and carefully back to the table where Bob, over more whiskey, slowly and gently laid out his plan.

~ ~ ~ ~ ~

The next morning, three of us phoned in sick. Bob went to work because he had an important meeting.

Around noon—a sunny day when a softball game and a cold six-pack of beer sounded good—Neil and Mike came over. They looked as bad as I felt, and no doubt looked myself.

We sat out on the patio eating the Hardee's lunch they'd bought. I'd need to play softball to work off some of the calories I was eating.

Birdsong and soft breezes and the smell of fresh cut grass should have made our patio time enjoyable. But I had to wonder if we'd ever enjoy anything again. I just kept seeing the body momentarily arced above the roaring waters of the dam; and dropping into white churning turbulence.

"You think we did the right thing?" Neil said.

"Now's a hell of a time to ask that," I said.

"Of course we did the right thing," Mike said. "What choice did we have? It was either that or get our asses arrested."

"So you don't have any regrets?" Neil said.

Mike sighed. "I didn't say that. I mean, I wish it hadn't happened in the first place."

"Maybe Aaron was right all along," Neil said.

"About what?"

"About going to the cops."

"Goddamn," Mike said, sitting up from his slouch. We all wore button-down shirts without ties and with the sleeves rolled up. Somehow there was something profane about wearing shorts and T-shirts on a workday. We even wore pretty good slacks. We were that kind of people. "Goddamn."

"Here he goes," Neil said.

"I can't believe you two," Mike said. "We should be happy that everything went so well last night—and what are we doing? Sitting around here pissing and moaning."

"That doesn't mean it's over," I said.

"Why the hell not?" Mike said.

"Because there's still one left."

"One what?"

"One burglar."

"So?"

"So you don't think he's going to get curious about what the hell happened to his partner?"

"What's he gonna do?" Mike said. "Go to the cops?"

"Maybe."

"Maybe? You're crazy. He goes to the cops, he'd be setting himself up for a robbery conviction."

"Not if he tells them we murdered his pal."

Neil said, "Aaron's got a point. What if this guy goes to the cops?"

"He's not going to the cops," Mike said. "No way he's going to the cops at all."

4

I was dozing on the couch, a Cubs game on the TV set, when the phone rang around nine that evening. I hadn't heard from Jan yet so I expected it would be her. Whenever we're apart, we call each other at least once a day.

The phone machine picks up on the fourth ring so I had to scramble to beat it.

"Hello?"

Nothing. But somebody was on the line. Listening.

"Hello?"

I never play games with silent callers. I just hang up. I did so now.

Two innings later, having talked to Jan, having made myself a tuna fish sandwich on rye, found a package of potato chips I thought we'd finished off at the poker game, and gotten myself a new can of beer, I sat down to watch the last inning. The Cubs had a chance of winning. I said a silent prayer to the God of Baseball.

The phone rang.

I mouthed several curses around my mouthful of tuna sandwich and went to the phone.

"Hello?" I said, trying to swallow the last of the bite.

My silent friend again.

I slammed the phone.

The Cubs got two more singles, I started on the chips and I had polished off the beer and was thinking of getting another one when the phone rang again.

I had a suspicion of who was calling and then saying nothing—but I didn't really want to think about it.

Then I decided there was an easy way to handle this situation. I'd just let the phone machine take it. If my anonymous friend wanted to talk to a phone machine, good for him.

Four rings. The phone machine took over, Jan's pleasant voice saying that we weren't home but would be happy to call you back if you'd just leave your number.

I waited to hear dead air then a click.

Instead a familiar female voice said: "Aaron, it's Louise. Bob—" Louise was Bob's wife. She was crying. I ran from the couch to the phone machine in the hall.

"Hello, Louise. It's Aaron."

"Oh, Aaron. It's terrible."

"What happened, Louise?"

"Bob—" More tears. "He electrocuted himself tonight out in the garage." She said that a plug had accidentally fallen into a bowl of water, according to the fire captain on the scene, and Bob hadn't noticed this and put the plug into the outlet and—

Bob had a woodcraft workshop in his garage, a large and sophisticated one. He knew what he was doing.

"He's dead, Aaron. He's dead."

"Oh, God, Louise. I'm sorry."

"He was so careful with electricity, too. It's just so hard to believe—"

Yes, I thought. Yes, it was hard to believe. I thought of last night. Of the burglars—one who'd died. One who'd gotten away.

"Why don't I come over?"

"Oh, thank you, Aaron, but I need to be alone with the children. But if you could call Neil and Mike—"

"Of course."

"Thanks for being such good friends, you and Jan."

"Don't be silly, Louise. The pleasure's ours."

"I'll talk to you tomorrow. When I'm—you know."

"Good night, Louise."

~ ~ ~ ~ ~

Mike and Neil were at my place within twenty minutes. We sat in the kitchen again, where we were last night.

I said, "Either of you get any weird phone calls tonight?"

"You mean just silence?" Neil said.

"Right."

"I did," Mike said. "Carrie was afraid it was that pervert who called all last winter."

"I did, too," Neil said. "Three of them."

"Then a little while ago, Bob dies out in his garage," I said. "Some coincidence."

"Hey, Aaron," Mike said. "Is that why you got us over here? Because you don't think it was an accident?"

"I'm sure it wasn't an accident," I said. "Bob knew what he was doing with his tools. He didn't notice a plug that had fallen into a bowl of water?"

"He's coming after us," Neil said.

"Oh, God," Mike said. "Not you, too."

"He calls us, gets us on edge," I said. "And then he kills Bob. Making it look like an accident."

"These are pretty bright people," Mike said sarcastically.

"You notice the burglar's eyes?" Neil said.

"I did," I said. "He looked very bright."

"And spooky," Neil said. "Never saw eyes like that before."

"I can shoot your theory right in the butt," Mike said.

"How?" I said.

He leaned forward, sipped his beer. I'd thought about putting out some munchies but somehow that seemed wrong given poor Bob's death and the phone calls. The beers we had to have. The munchies were too festive.

"Here's how. There are two burglars, right? One gets caught, the other runs. And given the nature of burglars, keeps on running. He wouldn't even know who was in the house last night, except for Aaron, and that's only because he's the owner and his name would be in the phone book. But he wouldn't know anything about Bob or Neil or me. No way he'd have been able to track down Bob."

I shook my head. "You're overlooking the obvious."

"Like what?"

"Like he runs off last night, gets his car and then parks in the alley to see what's going to happen."

"Right," Neil said. "Then he sees us bringing his friend out wrapped in a blanket. He follows us to the dam and watches us throw his friend in."

"And," I said, "everybody had his car here last night. Very easy for him to write down all the license numbers."

"So he kills Bob," Neil said. "And starts making the phone calls to shake us up."

"Why Bob?"

"Maybe he hates black people," I said.

Mike looked first at me and then at Neil. "You know what this is?"

"Here he goes," Neil said.

"No; no, I'm serious here. This is Catholic guilt."

"How can it be Catholic guilt when I'm Jewish?" Neil said.

"In a culture like ours, everybody is a little bit Jewish and a little bit Catholic, anyway," Mike said. "So you guys are in the throes of Catholic guilt. You feel bad about what we had to do last night—and we did have to do it, we really didn't have any choice—and the guilt starts to play on your mind. So poor Bob electrocutes himself accidentally and you immediately think it's the second burglar."

"He followed him," Neil said.

"What?" Mike said.

"That's what he did, I bet. The burglar. Followed Bob around all day trying to figure out what was the best way to kill him. You know, the best way that would look like an accident. So then he finds out about the workshop and decides it's perfect."

"That presumes," Mike said, "that one of us is going to be next."

"Hell, yes," Neil said. "That's why he's calling us. Shake us up. Sweat us out. Let us know that he's out there somewhere, just waiting. And that we're next."

"I'm going to follow you to work tomorrow, Neil," I said. "And Mike's going to be with me."

"You guys are having breakdowns. You really are," Mike said.

"We'll follow Neil tomorrow," I said. "And then on Saturday you and Neil can follow me. If he's following *us* around, then we'll see it. And then we can start following him. We'll at least find out who he is."

"And then what?" Mike said. "Suppose we do find out where he lives? Then what the hell do we do?"

Neil said, "I guess we worry about that when we get there, don't we?"

~ ~ ~ ~ ~

In the morning, I picked Mike up early. We stopped off for doughnuts and coffee. He's like my brother, not a morning person. Crabby. Our conversation was at a minimum, though he did say, "I could've used the extra hour's sleep this morning. Instead of this crap, I mean."

As agreed, we parked half a block from Neil's house. Also as agreed, Neil emerged exactly at 7:35. Kids were already in the wide suburban streets on skateboards and rollerblades. No other car could be seen, except for a lone silver BMW in a driveway far down the block.

We followed him all the way to work. Nobody followed him. Nobody.

When I dropped Mike off at his office, he said, "You owe me an hour's sleep."

"Two hours," I said.

"Huh?"

"Tomorrow, you and Neil follow me around."

"No way," he said.

There are times when only blunt anger will work with Mike. "It was your idea not to call the police, remember? I'm not up for any of your sulking, Mike. I'm really not."

He sighed: "I guess you're right."

I drove for two and a half hours Saturday morning. I hit a hardware store, a lumberyard, and a Kmart. At noon, I pulled into a McDonald's. The three of us had some lunch.

"You didn't see anybody even suspicious?"

"Not even suspicious, Aaron," Neil said. "I'm sorry."

"This is all bullshit. He's not going to follow us around."

"I want to give it one more chance," I said.

Mike made a face. "I'm not going to get up early, if that's what you've got in mind."

I got angry again. "Bob's dead, or have you forgotten?"

"Yeah, Aaron," Mike said. "Bob *is* dead. He got electrocuted. Accidentally."

I said, "You really think it was an accident?"

"Of course I do," Mike said. "When do you want to try it again?"

"Tonight. I'll do a little bowling."

"There's a fight on I want to watch," Mike said.

"Tape it," I said.

" 'Tape it,' " he mocked. "Since when did you start giving us orders?"

"Oh, for God's sake, Mike, grow up," Neil said. "There's no way that Bob's electrocution was an accident or a coincidence. He's probably not going to stop with Bob, either."

The bowling alley was mostly teenagers on Saturday night. There was a time when bowling was mostly a working-class sport. Now it's come to the suburbs and the white-collar people. Now the bowling lane is a good place for teenage boys to meet teenage girls.

I bowled two games, drank three beers, and walked back outside an hour later.

Summer night. Smell of dying heat, car exhaust, cigarette smoke, perfume. Sound of jukebox, distant loud mufflers, even more distant rushing train, lonely baying dogs.

Mike and Neil were gone.

I went home and opened myself a beer.

The phone rang. Once again, I was expecting Jan.

"Found the bastard," Neil said. "He followed you from your house to the bowling alley. Then he got tired of waiting and took off again. This time we followed *him*."

"Where?"

He gave me an address. It wasn't a good one.

"We're waiting for you to get here. Then we're going up to pay him a little visit."

"I need twenty minutes."

"Hurry."

Not even the silver touch of moonlight lent these blocks of crumbling stucco apartment houses any majesty or beauty. The rats didn't even bother to hide. They squatted red-eyed on the unmown lawns, amidst beer cans, and broken bottles, and wrappers from Taco John's, and used condoms that looked like deflated mushrooms.

Mike stood behind a tree.

"I followed him around back," Mike said. "He went up the fire escape on the back. Then he jumped on this veranda. He's in the back apartment on the right side. Neil's in the backyard, watching for him."

Mike looked down at my ball bat. "That's a nice complement," he said. Then he showed me his handgun. "To this."

"Why the hell did you bring that?"

"Are you kidding? You're the one who said he killed Bob."

That, I couldn't argue with.

"All right, "I said, "but what happens when we catch him?"

"We tell him to lay off us," Mike said.

"We need to go to the cops."

"Oh, sure. Sure we do." He shook his head. He looked as if he were dealing with a child. A very slow one. "Aaron, going to the cops now won't bring Bob back. And it's only going to get us in trouble."

That's when we heard the shout. It sounded like Neil.

Maybe five feet of rust-colored grass separated the yard from the alley that ran along the west side of the apartment house.

We ran down the alley, having to hop over an ancient drooping picket fence to reach the backyard where Neil lay sprawled, face down, next to a twenty-year-old Chevrolet that was tireless and up on blocks. Through the windshield, you could see the huge gouges in the seats where the rats had eaten their fill.

The backyard smelled of dog shit and car oil.

Neil was moaning. At least we knew he was alive.

"The sonofabitch," he said, when we got him to his feet. "I moved over to the other side, back of the car there, so he wouldn't see me if he tried to come down that fire escape. I didn't figure there was another fire escape on the side of the building. He must've come around there and snuck up on me. He tried to kill me but I had this—"

In the moonlight, his wrist and the switchblade knife he held in his fingers were wet and dark with blood. "I got him a couple of times in the arm. Otherwise, I'd be dead."

"We're going up there," Mike said.

"How about checking Neil first?" I said.

"I'm fine," Neil said. "A little headache from where he caught me on the back of the neck." He waved his bloody blade. "Good thing I had this."

The landlord was on the first floor. He wore Bermuda shorts and no shirt. He looked eleven or twelve months pregnant with little male titties and enough coarse black hair to knit a sweater with. He had a plastic-tipped cigarillo in the left corner of his mouth.

"Yeah?"

"Two-F," I said.

"What about it?"

"Who lives there?"

"Nobody."

"Nobody?"

"If you were the law, you'd show me a badge."

"I'll show you a badge," Mike said, making a fist.

"Hey," I said, playing good cop to his bad cop. "You just let me speak to this gentleman."

The guy seemed to like my reference to him as a gentleman. It was probably the only flattering name he'd never been called.

"Sir, we saw somebody go up there."

"Oh," he said, "the vampires."

"Vampires?"

He sucked down some cigarillo smoke. "That's what we call 'em, the missus and me. They're street people, winos and homeless and all like that. They know that sometimes some of these apartments ain't rented for a while, so they sneak up there and spend the night."

"You don't stop them?"

"You think I'd get my head split open for something like that?"

"I guess that makes sense." Then: "So nobody's renting it now?"

"Nope, it ain't been rented for three months. This fat broad lived there then. Man, did she smell. You know how fat people can smell sometimes? *She* sure smelled." He wasn't svelte.

Back on the front lawn, trying to wend my way between the mounds of dog shit, I said, " 'Vampires.' Good name for them."

"Yeah it is," Neil said. "I just keep thinking of the one who died. His weird eyes."

"Here we go again," Mike said. "You two guys love to scare the shit out of each other, don't you? They're a couple of nickel-dime crooks, and that's *all* they are."

"All right if Mike and I stop and get some beer and then swing by your place?"

"Sure," I said. "Just as long as Mike buys Bud and none of that generic crap."

"Oh, I forgot," Neil laughed. "He does do that when it's his turn to buy, doesn't he?"

"Yeah," I said, "he certainly does."

I was never sure what time the call came. Darkness. The ringing phone seemed part of a dream from which I couldn't escape. Somehow I managed to lift the receiver before the phone machine kicked in.

Silence. That special *kind* of silence.

Him. I had no doubt about it. The vampire, as the landlord had called him. The one who'd killed Bob. I didn't say so much as hello. Just listened, angry, afraid, confused.

After a few minutes, he hung up.

Darkness again; deep darkness, the quarter moon in the sky a cold golden scimitar that could cleave a head from a neck.

5

About noon on Sunday, Jan called to tell me that she was staying a few days extra. The kids had discovered archery and there was a course at the Y they were taking and wouldn't she please please *please* ask good old Dad if they could stay. I said sure.

I called Neil and Mike to remind them that at nine tonight we were going to pay a visit to that crumbling stucco apartment house again.

I spent an hour on the lawn. My neighbors shame me into it. Lawns aren't anything I get excited about. But they sort of shame you into it. About halfway through, Byrnes, the chunky advertising man who lives next door, came over and clapped me on the back. He was apparently pleased that I was a real human being and taking a real human being's interest in my lawn. As usual he wore an expensive T-shirt with one of his client products on it and a pair of Bermuda shorts. As usual he tried hard to be the kind of winsome neighbor you always had in sitcoms of the fifties. But I knew somebody who knew him. Byrnes had fired his number two man so he wouldn't have to keep paying the man's insurance. The man was unfortunately dying of cancer. Byrnes was typical of all the ad people I'd met. Pretty treacherous people who spent most of their time cheating clients out of their money and putting on awards banquets so they could convince themselves that advertising was actually an endeavor that was of consequence.

Around four *Hombre* was on one of the cable channels so I had a few beers and watched Paul Newman doing the best acting of his career. At least that was my opinion.

I was just getting ready for the shower when the phone rang.

He didn't say hello. He didn't identify himself. "Tracy call you?"

It was Neil. Tracy was Mike's wife. "Why should she call me?"

"He's dead. Mike."

"What?"

"You remember how he was always bitching about that elevator at work?"

Mike worked in a very old building. He made jokes about the antiquated elevators. But you could always tell the joke simply hid his fears. He'd gotten stuck innumerable times, and it was always stopping several feet short of the upcoming floor.

"He opened the door and the car wasn't there. He fell eight floors."

"Oh, God."

"I don't have to tell you who did it, do I?"

"Maybe it's time—"

"I'm way ahead of you, Aaron. I'll pick you up in half an hour. Then we go to the police. You agree?"

"I agree."

~ ~ ~ ~ ~

Late Sunday afternoon, the second precinct parking lot is pretty empty. We'd missed the shift change. Nobody came or went.

"We ask for a detective," Neil said. He was dark sportcoat-white shirt-necktie earnest. I'd settled for an expensive blue sport-shirt Jan had bought me for my last birthday.

"You know one thing we haven't considered?"

"You're not going to change my mind."

"I'm not *trying* to change your mind, Neil, I'm just saying that there's one thing we haven't considered."

He sat behind his steering wheel, his head resting on the back of his seat.

"A lawyer."

"What for?"

"Because we may go in there and say something that gets us in very deep shit."

"No lawyers," he said. "We'd just look like we were trying to hide something from the cops."

"You sure about that?"

"I'm sure."

"You ready?" I said.

"Ready."

~ ~ ~ ~ ~

The interior of the police station was quiet. A muscular bald man in a dark uniform sat behind a desk that read Information.

He said, "Help you?"

"We'd like to see a detective," I said.

"Are you reporting a crime?"

"Uh, yes," I said.

"What sort of crime?" he said.

I started to speak but once again lost my voice. I thought about all the reporters, about how Jan and the kids would be affected by it all. How my job would be affected. Taking a guy down to the basement and tying him up and then accidentally killing him—

Neil said: "Vandalism."

"Vandalism?" the cop said. "You don't need a detective, then. I can just give you a form." Then he gave us a leery look, as if he sensed we'd just changed our minds about something.

"In that case, could I just take it home with me and fill it out there?" Neil said.

"Yeah, I guess." The cop still watched us carefully now.
"Great."
'You sure that's what you wanted to report? Vandalism?"
"Yeah; yeah, that's exactly what we wanted to report," Neil said.
"Exactly."

~ ~ ~ ~ ~

"Vandalism?" I said, when we were back in the car.
"I don't want to talk right now."
"Well, maybe *I* want to talk."
"I just couldn't do it."
"No kidding."
He looked over at me. "You could've told him the truth. Nobody was stopping you."
I looked out the window. "Yeah, I guess I could've."
"We're going over there tonight. To the vampire's place."
"And do what?"
"Ask him how much he wants."
"How much he wants for what?" I said.
"How much he wants to forget everything. He goes on with his life, we go on with ours."
I had to admit, I 'd had a similar thought myself. Neil and I didn't know how to do any of this. But the vampire did. He was good at talking, good at harassing, good at violence.
"We don't have a lot of money to throw around."
"Maybe he won't *want* a lot of money. I mean, this guy isn't exactly sophisticated."
"He's sophisticated enough to make two murders look like accidents."
"I guess that's the point."
"I'm just not sure we should pay him anything, Neil."
"You got any better ideas?"
I didn't, actually; I didn't have any better ideas at all.

6

I spent an hour on the phone with Jan that afternoon. The last few days I'd been pretty anxious and she'd sensed it and now she was making sure that everything was all right with me. In addition to being wife and lover, Jan's also my best friend. I can't kid her. She always knows when something's wrong. I'd put off telling her about

Bob and Mike dying. I'd been afraid that I might accidentally say more than I should and make her suspicious. But now I had to tell her about their deaths. It was the only way I could explain my tense mood.

"That's awful," she said. "Their poor families."

"They're handling it better than you might think."

"Maybe I should bring the kids home early."

"No reason to, hon. I mean, realistically there isn't anything any of us can do."

"Two accidents in that short a time. It's pretty strange."

"Yeah, I guess it is. But that's how it happens sometimes."

"Are you going to be all right?"

"Just need to adjust is all." I sighed. "I guess we won't be having our poker games anymore."

Then I did something I hadn't intended. I started crying and the tears caught in my throat.

"Oh, honey," Jan said. "I wish I was there so I could give you a big hug."

"I'll be OK."

"Two of your best friends."

"Yeah." The tears were starting to dry up now.

"Oh, did I tell you about Tommy?" Tommy was our six-year-old.

"No, what?"

"Remember how he used to be so afraid of horses?"

"Uh-huh."

"Well, we took him out to this horse ranch where you can rent horses?"

"Uh-huh."

"And they found him a little Shetland pony and let him ride it and he loved it. He wasn't afraid at all." She laughed. "In fact, we could barely drag him home." She paused. "You're probably not in the mood for this, are you? I'm sorry, hon. Maybe you should go do something to take your mind off things. Is there a good movie on?"

"I guess I could check."

"Something light, that's what you need."

"Sounds good," I said. "I'll go get the newspaper and see what's on."

"Love you."

"Love you, too, sweetheart," I said.

I spent the rest of the afternoon going through my various savings accounts and investments. I had no idea what the creep would want to leave us alone. We could always threaten him with going to the police, though he might rightly point out that if we really wanted to do that, we would already have done it.

I settled in the five-thousand-dollar range. That was the maximum cash I had to play with. And even then I'd have to borrow a little from one of the mutual funds we had earmarked for the kids and college.

Five thousand dollars. To me, it sounded like an enormous amount of money, probably because I knew how hard I'd had to work to get it.

But would it be enough for our friend the vampire?

~ ~ ~ ~ ~

Neil was there just at dark. He parked in the drive and came in. Meaning he wanted to talk.

We went in the kitchen. I made us a couple of highballs and we sat there and discussed finances.

"I came up with six thousand," he said.

"I got five."

"That's eleven grand," he said. "It's got to be more cash than this creep has ever seen."

"What if he takes it and comes back for more?"

"We make it absolutely clear," Neil said, "that there is no more. That this is it. Period."

"And if not?"

Neil nodded. "I've thought this through. You know the kind of lowlife we're dealing with? A) He's a burglar which means, these days, that he's a junkie. B) If he's a junkie then that means he's very susceptible to AIDS. So between being a burglar and shooting up, this guy is probably going to have a very short lifespan."

"I guess I'd agree."

"Even if he wants to make our lives miserable, he probably won't live long enough to do it. So I think we'll be making just the one payment. We'll buy enough time to let nature take its course—his nature."

"What if he wants more than the eleven grand?"

"He won't. His eyes'll pop out when he sees this."

I looked at the kitchen clock. It was going on nine now.

"I guess we could drive over there."

"It may be a long night," Neil said.

"I know."

"But I guess we don't have a hell of a lot of choice, do we?"

~ ~ ~ ~ ~

As we'd done the last time we'd been here, we split up the duties. I took the backyard, Neil the apartment door. We waited until midnight. The rap music had died by now. Babies cried and mothers screamed; couples fought. TV screens flickered in dark windows.

I went up the fire escape slowly and carefully. We'd talked about bringing guns then decided against it. We weren't exactly marksmen and if a cop stopped us for some reason, we could be arrested for carrying unlicensed firearms. All I carried was a flashlight in my back pocket.

As I grabbed the rungs of the ladder, powdery rust dusted my hands. I was chilly with sweat. My bowels felt sick. I was scared. I just wanted it to be over with. I wanted him to say yes he'd take the money and then that would be the end of it.

The stucco veranda was filled with discarded toys—a tricycle, innumerable games, a space helmet, a Wiffle bat and ball. The floor was crunchy with dried animal feces. At least I hoped the feces belonged to animals and not human children.

The door between veranda and apartment was open. Fingers of moonlight revealed an overstuffed couch and chair and a floor covered with the debris of fast food. McDonald's sacks. Pizza Hut wrappers and cardboards. Arby's wrappers, and what seemed to be five or six dozen empty beer cans. Far toward the hall that led to the front door I saw four red eyes watching me; a pair of curious rats.

I stood still and listened. Nothing. No sign of life. I went inside. Tiptoeing.

I went to the front door and let Neil in. There in the murky light of the hallway, he made a face. The smell *was* pretty bad.

Over the next ten minutes, we searched the apartment. And found nobody.

"We could wait here for him," I said.

"No way."

"The smell?"

"The smell, the rats, God; don't you just feel unclean?"

"Yeah, guess I do."

"There's an empty garage about halfway down the alley. We'd have a good view of the back of this building."

"Sounds pretty good."

"Sounds better than this place, anyway."

This time, we both went out the front door and down the stairway. Now the smells were getting to me as they'd earlier gotten to Neil. Unclean. He was right.

We got in Neil's Buick, drove down the alley that ran along the west side of the apartment house, backed up to the dark garage, and whipped inside.

"There's a sack in back," Neil said. "It's on your side."

"A sack?"

"Brewskis. Quart for you, quart for me."

"That's how my old man used to drink them," I said. I was the only blue-collar member of the poker game club. "Get off work at the plant and stop by and pick up two quart bottles of Hamms. Never missed."

"Sometimes I wish I would've been born into the working class," Neil said.

I was the blue-collar guy and Neil was the dreamer, always inventing alternate realities for himself.

"No, you don't," I said, leaning over the seat and picking up the sack damp from the quart bottles. "You had a damned nice life in Boston."

"Yeah, but I didn't learn anything. You know I was eighteen before I learned about cunnilingus?"

"Talk about cultural deprivation," I said.

"Well, every girl I went out with probably looks back on me as a pretty lame lover. They went down on me but I never went down on them. How old were you when you learned about cunnilingus?"

"Maybe thirteen."

"See?"

"I learned about it but I didn't do anything about it."

"I was twenty years old before I lost my cherry," Neil said.

"I was seventeen."

"Bullshit."

"Bullshit what? I was seventeen."

"In sociology, they always taught us that blue-collar kids always lost their virginity a lot earlier than white-collar kids."

"That's the trouble with sociology. It tries to particularize from generalities."

"Huh?" He grinned. "Yeah, I always thought sociology was full of shit, too, actually. But you were really seventeen?"

"I was really seventeen."

I wish I could tell you that I knew what it was right away, the missile that hit the windshield and shattered and starred it, and then kept right on tearing through the car until the back window was also shattered and starred.

But all I knew was that Neil was screaming and I was screaming and my quart bottle of Miller's was spilling all over my crotch as I tried to hunch down behind the dashboard. It was a tight fit because Neil was trying to hunch down behind the steering wheel.

The second time, I knew what was going on: somebody was shooting at us. Given the trajectory of the bullet, he had to be right in front of us, probably behind the two dumpsters that sat on the other side of the alley.

"Can you keep down and drive this sonofabitch at the same time?"

"I can try," Neil said.

"If we sit here much longer, he's going to figure out we don't have guns. Then he's gonna come for us for sure."

Neil leaned over and turned on the ignition. "I'm going to turn left when we get out of here."

"Fine. Just get moving."

"Hold on."

What he did was kind of slump over the bottom half of the wheel, just enough so he could sneak a peek at where the car was headed.

There were no more shots.

All I could hear was the smooth-running Buick motor.

He eased out of the garage, ducking down all the time.

When he got a chance, he bore left.

He kept the lights off.

Through the bullet hole in the windshield I could see an inch or so of starry sky.

It was a long alley and we must have gone a quarter block before he said, "I'm going to sit up. I think we lost him."

"So do I."

"Look at that frigging windshield."

Not only was the windshield a mess, the car reeked of spilled beer.

"You think I should turn on the headlights?"

"Sure," I said. "We're safe now."

We were still crawling at maybe ten miles per hour when he pulled the headlights on.

That's when we saw him, silver of eye, dark of hair, crouching in the middle of the alley waiting for us. He was a good fifty yards ahead of us but we were still within range.

There was no place we could turn around.

He fired.

This bullet shattered whatever had been left untouched of the windshield. Neil slammed on the brakes.

Then he fired a second time.

By now, both Neil and I were screaming and cursing again.

A third bullet.

"Run him over!" I yelled, ducking behind the dashboard.

"What?" Neil yelled back.

"Floor it!"

He floored it. He wasn't even sitting up straight. We might have gone careening into one of the garages or Dumpsters. But somehow the Buick stayed in the alley. And very soon it was traveling eighty-five miles per hour. I watched the speedometer peg it.

More shots, a lot of them now, side windows shattering, bullets ripping into fender and hood and top.

I didn't see us hit him but I *felt* us hit him, the car traveling that fast, the creep so intent on killing us he hadn't bothered to get out of the way in time.

The front of the car picked him up and hurled him into a garage near the head of the alley.

We both sat up, watched as his entire body was broken against the edge of the garage, and he then fell smashed and unmoving to the grass.

"Kill the lights," I said.

"What?"

"Kill the lights and let's go look at him."

Neil punched off the headlights.

We left the car and ran over to him.

A white rib stuck bloody and brazen from his side. Blood poured from his ears, nose, mouth. One leg had been crushed and also showed white bone. His arms had been broken, too.

I played my flashlight beam over him.

He was dead, all right.

"Looks like we can save our money," I said. "It's all over now."

"I want to get the hell out of here."

"Yeah," I said. "So do I."

We got the hell out of there.

7

A month later, just as you could smell autumn on the summer winds, Jan and I celebrated our twelfth wedding anniversary. We drove up to Lake Geneva, in Wisconsin, and stayed at a very nice hotel and rented a Chris-Craft for a couple of days. This was the first time I'd been able to relax since the thing with the burglar had started.

One night when Jan was asleep, I went up on the deck of the boat and just watched the stars. I used to read a lot of Edgar Rice Burroughs when I was a boy. I always remembered how John Carter felt—that the stars had a very special destiny for him—and that night there on the deck, that was to be a good family man, a good stock-broker, and a good neighbor. The bad things were all behind me now. I imagined Neil was feeling pretty much the same way. Hot bitter July seemed a long ways behind us now. Fall was coming, bringing with it football and Thanksgiving and Christmas. July would recede even more with snow on the ground.

The funny thing was, I didn't see Neil much anymore. It was as if the sight of each other brought back a lot of bad memories. It was a mutual feeling, too. I didn't want to see him any more than he wanted to see me. Our wives thought this was pretty strange. They'd meet at the supermarket or shopping center and wonder why "the boys" didn't get together anymore. Neil's wife, Sarah, kept inviting us over to "sit around the pool and watch Neil pretend he knows how to swim." September was summer hot. The pool was still the center-piece of their life.

Not that I made any new friends. The notion of a midweek poker game had lost all its appeal. There was work and my family and little else.

Then one sunny Indian summer afternoon, Neil called and said, "Maybe we should get together again."

"Maybe."

"It's over, Aaron. It really is."

"I know."

"Will you at least think about it?"

I felt embarrassed. "Oh, hell, Neil. Is that swimming pool of yours open Saturday afternoon?"

"As a matter of fact, it is. And as a matter of fact, Sarah and the girls are going to be gone to a fashion show at the club."

"Perfect. We'll have a couple of beers."

'You know how to swim?"

"No," I said, laughing. "And from what Sarah says, you don't, ei-ther."

~ ~ ~ ~ ~

I got there about three, pulled into the drive, walked to the back where the gate in the wooden fence led to the swimming pool. It was eighty degrees and even from here I could smell the chlorine.

I opened the gate and went inside and saw him right away. The funny thing was, I didn't have much of a reaction at all. I just watched him. He was floating. Facedown. He looked pale in his red trunks. This, like the others, would be judged an accidental death. Of that I had no doubt at all.

I used the cellular phone in my car to call 911.

I didn't want Sarah and the girls coming back to see an ambulance and police cars in the drive and them not knowing what was going on.

I called the club and had her paged.

I told her what I'd found. I let her cry. I didn't know what to say. I never do.

In the distance, I could hear the ambulance working its way toward the Neil Solomon residence.

I was just about to get out of the car when my cellular phone rang. I picked up. "Hello?"

"There were three of us that night at your house, Mr. Bellini. You killed two of us. I recovered from when your friend stabbed me, remember? Now I'm ready for action. I really am, Mr. Billini."

Then the emergency people were there, and neighbors, too, and then wan, trembling Sarah. I just let her cry some more. Gave her whiskey and let her cry.

8

He knows how to do it, whoever he is.

He lets a long time go between late-night calls. He lets me start to think that maybe he changed his mind and left town. And then he calls.

Oh, yes, he knows just how to play this little game.

He never says anything, of course. He doesn't need to. He just listens. And then hangs up.

I've considered going to the police, of course, but it's way too late for that. Way too late.

Or I could ask Jan and the kids to move away to a different city with me. But he knows who I am and he'd find me again.

So all I can do is wait and hope that I get lucky, the way Neil and I got lucky the night we killed the second of them.

~ ~ ~ ~ ~

Tonight I can't sleep.

It's after midnight.

Jan and I wrapped presents until well after eleven. She asked me again if anything was wrong. We don't make love as much as we used to, she said; and then there are the nightmares. Please tell me if something's wrong. Aaron. Please.

I stand at the window watching the snow come down. Soft and beautiful snow. In the morning, a Saturday, the kids will make a snowman and then go sledding and then have themselves a good old-fashioned snowball fight, which invariably means that one of them will come rushing in at some point and accuse the other of some terrible misdeed.

I see all this from the attic window.

Then I turn back and look around the poker table. Four empty chairs. Three of them belong to dead men.

I look at the empty chairs and think back to summer.

I look at the empty chairs and wait for the phone to ring.

I wait for the phone to ring.

ANGIE

Roy said, "He heard us last night."

Angie said, "Heard what?"

"Heard us talking about Gina."

"No, he didn't. He was asleep."

"That's what I thought. But I went back to the can one time and I saw his door was open and I looked in there and he was sittin' up in bed, wide awake. Listenin'."

"He probably'd just woken up."

"He heard us talkin'."

"How do you know?"

"I asked him," Roy said.

"Yeah? And what did he say?"

"He said he didn't."

"See, I told ya."

"Well, he was lyin'."

"How do you know?" she said.

"He's my son, ain't he? That's how I know. I could tell by his face."

"So what if he did hear?"

Roy looked at her, astonished. "So what if he did? He'll go to the cops."

"The cops? Roy, you're crazy. He's nine years old and he's your son."

"That little bastard don't give two turds about me, Angie. He was strictly a mama's boy. And now that he knows. . ."

~ ~ ~ ~ ~

He didn't need to say it. Angie had been waitressing at a truck stop when she'd met Roy. He was living in a trailer with his son, Jason, and his wife, Gina. He went for Angie immediately. On her nights off, he'd take her to Cedar Rapids, where they'd go to a couple of dance clubs. They always had a great time except when Roy got real drunk and started trouble with black guys who were dating white girls. Roy had some friends who were always talking about blowing up places with blacks and Jews and gays in them. Roy always gave them a certain percentage of his robbery money. That's what Roy did. He robbed banks, usually small-town ones that were located on the edge of town. Roy was a pro. He figured everything out carefully in advance. He knew the exit routes and where the banks kept the video surveillance cameras, and he checked out the teller windows in advance to see which clerk looked most vulnerable. He'd served six years in Fort Madison for sticking up a gas station when he was nineteen. He was thirty-six now and vowed never to be caught again. What she liked about him was that he had a goal in life. There was this one bank in Des Moines where he said he could get half a million on a payroll Friday. They'd go to Vegas and then they'd go see this whites-only compound up in the Utah mountains. That was the only part that Angie didn't like. She didn't understand politics and Roy and his buddies always carrying on about Jews and gays and colored people bored her. She had a way of looking awake when she was really not awake. She did that practically every time Roy and his buddies started talking about some militia deal they had heard about and intended to join. The wife got wind of the courtship between Roy and Angie, though, and raised hell. She wouldn't give him a divorce, and she threatened to tell the cops about all his robberies all over the Midwest. So one rainy night he killed her.

Shoved a knife into her right breast, which silenced her, and then cut her throat. He loaded her into a body bag and packed a hundred pounds of hand weights in there with her and then drove his two-year-old Ford out to the river that very moonglow night and threw her in just below the dam. The only trouble Roy had was his son, Jason. The kid just kept wailin' and carryin' on about where's my mom, where's my mom? He hadn't wanted the kid in the first place, had beat the shit out of her, but she still wouldn't get an abortion. Even back then he'd had the dream of this big Des Moines bank on payroll Friday, and who wanted a kid along when you had all the cash with you? But Gina had her way and Roy was stuck with the little prick. And now Jason had overheard him talkin' about killin' his mother. Roy knew that somehow, some way, the little prick would turn him in.

Roy said, "Don't worry, I'll handle it."

She watched him carefully. "Sometimes you scare the shit out of me, Roy. You really do. He's your own flesh and blood."

"I didn't want him. Gina wanted him."

"And you killed Gina."

"For you," he said. "I killed her for you." Then, "Shit, honey, here we go again. Arguin'. This ain't what I want and it ain't what you want, either. You c'mere now." Then, "A kid like that, he's a ball and chain."

He liked it when she sat in his lap. He liked to feel her up to the point that his erection got so big and bulgy it was downright painful. She'd wriggle on it and make him even crazier. Then, as now, they'd go in on their big mussed sleepwarm bed and do the trick.

Afterward, today, he said, "I better get into town. I want to be there at noontime. See what the place is like around then."

He was scoping out a bank. He was planning to rob it day after tomorrow. Their cash supply was way way down. The trailer park manager was on Roy's ass for back rent. Roy said, "Don't say nothin' to him when he gets home from school."

"All right."

"You just let me handle everything."

"All right."

"It'll be better for us," Roy said, trying to make her feel better. "Haulin' that kid everywhere we go, that isn't the kind of life we want. We want to be free, babe. That's just the kind of people we are. Free."

Roy had killed people before and it had never bothered her. But never a kid before, that she knew of. And his own kid to boot.

He kissed her breasts a final time and then said, "I'll figure out what to do about Jason and then you'n me'll go dancin' tonight. Okay?"

"Okay, Roy."

Roy was gonna kill him for sure.

One day, when Angie was thirteen, her grandmother said, "That body of hers is gonna get her in trouble someday." The irony being that Grandmother herself had had a body just like it—killer breasts and hips that made young men weep in public—when she'd been young. And so had Angie's mother, the person Grandmother was talking to. The thing being that the worst trouble Grandmother had ever gotten in was getting knocked up by a soldier home on leave from WW2, a pregnancy that had brought Angie's mother, Suzie, into the world. The worst Suzie had ever gotten into, in turn, was getting knocked up by a Vietnam soldier home on leave, a pregnancy that had brought Angie into the world.

Angie, however, got into a lot more trouble than just spreading her sweet young thighs. She saw a TV show one night where this beautiful girl was referred to as a "kept woman," a woman who lounged about an expensive apartment all day, looking just great, while this older man paid her rent, gave her endless numbers of gifts, and practically groveled every time the kept woman was even faintly displeased. An Iowa girl with a wondrous body like Angie's, was it any wonder she'd want to be a kept woman, too?

When she was fifteen, she ran away from home in the company of a thirty-two-year-old woman from Omaha who took her to a hotel in Des Moines. Angie slept with ten men in three years and made just over a thousand dollars. One of the men had been black, and that gave her some pause. She could just hear her dad if he ever found out about her (A) screwing men for money or (B) screwing a black man for money.

She went back home. Her dad, who worked as an appliance service repair man for Al's American Appliances, didn't have the money for a private shrink so they sent her to the county Human Services Department, where she saw this counselor for free. She spent two hours filling out the Minnesota Multiphasic Personality Test, which just about bored her ass off. He kept peeking in the room and asking her if she was about done. That's what he pretended to do, anyway. What he was really doing was staring at her breasts. He'd fallen in love with them the moment they walked in the door. She ended up screwing him on the side. He had a wife who worked at Wal-Mart in Cedar Rapids and two little girls, one of whom was lame in some way and whom he got all sad about sometimes. He was thirty-eight and bald and felt guilty about screwing her and cheating on his wife and all but he said that her tits just made him dizzy when he touched them, just dizzy. He kept her in rap CDs. She loved rap. The way the gangsters in the rap videos took care of their girlfriends.

That's what she wanted. She wanted to meet some guy who'd give her a life of ease. A kept woman. No work. No hassle. No sweat. Just sit around some fancy apartment and read comic books and watch MTV and porno movies. She loved porno movies. The thing was, she didn't like sex very much, except for masturbating, but if sex was the price she had to pay for a life of ease, so be it.

She dropped the counselor as soon as she managed to get through high school. She got a job in Cedar Rapids as a clerk in a Target store. She lasted three weeks. She took her paycheck and bought a very sexy dress and then she started hanging out in the lawyer bars downtown. Her first couple of months, things went pretty good. She hadn't found a guy who'd make her an official kept woman, but she'd found several guys who'd give her a little money now and then, enough money for a nice little apartment and a six-year-old Oldsmobile.

But things did not go well after a time. She caught the clap and profoundly displeased a couple of the men who gave her money. Then she ran into two men who were long of tongue but short of wallet, a car salesman who drove them around in sleek new Caddies, and a supper club owner who wore her like a pinkie ring. They were full of promises but had no real money. The Caddie man had two wives and two alimonies; and the supper club man owed the IRS boys so much in back taxes, he could barely afford a pack of gum. He'd had a supper club over in Rock Island several years back, and he'd been charged with tax evasion, later dropped to a simple (if overwhelming) tax debt.

Then, the worst thing of all happened. On the night of her twenty-sixth birthday, Angie got busted for prostitution. She was in a downtown bar sitting with a couple of hookers she knew getting birthday party drunk, when one of the lawyers suggested they all go out to his houseboat. Well, they did, and the cops followed them. Angie insisted that she accepted gifts but never cash for sex per se but it was a distinction apparently too subtle for the minds of the gendarmes. They hated these two particular lawyers and were gleeful about arresting them. Cedar Rapids had a new police station and Angie was impressed with it. She saw a couple of cute young cops, too, and thought she wouldn't mind dating a cop. It was probably fun. She was booked and fingerprinted and charged. It all, like much of Angie's life, had a dream-like quality. She was just walking through it— as if her life was a TV show and she was simply watching it—the reality of her trouble not hitting her until the next day when her name appeared in the paper. The Cedar Rapids paper was read by everybody in her hometown. Angie called home and tried to explain. Her mother was in tears, her father enraged. They told her not, definitely not, to attend the family reunion two weekends hence.

Now it was two years later and Angie was living with Roy, who robbed banks and killed people when he thought it was necessary. She saw plainly now that he was never going to have the kind of money it took to make her a kept woman. Hell, he'd even hinted a few times that she should get another waitress job to help out with the rent and the food. Plus, there were the people he'd killed, three that she knew of for sure. The only one that really bothered her was his wife. Killing his wife was a real personal thing, and it scared Angie. Killing his own son scared her even more.

She spent the afternoon getting depressed about her bikinis. School would be out in a week. Swimming pools would be opening up. Time to flaunt her body. But this year there was too much of her body to flaunt. She'd put on twenty pounds. Ripples of cellulite could be seen on the back of her thighs. She wished now Roy hadn't talked her into getting his name tattooed on both her boobs.

At three-thirty, Jason came home. He was a skinny, sandy-haired kid with a lot of freckles and eyeglasses so thick they made you feel sorry for him. Kids like Jason always got picked on by other kids.

Something was wrong. He usually went to the refrigerator and got himself some milk and a piece of the pie Angie always kept on hand for both of them. Roy had a whiskey tooth, not a sweet tooth. Then Jason usually sat at the dining room table and watched Batman. But not today. He just muttered a greeting and went back to his little room and closed the door.

Something really was wrong and she figured she knew what it was. She slipped a robe on over her bikini—you shouldn't be around him, your tits hangin' out that way, Roy said whenever she wore a bikini around the trailer—and went back to his room and knocked gently. She could never figure out what he thought of her. He was almost always polite but never more than that.

"I'm asleep," he said.

She giggled. "If you were asleep, you couldn't say I'm asleep.'"

"I just don't feel like talkin', Angie."

She decided to risk it. "You heard us talkin' last night, didn't you, Jason?"

There was a long silence. "No."

"About your mom."

"No."

"About what happened to her."

There was another long silence. "He killed her. I heard him say so."

So Roy was right. The kid had heard.

She opened the door and went in. He lay on the bed. He still had his sneakers on. A Spawn comic book lay across his chest. Sunlight angled in through the dirty window on the west wall and picked out the blond highlights in his hair.

She went over and sat down next to him. The springs made a noise. She tried not to think about her weight, or how her bikinis fit her. She was definitely going on a diet. She was going to be a kept woman, and one thing a kept woman had to do was keep her body good.

She said, "I just wanted you to know that I didn't have nothin' to do with it, what he did, I mean."

"Yeah," he said. "I know."

"And I also wanted you to know that your daddy isn't a bad man."

"Yes, he is."

"Sometimes he is. But not all the time."

"He broke your rib, didn't he?"

"He didn't mean to hit me that hard. He was just drunk was all. If he'd been sober, he wouldn't have hit me that hard."

"They say in school that a man shouldn't hit a woman at all."

"Well," she said, "you know what your daddy says about schools. That they're run by Jews and gays and colored people."

He stared at her. "I'm gonna turn him in."

She got scared. "Oh, honey, don't you ever say that to your daddy." She knew that Roy was looking for an excuse, any excuse, to kill Jason. "Promise me you won't. He'd get so mad he'd—"

She didn't need to finish her sentence. She sensed that the kid knew what she was talking about.

She said, "Is that a good comic book?"

"Not as good as Batman."

"Then how come you don't get Batman?"

"I already read it for this month."

"Oh."

She leaned forward and kissed him on the forehead. She'd never done that before. He was a nice kid. "You remember what I said now. You never say anything in front of your daddy about turnin' him in. You hear me?"

"Yeah, I guess so."

"You take a nap now."

She stood up.

Her mother had once said, "You give a man plenty of starch and a good piece of meat, he'll never complain about you or your cookin'." Angie had told this to Roy once and he'd grinned at her and pawed one of her breasts and said, "All depends on what kind of meat you're talkin' about." At the time, Angie had found his remark hilarious. There was nothing to smile about as she made the Kraft cheese and macaroni while the pork chops sizzled in the oven.

He was going to kill his own son. She couldn't get over it. His own son.

Forty-five minutes later, the three of them ate dinner. As always, Jason said grace to himself the way his mom had taught him. While he did this, Roy made a face and rolled his eyes. Little sissy son-of-a-bitch, he'd drunkenly said to Jason one night, sayin' grace like that.

Roy said, "Guess what I found today?"

Angie said, "What?"

"I was talkin' to the boy."

"Oh," Angie said, irritated with his tone of voice. "Pardon me for living."

She got up from the table and carried her dishes to the sink.

"Guess what I found today?" Roy said to Jason.

"What?"

"A real great spot for fishin'."

"Oh."

"For you and me. I always wanted to teach you how to fish."

"I thought you hated to fish," Jason said.

"Not anymore. I love fishin', don't I, babe?"

"Yeah," Angie said from the sink, where she was cleaning off her plate. "He loves fishin'."

Angie knew immediately that Roy had figured out how to kill the kid. He hated fishing, and even more he hated to do anything with the kid.

After supper, Jason went into his room. Most kids would be out playing in the warm spring night. Not Jason. He had a little twelve-inch TV in there and he had a lot of X-Files novels, too. He was well set up.

While she was doing the dishes, and Roy was sitting at the table nursing a Hamms from the bottle and watching some skin on the Playboy Channel, she said, "You're gonna do it."

"Yes, I am."

"He's your own flesh and blood."

He came over and pressed against her. He had a hard-on. Seems he always had a hard-on. She didn't have no complaints in that department. He groped her and kissed her neck and said, "We're free kind of people, Angie. Free. And with the kid along, we'll never be free. Especially with what he knows about us. One phone call from him and we'll be in the slammer."

"But he's your own son."

Jason's door opened. He went to the john. Roy said, "You let me take care of it."

Twenty minutes later, Roy and Jason left. She couldn't think of any way to stop them without coming right out and warning Jason about what was going on.

She paced. She paced and gunned whiskey from a Smurfs glass. She was so agitated her heart felt like thunder in her chest and every few minutes her right arm jerked grotesquely.

And then she remembered the gun. She didn't even know what

kind of gun it was. One of her lawyer friends had given it to her once when one of her old boyfriends was hassling her. She'd shot it a few times. She knew how to use it. She kept it in the bureau underneath the crotchless panties Roy had bought her, his joke always being that he'd personally eaten the crotch out of them.

She got the gun and she went after them. Her only thought was the river. About half a mile on the other side of some hardwoods was a cliff and below it fast water that ran to a dam near Cedar Rapids. One time they'd been walking and Roy said it was a perfect place to throw a body. His cellmate, a lifer Roy had a lot of respect for, had said that while bodies did occasionally wash up right away, there was a better chance they'd give you a five-, six-day head start from the law.

The dying day was indigo in the sky, indigo and salmon pink and mauve spreading like a stain beneath a few northeasterly thunderheads and a biting wind that tasted of rain. Rainstorms always scared her. When she was little, she'd always hidden in the closet, her two older sisters laughing at her, scaredy-pants, scaredy-pants. But she didn't care. She'd hidden anyway.

The way she found them, they were sitting on a picnic table near the cliff, father and son, just talking. Darkness was slowly making them grainy, and soon would make them invisible.

Roy said, "What the hell you doing here?"

"She can be here if she wants to," Jason said.

She smiled. The kid liked her and that made her feel good.

"I guess I need to go to the bathroom," Jason said.

He walked over to the hardwoods and disappeared.

"I was afraid you already did something to him," Angie said.

He looked at her. Shrugged. "It's harder than I thought it would be."

"He's your own flesh and blood."

"Yeah, yeah, I guess that's it. I started to do it a couple times but I couldn't go through with it. I mean, it's not like shootin' a stranger or anything."

"Let's go back."

He shook his head. "Oh, no. You go back alone."

"But if you can't do it, why you want to stay out here?"

"I didn't say I can't do it. I just said it's harder than I thought it was. It's just gonna take me a little time is all. Now, you get that sweet ass of yours back home and wait for me. We'll be pullin' out tonight."

"Pullin' out?"

They could see Jason coming back toward them.

"Yeah," Roy said in a whispering voice, "school'll be askin' questions, him not around anymore. Better off pullin' out tonight."

Jason walked up. "Dad tell you there's twenty-pound fish in that river?"

"Yeah," she said, "that's what he said."

"Angle's got to get back home. She's makin' us a surprise."

"A surprise?" Jason said, excited. "What kinda surprise?"

"Well, if she tells ya, it won't be much of a surprise, will it?"

Jason grinned. "No, I guess not."

"You head home, babe," Roy said. "We'll be up'n a while."

She wanted to argue but you didn't argue with Roy. You didn't argue and win, anyway. And you got bruises and bumps and breaks for not winning.

"Guess I better go," she said.

"I can't wait to see the surprise," Jason said.

She went back but she didn't go home. She stood inside the hardwoods, inside the shadows, inside the night, and watched them.

He couldn't do it. That's what she was hoping. That when it came right down to it, he just couldn't do it. She said a couple of prayers.

But he did it. Pulled the gun out, grabbed Jason by the shoulder and started dragging him across the grassy space between picnic table and cliff.

All this was instinct: her running, her screaming. Roy looked real pissed when he saw her. He got distracted from the kid and the kid tried wrestling himself away, swinging his arms wild, trying to kick, trying to bite.

Roy didn't have any warning about her gun. She got up close to him and jerked it out of the back pocket of her Levi's and killed him point-blank. Three bullets in the side of the head.

He went over on his side and shit his pants before he hit the ground. The smell was awful.

The weird thing was how the kid reacted. You'd think he'd be grateful that she'd killed the son-of-a-bitch. But he knelt next to Roy and wailed and rocked back and forth and held a dead cold white hand in his hand and then wailed some more.

Maybe, she thought, maybe it was because his mom was dead, too. Maybe losin' both your folks, maybe it was too much to handle, even if your own flesh-and-blood dad had tried to kill you.

She dragged Roy over and pushed him off the cliff into the river. The stars were on the water tonight and the choppy waves glistened.

She dragged the boy away. He fought at first, biting, kicking, wrestling, and all. She let him have a good hard slap, though, and that settled him down. He kept cryin' but he did what she told him. "How you doin'?"

"All right."

"You hungry?"

"Sort of, I guess."

"You'll like Colorado. Wait till you see the mountains."

"You didn't have to kill him."

"He was gonna kill you."

He didn't say anything for a long time. They were nearing the Nebraska border. The land was getting flatter. Cows, crying with prairie sorrow, tossed in their earthen beds, while night birds collected chorus-like in the trees, making the leafy branches thrum with their song. It was nice with the windows rolled down and all the summery Midwest roaring in your ears.

Sixty-three miles before they hit the border, just after ten o'clock, they found the Empire Motel, one of those 1950s jobs with the office in the middle and eight stucco-sided rooms fanned out on either side.

Angle rented a room and bought a bunch of candy and potato chips from the vending machine. She rented a sci-fi video from the manager for Jason.

She got him into the shower and then into bed and played the movie for him. He didn't last long. He was asleep in no time. She turned out the lights and got into bed herself. She was tired. Or thought she was, anyway. But she couldn't sleep. She lay there and thought about Roy and about when she was a little girl and about being a kept woman. It had to happen for her someday. It just had to. Then she remembered what she'd looked like in those bikinis. God, she really had to go on a diet.

She lay like this for an hour. Then she heard car doors opening and male laughter. She decided to go peek out the window. Two nice-looking, nicely dressed guys were carrying a suitcase each into a room two doors away. They were driving this just-huge new Lincoln. Sight of them made her agitated. She wanted a drink and to hear some music. Maybe dance a little. And laugh. She needed a good laugh.

Fifteen minutes later, she was fixed up pretty good, white tank top and red short-shorts, the ones where her cheeks were exposed to erotic perfection, her hair all done up nice, and enough perfume so that she smelled really good. The kid wouldn't miss her. He'd be fine. He'd be sleeping and the door would be locked and he'd be just fine.

Their names were Jim Durbin and Mike Brady. They were from Cedar Rapids and they owned a couple of computer stores and they were going to open a big new one in Denver.

Ordinarily, Jim would fly but Mike was scared to fly. And ordinarily, they would stay in a nicer motel than this but they couldn't find anything else on the road. Her excuse for knocking on their door this late was the front office didn't have a cigarette machine and she was out and she heard them still up and she wondered if either of them had a few cigarettes they'd loan her. Jim said he didn't smoke but Mike did.

Jim said he'd been trying for years to get Mike to quit. How do you like that? Jim said. Guy doesn't mind risking lung cancer every day of his life but he won't get on an airplane?

They had a nice bottle of I. W. Harper and invited her in.

It was obvious Mike was interested in her. Jim was married. Mike was just going through a divorce he called "painful." He said his wife ended up running off with this doctor she was on this charity committee with. Jim said Mike needed a good woman to rebuild Mike's self-esteem. That was a word Angie heard a lot. She liked the daytime talk shows and they talked a lot about self-esteem. There was a transvestite prostitute on just last week, as a matter of fact, and Angie felt sorry for the poor thing. He/she said that's all he/she was looking for, self-esteem.

Angie got sort of drunk and spent her time talking to Mike while Jim took a shower and got ready for bed. Angie could tell he was taking a real long time to give Mike and her a chance to be alone. And then they were making out and his hands were all over her and then she was down on her knees next to his bed and doing him and he was gasping and groaning and bucking and just going crazy and it made her feel powerful and wonderful to make a man this happy, especially a broken-hearted one.

When Jim came back, wearing a red terry-cloth robe and rubbing his crew cut with a white towel, Angie and Mike were sitting in chairs and having another drink.

"So, what's going on?" Jim said.

"Well," Mike said, and he looked like a teenager, excited and nervous at the same time, "I was going to ask Angie if she'd like to come to Denver with me. Spend a couple of weeks while we get the grand opening all set up and everything."

Jim said, still rubbing his crew cut with the white towel, "This is a guy who does everything first-class, Angie, let me tell you. You should see his condo. The view of the city. Unbelievable."

"You like Jet Skiing?" Mike said.

"Sure," Angie said, though she wasn't exactly sure what it was.

"Well, I've got two Jet Skis and they're a ball. Believe me, we could have a lot of fun. You could stay at my condo and do what you like during the day—shop or whatever—and then at night, we'll get together again."

Jim said, "God, Angie, you're a miracle worker. This sounds like my old buddy Mike Brady. I haven't heard him sound this happy in three or four years."

Mike grinned. "Maybe I'm in love." And he leaned over and slid his arm around Angie's neck and gave her a big whiskey kiss on the mouth.

All she could think of was how strange it was. Maybe she'd met the man who was going to make her into a kept woman. And this one wasn't married, either. He could marry her somewhere down the line.

She said, "Wait till I tell Jason."

Mike gave her a funny look. "Jason? Who's Jason?"

Jim came over, too. "Yeah, who's Jason?"

"Oh, sort of my stepson, I guess you'd say."

"You're traveling with a kid?" Mike said.

"Yeah."

Mike didn't have to say anything. It was all in his face.

He'd been outlining an orgy of activities and she went and ruined it all with reality. A kid. A fucking kid.

"Oh," Mike said, finally.

"He's a real nice kid," Angie said. "Real quiet and everything."

"I'm sure he's a nice kid, Angie," Jim said. "But I don't think that's what Mike had in mind. Nothing against kids, you understand. I've got two of my own and Mike's got three."

"I love kids," Mike said, as if somebody had accused him otherwise.

"He wouldn't be any trouble," Angie said. "He really wouldn't."

Mike and Jim looked at each other and Jim said, looking at Angie now, "You know what we should do? Why don't we take your phone number, you know where you're staying in Omaha and everything, and then Mike can give you a call when he gets settled into his condo?"

Mike didn't have nerve enough to say good-bye so Jim was doing it for him.

A ball and chain, she remembered Roy said about Jason. Mike wasn't going to call. Jim was just saying that. And she'd be somewhere in Omaha, maybe with a waitress job or something. And pretty soon school would roll around and she'd have to worry about school clothes and getting him enrolled in a new school and everything. While somebody else would be living with Mike in his Denver condo, and Jet Skiing, whatever that was, and using Mike's American Express to buy new clothes and stuff.

She said, "You know if there's a river around here somewhere?"

"A river?" Jim said.

"Yes," she said. "A river."

Next morning at seven A.M. she knocked on the door. A sleepy pajamaed Jim opened it. "Hey," he said. "How's it goin'?" He sounded a little leery of seeing her. He'd obviously hoped they'd put the Denver matter to rest last night.

"Guess what?" she said.

"What?"

"I said I was sort of Jason's stepmother? Well, actually, I'm his aunt. My sister lives about ten miles from here and has troubles with depression. She wanted me to take him for a while but she stopped by the room here real early this morning and picked him up. Said she was feeling a lot better."

Mike could be seen over Jim's shoulder now. He said, excited, "So you don't have the kid anymore?"

"Free, white and twenty-one," she said.

"You're going to Denver!" he said.

Jim said, "I'm going to get some breakfast down the road. I'll be back in an hour or so."

He got dressed quick and left.

They did it their first time right in Mike's mussed bed. Only once or twice did she think of the kid, and how she'd smothered him in the room. She hadn't had any trouble finding the river. She had to give it to Roy. The ball-and-chain business. She had liked the kid but he really was a ball and chain.

A few hours later, they left for Denver. That night, they had spare ribs for supper at a roadside place. They drank a lot of wine, or vino, as Jim kept calling it, and Mike as a joke licked some of the rib sauce off her fingers. She was scared about later, when she went to sleep. Maybe she'd have nightmares about the kid. But she snuggled up to Mike real good and after they made love, they lay in the darkness sharing his cigarette and talking about Denver and she ended up not having any dreams at all.

EN FAMILLE

By the time I was eight years old, I'd fallen disconsolately in love with any number of little girls who had absolutely no interest in me. These were little girls I'd met in all the usual places, school, playground, neighborhood.

Only the girl I met at the racetrack took any interest in me. Her name was Wendy and, like me, she was brought to the track three or four times a week by her father, after school in the autumn months, during working hours in the summer.

Ours was one of those impossibly romantic relationships that only a young boy can have (all those nights of kissing pillows while pretending it was her—this accompanied by one of those swelling romantic songs you hear in movies with Ingrid Bergman and Cary Grant—how vulnerable and true and beautiful she always was in my mind's perfect eye). I first saw her the spring of my tenth year, though we saw each other at least three times a week. But she was always with me, this girl I thought about constantly, and dreamed of nightly, the melancholy little blonde with the slow sad blue eyes and the quick sad smile.

I knew all about the sadness I saw in her. It was my sadness, too. Our fathers brought us to the track in order to make their gambling more palatable to our mothers. How much of a vice could it be if you took the little one along? The money lost at the track meant rent going unpaid, grocery store credit cut off, the telephone frequently disconnected. It also meant arguing. No matter how deeply I hid in the closet, no matter how many pillows I put over my head, I could still hear them shrieking at each other. Sometimes he hit her. Once he even pushed her down the stairs and she broke her leg. Despite all this, I wanted them to stay together. I was terrified they would split up. I loved them both beyond imagining. Don't ask me why I loved him so much. I have no idea.

The day we first spoke, the little girl and I, that warm May afternoon in my fifteenth year, a black eye spoiled her very pretty, very pale little face. So he'd finally gotten around to hitting her. My father had gotten around to hitting me years ago. They got so frustrated over their gambling, their inability to *stop* their gambling, that they grabbed the first person they found and visited all their despair on him.

She was coming up from the seats in the bottom tier where she and her father always sat. I saw her and stepped out into the aisle.

"Hi," I said after more than five years of us watching each other from afar.

"Hi."

"I'm sorry about your eye."

"He was pretty drunk. He doesn't usually get violent. But it seems to be getting worse lately." She looked back at her seats. Her father was glaring at us. "I'd better hurry. He wants me to get him a hot dog."

"I'd like to see you sometime."

She smiled, sad and sweet with her black eye. "Yeah, me, too."

I saw her the rest of the summer but we never again got the chance to speak. Nor did we make the opportunity. She was my narcotic. I thought of no one else, wanted no one else. The girls at school had no idea what my home life was like, how old and worn my father's gambling had made my mother, how anxious and angry it had made me. Only Wendy understood.

Wendy Wendy Wendy. By now, my needs having evolved, she was no longer just the pure dream of a forlorn boy. I wanted her carnally, too. She'd become a beautiful young woman.

Near the end of that summer an unseasonable rainy grayness filled the skies. People at the track took to wearing winter coats. A few races had to be called off. Wendy and her father suddenly vanished.

I looked for them every day, and every night trudged home feeling betrayed and bereft. "Can't find your little girlfriend?" my father said. He thought it was funny.

Then one night, while I was in my bedroom reading a science fiction magazine, he shouted: "Hey! Get out here! Your girlfriend's on TV!"

And so she was.

"Police announce an arrest in the murder of Myles Larkin, who was found stabbed to death in his car last night. They have taken Larkin's only child, sixteen-year-old Wendy, into custody and formally charged her with the murder of her father."

I went twice to see her but they wouldn't let me in. Finally, I learned the name of her lawyer, lied that I was a shirttail cousin, and he took me up to the cold concrete visitors' room on the top floor of city jail.

Even in the drab uniform the prisoners wore, she looked lovely in her bruised and wan way.

"Did he start beating you up again?" I asked.

"No."

"Did he start beating up your mother?"

"No."

"Did he lose his job or get you evicted?"

She shook her head. "No. It was just that I couldn't take it anymore. I mean, he wasn't losing any more or any less money at the track, it was just I—I snapped. I don't know how else to explain it. It was like I saw what he'd done to our lives and I—I snapped. That's all—I just snapped."

She served seven years in a minimum-security women's prison upstate during which time my parents were killed in an automobile accident. I finished college, got married, had a child and took up the glamorous and adventurous life of a tax consultant. My wife, Donna, knew about my mental and spiritual ups and downs. Her father had been an abusive alcoholic.

I didn't see Wendy until twelve years later, when I was sitting at the track with my seven-year-old son. He didn't always like going to the track with me—my wife didn't like me going to the track at all—so I'd had to fortify him with the usual comic books, candy and a pair of "genuine" Dodgers sunglasses.

Between races, I happened to look down at the seats Wendy and her father usually took, and there she was. Something about the cock of her head told me it was her.

"Can we go, Dad?" my son, Rob, said. "It's so boring here."

Boring? I'd once tried to explain to his mother how good I felt when I was at the track. I was not the miserable, frightened, self-effacing owner of Advent Tax Systems (some system—me and my low-power Radio Shack computer and software). No. . .when I was at the track I felt strong and purposeful and optimistic, and frightened of nothing at all. I was pure potential—potential for winning the easy cash that was the mark of men who were successful with women, and with the competitors, and with their own swaggering dreams.

"Please, Dad. It's really boring here. Honest."

But all I could see, all I could think about, was Wendy. I hadn't seen her since my one visit to jail. Then I noticed that she, too, had a child with her, a very proper-looking little blond girl whose head was cocked at the odd and fetching angle so favored by her mother.

We saw each other a dozen more times before we spoke.

Then: "I knew I'd see you again someday."

Wan smile. "All those years I was in prison, I wasn't so sure." Her daughter came up to her then and Wendy said: "This is Margaret."

"Hello, Margaret. Glad to meet you. This is my son, Rob."

With the great indifference only children can summon, they nodded hellos.

"We just moved back to the city," Wendy explained. "I thought I'd show Margaret where I used to come with my father." She mentioned her father so casually, one would never have guessed that she'd murdered the man.

Ten more times we saw each other, children in tow, before our affair began.

April 6 of that year was the first time we ever made love, this in a motel where the sunset was the color of blood in the window, and a woman two rooms away wept inconsolably. I had the brief fantasy that it was my wife in that room.

"Do you know how long I've loved you?" she said.

"Oh, God, you don't know how good it is to hear that."

"Since I was eight years old."

"For me, since I was nine."

"This would destroy my husband if he ever found out."

"The same with my wife."

"But I have to be honest."

"I want you to be honest."

"I don't care what it does to him. I just want to be with you."

In December of that year, my wife, Donna, discovered a lump in her right breast. Two weeks later she received a double mastectomy and began chemotherapy.

She lived nine years, and my affair with Wendy extended over the entire time. Early on, both our spouses knew about our relationship. Her husband, an older and primmer man than I might have expected, stopped by my office one day in his new BMW and threatened to destroy my business. He claimed to have great influence in the financial community.

My wife threatened to leave me but she was too weak. She had one of those cancers that did not kill her but that never left her alone, either. She was weak most of the time, staying for days in the bedroom that had become hers, as the guest room had become mine. Whenever she became particularly angry about Wendy, Rob would fling himself at me, screaming how much he hated me, pounding me with fists that became more powerful with each passing year. He hated me for many of the same reasons I'd hated my own father, my ineluctable passion for the track, and the way there was never any security in our lives, the family bank account wholly subject to the whims of the horses that ran that day.

Wendy's daughter likewise blamed her mother for the alcoholism that had stricken the husband. There was constant talk of divorce but their finances were such that neither of them could quite afford it. Margaret constantly called Wendy a whore, and only lately did Wendy realize that Margaret sincerely meant it.

Two things happened the next year. My wife was finally dragged off into the darkness, and Wendy's husband crashed his car into a retaining wall and was killed.

Even on the days of the respective funerals, we went to the track.

"He never understood."

"Neither did she," I said.

"I mean why I come here."

"I know."

"I mean how it makes me feel alive."

"I know."

"I mean how nothing else matters."

"I know."

"I should've been nicer to him, I suppose."

"I suppose. But we can't make a life out of blaming ourselves. What's happening. Happened. We have to go on from here."

"Do you think Rob hates you as much as Margaret hates me?"

"More, probably," I said. "The way he looks at me sometimes, I think he'll probably kill me someday."

But it wasn't me who was to die.

All during Wendy's funeral, I kept thinking of those words. Margaret had murdered her mother just as Wendy had killed her father. The press made a lot of this.

All the grief I should have visited upon my dead wife I visited upon my dead lover. I went through months of alcoholic stupor. Clients fell away; rent forced me to move from our nice suburban home to a small apartment in a section of the city that always seemed to be on fire. I didn't have to worry about Rob anymore. He got enough loans for college and wanted nothing to do with me.

Years and more years, the track the only constant in my life. Many times I tried to contact Rob through the alumni office of his school but it was no use. He'd left word not to give his current address to his father.

There was the hospital and, several times, the detox clinic. There was the church in which I asked for forgiveness, and the born-again rally at which I proclaimed my happiness in the Lord.

And then there was the shelter. Five years I lived there, keeping the place painted and clean for the other residents. The nuns seemed to like me.

My teeth went entirely, and I had to have dentures. The arthritis in my foot got so bad that I could not wear shoes for days at a time. And my eyesight, beyond even the magic of glasses, got so bad that when I watched the horse races on TV, I couldn't tell which horse was which.

Then one night I got sick and threw up blood and in the morning one of the sisters took me to the hospital where they kept me overnight. In the morning the doctor came in and told me that I had stomach cancer. He gave me five months to live.

There were days when I was happy about my death sentence. Looking back, my life seemed so long and sad, I was glad to have it over with. Then there were days when I sobbed about my death sentence, and hated the God the nuns told me to pray to. I wanted to live to go back to the track again and have a sweet, beautiful winner.

Four months after the doctor's diagnosis, the nuns put me in bed and I knew I'd never walk on my own again. I thought of Donna, and her death, and how I'd made it all the worse with the track and Wendy.

The weaker I got, the more I thought about Rob. I talked about him to the nuns. And then one day he was there.

He wasn't alone, either. With him was a very pretty dark-haired woman and a seven-year-old-boy who got the best features of both his mother and father.

"Dad, this is Mae and Stephen."

"Hello, Mae and Stephen. I'm very glad to meet you. I wish I was better company."

"Don't worry about that," Mae said. "We're just happy to meet you."

"I need to go to the bathroom," Stephen said.

"Why don't I take him, and give you a few minutes alone with your dad?" Mae said.

And so, after all these years, we were alone and he said, "I still can't forgive you, Dad."

"I don't blame you."

"I want to. But somehow I can't."

I took his hand. "I'm just glad you turned out so well, son. Like your mother and not your father."

"I loved her very much."

"I know you did."

"And you treated her very, very badly."

All his anger. All these years.

"That's a beautiful wife and son you've got."

"They're my whole life, everything that matters to me."

I started crying; I couldn't help it. Here at the end I was glad to know he'd done well for himself and his family.

"I love you, Rob."

"I love you, too, Dad."

And then he leaned down and kissed me on the cheek and I started crying harder and embarrassed both of us.

Mae and Stephen came back.

"My turn," Rob said. He patted me on the shoulder. "I'll be back soon."

I think he wanted to cry but wanted to go somewhere alone to do it.

"So," Mae said, "are you comfortable?"

"Oh, very."

"This seems like a nice place."

"It is."

"And the nuns seem very nice, too."

"Very nice." I smiled. "I'm just so glad I got to see you two."

"Same here. I've wanted to meet you for years."

"Well," I said, smiling. "I'm glad the time finally came."

Stephen, proper in his white shirt and blue trousers and neatly combed dark hair, said, "I just wish you could go to the track with us sometime, Grandpa."

She didn't have to say anything. I saw it all in the quick certain pain that appeared in her lovely gray eyes.

"The race track, you mean?" I said.

"Uh-huh. Dad takes me all the time, doesn't he, Mom?"

"Oh, yes," she said, her voice toneless. "All the time."

She started to say more but then the door opened up and Rob came in and there was no time to talk.

There was no time at all.

TURN AWAY

On Thursday she was there again. (This was on a soap opera he'd picked up by accident looking for a western movie to watch since he was all caught up on his work.) Parnell had seen her Monday but not Tuesday then not Wednesday either. But Thursday she was there again. He didn't know her name, hell it didn't matter, she was just this maybe twenty-two twenty-three year old who looked a lot like a nurse from Enid, Oklahoma he'd dated a couple of times (Les Elgart had been playing on the Loop) six seven months after returning from WWII.

Now this young look-alike was on a soap opera and he was watching.

A frigging soap opera.

He was getting all dazzled up by her, just as he had on Monday, when the knock came sharp and three times, almost like a code.

He wasn't wearing the slippers he'd gotten recently at K-mart so he had to find them, and he was drinking straight from a quart of Hamms so he had to put it down. When you were the manager of an apartment building, even one as marginal as the Alma, you had to go to the door with at least a little "decorousness," the word Sgt. Meister, his boss, had always used back in Parnell's cop days.

It was 11:23 A.M. and most of the Alma's tenants were at work. Except for the ADC mothers who had plenty of work of their own kind what with some of the assholes down at Social Services (Parnell had once gone down there with the Jamaican woman in 201 and threatened to punch out the little bastard who was holding up her check), not to mention the sheer simple burden of knowing the sweet innocent little child you loved was someday going to end up just as blown-out and bitter and useless as yourself.

He went to the door, shuffling in his new slippers which he'd bought two sizes too big because of his bunions.

The guy who stood there was no resident of the Alma. Not with his razor-cut black hair and his three-piece banker's suit and the kind of melancholy in his pale blue eyes that was almost sweet and not at all violent. He had a fancy mustache spoiled by the fact that his pink lips were a woman's.

"Mr. Parnell?"

Parnell nodded.

The man, who was maybe thirty-five, put out a hand. Parnell took it, all the while thinking of the soap opera behind him and the girl who looked like the one from Enid, Oklahoma. (Occasionally he bought whack-off magazines but the girls either looked too easy or too arrogant so he always had to close his eyes anyway and think of somebody he'd known in the past.) He wanted to see her, fuck this guy. Saturday he would be sixty-one and about all he had to look forward to was a phone call from his kid up the Oregon coast. His kid, who, God rest her soul, was his mother's son and not Parnell's, always ran a stopwatch while they talked so as to save on the phone bill. Hi Dad Happy Birthday and It's Been Really Nice Talking To You. I-Love-You-Bye.

"What can I do for you?" Parnell said. Then as he stood there watching the traffic go up and down Cortland Boulevard in baking July sunlight, Parnell realized that the guy was somehow familiar to him.

The guy said, "You know my father."

"Jesus H. Christ—"

"—Bud Garrett—"

"—Bud. I'll be goddamned." He'd already shaken the kid's hand and he couldn't do that again so he kind of patted him on the shoulder and said, "Come on in."

"I'm Richard Garrett."

"I'm glad to meet you, Richard."

He took the guy inside. Richard looked around at the odds and ends of furniture that didn't match and at all the pictures of dead people and immediately put a smile on his face as if he just couldn't remember when he'd been so enchanted with a place before, which meant of course that he saw the place for the dump Parnell knew it to be.

"How about a beer?" Parnell said, hoping he had something besides the generic stuff he'd bought at the 7-11 a few months ago.

"I'm fine, thanks."

Richard sat on the edge of the couch with the air of somebody waiting for his flight to be announced. He was all ready to jump up. He kept his eyes downcast and he kept fiddling with his wedding ring. Parnell watched him. Sometimes it turned out that way. Richard's old man had been on the force with Parnell. They'd been best friends. Garret, Sr. was a big man, six-three and fleshy but strong, a brawler and quite right. But his son. . .sometimes it turned out that way. He was manly enough, Parnell supposed, but there was an air of being trapped in himself, of petulance, that put Parnell off.

Three or four minutes of silence went by. The soap opera ended with Parnell getting another glance of the young lady. Then a "CBS Newsbreak" came on. Then some commercials. Richard didn't seem to notice that neither of them had said anything for a long time. Sunlight made bars through the Venetian blinds. The refrigerator thrummed. Upstairs but distantly a kid bawled.

Parnell didn't realize it at first, not until Richard sniffed, that Bud Garrett's son was either crying or doing something damn close to it.

"Hey, Richard, what's the problem?" Parnell said, making sure to keep his voice soft.

"My, my Dad."

"Is something wrong?"

"Yes."

"What?"

Richard looked up with his pale blue eyes. "He's dying."

"Jesus."

Richard cleared his throat. "It's how he's dying that's so bad."

"Cancer?"

Richard said, "Yes. Liver. He's dying by inches."

"Shit."

Richard nodded. Then he fell once more into his own thoughts. Parnell let him stay there a while, thinking about Bud Garrett. Bud had left the force on a whim that all the cops said would fail. He started a rent-a-car business with a small inheritance he'd come into. That was twenty years ago. Now Bud Garrett lived up in Woodland Hills and drove the big Mercedes and went to Europe once a year. Bud and Parnell had tried to remain friends but beer and champagne didn't mix. When the Mrs. had died Bud had sent a lavish display of flowers to the funeral and a note that Parnell knew to be sincere but they hadn't had any real contact in years.

"Shit," Parnell said again.

Richard looked up, shaking his head as if trying to escape the aftereffects of drugs. "I want to hire you."

"Hire me? As what?"

"You're a personal investigator aren't you?"

"Not anymore. I mean I kept my ticket—it doesn't cost that much to renew it—but hell I haven't had a job in five years." He waved a beefy hand around the apartment. "I manage these apartments."

From inside his blue pin-striped suit Richard took a sleek wallet.

He quickly counted out five one hundred dollar bills and put them on the blond coffee table next to the stack of Luke Short paperbacks. "I really want you to help me."

"Help you do what?"

"Kill my father."

Now Parnell shook his head. "Jesus, kid, are you nuts or what?"

Richard stood up. "Are you busy right now?"

Parnell looked around the room again. "I guess not."

"Then why don't you come with me?"

"Where?"

~ ~ ~ ~ ~

When the elevator doors opened to let them out on the sixth floor of the hospital, Parnell said, "I want to be sure that you understand me."

He took Richard by the sleeve and held him and stared into his pale blue eyes. "You know why I'm coming here, right?"

"Right."

"I'm coming to see your father because we're old friends. Because I cared about him a great deal and because I still do. But that's the only reason."

"Right."

Parnell frowned. "You still think I'm going to help you, don't you?'

"I just want you to see him."

On the way to Bud Garrett's room they passed an especially good-looking nurse. Parnell felt guilty about recognizing her beauty. His old friend was dying just down the hall and here Parnell was worrying about some nurse.

Parnell went around the corner of the door. The room was dark. It smelled sweet from flowers and fetid from flesh literally rotting.

Then he looked at the frail yellow man in the bed. Even in the shadows you could see his skin was yellow.

"I'll be damned," the man said.

It was like watching a skeleton talk by some trick of magic.

Parnell went over and tried to smile his ass off but all he could muster was just a little one. He wanted to cry until he collapsed. You sonofabitch, Parnell thought, enraged. He just wasn't sure whom he was enraged with. Death or God or himself—or maybe even Bud himself for reminding Parnell of just how terrible and scary it could get near the end.

"I'll be damned," Bud Garrett said again.

He put out his hand and Parnell took it. Held it for a long time.

"He's a good boy, isn't he?" Garrett said, nodding to Richard.

"He sure is."

"I had to raise him after his mother died. I did a good job, if I say so myself."

"A damn good job, Bud."

This was a big private room that more resembled a hotel suite. There was a divan and a console tv and a dry bar. There was a Picasso lithograph and a walk-in closet and a deck to walk out on. There was a double-sized water bed with enough controls to drive a space ship and big stereo and a bookcase filled with hardcovers. Most people Parnell knew dreamed of living in such a place. But Garrett was dying in it.

"He told you," Garret said.

"What?" Parnell spun around to face Richard, knowing suddenly the worst truth of all.

"He told you."

"Jesus, Bud, you sent him, didn't you?"

"Yes. Yes, I did."

"Why?"

Parnell looked at Garrett again. How could somebody who used to have a weight problem and who could throw around the toughest drunk the barrio ever produced get to be like this? Nearly every time he talked he winced. And all the time he smelled. Bad.

"I sent for you because none of us is perfect," Bud said.

"I don't understand."

"He's afraid."

"Richard?"

"Yes."

"I don't blame him. I'd be afraid too." Parnell paused and stared at Bud. "You asked him to kill you, didn't you?"

"Yes. It's his responsibility to do it."

Richard stepped up to his father's bedside and said, "I agree with that, Mr. Parnell. It is my responsibility. I just need a little help is all."

"Doing what?"

"If I buy cyanide, it will eventually be traced to me and I'll be tried for murder. If you buy it, nobody will ever connect you with my father."

Parnell shook his head. "That's bullshit. That isn't what you want me for. There are a million ways you could get cyanide without having it traced back."

Bud Garrett said, "I told him about you. I told him you could help give him strength."

"I don't agree with any of this, Bud. You should die when it's your time to die. I'm a Catholic."

Bud laughed hoarsely. "So am I, you asshole." He coughed and said, "The pain's bad. I'm beyond any help they can give me. But it could go on for a long time." Then, just as his son had an hour ago, Bud Garrett began crying almost imperceptibly. "I'm scared, Parnell. I don't know what's on the other side but it can't be any worse than this." He reached out his hand and for a long time Parnell just stared at it but then he touched it.

"Jesus," Parnell said. "It's pretty fucking confusing, Bud. It's pretty fucking confusing."

Richard took Parnell out to dinner that night. It was a nice place. The table cloths were starchy white and the waiters all wore shiny shoes. Candles glowed inside red glass.

They'd had four drinks apiece, during which Richard told Parnell about his two sons (six and eight respectively) and about the perils and rewards of the rent-a-car business and about how much he liked windsurfing even though he really wasn't much good at it.

Just after the arrival of the fourth drink, Richard took something from his pocket and laid it on the table.

It was a cold capsule.

"You know how the Tylenol Killer in Chicago operated?"

Parnell nodded.

"Same thing," Richard said. "I took the cyanide and put it in a capsule."

"Christ. I don't know about it."

"You're scared too, aren't you?"

"Yeah, I am."

Richard sipped his whiskey-and-soda. With his regimental striped tie he might have been sitting in a country club. "May I ask you something?"

"Maybe."

"Do you believe in God?"

"Sure."

"Then if you believe in God, you must believe in goodness, correct?"

Parnell frowned. "I'm not much of an intellectual, Richard."

"But if you believe in God, you must believe in goodness, right?"

"Right."

"Do you think what's happening to my father is good?"

"Of course I don't."

"Then you must also believe that God isn't doing this to him—right?"

Richard held up the capsule. Stared at it. "All I want you to do is give me a ride to the hospital. Then just wait in the car down in the parking lot."

"I won't do it."

Richard signaled for another round.

"I won't god damn do it," Parnell said.

~ ~ ~ ~ ~

By the time they left the restaurant Richard was too drunk to drive. Parnell got behind the wheel of the new Audi. "Why don't you tell me where you live? I'll take you home and take a cab from there."

"I want to go to the hospital."

"No way, Richard."

Richard slammed his fist against the dashboard. "You fucking owe him that, man!" he screamed.

Parnell was shocked, and a bit impressed, with Richard's violent side. If nothing else, he saw how much Richard loved his old man.

"Richard, listen."

Richard sat in a heap against the opposite door. His tears were dry ones, choking ones. "Don't give me any of your speeches." He wiped snot from his nose on his sleeve. "My Dad always told me what a tough guy Parnell was." He turned to Parnell, anger in him again. "Well, I'm not tough, Parnell, and so I need to borrow some of your toughness so I can get that man out of his pain and grant him his one last fucking wish. DO YOU GOD DAMN UNDERSTAND ME?"

He smashed his fist on the dashboard again.

Parnell turned on the ignition and drove them away.

When they reached the hospital, Parnell found a parking spot and pulled in. The mercury vapor lights made him feel as though he were on Mars. Bugs smashed against the windshield.

"I'll wait here for you," Parnell said.

Richard looked over at him. "You won't call the cops?"

"No."

"And you won't come up and try to stop me?"

"No."

Richard studied Parnell's face. "Why did you change your mind?"

"Because I'm like him."

"Like my father?"

"Yeah. A coward. I wouldn't want the pain either. I'd be just as afraid."

All Richard said, and this he barely whispered, was "Thanks."

~ ~ ~ ~ ~

While he sat there Parnell listened to country western music and then a serious political call-in show and then a call-in show where a lady talked about Venusians who wanted to pork her and then some salsa music and then a religious minister who sounded like Foghorn Leghorn in the old Warner Brothers cartoons.

By then Richard came back.

He got in the car and slammed the door shut and said, completely sober now, "Let's go."

Parnell got out of there.

They went ten long blocks before Parnell said, "You didn't do it, did you?"

Richard got hysterical. "You sonofabitch! You sonofabitch!"

Parnell had to pull the car over to the curb. He hit Richard once, a fast clean right hand, not enough to make him unconscious but enough to calm him down.

"You didn't do it, did you?"

"He's my father, Parnell. I don't know what to do. I love him so much I don't want to see him suffer. But I love him so much I don't want to see him die, either."

Parnell let the kid sob. He thought of his old friend Bud Garrett and what a good goddamn fun buddy he'd been and then he started crying, too.

~ ~ ~ ~ ~

When Parnell came down Richard was behind the steering wheel.

Parnell got in the car and looked around the empty parking lot and said, "Drive."

"Any place especially?"

"Out along the East River road. Your old man and I used to fish off that little bridge there."

Richard drove them. From inside his sportcoat Parnell took the pint of Jim Beam.

When they got to the bridge Parnell said, "Give me five minutes alone and then you can come over, ok?"

Richard was starting to sob again.

Parnell got out of the car and went over to the bridge. In the hot night you could hear the hydroelectric dam half a mile downstream and smell the fish and feel the mosquitoes feasting their way through the evening.

He thought of what Bud Garrett had said, "Put it in some whiskey for me, will you?"

So Parnell had obliged.

He stood now on the bridge looking up at the yellow circle of moon thinking about dead people, his wife and many of his WWII friends, the rookie cop who'd died of a sudden tumor, his wife with her rosary-wrapped hands. Hell, there was probably even a chance that nurse from Enid, Oklahoma was dead.

"What do you think's on the other side?' Bud Garrett had asked just half-an-hour ago. He'd almost sounded excited. As if he were a farm kid about to ship out with the Merchant Marines.

"I don't know," Parnell had said.

"It scare you, Parnell?"

"Yeah," Parnell had said. "Yeah it does."

Then Bud Garrett had laughed. "Don't tell the kid that. I always told him that nothin' scared you."

~ ~ ~ ~ ~

Richard came up the bridge after a time. At first he stood maybe a hundred feet away from Parnell. He leaned his elbows on the concrete and looked out at the water and the moon. Parnell watched him, knowing it was all Richard, or anybody, could do.

Look out at the water and the moon and think about dead people and how you yourself would soon enough be dead.

Richard turned to Parnell then and said, his tears gone completely now, sounding for the first time like Parnell's sort of man, "You know, Parnell, my father was right. You're a brave sonofabitch. You really are."

Parnell knew it was important for Richard to believe that—that there were actually people in the world who didn't fear things the way most people did—so Parnell didn't answer him at all.

He just took his pint out and had himself a swig and looked some more at the moon and the water.

STALKER

1

Eleven years, two months, and five days later, we caught him. In an apartment house on the west edge of Des Moines. The man who had raped and murdered my daughter.

Inside the rental Pontiac, Slocum said, "I can fix it so we have to kill him." The dramatic effect of his words was lost somewhat when he waggled a bag of Dunkin' Donuts at me.

I shook my head, "No."

"No to the donuts. Or no to killing him?"

"Both."

"You're the boss."

I suppose I should tell you about Slocum. At least two hundred pounds overweight, given to western clothes too large for even his bulk (trying to hide that slope of belly, I suppose), Slocum is thirty-nine, wears a beard the angriest of Old Testament prophets would have envied, and carries at all times in his shoulder holster a Colt King Cobra, one of the most repellent-looking weapons I've ever seen. I don't suppose someone like me—former economics professor at the state university and antigun activist of the first form—ever quite gets used to the look and feel and smell of such weapons. Never quite.

I had been riding shotgun in an endless caravan of rented cars, charter airplanes, Greyhound buses, Amtrak passenger cars, and even a few motorboats for the past seven months, ever since that day in Chicago when I turned my life over to Slocum the way others turned their lives over to Jesus or Republicanism.

I entered his office, put twenty-five thousand dollars in cash on his desk, and said, "Everybody tells me you're the best. I hope that's true, Mr. Slocum."

He grinned at me with teeth that Red Man had turned the color of peach wine. "Fortunately for you, it is true. Now what is it you'd like me to do?" He turned down the Hank Williams Jr. tape he'd been listening to and waved to me, with a massive beefy hand bearing two faded blue tattoos, to start talking.

I had worked with innumerable police departments, innumerable private investigators, two soldiers of fortune, and a psychic over the past eleven years in an effort to find the man who killed my daughter.

That cold, bright January day seven months ago, and as something of a last resort, I had turned to a man whose occupation sounded far too romantic to be any good to me: Slocum was a bounty hunter.

"Maybe you should wait here."

"Why?" I said.

"You know why."

"Because I don't like guns? Because I don't want to arrange it so we have to kill him?"

"It could be dangerous."

"You really think I care about that?"

He studied my face. "No, I guess you don't."

"I just want to see him when he gets caught. I just want to see his expression when he realizes he's going to go to prison for the rest of his life."

He grinned at me with his stained teeth. "I'd rather see him when he's been gut-shot. Still afraid to die but at the same time wanting to. You know? I gut-shot a gook in Nam once and watched him the whole time. It took him an hour. It was one long hour, believe me."

Staring at the three-story apartment house, I sighed. "Eleven years."

"I'm sorry for all you've gone through."

"I know you are, Slocum. That's one of the things a good liberal like me can't figure out about a man like you."

"What's that?"

"How you can enjoy killing people and still feel so much compassion for the human race in general."

He shrugged. "I'm not killing humanity in general, Robert. I'm killing animals." He took out the Cobra, grim gray metal almost glowing in the late June sunlight, checked it, and put it back. His eyes scanned the upper part of the red brick apartment house. Many of the screens were torn and a few shattered windows had been taped up. The lawn needed mowing and a tiny black baby walked around wearing a filthy too-small t-shirt and nothing else. Twenty years ago this had probably been a very nice middle-class place. Now it had the feel of an inner-city housing project.

"One thing," he said, as I started to open the door. He put a meaty hand on my shoulder for emphasis.

"Yes?"

"When this is all over—however it turns out—you're going to feel let down."

"You maybe; not me. All I've wanted for the past eleven years was finding Dexter. Now we have found him. Now I can start my life again."

"That's the thing," he said. "That's what you don't understand."

"What don't I understand?"

"This has changed you, Robert. You start hunting people—even when you've got a personal stake in it—and it changes you."

I laughed. "Right. I think this afternoon I'll go down to my friendly neighborhood recruiting office and sign up for Green Beret school."

Occasionally, he got irritated with me. Now seemed to be one of those times. "I'm just some big dumb redneck, right, Robert? What would I know about the subtleties of human psychology, right?"

"Look, Slocum, I'm sorry if—"

He patted his Cobra. "Let's go."

2

They found her in a grave that was really more of a wide hole up in High Ridge forest where the scrub pines run heavy down to the river. My daughter Debbie. The coroner estimated she had been there at least thirty days. At the time of her death she'd been seventeen.

This is the way the official version ran: Debbie, leaving her job at the Baskin-Robbins, was dragged into a car, taken into the forest, raped, and killed. Only when I pressed him on the subject did the coroner tell me the extent to which she had been mutilated, the mutilation coming, so far as could be determined, after she had died. At the funeral the coffin was closed.

At the time I had a wife—small, tanned, intelligent in a hard sensible way I often envied, quick to laugh, equally quick to cry—and a son. Jeff was twelve the year his sister died. He was seventeen when he died five years later.

When you're sitting home watching the sullen parade of faceless murders flicker and die on your screen—the weeping mother of the victim, the carefully spoken detective in charge, the sexless doll-like face of the reporter signing off on the story—you don't take into account the impact that the violent death of a loved one has on a family. I do; after Debbie's death, I made a study of the subject. Like so many things I've studied in my life, I ended up with facts that neither enlightened nor comforted. They were just facts.

My family's loss was measured in two ways—my wife's depression (she came from a family that suffered mental illness the way some families suffered freckles) and my son's wildness.

Not that I was aware of either of these problems as they began to play out. When it became apparent to me that the local police were never going to solve the murder—their entire investigation centered on an elusive 1986 red Chevrolet—I virtually left home. Using a generous inheritance left to me by an uncle, I began—in tandem with the private eyes and soldiers of fortune and psychics I've already mentioned—to pursue my daughter's killer. I have no doubt that my pursuit was obsessive, and clinically so. Nights I would lie on the strange, cold, lonely bed of a strange, cold, lonely motel room thinking of tomorrow, always tomorrow, and how we were only hours away from a man we now knew to be one William K. Dexter, age thirty-seven, twice incarcerated for violent crimes, unduly attached to a very aged mother, perhaps guilty of two similar killings in two other Midwestern states. I thought of nothing else—so much so that sometimes, lying there in the motel room, I wanted to take a butcher knife and cut into my brain until I found the place where memory dwelt—and cut it away. William K. Dexter was my only thought.

During this time, me gone, my wife began a series of affairs (I learned all this later) that only served to increase the senseless rage she felt (she seemed to resent the men because they could not give her peace)—she still woke up screaming Debbie's name. Her drinking increased also and she began shopping around for new shrinks the way you might shop around for a new car. A few times during her last two months we made love when I came home on the weekend from pursuing Dexter in one fashion or another—but afterward it was always the same. "You weren't a good father to her, Robert." "I know." "And I wasn't a good mother. We're such goddamned selfish people." And then the sobbing, sobbing to the point of passing out (always drunk of course) in a little-girl pile in the bathroom or the center of the hardwood bedroom floor.

Jeff found her. Just home from school, calling her name, not really expecting her to be there, he went upstairs to the TV room for the afternoon ritual of a dance show and there he found her. The last images of a soap opera flickering on the screen. A drink of bourbon in the Smurf glass she always found so inexplicably amusing. A cigarette guttering out in the ashtray. Dressed in one of Jeff's T-shirts with the rock-and-roll slogan on its front and a pair of designer jeans that pointed up the teenage sleekness of her body. Dead. Heart attack.

On the day of her funeral, up in the TV room where she'd died, I was having drinks of my own, wishing I had some facts to tell me what I should be feeling now. . .when Jeff came in and sat down next to me and put his arm around my neck the way he used to when he was three or four. "You can't cry, can you, Dad?" All I could do was sigh. He'd been watching me. "You should cry, Dad. You really should. You didn't even cry when Debbie was killed. Mom told me." He said all this in the young man's voice I still couldn't quite get used to—the voice he used so successfully with ninth-grade girls on the phone. He wasn't quite a man yet but he wasn't a kid, either. In a moment of panic I felt he was an imposter, that this was a joke; where was my little boy? "That's all I do, Dad. Is cry, I mean. I think it helps me. I really do."

So I'd tried, first there with Jeff in the TV room, later alone in my bedroom. But there were just dry choking sounds and no tears at all. At all. I would think of Debbie, her sweet soft radiance; and of my wife, the years when it had been good for us, her so tender and kind in the shadows of our hours together; and I wanted to cry for the loss I felt. But all I could see was the face of William K. Dexter. In some way, he had become more important to me even than the two people he'd taken from me.

Jeff died three years later, wrapped around a light pole on the edge of a country park, drugs and vodka found in the front seat of the car I'd bought him six months earlier.

Left alone at the wake, kneeling before his waxen corpse, an Our Father faint on my lips, I'd felt certain I could cry. It would be a tribute to Jeff; one he'd understand; some part of the process by which he'd forgive me for being gone so much, for pursuing William K. Dexter while Jeff was discovering drugs and alcohol and girls too young to know about nurturing. I put out my hand and touched his cheek, his cold waxen cheek, and I felt something die in me. It was the opposite of crying, of bursting forth with poisons that needed to be purged. Something was dead in me and would never be reborn.

It was not too long after this that I met Frank Slocum and it was not long after Slocum took the case that we began to close inexorably in on William K. Dexter.

And soon enough we were here, at the apartment house just outside Des Moines.

Eleven years, two months, and five days later.

3

The name on the hallway mailbox said Severn, George Severn. We knew better, of course.

Up carpeted stairs threadbare and stained, down a hallway thick with dusty sunlight, to a door marked 4-A.

"Behind me," Slocum whispered, waving me to the wall.

For a moment, the only noises belonged to the apartment building; the thrum of electricity snaking through the walls; the creak of roof in summer wind; a toilet exploding somewhere on the floor below us.

Slocum put a hefty finger to his thick mouth, stabbing through a thistle of beard to do so. Sssh.

Slocum stood back from the door himself. His Cobra was in his hand, ready. He reached around the long way and set big knuckles against the cheap faded pine of the door.

On the other side of the door, I heard chair legs scrape against tile.

Somebody in there.

William K. Dexter.

Chair legs scraped again; footsteps. They did not come all the way to the door, however, rather stopped at what I imagined was probably the center of the living room.

"Yeah?"

Slocum put his finger to his lips again. Reached around once more and knocked.

"I said 'Yeah'. Who the hell is it?"

He was curious about who was in the hall, this George Severn was, but not curious enough to open the door and find out.

One more knock. Quick rap really; nothing more.

Inside, you could sense Severn's aggravation.

"Goddammit," he said and took a few loud steps toward the door but then stopped.

Creak of floor; flutter of robin wings as bird settled on hallway window; creak of floor again from inside the apartment.

Slocum held up a halting hand. Then he pantomimed Don't Move with his lips. He waited for my reaction. I nodded.

He looked funny, a man as big as he was, doing a very broad, cartoon version of a man walking away. Huge noisy steps so that it sounded as if he were very quickly retreating. But he did all this in place. He did it for thirty seconds and then he eased himself flat back against the wall. He took his Cobra and put it man-high on the edge of the door frame.

Severn didn't come out in thirty seconds but he did come out in about a minute.

For eleven years I'd wondered what he'd look like. Photos deceive. I always pictured him as formidable. He would have to be, I'd reasoned; the savage way he'd mutilated her. . . He was a skinny fortyish man in a stained white T-shirt and Levis that looked a little too big. He wore the wide sideburns of a hillbilly trucker and the scowl of a mean drunk. He stank of sleep and whiskey. He carried a butcher knife that appeared to be new. It still had the lime-green price sticker on the black handle.

When he came out of his apartment, he made the mistake of looking straight ahead.

Slocum did two things at the same time: slammed the Cobra's nose hard against Severn's temple and yanked a handful of hair so hard, Severn's knees buckled. "You're dead, man, in case you haven't figured it out already," Slocum said. He seemed enraged; he was a little frightening to watch.

He grabbed some more hair and then he pushed Severn all the way back into his apartment.

4

Slocum got him on a straight-backed chair, hit him so hard in the mouth that you could hear teeth go, and then handcuffed him, still in the chair, to the aged Formica dining-room table.

Slocum then cocked his foot back and kicked Severn clean and hard in the ribs. Almost immediately, Severn's mouth started boiling with red mucus that didn't seem quite thick enough to be blood.

Slocum next went over to Severn and ripped his T-shirt away from his shoulder. Without a word, Slocum motioned me over.

With his Cobra, Slocum pointed to a faded tattoo on Severn's right shoulder. It read: *Mindy* with a rose next to it. Not many men had such a tattoo on their right shoulder. It was identical to the one listed in all of Severn's police records.

Slocum slapped him with stunning ferocity directly across the mouth, so hard that both Severn and his chair were lifted from the floor.

For the first time, I moved. Not to hit Severn myself but to put a halting hand on Slocum's arm. "That's enough."

"We've got the right guy!" It was easy to see he was crazed in some profound animal way I'd never seen in anybody before.

"I know we do."

"The guy who killed your daughter!"

"I know," I said, "but—"

"But what?"

I sighed. "But I don't want to be like him and if we sat here and beat him, that's exactly what we'd be. Animals—just like him."

Slocum's expression was a mixture of contempt and disbelief. I could see whatever respect he'd had for me—or perhaps it had been nothing more than mere pity—was gone now. He looked at me the same way I looked at him—as some alien species.

"Please, Slocum," I said.

He got one more in, a good solid right hand to the left side of Severn's head. Severn's eyes rolled and he went out. From the smell, you could tell he'd wet his pants.

I kept calling him Severn. But of course he wasn't Severn. He was William K. Dexter.

Slocum went over to the ancient Kelvinator, took out a can of Hamms and opened it with a great deal of violence, and then slammed the refrigerator door.

"You think he's all right?" I said.

"What the hell's that supposed to mean?"

"It means did you kill him?"

"Kill him?" He laughed. The contempt was back in his voice. "Kill him? No, but I should have. I keep thinking of your daughter, man. All the things you've told me about her. Not a perfect kid—no kid is—but a real gentle little girl. A girl you supposedly loved. Your frigging daughter, man." He sloshed his beer in the general direction of Dexter. "I should get out my hunting knife and cut his balls off. That's what I should do. And that's just for openers. Just for openers."

He started pacing around, then, Slocum did, and I could gauge his rage. I suppose at that moment he wanted to kill us both—Dexter for being an animal, me for being a weakling—neither of us the type of person Slocum wanted in his universe.

The apartment was small and crammed with threadbare and wobbly furniture. Everything had been burned with cigarettes and disfigured with beer-can rings. The sour smell of bad cooking lay on the air; sunlight poured through filthy windows; and even from here you could smell the rancid odors of the bathroom. On the bureau lay two photographs, one of a plump woman in a shabby housedress standing with her arm around Dexter, obviously his mother; and a much younger Dexter squinting into the sun outside a gray metal barracks where he had served briefly as an army private before being pushed out on a mental.

Peeking into the bedroom, I found the centerfolds he'd pinned up. They weren't the centerfolds of the quality men's magazines where the women were beautiful to begin with and made even more so with careful lighting and gauzy effects; no, these were the women of the street, hard-eyed, flabby-bodied, some even tattooed like Dexter himself. They covered the walls on either side of his sad little cot where he slept in a room littered with empty beer cans and hard-crusted pizza boxes. Many of the centerfolds he'd defaced, drawing penises in black ballpoint aimed at their vaginas or their mouths, or putting huge blood-dripping knives into their breasts or eyes or even their vaginas. All I could think of was Debbie and what he'd done to her that long ago night. . .

A terrible, oppressive nausea filled me as I backed out of the bedroom and groped for the couch so I could sit down.

"What's the matter?" Slocum said.

"Shut up."

"What?"

"Shut the fuck up!"

I sank to the couch—the sunlight through the greasy window making me ever warmer—and cupped my hands in my face and swallowed again and again until I felt the vomit in my throat and esophagus and stomach recede.

I was shaking, chilled now with sweat.

"Can you wake him up?"

"What?"

"Can you wake him up?"

"Sure," Slocum said, "Why?"

"Because I want to talk to him."

Slocum gulped the last of his beer, tossed the can into a garbage sack overflowing with coffee grounds and tomato rinds, and then went over to the sink. He took down a big glass with the Flintstones on it and filled it with water, then took the glass over to where he had Dexter handcuffed. With a certain degree of obvious pleasure, he threw the water across Dexter's head. He threw the glass—as if it were now contaminated—into the corner where it shattered into three large jagged pieces.

He grabbed Dexter by the hair and jerked his head back.

Groaning, Dexter came awake.

"Now what?" Slocum said, turning to me.

"Now I want to talk to him."

"Talk to him," Slocum said. "Right."

He pointed a large hand at Dexter as if he were a master of cere-monies introducing the next act.

It wasn't easy, getting up off that couch and going over to him. In a curious way, I was terrified of him. If I pushed him hard enough, he would tell me the exact truth about the night. The truth in detail. What she had looked like and sounded like—her screams as he raped her; her screams as she died—and then I would have my facts. . .but facts so horrible I would not be able to live with them. How many times—despite myself—I had tried to recreate that night. But there would be no solace in this particular truth; no solace at all.

I stood over him. "Have you figured out who I am yet?"

He stared up at me. He started crying. "Hey, man, I never did nothing to you."

"You raped and killed a girl named Debbie eleven years ago."

"I don't know what you're talking about, man. Honest. You got the wrong guy."

I knew by the way I studied his face—every piece of beard stub-ble, the green matter collected in the corners of his eyes, the dandruff flaked off at the front of his receding hairline—that I was trying to learn something about him, something that would grant me peace after all these years.

A madman, this Dexter, and so not quite responsible for what he'd done and perhaps even deserving of pity in my good liberal soul.

But he didn't seem insane, at least not insane enough to move me in any way. He was just a cheap trapped frightened animal.

"Really, man; really I don't know what the hell you're talking about."

"I've been tracking you for eleven years now—"

"Jesus, man; listen—"

"You're going to hate prison, Dexter. Or maybe they'll even exe-cute you. Did you ever read anything about the injections they give? They make it sound so humane but it's the waiting, Dexter. It's the waiting—"

"Please," he said, "please," and he writhed against his handcuffs, scraping the table across the floor in the process.

"Eleven years, Dexter," I said.

I could hear my voice, what was happening to it—all my feelings about Dexter were merging into my memories of those defaced cen-terfolds in his bedroom—and Slocum must have known it too, with his animal wisdom, known at just what moment I would be right for it because just then and just so the Cobra came into my hands and I shot Dexter once in the face and once in the chest and I

5

Slocum explained to me—though I really wasn't listening—that they were called by various names (toss guns or throw away guns) but they were carried by police officers in case they wanted to show that the person they'd just killed had been armed.

From a holster strapped to his ankle, Slocum took a .38, wiped it clean of prints, and set it next to Dexter's hand.

Below and to the side of us the apartment house was a frenzy of shouts and cries—fear and panic—and already in the distance sirens exploded red on the soft blue air of the summer day.

6

That evening I cried.

I sat in a good room in a good hotel with the air-conditioning going strong, a fine dinner and many fine drinks in my belly, and I cried.

Wept, really.

Whatever had kept me from crying for my daughter and then my wife and then my son was gone now and so I could love and mourn them in a way I'd never been able to. I thought of each of them—their particular ways of laughing, their particular sets of pleasures and dreams, their particular fears and apprehensions—and it was as if they joined me there in that chill antiseptic hotel room, Debbie in her blue sweater and jeans, my wife in her white linen sheath, Jeff in his Kiss T-shirt and chinos—came around in the way the medieval church taught that angels gathered around the bed of a dying person. . .only I wasn't dying.

My family was there to tell me that I was to live again. To seek some sort of peace and normalcy after the forced march of these past eleven years.

"I love you so much," I said aloud to each of them, and wept all the more; "I love you so much."

And then I slept.

7

"I talked to the district attorney," Slocum said in the coffee shop the following morning. "He says it's very unlikely there will be any charges."

"He really thought Dexter was armed?"

"Wouldn't you? A piece of trash like Dexter?"

I stared at him. "You know something terrible?"

"What?"

"I don't feel guilty."

He let go with one of those cigarette-raspy laughs of his. "Good."

Then it was his turn to stare at me, there in the hubbub of clattering dishes and good sweet coffee smells and bacon sizzling on the grill. "So what now?"

"See if I can get my job back."

"At the university?"

"Umm-hmm."

He kept staring. "You don't feel any guilt do you?"

"No. I mean, I know I should. Whatever else, he was a human being. But—"

He smiled his hard Old Testament smile. "Now don't you go giving me any of those mousy little liberal 'buts,' all right?"

"All right."

"You just go back and live your life and make it a good one."

"I owe you one hell of a lot, Slocum."

He put forth a slab of hand and a genuine look of affection in his eyes. "Just make it a good one," he said. "Promise?"

"Promise."

"And no guilt?"

"No guilt."

He grinned. "I knew I could make a man out of you."

8

Her name was Anne Stevens and she was to dominate my first year back at the university. Having met at the faculty picnic—hot August giving way to the fierce melancholy of Indian summer—we began what we both hoped (her divorced; me not quite human yet) would be a pleasant but slow-moving relationship. We were careful to not introduce real passion, for instance, until we both felt certain we could handle it, about the time the first of the Christmas decorations blew in the gray wind of Harcourt Square.

School itself took some adjusting. First, there was the fact that the students seemed less bright and inquisitive, more conservative than the students I remembered. Second, the faculty had some doubts about me; given my experiences over the past eleven years, they wondered how I would fit into a setting whose goals were at best abstract. I wondered, too. . .

After the first time we made love—Anne's place, unplanned, satisfying if slightly embarrassing—I went home and stared at the photograph of my wife I keep on my bureau. In whispers, I apologized for what I'd done. If I'd been a better husband I would have no guilt now. But I had not, alas, been a better husband at all. . .

In the spring, a magazine took a piece on inflation I wrote and the academic dean made a considerable fuss over this fact. Also in the spring Anne and I told each other that we loved each other in a variety of ways, emotionally, sexually, spiritually. We set June 23 as our wedding day.

It was on May 5 that I saw the item in the state newspaper. For the following three weeks I did my best to forget it, troubling as it was. Anne began to notice a difference in my behavior, and to talk about it. I just kept thinking of the newspaper item and of something Slocum had said that day when I killed Dexter.

In the middle of a May night—the breeze sweet with the newly blooming world—I typed out a six-page letter to Anne, packed two bags, stopped by a 7-11 and filled the Volvo and dropped Anne's letter in a mailbox, and then set out on the Interstate.

Two mornings later, I walked up a dusty flight of stairs inside an apartment house. A Hank Williams, Jr. record filled the air.

To be heard above the music, I had to pound.

I half-expected what would happen, that when the door finally opened a gun would be shoved in my face. It was.

A Cobra.

I didn't say anything. I just handed him the news clipping. He waved me in—he lived in a place not dissimilar from the one Dexter had lived in—read the clipping as he opened an 8:48 A.M. beer.

Finished reading it, he let it glide to the coffee table that was covered with gun magazines.

"So?"

"So I want to help him. I don't want him to go through what I did."

"You know him or something?"

"No."

"Just some guy whose daughter was raped and killed and the suspect hasn't been apprehended."

"Right."

"And you want what?"

"I've got money and I've got time. I quit my job."

"But what do you want?"

"I want us to go after him. Remember how you said that I'd changed and that I didn't even know it?"

"Yeah, I remember."

"Well, you were right. I have changed."

He stood up and stated laughing, his considerable belly shaking beneath his Valvoline T-shirt. "Well, I'll be goddamned, Robert. I'll be goddamned. I did make a man out of you, after all. So how about having a beer with me?"

At first—it not being nine A.M. yet—I hesitated. But then I nodded my head and said, "Yeah, Slocum. That sounds good. That really sounds good."

THE REASON WHY

I'm scared."

   "This was your idea, Karen."

   "You scared?"

"No."

"You bastard."

"Because I'm not scared I'm a bastard?"

"You not being scared means you don't believe me."

"Well."

"See. I knew it."

"What?"

"Just the way you said 'Well.' You bastard."

I sighed and looked out at the big red brick building that sprawled over a quarter mile of spring grass turned silver by a fat June moon. Twenty-five years ago a 1950 Ford fastback had sat in the adjacent parking lot. Mine for two summers of grocery store work.

We were sitting in her car, a Volvo she'd cadged from her last marriage settlement, number four if you're interested, and sharing a pint of bourbon the way we used to in high school when we'd been more than friends but never quite lovers.

The occasion tonight was our twenty-fifth class reunion. But there was another occasion, too. In our senior year a boy named Michael Brandon had jumped off a steep clay cliff called Pierce Point to his death on the winding river road below. Suicide. That, anyways, had been the official version.

A month ago Karen Lane (she had gone back to her maiden name these days, the Karen Lane-Cummings-Todd-Brown-Lemay getting a tad too long) had called to see if I wanted to go to dinner and I said yes, if I could bring Donna along, but then Donna surprised me by saying she didn't care to go along, that by now we should be at a point in our relationship where we trusted each other ("God, Dwyer, I don't even look at other men, not for very long anyway, you know?"), and Karen and I had had dinner and she'd had many drinks, enough that I saw she had a problem, and then she'd told me about something that had troubled her for a long time. . .

In senior year she'd gone to a party and gotten sick on wine and stumbled out to somebody's backyard to throw up and it was there she'd overheard the three boys talking. They were earnestly discussing what happened to Michael Brandon the previous week and they were even more earnestly discussing what would happen to them if "anybody ever really found out the truth."

"It's bothered me all these years," she'd said over dinner a month earlier. "They murdered him and they got away with it."

"Why didn't you tell the police?"

"I didn't think they'd believe me."

"Why not?"

She shrugged and put her lovely little face down, dark hair covering her features. Whenever she put her face down that way it meant that she didn't want to tell you a lie so she'd just as soon talk about something else.

"Why not, Karen?"

"Because of where we came from. The Highlands."

The Highlands is an area that used to ring the iron foundries and factories of this city. Way before pollution became a fashionable concern, you could stand on your front porch and see a peculiarly beautiful orange haze on the sky every dusk. The Highlands had bars where men lost ears, eyes, and fingers in just garden-variety fights, and streets where nobody sane ever walked after dark, not even cops unless they were in pairs. But it wasn't the physical violence you remembered so much as the emotional violence of poverty. You get tired of hearing your mother scream because there isn't enough money for food and hearing your father scream back because there's nothing he can do about it. Nothing.

Karen Lane and I had come from the Highlands, but we were smarter and, in her case, better looking than most of the people from the area, so when we went to Wilson High School—one of those nightmare conglomerates that shoves the poorest kids in a city in with the richest—we didn't do badly for ourselves. By senior year we found ourselves hanging out with the sons and daughters of bankers and doctors and city officials and lawyers and riding around in new Impala convertibles and attending an occasional party where you saw an actual maid. But wherever we went, we'd manage for at least a few minutes to get away from our dates and talk to each other. What we were doing, of course, was trying to comfort ourselves. We shared terrible and confusing feelings—pride that we were acceptable to those we saw as glamorous, shame that we felt disgrace for being from the Highlands and having fathers who worked in factories and mothers who went to Mass as often as nuns and brothers and sisters who were doomed to punching the clock and yelling at ragged kids in the cold factory dusk. (You never realize what a toll such shame takes till you see your father's waxen face there in the years-later casket.)

That was the big secret we shared, of course, Karen and I, that we were going to get out, leave the place once and for all. And her brown eyes never sparkled more Christmas-morning bright than at those moments when it all was ahead of us, money, sex, endless thrills, immortality. She had the kind of clean good looks brought out best by a blue cardigan with a line of white buttons at the top and a brown suede car coat over her slender shoulders and moderately tight jeans displaying her quietly artful ass. Nothing splashy about her. She had the sort of face that snuck up on you. You had the impression you were talking to a pretty but in no way spectacular girl, and then all of a sudden you saw how the eyes burned with sad humor and how wry the mouth got at certain times and how the freckles enhanced rather than detracted from her beauty and by then of course you were hopelessly entangled. Hopelessly.

This wasn't just my opinion, either. I mentioned four divorce settlements. True facts. Karen was one of those prizes that powerful and rich men like to collect with the understanding that it's only something you hold in trust, like a yachting cup. So, in her time, she'd been an ornament for a professional football player (her college beau), an orthodontist ("I think he used to have sexual fantasies about Barry Goldwater"), the owner of a large commuter airline ("I slept with half his pilots; it was kind of a company benefit"), and a sixty-nine-year-old millionaire who was dying of heart disease ("He used to have me sit next to his bedside and just hold his hand—the weird thing was that of all of them, I loved him, I really did—and his eyes would be closed and then every once in a while tears would start streaming down his cheeks as if he was remembering something that really filled him with remorse; he was really a sweetie, but then cancer got him before the heart disease and I never did find out what he regretted so much, I mean if it was about his son or his wife or what"), and now she was comfortably fixed for the rest of her life and if the crow's feet were a little more pronounced around eyes and mouth and if the slenderness was just a trifle too slender (she weighed, at five-three, maybe ninety pounds and kept a variety of diet books in her big sunny kitchen), she was a damn good-looking woman nonetheless, the world's absurdity catalogued and evaluated in a gaze that managed to be both weary and impish, with a laugh that was knowing without being cynical.

So now she wanted to play detective.

I had some more bourbon from the pint—it burned beautifully—and said, "If I had your money, you know what I'd do?"

"Buy yourself a new shirt?"

"You don't like my shirt?"

"I didn't know you had this thing about Hawaii?"

"If I had your money I'd just forget about all of this."

"I thought cops were sworn to uphold the right and the true."

"I'm an ex-cop."

"You wear a uniform."

"That's for the American Security Agency."

She sighed. "So I shouldn't have sent the letters?"

"No."

"Well, if they're guilty, they'll show up at Pierce Point tonight."

"Not necessarily."

"Why?"

"Maybe they'll know it's a trap. And not do anything."

She nodded to the school. "You hear that?"

"What?"

"The song?"

It was Bobby Vinton's "Roses are Red."

"I remember one party when we both hated our dates and we ended up dancing to that over and over again. Somebody's basement. You remember?"

"Sort of, I guess," I said.

"Good. Let's go in the gym and then we can dance to it again."

Donna, my lady friend, was out of town attending an advertising convention. I hoped she wasn't going to dance with anybody else because it would sure make me mad.

I started to open the door and she said, "I want to ask you a question."

"What?" I sensed what it was going to be so I kept my eyes on the parking lot.

"Turn around and look at me."

I turned around and looked at her. "Okay."

"Since the time we had dinner a month or so ago I've started receiving brochures from Alcoholics Anonymous in the mail. If you were having them sent to me, would you be honest enough to tell me?"

"Yes, I would."

"Are you having them sent to me?"

"Yes, I am."

"You think I'm a lush?"

"Don't you?"

"I asked you first."

So we went into the gym and danced.

~ ~ ~ ~ ~

Crepe of red and white, the school colors, draped the ceiling; the stage was a cave of white light on which stood four balding fat guys with spit curls and shimmery gold lamé dinner jackets (could these be the illegitimate sons of Bill Haley?) playing guitars, drum, and saxophone; on the dance floor couples who'd lost hair, teeth, jaw lines, courage, and energy (everything, it seemed, but weight) danced to lame cover versions of "Breaking Up Is Hard To Do" and "Sheila," "Run-Around Sue" and "Running Scared" (tonight's lead singer sensibly not even trying Roy Orbison's beautiful falsetto) and then, they broke into a medley of dance tunes—everything from "Locomotion" to "The Peppermint Twist"—and the place went a little crazy, and I went right along with it.

"Come on," I said.

"Great."

We went out there and we burned ass. We'd both agreed not to dress up for the occasion so we were ready for this. I wore the Hawaiian shirt she found so despicable plus a blue blazer, white socks and cordovan penny-loafers. She wore a salmon-colored Merikani shirt belted at the waist and tan cotton fatigue pants and, sweet Christ, she was so adorable half the guys in the place did the kind of double-takes usually reserved for somebody outrageous or famous.

Over the blasting music, I shouted, "Everybody's watching you!"

She shouted right back, "I know! Isn't it wonderful?"

The medley went twenty minutes and could easily have been confused with an aerobics session. By the end I was sopping and wishing I was carrying ten or fifteen pounds less and sometimes feeling guilty because I was having too much fun (I just hoped Donna, probably having too much fun, too, was feeling guilty), and then finally it ended and mate fell into the arms of mate, hanging on to stave off sheer collapse.

Then the head Bill Haley clone said, "Okay, now we're going to do a ballad medley," so then we got everybody from Johnny Mathis to Connie Francis and we couldn't resist that, so I moved her around the floor with clumsy pleasure and she moved me right back with equally clumsy pleasure. "You know something?" I said.

"We're both shitty dancers?"

"Right."

But we kept on, of course, laughing and whirling a few times, and then coming tighter together and just holding each other silently for a time, two human beings getting older and scared about getting older, remembering some things and trying to forget others and trying to make sense of an existence that ultimately made sense to nobody, and then she said, "There's one of them."

I didn't have to ask her what "them" referred to. Until now she'd refused to identify any of the three people she'd sent the letters to.

At first I didn't recognize him. He had almost white hair and a tan so dark it looked fake. He wore a black dinner jacket with a lacy shirt and a black bow tie. He didn't seem to have put on a pound in the quarter century since I'd last seen him.

"Ted Forester?"

"Forester," she said. "He's president of the same savings and loan his father was president of."

"Who are the other two?"

"Why don't we get some punch?"

"The kiddie kind?"

"You could really make me mad with all this lecturing about alcoholism."

"If you're really not a lush then you won't mind getting the kiddie kind."

"My friend, Sigmund Fraud."

We had a couple of pink punches and caught our respective breaths and squinted in the gloom at name tags to see who we were saying hello to and realized all the terrible things you realize at high school reunions, namely that people who thought they were better than you still think that way, and that all the sad people you feared for—the ones with blackheads and low IQs and lame left legs and walleyes and lisps and every other sort of unfair infirmity people get stuck with—generally turned out to be deserving of your fear, for there was melancholy in their eyes tonight that spoke of failures of every sort, and you wanted to go up and say something to them (I wanted to go up to nervous Karl Carberry, who used to twitch—his whole body twitched—and throw my arm around him and tell him what a neat guy he was, tell him there was no reason whatsoever for his twitching, grant him peace and self-esteem and at least a modicum of hope; if he needed a woman, get him a woman, too), but of course you didn't do that, you didn't go up, you just made edgy jokes and nodded a lot and drifted on to the next piece of human carnage.

"There's number two," Karen whispered.

This one I remembered. And despised. The six-three blond movie-star looks had grown only slightly older. His blue dinner jacket just seemed to enhance his air of malicious superiority. Larry Price. His wife Sally was still perfect, too, though you could see in the lacquered blond hair and maybe a hint of face-lift that she'd had to work at it a little harder. A year out of high school, at a bar that took teenage IDs checked by a guy who must have been legally blind, I'd gotten drunk and told Larry that he was essentially an asshole for beating up a friend of mine who hadn't had a chance against him. I had the street boy's secret belief that I could take anybody whose father was a surgeon and whose house included a swimming pool. I had hatred, bitterness, and rage going, right? Well, Larry and I went out into the parking lot, ringed by a lot of drunken spectators, and before I got off a single punch, Larry hit me with a shot that stood me straight up, giving him a great opportunity to hit me again. He hit me three times before I found his face and sent him a shot hard enough to push him back for a time. Before we could go at it again, the guy who checked IDs got himself between us. He was madder than either Larry or me. He ended the fight by taking us both by the ears (he must have trained with nuns) and dragging us out to the curb and telling neither of us to come back.

"You remember the night you fought him?"

"Yeah."

"You could have taken him, Dwyer. Those three punches he got in were just lucky."

"Yeah, that was my impression, too. Lucky."

She laughed. "I was afraid he was going to kill you."

I was going to say something smart, but then a new group of people came up and we gushed through a little social dance of nostalgia and lies and self-justifications. We talked success (at high school reunions, everybody sounds like Amway representatives at a pep rally) and the old days (nobody seems to remember all the kids who got treated like shit for reasons they had no control over) and didn't so-and-so look great (usually this meant they'd managed to keep their toupees on straight) and introducing new spouses (we all had to explain what happened to our original mates; I said mine had been eaten by alligators in the Amazon, but nobody seemed to find that especially believable) and in the midst of all this, Karen tugged my sleeve and said, "There's the third one."

Him I recognized, too. David Haskins. He didn't look any happier than he ever had. Parent trouble was always the explanation you got for his grief back in high school. His parents had been rich, truly so, his father an importer of some kind, and their arguments so violent that they were as eagerly discussed as who was or was not pregnant. Apparently David's parents weren't getting along any better today because although the features of his face were open and friendly enough, there was still the sense of some terrible secret stooping his shoulders and keeping his smiles to furtive wretched imitations. He was a paunchy balding little man who might have been a church usher with a sour stomach.

"The Duke of Earl" started up then and there was no way we were going to let that pass so we got out on the floor; but by now, of course, we both watched the three people she'd sent letters to. Her instructions had been to meet the anonymous letter writer at nine-thirty at Pierce Point. If they were going to be there on time, they'd be leaving soon.

"You think they're going to go?"

"I doubt it, Karen."

"You still don't believe that's what I heard them say that night?"

"It was a long time ago and you were drunk."

"It's a good thing I like you because otherwise you'd be a distinct pain in the ass."

Which is when I saw all three of them go stand under one of the glowing red EXIT signs and open a fire door that led to the parking lot.

"They're going!" she said.

"Maybe they're just having a cigarette."

"You know better, Dwyer. You know better."

Her car was in the lot on the opposite side of the gym.

"Well, it's worth the drive even if they don't show up. Pierce Point should be nice tonight."

She squeezed against me and said, "Thanks, Dwyer. Really."

So we went and got her Volvo and went out to Pierce Point where twenty-five years ago a shy kid named Michael Brandon had fallen or been pushed to his death.

Apparently we were about to find out which.

~ ~ ~ ~ ~

The river road wound along a high wall of clay cliffs on the left and a wide expanse of water on the right. The spring night was impossibly beautiful, one of those moments so rich with sweet odor and even sweeter sight you wanted to take your clothes off and run around in some kind of crazed animal circles out of sheer joy.

"You still like jazz," she said, nodding to the radio.

"I hope you didn't mind my turning the station."

"I'm kind of into country."

"I didn't get the impression you were listening."

She looked over at me. "Actually, I wasn't. I was thinking about you sending me all of those AA pamphlets."

"It was arrogant and presumptuous and I apologize."

"No, it wasn't. It was sweet and I appreciate it."

The rest of the ride, I leaned my head back and smelled flowers and grass and river water and watched moonglow through the elms and oaks and birches of this new spring. There was a Dakota Staton song, "Street of Dreams," and I wondered as always where she was and what she was doing, she'd been so fine, maybe the most unappreciated jazz singer of the entire fifties.

Then we were going up a long, twisting gravel road. We pulled up next to a big park pavilion and got out and stood in the wet grass, and she came over and slid her arm around my waist and sort of hugged me in a half-serious way. "This is probably crazy, isn't it?"

I sort of hugged her back in a half-serious way. "Yeah, but it's a nice night for a walk so what the hell."

"You ready?"

"Yep."

"Let's go then."

So we went up the hill to the Point itself, and first we looked out at the far side of the river where white birches glowed in the gloom and where beyond you could see the horseshoe shape of the city lights. Then we looked down, straight down the drop of two hundred feet, to the road where Michael Brandon had died.

When I heard the car starting up the road to the east, I said, "Let's get in those bushes over there."

A thick line of shrubs and second-growth timber would give us a place to hide, to watch them.

By the time we were in place, ducked down behind a wide elm and a mulberry bush, a new yellow Mercedes sedan swung into sight and stopped several yards from the edge of the Point.

A car radio played loud in the night. A Top 40 song. Three men got out. Dignified Forester, matinee-idol Price, anxiety-tight Haskins.

Forester leaned back into the car and snapped the radio off. But he left the headlights on. Forester and Price each had cans of beer.

Haskins bit his nails.

They looked around in the gloom. The headlights made the darkness beyond seem much darker and the grass in its illumination much greener. Price said harshly, "I told you this was just some kind of goddamn prank. Nobody knows squat."

"He's right. He's probably right," Haskins said to Forester. Obviously he was hoping that was the case.

Forester said, "If somebody didn't know something, we would never have gotten those letters."

She moved then and I hadn't expected her to move at all. I'd been under the impression we would just sit there and listen and let them ramble and maybe in so doing reveal something useful.

But she had other ideas.

She pushed through the undergrowth and stumbled a little and got to her feet again and then walked right up to them.

"Karen!" Haskins said.

"So you did kill Michael," she said.

Price moved toward her abruptly, his hand raised. He was drunk and apparently hitting women was something he did without much trouble.

Then I stepped out from our hiding place and said, "Put your hand down, Price."

Forester said, "Dwyer."

"So," Price said, lowering his hand, "I was right, wasn't I?" He was speaking to Forester.

Forester shook his silver head. He seemed genuinely saddened. "Yes, Price, for once your cynicism is justified."

Price said, "Well, you two aren't getting a goddamned penny, do you know that?"

He lunged toward me, still a bully. But I was ready for him, wanted it. I also had the advantage of being sober. When he was two steps away, I hit him just once and very hard in the solar plexus. He backed away, eyes startled, and then he turned abruptly away.

We all stood looking at one another, pretending not to hear the sounds of violent vomiting on the other side of the splendid new Mercedes.

Forester said, "When I saw you there, Karen, I wondered if you could do it alone."

"Do what?"

"What?" Forester said. "What? Let's at least stop the games. You two want money."

"Christ," I said to Karen, who looked perplexed, "they think we're trying to shake them down."

"Shake them down?"

"Blackmail them."

"Exactly," Forester said.

Price had come back around. He was wiping his mouth with the back of his hand. In his other hand he carried a silver-plated .45, the sort of weapon professional gamblers favor.

Haskins said, "Larry, Jesus, what is that?"

"What does it look like?"

"Larry, that's how people get killed." Haskins sounded like Price's mother.

Price's eyes were on me. "Yeah, it would be terrible if Dwyer here got killed, wouldn't it?" He waved the gun at me. I didn't really think he'd shoot, but I sure was afraid he'd trip and the damn thing would go off accidentally. "You've been waiting since senior year to do that to me, haven't you, Dwyer?"

I shrugged. "I guess so, yeah."

"Well, why don't I give Forester here the gun and then you and I can try it again."

"Fine with me."

He handed Forester the .45. Forester took it all right, but what he did was toss it somewhere into the gloom surrounding the car. "Larry, if you don't straighten up here, I'll fight you myself. Do you understand me?" Forester had a certain dignity and when he spoke, his voice carried an easy authority. "There will be no more fighting, do you both understand that?"

"I agree with Ted," Karen said.

Forester, like a teacher tired of naughty children, decided to get on with the real business. "You wrote those letters, Dwyer?"

"No."

"No?"

"No. Karen wrote them."

A curious glance was exchanged by Forester and Karen.

"I guess I should have known that," Forester said.

"Jesus, Ted," Karen said, "I'm not trying to blackmail you, no matter what you think."

"Then just exactly what are you trying to do?"

She shook her lovely little head. I sensed she regretted ever writing the letters, stirring it all up again. "I just want the truth to come out about what really happened to Michael Brandon that night."

"The truth," Price said. "Isn't that goddamn touching?"

"Shut up, Larry," Haskins said.

Forester said, "You know what happened to Michael Brandon?"

"I've got a good idea," Karen said. "I overheard you three talking at a party one night."

"What did we say?"

"What?"

"What did you overhear us say?"

Karen said, "You said that you hoped nobody looked into what really happened to Michael that night."

A smile touched Forester's lips. "So on that basis you concluded that we murdered him?"

"There wasn't much else to conclude."

Price said, weaving still, leaning on the fender for support, "I don't goddamn believe this."

Forester nodded to me. "Dwyer, I'd like to have a talk with Price and Haskins here, if you don't mind. Just a few minutes." He pointed to the darkness beyond the car. "We'll walk over there. You know we won't try to get away because you'll have our car. All right?"

I looked at Karen.

She shrugged.

They left, back into the gloom, voices receding and fading into the sounds of crickets and a barn owl and a distant roaring train.

"You think they're up to something?"

"I don't know," I said.

We stood with our shoes getting soaked and looked at the green green grass in the headlights.

"What do you think they're doing?" Karen asked.

"Deciding what they want to tell us."

"You're used to this kind of thing, aren't you?"

"I guess."

"It's sort of sad, isn't it?"

"Yeah, it is."

"Except for you getting the chance to punch out Larry Price after all these years."

"Christ, you really think I'm that petty?"

"I know you are. I know you are."

Then we both turned to look back to where they were. There'd been a cry and Forester shouted, "You hit him again, Larry, and I'll break your goddamn jaw." They were arguing about something and it had turned vicious.

I leaned back against the car. She leaned back against me. "You think we'll ever go to bed?"

"I'd sure like to, Karen, but I can't."

"Donna?"

"Yeah. I'm really trying to learn how to be faithful."

"That been a problem?"

"It cost me a marriage."

"Maybe I'll learn how someday, too."

Then they were back. Somebody, presumably Forester, had torn Price's nice lacy shirt into shreds. Haskins looked miserable.

Forester said, "I'm going to tell you what happened that night."

I nodded.

"I've got some beer in the back seat. Would either of you like one?"

Karen said, "Yes, we would."

So he went and got a six pack of Michelob and we all had a beer and just before he started talking he and Karen shared another one of those peculiar glances and then he said, "The four of us—myself, Price, Haskins, and Michael Brandon—had done something we were very ashamed of."

"Afraid of," Haskins said.

"Afraid that if it came out, our lives would be ruined. Forever," Forester said.

Price said, "Just say it, Forester." He glared at me.

"We raped a girl, the four of us.

"Brandon spent two months afterward seeing the girl, bringing her flowers, apologizing to her over and over again, telling her how sorry we were, that we'd been drunk and it wasn't like us to do that and—" Forester sighed, put his eyes to the ground. "In fact we had been drunk; in fact it wasn't like us to do such a thing—"

Haskins said, "It really wasn't. It really wasn't."

For a time there was just the barn owl and the crickets again, no talk, and then gently I said, "What happened to Brandon that night?"

"We were out as we usually were, drinking beer, talking about it, afraid the girl would finally turn us into the police, still trying to fig- ure out why we'd ever done such a thing—"

The hatred was gone from Price's eyes. For the first time the matinee idol looked as melancholy as his friends. "No matter what you think of me, Dwyer, I don't rape women. But that night—" He shrugged, looked away.

"Brandon," I said, "You were going to tell me about Brandon."

"We came up here, had a case of beer or something, and talked about it some more, and that night," Forester said, "that night Bran- don just snapped. He couldn't handle how ashamed he was or how afraid he was of being turned in. Right in the middle of talking—"

Haskins took over. "Right in the middle, he just got up and ran out to the Point." He indicated the cliff behind us. "And before we could stop him, he jumped."

"Jesus," Price said, "I can't forget his screaming on the way down. I can't ever forget it."

I looked at Karen. "So what she heard you three talking about outside the party that night wasn't that you'd killed Brandon but that you were afraid a serious investigation into his suicide might turn up the rape?"

Forester said, "Exactly." He stared at Karen. "We didn't kill Michael, Karen. We loved him. He was our friend."

But by then, completely without warning, she had started to cry and then she began literally sobbing, her entire body shaking with some grief I could neither understand nor assuage.

I nodded to Forester to get back in his car and leave. They stood and watched us a moment and then they got into the Mercedes and went away, taking the burden of years and guilt with them.

~ ~ ~ ~ ~

This time I drove. I went far out the river road, miles out, where you pick up the piney hills and the deer standing by the side of the road.

From the glove compartment she took a pint of J&B, and I knew better than to try and stop her.

I said, "You were the girl they raped, weren't you?"

"Yes."

"Why didn't you tell the police?"

She smiled at me. "The police weren't exactly going to believe a girl from the Highlands about the sons of rich men."

I sighed. She was right.

"Then Michael started coming around to see me. I can't say I ever forgave him, but I started to feel sorry for him. His fear—" She shook her head, looked out the window. She said, almost to herself, "But I had to write those letters, get them there tonight, know for sure if they killed him." She paused. "You believe them?"

"That they didn't kill him?"

"Right."

"Yes, I believe them."

"So do I."

Then she went back to staring out the window, her small face childlike there in silhouette against the moonsilver river. "Can I ask you a question, Dwyer?"

"Sure."

"You think we're ever going to get out of the Highlands?"

"No," I said, and drove on faster in her fine new expensive car. "No, I don't."

THE WAY IT USED TO BE

PRIVATE COON HUNTING

That's all the note said, the note passed three desks back in last hour study hall, that lazy hour when half the students dozed off.

When Boze Douglas opened the note and read the three words, he smiled. No doubt who'd sent the note. No doubt what it meant. No doubt.

Boze kept right on smiling.

He couldn't concentrate on his comic book any more. Boze was a master at laying a comic book inside a textbook and then pretending to be studying his ass off. He liked superheroes especially. In his own mind, he was a superhero. The fact that nobody else at Duncan County Consolidated saw him as a superhero only proved what lame bastards they were. Duncan County Consolidated was one of those country high schools where kids from five small towns went to school together. Farm kids, too. Lots and lots of farm kids. Kids who didn't know, kids who weren't cool, not the way Boze and his friend Gunner (aka Eugene) Preston were cool. Boze and Gunner were wearing nose rings and earrings long before anybody else at Duncan County Consolidated was. And they were way into heavy music and street drugs before most of the other kids, too. And they were tough. Even the big loping farm boys were smart enough to walk clear of Boze and Gunner. Most students—and teachers—considered them dangerous and, man, they loved that shit, people seeing them as dangerous. Absolutely loved it.

"He's gonna be surprised," Gunner said, lighting up a Camel as soon as they cleared the school door.

There was a big football game tonight and so part of the east parking lot was given over to last minute work on the float where the King and Queen would sit tonight. King and Queen, Boze thought. That was crap for little kids. King and Queen. In the distance, he could hear the marching band practicing in the field to the north of the large red brick school. He had to admit, reluctantly, that marching band music still gave him a little-kid thrill. He'd always liked parades. His father had always taken him to parades. . .at least when he was sober. But padre was long gone. Living over in Keokuk with wife number three, selling mobile homes. Now, marching band music—as much as it still secretly thrilled Boze—embarrassed him, too.

Then they were in Boze's five-year-old Firebird and driving fast. This was the best way for Boze to avoid thinking about things—thinking about long-gone Dad, thinking about all the bullshit his sixteen-year-old sister Angie had fallen into—driving fast. Not even drugs were as good as driving fast.

Farm fields in sunny October. Pumpkins and scarecrows and the green John Deere working the hills, preparing for spring planting. And that melancholy smoky smell down from the hills where the trees were on fire with colours so beautiful—reds and yellows and golds and ambers—that they were almost painful to see.

And Angie—little Angie, his own little sister—was going out with a black guy. He still couldn't believe it, though he knew it was absolutely true.

Boys could handle going to Cedar Rapids. There were a lot of temptations for farm kids in a town that size but boys knew how to stay away from them. Or if they couldn't handle them, it still wasn't so bad. They were boys, after all. A white boy and a black girl going out together, much as Boze was against such a thing, that was all right. No harm done. The boy wasn't likely to get all emotional with the black girl. But a white girl with a black boy. . .once you go black, you'll never go back? Wasn't that what he'd heard his old man say to a friend of his, laughing and winking, one beery night?

Boze drove a good ten miles out into the countryside. He hit 104 mph crossing the old Miller bridge. Even the horses and the cows and the sheep seemed to stand still and watch with awe as the Firebird blazed by. The radio was up all the way. Country music all the way. He used to listen to rock but now it was all fairies or coons. Now he was strictly country. On the way back to town, Gunner said, "You scared?"

"About what?"

"You know. Tonight."

Boze looked over at him. "No. But you are."

"Bullshit."

"Bullshit yourself, man. If you weren't scared, you wouldn't have brought it up."

"I just mean we could get caught there. You know, down there with all those black bastards."

"Yeah, we could. But we're not gonna. We're gonna do it and get the hell out of there." That was Gunner for you. Everybody thought he was like this really fearless dude. But he wasn't. He talked big and he had big ideas. But when it came to actually doing them, Boze was the one who always led the way. Gunner wouldn't have done anything if Boze didn't drag him along.

Boze dropped Gunner off. Gunner lived in a small housing development. Most of the people here worked in nearby Amana—factory jobs and good paying ones. New or at least newer cars in the drives now that the day shift was over. And new siding on a lot of the houses. Boze had always envied Gunner his industrious and sober old man. Gunner had it made here and didn't seem to know it. As he was getting out of the car, Gunner said, "I'm really not scared, man. I'm really not." "Then you'll do it?"

"Fuckin' right." Trying to sound tough, hard. But Boze could see the fear in his eyes. This was a couple steps up the criminal ladder from the shoplifting and minor vandalism they were usually into. This was quite a ways up the criminal ladder, in fact.

"I'll pick you up at seven," Boze said.

"Cool," Gunner said, closing the door. Cool, Boze thought to himself as the Firebird squealed away from the curb. Sometimes Gunner was such a lame, he couldn't believe it.

Mom wasn't home yet. Sometimes Al at the restaurant, a slow afternoon, he'd let her off a little early and pay her for the whole day. Mom liked Al despite the fact that the old bastard was always putting the moves on her. He wasn't alone, of course, Al wasn't, Mom being a good-looking woman and lots of men hitting on her. But she said it was "sweet," a seventy-two-year-old guy hitting on a thirty-eight-year-old woman. Plus, it was the best waitressing job she'd ever had. Great tips and nice family-style restaurant. She'd burned out on butt-pinching truck stops and stingy-ass truck drivers.

On a sunny day like this one, the trailer park didn't look so bad. The dirt roads winding between the half mile of mobile homes were dry and not muddy; and fresh wash hanging on clotheslines looked white and clean; and even the battered trailers themselves—screens missing, some graffiti here and there, cracked windows taped up—looked reasonably clean and tidy, tiny strips of lawns covered with dirt roads.

When he got inside, he heard music coming from Angie's room. Rap music. He should have taken that as a sign for sure, last year when she'd started listening to that crap. White girls, at least not good white girls, didn't listen to blacks who couldn't (a) sing (b) write songs, or (c) look like anything but the street punks they were.

At least she'd cleaned up the house. Angie was the neat freak of the family, mostly because she had friends over a lot— she even had a couple of fairly rich friends from in town; she was a friendly and bright and popular girl, she was—and she hated it the way Mom and Boze always left ashtrays overflowing and half-drunk cans of beer and pop strewn everywhere. Not to mention magazines and newspapers and even the occasional half-eaten sandwich. Dad was a neat freak too, unlikely as that was. Angie had inherited the tendency from him.

He knocked on her door and then pushed in without waiting for her to answer.

"Damn you!" she cried when he burst in.

She was standing at her bureau mirror, combing her long, chestnut-coloured hair. Her hair was her pride, as were the high proud breasts she'd sprouted last summer. She was dressed only in a white slip now. Despite the anger he felt—how the hell could she go out with a black guy, anyway?—he wished now he hadn't broken in like this. He felt uncomfortable seeing his fetching sister half-undressed this way. He wanted to think of her the way he used to. . .as a sweet little kid he was always very protective of. He'd even walked to school with her, to make sure she was all right, even though the other boys used to make fun of him. When it started to storm, he'd always panicked, searched frantically through the trailer park until he had her inside and safe. And when she'd been sick with flu or a sore throat or something, he'd always brought her stupid little gifts, and tried to make her laugh so she'd feel better. And then she changed. Last year, it was. Maybe it was her breasts. Maybe her breasts had made her crazy or something. Suddenly, she resented all his fondness, all his protectiveness. How many times in the past year had she screamed at him. It's my life and I'll do what I damned well please! He always felt vaguely sick—even mysteriously fearful—when she screamed this. He felt deserted, more alone than he ever had in his life, even more alone than when Mom and Dad split up six years ago.

And now she was going out with a black guy.

"I'm really getting tired of this, Boze," she said. "You're supposed to knock."

He kept his eyes from her as much as he could. What he really wanted to do was say it. Say he knew about the black guy he had seen pulling away from the trailer here on two different occasions. Linn County plates. Cedar Rapids. Boze hadn't gotten all that good a look at him. But he didn't have to. The guy was black, wasn't he? Wasn't that enough?

But Boze didn't say it because if he did say it she'd run right to Mom and tell her everything, and Mom didn't need any more grief than she already had. It wasn't easy, holding the family together this way, let alone your daughter going out with a black guy. Obviously, there was no way Angie was going to tell Mom—I been going out with this black guy, Mom. And wouldn't Mom just love that? Mom knew a lot about men and men problems. She'd dated a lot of different guys since Dad left. She knew all the ways a woman could get screwed up over a man. And that certainly included dating someone not of your own race. Mom would tear Angie a new one if she ever found out about the black guy.

Boze decided to be coy. "Where you going tonight?"

"Out."

"I know 'out.' I mean where?"

She looked angry a moment and then she smiled sentimentally at him in the mirror. She was putting on bright red lipstick. Blood red. The color she'd be if the black guy ever cut her up with his switchblade. Boze knew all about black guys and their knives. "I'm not six years old any more, Boze. You don't have to protect me."

"I have to protect you more than ever," he said gently.

She turned and came over to him. He tried not to look at her breasts loose beneath her white silk slip. No bra. She kissed him. "I'm sorry I got so mad a minute ago."

"It's all right."

"No, it isn't." She leaned forward and kissed him on the cheek. She smelled sweetly of perfume. It was like she wasn't his sister at all. She was as full of wiles as any other girl, now. He felt sad for some reason. He wanted her to be six or seven or eight again, and have her tiny hand in his, and be helping her. He'd liked to help her. It made him feel important somehow. He hadn't felt important much lately at all. "And since you asked," she said, withdrawing, going back to the mirror and the comb and her hair, "I'm going to Cedar Rapids with Donna and Heather."

"You should stay away from that place."

She watched him coolly in the mirror. "So should you. You're the one who got in trouble there. Not me." The edge was back in her voice now.

He was about to defend himself—pointing out that all he got charged with that time was underage drinking and public intoxication, not exactly murder one—when the front door opened and Mom said, "Hi, kids!"

It was always good to hear her voice. "Hi!" they both said back to her.

Mom set the sack of groceries on the table and then walked back to the bedroom. "How do vegetable burgers and a salad sound for tonight?"

She smelled of perfume, too, and then Boze realized that Angie was wearing Mom's perfume. Mom was short, slender, with long, dark hair and turquoise eyes. She usually wore jeans and crisp white blouses and argyle socks and a pair of comfortable walking shoes. The saddest he'd ever seen her was when Dad gave her that black eye that time. Usually when he beat her up, you couldn't see anything. But the black eye had really embarrassed her. That had been near the end of the marriage.

Mom said, "I take it you're both going out tonight?"

Boze smiled. "No, I thought I'd stay home and do a little knitting."

Mom loved it when he joked with her. When her marriage had been good, before Dad really got going on the booze, Dad had kidded around a lot with her, too. "Oh, you," she said, poking Boze in the ribs. But she looked tired, despite the smile and the kidding, and sometimes he worried about her, how tired and suddenly old she could look. A great sorrow overcame him at such times and all he could think of was funeral homes when he was little, the mysterious adult ritual of putting the dead to rest, the choking-sweet smell of flowers and the whiskey-breath of the working men as they bent down to kiss their little nephews and nieces and the smell of his mother's Kleenex damp with Hail Mary tears when she'd knelt next to the coffin.

Half an hour later, they ate. The burgers were delicious. Part of the time Boze looked out the window. Dusk was falling and it was beautiful, the sky gorgeous golds and salmon pinks and rich purples behind a few full thunderheads. Dusk made Boze sad, too, but it was a good sad somehow, not a bad sad like with Angie or Mom or Dad or Molly Cantrell when he was in love with her last year. That was just one more crazy thing in an already crazy world; how there could be good sads and bad sads. But it wasn't the kind of thing you ever talked about because people would think you were crazy.

Mom said, "You remember you're supposed to be home by eleven tonight?"

"Oh, Mom," Angie said. "That's not fair."

"It certainly is fair, Angie," Mom said. "You were late last Friday night by an hour, so tonight I'm taking an hour off the time you're supposed to be in."

"But eleven o'clock. Nobody else has to come in by eleven o'clock."

"I'm sorry, Angie. But that's the way it's got to be."

Boze lifted weights for twenty minutes while he watched The Nashville Channel (say what you want, Dwight Yoakam was still the coolest of all the male country singers) and then he took a shower and then he got dressed for the night. He put change and a ten dollar bill in his right pocket (Mom always gave him a ten dollar bill on Friday) and his twelve-inch switchblade in his left pocket. Anything over twelve inches, the cops could bust your ass for carrying an illegal weapon. There was a small grey metal lockbox in there. He opened it up. The .38 snub nose pistol looked as imposing as ever. Mom'd kick his ass if she ever found out he had it. Same way she'd kick Angie's ass if she ever found out Angie was going out with the black guy.

He loaded the .38 and stuffed it down the front of his pants. Down in black town, man, you couldn't have enough weapons. Not on a Friday night, you couldn't.

Angie was in the living room still arguing with Mom about eleven o'clock. Boze gave Mom a kiss on the cheek. Angie looked beautiful, purple blouse, hip-hugger slacks, high heels. Her sexuality was overwhelming. He imagined black hands on that white flesh. The image sickened him.

"You've got hours, too, Boze, don't forget," Mom said. "Twelve o'clock."

Boze grinned. "You make a great boot camp instructor, I ever tell you that?"

Mom grinned back. "Many times."

Then Boze was out of there. In the car. Driving fast on empty country roads just as the half-moon was rising above the cornfields and all the little farmhouses whose lights seemed curiously lonely in the gloom. Dwight Yoakam was singing his ass off. Boze had half an hour by himself driving this way—a can of beer from the trunk in one hand, a cigarette in the other—just driving, driving fast all by himself before he had to pick up Gunner.

~ ~ ~ ~ ~

There was a certain part of the Interstate when you were coming into Cedar Rapids. . .if you looked fast enough, it was like coming into a really big city. . .the way three or four tall buildings were silhouetted against the moon. . .and the way the neon chain of lights seemed to stretch forever into the prairie night and the way cross-town traffic was almost bumper-to-bumper on a Friday night like this.

Boze waited until they pulled up in front of the pool hall before he told Gunner. He just wanted to see his face. See how pale he would turn. See how sick and scared he would look. While they had bad reputations for being dangerous, Boze was the only truly dangerous one of the duo. And both of them knew that.

"Guess what I brought tonight?"

"What?" Gunner said.

"Guess."

"You steal some more booze from your Mom?"

"Huh-uh. Somethin' else."

"Shit. I hate guessin' games, Boze."

"My .38."

Boze got the reaction he wanted. Instant terror on Gunner's face.

"Are you crazy, man? A gun?" Gunner said.

"Scare him a little."

"You know what the cops'd do to us if they found a gun on you?"

"They've all got guns down there. We'll need one, too."

"This is the kinda shit they put you in jail for, man."

Boze was suddenly tired of Gunner's whining. Boze really was the only dangerous one here. He felt especially dangerous tonight, the .38 stuffed down the front of his jeans this way. That black was never going to bother Angie again, that was for sure.

"C'mon," Boze said, "let's go shoot some pool."

Boze loved the atmosphere of the place. It was mostly bikers and they looked fierce as hell in their beards and tattoos and their chains and leather vests. They never bothered Boze and Gunner either, which Boze thought was pretty cool. Just let them play. There was a good jukebox, too, a lot of heavy metal from the seventies and eighties, the only kind of rock and roll Boze could stand. No blacks.

They shot for two hours. Gunner was lame as usual. Especially so tonight. Boze could see the gun thing was really working on him. Gunner could barely concentrate on his game. Gunner kept running back to the john all the time. Pissing. Nerves.

When they were out in the night air again, leaning on the Firebird and smoking cigarettes and watching the Friday night traffic, all the beautiful wan city girls cruising past and gracing Boze and Gunner with the most disinterested of glances, and the whole city redolent of fuming ripe Indian summer, Gunner said, "Man, that gun of yours scares me."

"Don't be such a chickenshit."

"I didn't sign on for no gun, man."

"We're gonna scare him a little is all."

Gunner looked at Boze. "Really?"

"Really."

"You give me your word, Boze?"

"I give you my word."

"You better not use that thing," Gunner said. "You better not, man."

~ ~ ~ ~ ~

Another planet.

At least that's what it felt like to Boze. Everything looked darker, for one thing. The lights in the houses didn't seem to burn quite so bright. The glow of TV sets seemed dulled, somehow. Even the headlights of the battered cars that prowled the streets like wounded animals. . .even they had a gauzy, faint cast to them. Boze had expected a lot of noise. Shadowland. Blacks dancing in the street maybe to rap music and throwing their doped-up bodies this way and that. But the streets were mostly empty. And dark. And silent. The only sound was the occasional car radio thundering rap music.

The little houses seemed to cower in the night as they had cowered ever since they'd been built.

Another planet.

The houses small, hunched together. Large empty lots here and there. The occasional brand new car parked proudly in a driveway. Eyes, gang eyes, peering at Boze and Gunner as they passed by in their white-boy tourist arrogance. Don't belong here motherfucker. Don't belong here. Even Boze now feeling a tightening in his groin, a hammering in his heart.

The way Boze'd known how to find the black guy was because he'd followed him. Saw the guy pulling away from the trailer one day and whipped around and followed him all the way back to Cedar Rapids. Twenty or so the guy was, no flashy black clothes bullshit or any of that. Kinda straight-looking, actually. But still a coon. Boze'd followed him right to his door. Boze wondered if he lived with his folks. Guy pulled into his driveway and never seemed to notice Boze at all. Boze just went right on by. But he sure knew where to come next time. He sure did.

This was next time.

Boze parked half a block away. They had to be careful of the gang members they'd seen here and there. Or maybe they weren't really gang members. Just kids. But kids who'd gladly whump on two country boys like themselves.

Boze figured it'd be safer if they took the alley. In the moonlight the garages spoke of other eras, dating all the way back to the twenties when cars had been big and boxy. Cats sat on garbage cans watching them. Boze whispered to them. He liked cats.

"So when we get there—" Gunner was saying.

"Real simple, man," Boze said. "When we get there, we try the back door. If his car's there, we go inside and scare the shit out of him."

"Scare him and that's all?"

"That's all."

"And if he's not there—"

"Then we leave him a note and tell him to leave Angie alone."

"I just wish you didn't have that gun, man."

"The gun's just for show, Gunner. Just fucking relax, will you?"

Boze recognized the house from the back. How many dark green houses were there on this block?

He also recognized something else. The dude's car. The same one Boze had followed here.

"The lights're out," Gunner said, as if Boze was blind and couldn't see for himself.

"Yeah," Boze said.

The lights out and Angie inside. . .well, just as Boze wasn't blind, he also wasn't stupid. He didn't have to wonder much about what his sister was doing.

"You really sure you want to do this?" Gunner said.

"Really sure."

"I'm scared, Boze."

"You bastard."

"I can't help it. The gun and everything, man. What if he has a gun."

"Yeah, but we're gonna surprise him. He won't have time to pull a gun."

"I can't help it, Boze. I'm just scared." Gunner sounded on the edge of crying. Little-boy crying. The bogey-man was after him.

Then Gunner said, "I'm goin' back to the car, Boze."

"You're shittin' me."

"I can't do it, Boze. Not breakin' in like this. And havin' a gun and everything."

"You really are a chickenshit."

"I don't even care if I have to walk home, Boze. I'm goin'. I really am. I just don't want to do this."

Boze just shook his head, couldn't friggin' believe it, and watched Gunner walk away.

Then he sighed. He was the dangerous one, after all, and should've realized that a long time ago. Gunner wasn't dangerous. He just liked pretending he was. But somehow Boze couldn't hate him. They'd grown up together. He said, "Just wait in the car, man. I won't be long." Gunner, shambling moon-outlined against the ancient sagging garages that smelled of so many dusty and decaying decades, stopped and turned back. "You better leave this one alone, Boze. I just got a feeling. A real bad feeling. The gun and all, man. That gun's gonna get you in trouble. It really is."

Then he was gone, caught up in shadows, and then he was vanished, one with the night.

Boze took the gun from inside his belt. He was gonna scare the guy. And kick Angie's ass out. That was all. Nothing more.

He walked to the back door, ducking under a clothesline. The support poles were rusty. There were dried dog turds on the autumn-brown grass.

He heard it, then. Coming from inside. Music. Faint. Not rap but black. Definitely black. That heavy bass. That rhythm and blues beat. A sexy black song. For lovers. The fucker. The black fucker. He gripped his gun tighter.

There was a small screened-in porch, the screening old and brown and curling up from the edges. He went up on the steps and went inside. The porch was empty except for three flats of empty Budweiser cans waiting to be cashed in at a supermarket.

The music was louder. And for the first time, he heard voices. The voices were even fainter than the music. Coming from inside.

He peered between the curtains hanging in the back door. A kitchen. Dishes piled high. Beer cans all over the place. No, the guy didn't live here with his mother. He lived here alone. Bachelor pad.

Boze tried the doorknob. Locked.

He stood still for a moment, considering the various ways he could get inside. Easiest would be just breaking down the frigging door. But he wanted to surprise the guy. Just to see his face. How scared he'd be.

Boze took out his switchblade and went to work. The lock mechanism was very old and vulnerable. There was no skill or grace in what Boze did. He simply jiggled and jammed and twisted and jabbed the point of his switchblade around inside until the doorknob turned all the way to the right. He went inside.

Cigarette smoke. Stale beer. Even staler wine. Pizza. Vomit. For sure, the guy lived alone. Nobody's mother would put up with this kind of crap.

He heard them much more clearly now. The voices. Coming from the other part of the house. Boy and girl voices. Having-sex voices. Boze felt sick.

He gripped the gun even tighter and started walking carefully through the small house. Didn't want to bang into something and give himself away. Not that they'd be able to hear. Not with the soft, sexy music going. Not with the sex they were having, the unmistakable sounds of pleasure that seemed at least occasionally to also include pain.

And then he couldn't take it anymore, couldn't take the idea of those black hands all over his little sister's white body. He jerked his gun up and ran straight into the lone bedroom off the living room. Ran straight in swearing and screaming and threatening. Ran straight in and put the gun right in the guy's face.

Right in the fucker's face.

Then all three of them were swearing and screaming.

~ ~ ~ ~ ~

Angie got home right at eleven o'clock, the way Mom had told her to. She was sort of drunk. Her clothes were wrinkled and her make-up was a mess.

But Boze didn't care. He just sat in the recliner staring at the TV—country western videos—and sipping from the fifth of Old Grandad he'd found up in the cupboard.

Even drunk, Angie could tell something was wrong. "You all right?"

"Yeah." But he wasn't all right and that was clear.

"I think I had too much to drink tonight."

He raised his eyes to her. "Yeah? No shit? I could hardly tell."

"I hate it when you're sarcastic."

He started watching videos again.

She stood and stared at him for a time and then she all of a sudden clamped her hand over her mouth and rushed into the bathroom and puked all over the place.

He wasn't going to help her but then he stood up anyway and went into the bathroom and took down a wash cloth and got it hot and soapy and then he wiped off her face and got her all cleaned up. She was sagging, drunk and drained, against the far wall. He got her arm around him and half-carried her into her bed. He got her dress off and put her to bed with her slip and panties. He wanted her to be a little girl again. And him to be a little boy again. But time didn't let you go back. It always pushed you on ahead in the darkness. And there was always something terrible waiting there for you in that darkness. Sometimes there were good things but they were never good enough to compensate for the bad things. For how people changed on you. For how people let you down.

He went into the bathroom and cleaned it all up.

Then he went back to the living room and sat in the recliner again and drank whiskey and stared at the TV. He should be tearing this fucking place apart is what he should be doing. But somehow he didn't have the energy.

She didn't get home until nearly three a.m.

Boze still sat in the recliner. He'd finished the bourbon and was now drinking the remnants of the scotch.

When she saw him from the doorway, she said, quietly. "I'm sorry you had to find out that way. I mean, I probably should be mad at you for breaking in that way but—"

She shook her head. She looked very sad. "Roger's a very nice guy. He comes into the restaurant all the time on his way back from Iowa City. That's how we met."

Boze looked up and smirked. "That's his name? A black guy named Roger?"

"Oh, God, Boze. He's a very nice man. He's assistant professor at Iowa."

"And he lives in a place like that, all those beer cans and shit?"

She came into the trailer, closing the door behind her.

"He had a birthday party for his nephew earlier. That's why the mess. He'll clean it up tomorrow. He really will."

She came over to him and stood above him. "I want you to give me the gun, Boze. You terrified us tonight. I just couldn't believe it when I saw you standing there."

He looked straight up at her, all his hatred and hurt in his eyes, and said, "My own mother, sleeping with a fucking jig." She slapped him, then, harder than she'd ever slapped him in her life. Boze should have been the one who cried, the slap and all being hard.

But it was Mom who cried. Mom who went into the bedroom and quietly closed the door and cried and cried and cried.

Boze just sat in the living room all by himself and didn't cry at all.

BROTHERS

1

When I rolled into the precinct just before eleven that humid August night, I saw my brother Michael walking out the west door.

I'd been able to get him on the force seven years ago, despite a still ongoing hiring freeze, and he was generally doing well. It didn't hurt that at the time I'd just received an award for stopping a man who'd just killed three people in a convenience store. I'd chased him in my car, warning him in the dark alley to stop running. He had turned around and put three bullets in my windshield. I ran him over and killed him.

I'd asked the commander a few times before about hiring Michael. He knew about Michael's past and problems. He'd always said, "Let me think about it."

Since joining the department, Michael had become a dutiful cop. On other matters, which he insisted weren't my business, he wasn't doing well at all.

He worked the same shift I did but he was already in civvies, a crisp white short-sleeved shirt, dark slacks, and a brisk, slightly wood-scented cologne.

He must have been lost in his own thoughts, because he didn't see me until I almost walked into him.

"Hey," he said, looking up. "Didn't see you."

"I wanted to apologize for the other night."

He grinned the grin that had won him a hundred hearts. My little brother got the family's blond good looks. I got the family's work ethic. Or, as our mother always put it, "Little Mike got the looks, but Chet got the maturity." In her maternal way, she tried to pretend that both attributes were equal. Maturity, in case you hadn't noticed, has yet to get even one female into a bed.

He clapped me on the arm. "Hell, Chet, we're brothers. You were just looking out for me the way you have since Mom died."

When I was sixteen and Michael was twelve, Mom drowned in

the YMCA pool after suffering a stroke. Freak accident. The news reports called it that, the Y called it that, the coroner called it that, the priest at the burial site called it that, everybody at the wake called it that. Even fourteen years later I wince when I hear that term.

Dad took over. Or tried. But he'd always been a better cop than a father. It was from his side of the family that the good blond looks came. For twenty-one years of marriage, Mom had been able to pretend that all the nights Dad spent carousing with other cops were spent bowling and playing nickel-dime poker. The only time I'd ever heard them argue about those nights was when a drunk lady called at two am and demanded to talk to my Dad. Bowling alleys don't make those kind of calls.

Other cops, male and female, walked around us now, good nights and good-byes on the air thick as the fireflies.

"I'm not mad, Chet. I just want to run my own life. You don't need to play dad anymore."

And I had been his Dad for five years. Made sure he got a B average, made sure he wasn't into drugs or alcohol, made sure he wasn't hanging around with the wrong boys, made sure he honored the curfew hours I set for him.

Dad spent more and more time away from the house. He got himself what he called a " woman friend" and half-ass moved in with her. One night when he was home and puke-drunk, I heard him sobbing—literally, sobbing—in the bedroom he'd shared with Mom all those years. I went in and dragged him to the bathroom and got him cleaned up and then ripped the covers with the vomit on it off and got him settled in. He grabbed my hand and gripped it hard, the way he used to. He didn't seem to realize that these days my grip was a lot harder than his. Before he passed out, he said: "You gotta watch Michael. He's gonna turn out just like me. And I was such a shitty husband to your poor mother, Chet." He started sobbing again. He wouldn't let go of my hand. "I'm goin' to hell, Chet, the way I treated that woman, always sneakin' off for some strange broad. You got to know that I loved her. She was the only woman I ever truly loved. Those bitches I ran around with didn't mean nothing to me. They really didn't."

~ ~ ~ ~ ~

Michael said, "It's just this little thing I'm having on the side is all. It'll wear itself out."

"That's what you said four months ago."

His face hardened. His tactic was to be amiable, kid you away from serious talk. But since that hadn't worked, he coasted for awhile on irritation that would soon become real anger if he wasn't careful. "Look, I admit I screwed up my life back there when I first left home. I gambled, I did some drugs, I married the wrong woman, I couldn't hold a job—and I let you take over my life the same way you did when I was a kid. And that really helped, Chet. And I'm really grateful for it. I mean, how could I not be? You found my second wife for me, you got me on the force, and you managed to find a bank that would give me a mortgage even with *my* credit rating." He put both of his hands on my shoulders. He was three inches taller than I was. "I owe you everything, Chet. Everything. But this time—" He shook his head. Then he shot me the Michael grin again. "This time it isn't any of your business. All right? I know what I'm doing? I'm not going to hurt Laura or the kids. That I promise. But I'm in this thing and I just have to play it out is all." His hands shook my shoulders with mock fondness—mock because he was sick of me trying to drag him away from the affair he was having. The affair that had put him right back into gambling, drinking too much, even getting into a few fights. Fights can get you kicked off the force.

He took his hands down. "So can we leave it like that, Chet? Please? I'll handle it, everything'll be cool, and we'll get together at Jen's birthday party a couple weeks from now and everything'll be fine. All right?"

He walked away before I could say anything, got in his car, and drove off. I hadn't known until that moment that he'd bought himself a new Pontiac GTO. I didn't know another uniformed officer who could afford a new GTO and have any money left over for the wife and kids.

~ ~ ~ ~ ~

The call came a few months later. Laura, Michael's wife.

"I'm sure you're watching the football game," she said. I'd met her years ago at a grade school. I had been there to tell the kids about being a policeman. Laura was a slender, dark-haired young woman with a very pretty face spoiled only by a quick, nervous smile that revealed the stress she always seemed to feel. This was at the time when Michael had neared the end of his problems—no job, into some gamblers for several thousand dollars, and drinking way more than he should have been. Laura herself was just getting through a divorce, a husband who'd run around on her. Neither of them wanted to meet each other, but I stage-mothered the relationship until it found its own way.

"Actually, no. Joan's volunteering at the hospital tonight, so I'm here with the kids. I just cattle-prodded them into bed, in fact."

A strained laugh. "They're just like ours. They hate going to bed." Then: "Could we talk a little, Chet?"

"Sure. That's what brothers-in-law are for."

So this was to be the night. I knew that it would happen and that when it happened a whole lot of things would change. I thought of what Dad had told me the night he'd drunkenly admitted he'd been such a terrible husband and that I was to keep Michael from repeating Dad's mistakes. I wondered how much Laura knew. I was about to find out.

"I don't think Michael loves me anymore."

"Oh, come on. You know better than that."

"He used to come straight home after work. He'd only hang out at that cop bar once a week. But now—three or four nights a week he doesn't get home until three in the morning. And he hasn't had much to drink. That's what makes me suspicious."

"I guess I'm not following you there."

"Well, he always tells me he's just at the bar with the boys. Well, first of all, the bar closes at two, and it's only about a mile away. It sure doesn't take him that long to drive home. But even worse than that—he's never drunk."

"Well, that's a good thing, isn't it, that he's cut back on his drinking?" I tried to put a smile into it.

"But I know him well enough that if he was at that bar, he'd be drunk when he came home." Cop wives always say "that bar" when referring to the Golden Chalice. They hate it because they know all about the cop groupies who hang out there.

She said: "Would you talk to him, Chet?"

"I'd be happy to. But you know how he resents me sometimes."

"You know how I feel about that. And I've told him so. You were in a situation where you were forced to be his father. You had to give up a lot of things other boys your age got to do—and all for his sake. I always tell him that."

"I appreciate it, Laura. But that doesn't mean he'll be any happier if I butt into your marriage."

A long pause: "Then how about a little spying?"

"Spying?"

"Just seeing what he's up to after your shift ends. Where he goes and things like that." This time her laugh was real but sad. "I know this is awful. I'd sure resent it if somebody spied on me. But our marriage—it hasn't been any good for quite a while."

For a moment I was back in the parking lot and Michael was explaining to me, as if I was slightly retarded, how everything was under control. He had his mistress and he had his family, and according to him, he was doing well by both of them.

"Maybe I shouldn't have called, Chet. I'm just so—"

She started crying. I let her get through the worst of it. Michael was doing it all over again. He'd lost a first wife who'd been every bit the player he was. But this woman was different. Only through her had he finally put his life on track. And now he was turning away from her.

"I'm sorry, Chet," when the tears became sniffles. "I just feel so isolated, I guess. I'm sorry I called."

"Tell you what. I'm going to do a little looking around. I'll be back to you in a day or so."

"I'm sorry I'm so needy, Chet."

"I'm needy, too. I want to find out what's going on. We've both got a stake in this, Laura, believe me." I made a joke of it before hanging up: "I didn't spend all those years raising him so he'd act this way."

2

Three o'clock a.m. Sitting in my boxers. Staring at the glow of the guttering fire we'd set to chase the autumn cold away.

I heard Jen coming down the stairs, her slippers flapping with each step. When she reached the living room, I said, "Leave the lights off, please."

She came over, the hem of her long cotton robe whispering across the hardwood floor. She sat on her haunches next to my armchair. Bare branches scraped the windows in the whistling wind. Shadow goblins played on the walls.

"So what seems to be troubling our baby boy tonight?"

"Sometimes I *wish* I was a baby boy." Then: "Michael. Of course."

She touched my wide coarse hand with her long smooth one. "Now I'm going out to the kitchen and get that .45 you taught me how to shoot. And then I'm going to come back and kill one of us. And at this point I really don't care which one of us it is. Because if I ever hear that you're brooding about him again—"

"He's my brother."

"Oh, yes, and you swore to your father you'd raise him right."

"Don't make fun of that. I gave him my word."

"Yes, and that was the right thing to do. When Michael was still a boy. But he's almost thirty now. He has a wife and two children. You got him a job, you found him a wife, and you've been playing daddy to him right straight through. It's not right, honey. Or normal."

For some reason that irritated me. Normal. What was abnormal about taking care of your kid brother?

"If I don't take care of him, who will?"

"Oh, let's see—maybe himself. He's an adult, Chet. At least that's what it says on his driver's license. You have your own family and your own problems you need to take care of. You can't keep spending all your time on him. It's unnatural."

Abnormal. Unnatural.

"You know how selfish that sounds?"

"Selfish? What're you talking about?"

"That I shouldn't worry about my own little brother?"

"Worry, fine. But try to turn his life around—no way." Her hand had pulled from mine a minute ago. Now she used it as a lever on the arm of the chair to pull herself up. "You know I don't like him. But sometimes I can't help myself—I feel sorry for him, the way you're always putting yourself in his business. I understand why he resents you, Chet. I really do."

And then the line I hated most where my little brother was concerned: "You could always see the police shrink. I really think it's something you should talk through. We've been arguing about this since we first started dating. And it never seems to get any better."

"And you never stop saying that I should see the police shrink."

She was all done with banter. Tears trembled in her voice. "You ever think that's because I love you? You ever think how tired I am of all this? And I meant what I said about Michael. I feel sorry for him sometimes. I really do. But if he's going to screw up his life, that's his business."

"If it's his business, why did Laura call me today and tell me she's worried about their marriage?"

"Laura called you?"

"That's right. So if I'm butting in, it's because she asked me to."

"Oh, great," Jen said. "Now we've got her pulling you into their lives. This whole thing is insane." She started to walk back to the stairs. "I'm going to sleep on the couch in the TV room. You need your sleep, so you take the bed."

I started to object but she stopped me.

"I'm too tired to argue about it, Chet. I'm taking the couch. I'll grab a blanket from the closet upstairs." Six steps up the staircase, she said, in a gentler tone, "I'll see you in the morning."

3

I spent the next few days finding out what I could about Jane Cameron and found nothing I liked.

You couldn't call her rich, I suppose, but she did have the remains of a large inheritance to rely on if she needed it for her business, which was public relations. You would have to call her beautiful. College girl beautiful, though she was mid-thirties—fine, clean features; gym-trim body; and a radiant blonde presence in any environment. A ten-year-old daughter conveniently locked away at a boarding school in Vermont. Two husbands, several lovers, at least three of whom had been married at the time. A few very public and very angry scenes with angry wives.

As I sat at my computer looking at her photos, I realized what my little brother was living out here. He'd met her the night a jilted lover of hers had assaulted her in the lobby of her expensive condo. Michael and his partner were the first on the scene. It probably hadn't taken long for Michael to find himself in the sort of bad movie he used to star in frequently. Married cop intrigued by fashionable, vulnerable beauty, cheats on family, honor, good sense.

For three nights, I followed him. Twice he left work to meet her at the bar across the street from her condo, the bar where all the successful young lawyers in town like to do their cheating. An hour of drinks there and back across the street to her condo. The third night, still in uniform, he went straight home. In my talk with Laura, she'd said this was his standard pattern. Somehow, she didn't think any of this had to do with a woman. I guess she just couldn't face what was really going on.

One night I took my camera and got some good snaps of them making out in the parking lot of the café.

I put them in a manila envelope and set them in the front seat of his new Pontiac.

The next night, when I got off shift, I found them sitting on the front seat of my own car.

He came over, still in uniform, and slid into the shotgun seat.

"You really think I wouldn't figure out you were behind this bullshit?"

"I wanted you to know, Michael. If you hadn't figured it out, I would've told you."

"You're insane, you know that? Clinically, I mean. Off your damned rocker."

"You know anything about her, Michael?"

"Sure I know about her. She's a very beautiful and a very successful woman."

"And she has a lot of enemies."

"That's because she's so successful."

"That's because she's slept with so many important men around town."

"People change."

I couldn't help it. I laughed.

"In Japan they get their hymens sewn back in for the wedding. She thinking of doing that, is she?"

"Be careful here, man. You may still be able to take me but I can still put a lot of hurt on you."

I stared straight ahead. Sighed.

"So now it's supposed to be serious, Michael?"

"Isn't 'supposed to be.' Is."

"I thought it was going to end."

Now it was Michael who stared straight ahead and sighed.

"I'm not sure what to do, Chet."

"Take out that picture of your kids in your billfold and look at it for awhile. That'll tell you what to do."

Silence for a time.

"You know how good a woman you've got in that wife of yours, Michael."

"Of course I know."

"And you treat her like this, anyway?"

"We're different is all, Chet. You and me, I mean. You're satisfied to sit home and watch TV and I want—"

"Excitement."

"Not exactly. Not the way you mean. Not running around and getting all boozed up and hanging out in clubs. It's just—I'm starting to feel old, Chet. I'm young. But when I met Jane I realized that I'd mentally become an old man. She didn't make me feel young exactly, but I didn't feel old anymore, either. I'm a better cop now because of her. I know that sounds funny but it isn't. She really thinks it's true. I'm even thinking about taking the test for detective."

"Laura wanted you to do that two years ago."

"Yeah, but with Laura it was different. It was just because I'd make more money. But with Jane being a detective isn't just about that, it's because being a detective is—"

"Cool."

"God, Chet, you don't understand any of this."

"I don't think you do, either. You're getting a nice piece of ass on the sly and you think it's worth destroying your family for."

"I'm going to go now. I can't sit here and let you lay all this on me. Remember when I called you the Pope once? Well, you haven't changed. You think you can run my life from this big ass throne you sit on. But it doesn't work that way anymore, Chet. Maybe I am screwing up my life. I'm not stupid. I know what I'm doing is wrong. But right now I can't pull myself out of it. But you playing Pope isn't helping. You can't order me around anymore, Chet."

He opened the car door.

"Let me ask you one thing. It's my place to tell Laura. Not yours. So until I tell her about this, don't say anything to her. All right?"

I just stared at my big hands on the steering wheel.

"All right, Chet?" The anger coming back into his voice.

I could barely whisper. "All right, Michael."

4

The next day, I started following her. I wanted to see where the best place was to have the conversation she was forcing on me.

Didn't take me long to figure out that there would be no opportunity to confront her during the day. Meetings all over town with her various important clients. I couldn't afford to brace her in any sort of public way.

Nothing to stop me wearing my uniform on my night off, though.

I had to make sure she was alone. I sat across the street from her fifteen-story condo. She swept her Jag—what else?—into the underground parking garage just after nine that night. She was alone.

I pulled in four spaces down from her. I reached the elevator before she did.

In the shadowy light, she wasn't able to see even my faint resemblance to Michael.

"Did something happen here tonight?" she said.

She looked especially fine this evening in a silver suit, her golden hair pulled into a loose chignon.

"Happen?"

"When I saw your uniform, I thought maybe something had happened in the building tonight."

"Oh, no, ma'am. I'm here on my own. I'm just going to see

somebody in the building."

She smiled. "Well, I love having a police officer around. Makes me feel very safe."

The elevator door opened. We climbed in.

Then she said: "That's funny."

"What is?"

"Why you aren't in the lobby getting checked in by Lenny? He checks everybody in. Even cops."

I had been demoted from police officer to cop. She was smart. She knew there was something wrong with this situation.

I said, "I'll bet you said that to my brother."

"Your brother? What're you talking about?"

A bit of panic—just enough to be gratifying—shone in those azure eyes.

She didn't know it, but she'd already lost control of the situation. It was almost disappointing. I thought she'd be a lot tougher.

~ ~ ~ ~ ~

After she'd brought us whiskey sours, she sat on the divan across from my chair and said, "I hope you realize that all I have to do is pick up the phone and call my friend the police commissioner and your days as a cop are long gone, sweetie."

"And if that happens, 'sweetie,' then I'll get somebody to help me get me a computer file of some of your messes we've had to help you with—especially a certain group of pissed off wives—and I'll download that file straight to a friend of mine who's a reporter at KBST. And I'll do the same thing if you don't agree to break it off with my brother right away."

She smirked. "You're going to blackmail me out of seeing your brother?" She didn't wait for me to answer. "I can't believe you two are brothers. Michael's so handsome and intense and you're so—" She hesitated. "I may as well be upfront with you. You scare me."

"Good. I should scare you. You've got good instincts."

She exhaled harshly. I tried not to notice the way her long sleek legs were stretched out on the divan or the sheer blouse she wore now, having discarded the coat to her suit. She kept a single shoe on a single big toe, dangling there. Like my brother's future.

"You'll dump him someday, anyway."

"I've been dumped, too, you know."

"Any tears go with this story?"

"It's true, you bastard, whether you believe it or not. I was dumped—twice in fact—and I got hurt just like anybody else would. You make me sound like some sort of professional heartbreaker. I have parents I see three times a month and I have a daughter I love very much."

"So much you put her in boarding school."

Her eyes narrowed. She just watched me for a time, as if she was observing something in nature she'd never seen before. "Michael told me you were like this. So god damned judgmental. He calls you 'The Pope.' "

"I'm judgmental about women who break up marriages."

"Michael told me you had an affair when you were about his age. Aren't you a little hypocritical here?"

I felt my cheeks burn. "I made up for it. I've never put a hand to another woman since."

"Mass three times a week? Confession every Saturday? Coach a Little League Team? The perfect husband and father."

I finished my drink and set it down. "Thanks for the drink. I want to hear Michael tell me that you've broken it off."

"What if I don't?"

"We've already discussed that."

"You'll ruin me."

I waited until I was on my feet. "I'll sure give it my best shot."

"I really do love Michael. I've never claimed to be anything other than what I am—a selfish, spoiled woman. But this time, with Michael—I really do love him. I never thought I'd do it again."

"Do what again?"

"Let somebody get me pregnant. I didn't want to be owned by a man or by a child. But with Michael—I stopped taking my birth control. I went to the doctor's last week. I haven't even told Michael yet. I want this child. I want Michael, too. But if I can't have him, at least I'll have his child."

I shrugged. I was trying to make sense of all this. But there was no sense to be made of it, none of it. A little fling, every man did it once in a while. Back when it started it had seemed nothing more than that. But now I was listening to her tell me that she was carrying Michael's baby.

All I could think of was poor Laura and the kids. I turned the knob on the door leading to the hall. I wanted to say something nasty. But then an old man's weariness overcame me. I didn't seem to have any strength left at all. Then words came: "I'll pay for an abortion. And Michael doesn't have to know about it."

She laughed. "You won't believe this, Mr. High and Mighty, but

I don't believe in abortion. I may be a slut in your eyes but I'm still a good little Catholic girl."

I turned my eyes back to hers and with the last of my strength, I said: "Then walk out of his life. He doesn't have the strength, but you do."

"That's the terrible thing," she said. "I don't have the strength, either."

5

The next afternoon I tried to find my brother before his shift started. Sometimes he had coffee down the street at a luncheonette. He wasn't there. He wasn't in the precinct locker room, either.

"You didn't happen to see my brother, did you?" I asked Keller, who was spelling the watch commander who was in Vegas at a police convention. Don't think there hadn't been a lot of jokes about holding a cop convention in Vegas.

"Bad sore throat and fever. Home sick."

"He call in himself?"

He gave me a sharp look.

"No, his wife did. Man, you gotta give the kid some breathing room, Chet. He calls in or Laura calls in. What's the difference?"

"Just curious."

He shook his head and walked on. It was clear that Michael had done a good job with the other cops at the precinct, letting them know that I was always interfering in his life.

There was no answer at his house. I didn't leave a message on his machine. If he'd actually told Linda about his affair, this wasn't a hopeful sign. A number of paranoid ideas shook me, the one that kept repeating being where the wife, the kids off at school, goes insane and kills her unfaithful husband. It happens.

At the end of my shift, I got in my car and drove out there. A lone lamp lit the house, downstairs, the family room. Michael's car was gone. I went to the front door and knocked.

I could see her through the glass slat in the door. She was curled up in the corner of the couch. She wore a pair of faded pink cotton pajamas. With her short dark hair and sweet face, she could have been a college girl. The TV was on but the sound was off and she wasn't watching it anyway. Screen colors flickered across the living room.

I knocked again. This time she looked up. I walked over to the window and waved. She got up off the couch, buttoning the top of her pajama shirt and came to the door.

She let me in but said nothing. She went back to the couch and sat down. "You could've told me. Then this wouldn't have come as such a shock tonight."

I sat down in an armchair across from her. "It would've been just as much of a shock if *I'd* warned you."

She raised her head, closed her eyes, as if invisible rain was spattering her face. "This is so unreal." She opened her eyes, lowered her head, looked at me. "In case you don't think I got hysterical, I did. There's broken glass all over the kitchen floor. The kids are at my sister's house. I didn't trust myself enough to keep them here tonight."

"Don't do anything nuts."

She shrugged. "I never do anything nuts, Chet. You know that. I'm not dramatic in any way. Or exciting. That's what he said she was. Exciting." Then. "Damn, I wish I had a cigarette."

"No, you don't. You quit five years ago. Keep it that way."

"And all my self-pity."

"You're entitled."

"I just keep thinking about all the people who have it worse than me. And here I am feeling sorry for myself."

"That never works. Believe me, I've been trying it all my life. Just because somebody's crippled or blind or has cancer doesn't help me at all."

She made a face. "We could always have sex."

"You frowned when you said that. Meaning that you know better than that."

"I have these fantasies that he walks in on me when I'm having sex with somebody and make him jealous and then he realizes what a good thing he's lost."

"You're in shock right now."

"That's funny you should say that. That's sort of how I feel. So shocked I don't know what to do with myself. I can't even get drunk. Two drinks and I throw up."

"You have any tranquilizers?"

"I've taken two already. This is the best they can do for me, I guess." Something changed, then. I wasn't sure what. The eyes were no longer vulnerable or sad. They reflected anger.

"I'm probably just lashing out here, Chet. But I need to say something to you, something I should've said a long time ago."

"Lash away. You'll feel better."

She took a deep breath and said, "This'll probably make you

mad."

I was thinking she was going to tear into me for keeping the truth from her.

Instead, she said, "You didn't help my marriage any by constantly being on Michael's back."

The anger was swift, sure. I guess I'd been told too often in too short a time how I was doing badly by my little brother.

"I don't think that's fair, Laura."

"I just had to say it."

"Did it make you feel better?"

"Maybe. But it made you mad."

"No, it didn't."

She smiled. "You're grinding your jaw muscles and your hands are fists. I'd say those are signs you're pretty pissed off."

"Irked, irritated, maybe. But not pissed off." Then: "I was just trying to help you kids."

"That's just it. We're not kids, Chet. We're grown-ups. But you'd never acknowledge that. You were always checking on him at the precinct and giving him advice on handling his money and telling him who to hang out with and not hang out with and—God, I remember the time when your aunt died and you told him right in front of everybody at the funeral that he shouldn't have worn a tan suit to the wake. But that was the only suit he owned, Chet. And the time you saw our girls playing wiffle ball and you told him you thought they should be playing more feminine games. And when you got on his case about where we went to church, that it was better to go to St. Joe's because that's where the shift commander went. It just never ended, Chet."

I suppose, looking back, that's when it started, this black feeling. And that's the only way I can describe it. It was anger in such volume that I could barely breathe holding it back.

I said, "You ever hear the expression 'No good deed ever goes unpunished.' I used to think that was just a funny line. But it isn't. It's the truth."

"Now who's feeling sorry for himself? We're just talking here, having a conversation."

"Is that what this is, Laura, just a conversation?"

"All I meant was that you need to let him go. I hate that bitch he's in love with but even with them, Chet—you have to let them have their own lives. You can't be his father anymore." She hesitated. "He told me they're going to move away. He said he's giving notice to the commander tomorrow that he'll be leaving."

"Oh," I said, "just great." And the anger made my breathing short again. Gave me a sudden stabbing headache just above my left eye. Made every taut muscle in my body scream for release. "You know how hard I had to work on get him on the force? All the trouble he'd been in, and I had to promise that he'd straightened out and really wanted to be a cop. And now he's throwing it all away."

"It's his choice, Chet. His choice. He's a grown man. Right now I'd like to get that gun of his and empty it into his heart. And then I'd do the same to her. I hurt so much right now I don't know what to do. But it's his choice and you've got to let him make it."

"Oh, right. I get him through high school, studying with him every night so he'll get good grades. And then I get him through a couple of years of college until he starts hanging out with punks. And then I get him on the road to recovery and introduce him to you. And you're everything a man would want in a wife. And he throws it all over for some slut. And I'm supposed to like it."

"You don't like it any more than I do, Chet. But you've got to let go now. He's in love with her and he's moving away and there's nothing we can do about it."

I stood up.

"Where're you going?"

"I'm not sure."

"I didn't mean to chase you off."

"Oh, no, of course you didn't. All the things I've done for you two over the years and this is what you say to me." I went to the front door, opened it. "You aren't chasing me away, Laura. *I'm* chasing me away."

6

I didn't count the beers. I was careful to stay under what I considered my own legal limit, but that didn't mean I was sober.

A little bar near the old stadium. Dark, anonymous. I found myself salting my beer the way the old man had. He used to take me to the neighborhood tavern with him. Those were my favorites times, the few occasions when I got to be alone with my old man. He took Michael places than he'd take me. But in the tavern I'd sit on the stool next to him and he'd pop peanuts in his mouth and sprinkle salt in his beer. I always wanted people to know he was a cop because I was so proud of him. But he never wore his uniform when he went drinking. He said it just caused trouble. I'd always wondered what he meant by that. If somebody gave him trouble, couldn't he just shoot him? That was how my eight-year-old mind worked. Nobody could insult cops.

But I made the mistake he'd avoided. Early on I wore my uniform into a few non-cop bars and paid for it. No fights or anything but a couple hours of vague insults grinding into my ear canal. Everybody, especially drunks, has a good stock of anti-police stories.

I had one more beer than I should have and went out to my car.

And that was when it happened. A lot of it was the rain. It came down in such force—it sounded like hail by then—that it hammered the metal of cars and overflowed gutters within minutes. My wipers started straining after just a few blocks. I wasn't sure where I was going. But I was in a hell of a hurry to get there.

7

You certainly can't call this first degree murder, my lawyer told the press the next day. *It was a terrible accident. A terrible, terrible accident. I doubt the D.A.'s even going to bring charges. You wait and see.*

I can honestly say that I wasn't even aware where I was after I left the tavern. I just instinctively took the usual way home. I forgot entirely that I'd be passing by her condo. I just wanted to be home, in my own bed, slipping into darkness.

She could have been anybody. I don't expect you to believe that but it's true. Wrong time, wrong place.

They were coming from the yuppie bar across from her condo, covering their heads with newspapers they must have dragged along from inside.

And there was this person stepping into the beam of my headlights—and I was slamming on the brakes—and then there was this other figure reaching for her, jerking her back from the path of my car but in doing so he himself stumbled and fell into the way of my skidding car and—

~ ~ ~ ~ ~

Daniel Ahearn, my lawyer, says to me, "You wait right here and I'm going to let her have two minutes with you."

"You going to be here, too?"

"Are you crazy? Of course I'm going to be here. But she's been calling and coming up here all day long."

"I'm afraid to see her."

"Chet, look, what happened was an honest accident, just the way you told me, right?"

He knew better and I knew better. But I had to keep repeating the story so eventually I'd believe it, too.

I'd seen her running out into the street and then I was back in that alley where I ran the killer down that time. All the misery she'd caused. Poor Laura and the kids. And ruining Michael's life after he'd tried so hard to be trustworthy and sober again and—

But then Michael had suddenly pulled her back and tripped in front of my car and by then I couldn't stop and the sound he made when the car hit him—I knew he was dead; I knew he was dead.

"So she's going to come in here and go all hysterical on you and accuse you of being a murderer and going to the gas chamber. But you're going to do what?"

"I'm just going to sit here and calmly tell her that I'm sorry. That it really was an accident. That it was just this terrible coincidence that I happened to be driving by that night."

"And that's when I say, 'I hate to put it this way, Jane, but his loss is as big as yours, wouldn't you say? He accidentally killed his own brother.' So, you ready?"

"I'm ready."

"Remember, just keep taking a lot of good long breaths to keep yourself cool."

I took a good long breath.

"That's right," he said, "just like that."

He patted me on the shoulder and then he went through the door to the reception area.

She was already screaming and sobbing when he brought her in.

She stood in front of me like an interrogator. She didn't talk. Between sobs, she shouted. "You think you're going to get away with this, don't you, Chet? Well, you're not. Not when the D.A. gets all the witnesses lined up. Even his wife's going to testify against you, you know that, Chet? Do you know that? As much as she hates me, she's going to testify against you?"

And that was when she slapped me. I couldn't tell if it was skill or luck but I sure felt it.

She touched her stomach. "Thanks to you, your brother's baby won't have a father. Maybe you think about that when you're in prison, Chet. His poor little kid without a father." She started crying again. "This was supposed to be so good, so happy for the three of us. But you couldn't let that happen, could you, Chet? You had to make sure your little brother did just what you wanted him to, didn't you?

So you killed him! Your own brother! You killed him!"

She spat at me. It covered my nose and immediately dripped down to my upper lip. My lawyer stepped in then and started dragging her to the door. She was still screaming in the outer office. I imagine the wealthy clients sitting in the reception room were wondering what was going on.

When he came back and closed the door, he said, "That is one nasty bitch."

"She said my sister-in-law's going to testify against me."

He waved me off. "She doesn't know what she's talking about, Chet. You think she wants her kids to hear about what kind of man your brother was?"

"How about bond?"

"Just what I predicted. Judge said no bond. You're on your own recognizance. I brought along all your awards and commendations. Nobody thinks you ran Michael down on purpose. It was raining and dark and he just stepped too far out into the street. His blood alcohol was way over the limit. I'm not arrogant enough to call this a slam dunk. No serious criminal case is. But I can practically guarantee you you'll never see prison. You'll be free."

That was the word that was supposed to make me feel better. Free. I kept thinking about it all the way home and all the way through our quiet dinner and even when we were in bed and when I couldn't respond to Jen as I usually do.

Free. But I knew better than that now, didn't I?

THE MOVING COFFIN

On that rainy Tuesday morning, half an hour after a car splashed me with mud, fifteen minutes after my left foot sank into a watery hole, my parole officer said, "Three times."

"Three times?"

"That you snuck off last week."

I started to defend myself, but all that came out was a sneeze. "It's really miserable out there, isn't it?" he said.

I'd always assumed that parole officers would be dour old gentlemen who wanted nothing more than to unnerve and exasperate their charges every time they got a chance.

Mr. DeConcini was not that way at all. His thirty extra pounds and bright blue eyes gave him a jolly effect, for one thing, and the yellow ties he favored continued the sense of quiet merriment. His personality was pretty much like that, too. Here we sat in an office filled with murderers, rapists, perverts, and armed-robbery types, and Mr. DeConcini managed to be relentlessly friendly, like a campaigning politician on speed.

"You know what I told him, Bob?"

"Told my boss?"

"Right. I said, if Bob disappeared for a few hours last week, he had a darn good reason. That's exactly what I told him."

"Well, I really appreciate that, Mr. DeConcini."

"Ralph."

"I really appreciate that, Ralph."

I sneezed again.

"Kleenex?"

"Thank you."

"So where did you go?"

"You really have to know?"

"I really have to know, Bob. I really do. I have a boss, too, you know."

"I went to church."

At first he didn't react. Just sat there looking at me. Then he sat up straight in his seat and said, "You wouldn't play with my feelings, would you, Bob?"

"No, Ralph, I wouldn't play with your feelings."

"I've been after you for months to get next to the Lord, and now you mean you've gone and done it?"

"Gone and done it, Ralph. Gone and done it."

He looked as if he were about to cry. Ralph had always liked me because I wasn't like, as he'd explained on my first visit, "the rest." By that he meant that I had a college degree in business and that before I became prisoner number 4832, I'd been an executive in a research company.

He looked at me and gave me one of those crinkly smiles people in TV commercials are always giving each other. His bright blue eyes watered a bit too.

"Good Lord, Bob, this is the moment a parole officer like myself lives for."

"It is?"

"Of course. A parolee who's renouncing his old ways and affirming his new ways by going to church three times in the middle of the day? This is going to be our lead story in next month's newsletter. We got one of those desktop publishing deals, so we can get it out monthly now. A parolee who's had the calling from God. It's just great."

You really believe that story I just gave you? I wanted to say. But not being crazy, at least not in that way, I decided to keep quiet.

"Mr. Carlson will be happy to hear about this."

"I hope so. I don't want to lose my job, Ralph."

"He'll be relieved, too. He thinks you're a real good worker. Says you look nice in the clothes, too. And that counts in an upscale store like that. You know that's probably the most expensive store in the city."

"I've checked. It is."

"And you're their top salesman already—after only four months. I'm going to mention that in the newsletter story, too."

"Good."

He leaned close, as if he were going to confide in me one of the universe's most important secrets.

"See all those people over there?"

"The parolees?" I said, scanning the line of sad and shabby and sometimes frightening men who sat angry and beaten and resentful in their bright plastic chairs.

He nodded. "Yeah, I see them, Ralph."

"Hopeless," he said. "They're hopeless."

Then he sat up straight, his desk an oasis of orderliness in a vast gray room of cluttered desks and even more cluttered lives.

"If I was a betting man, Bob, I'd bet you were the only one who'll go completely straight the rest of his life."

"I appreciate you saying that."

"The recidivism rate is terrible. But you. . ."

The merry smile again.

"You always make my day, Bob. I feel that there's a little hope left in the world when you're around. I always tell my wife about you. I always say that on the days when Bob comes in, I feel like I'm actually accomplishing something."

"That's nice of you, Ralph." I checked my watch. "Well, I guess I'd better be getting back. I wanted to use my lunch hour so I wouldn't take any more hours away from the job."

"You're thinking like executive material already, Bob. Already."

We stood up and shook hands in a solemn and sort of corny way and then I turned to go and Ralph said, "No, sir, if there's one man I don't have to worry about, it's Bob."

I nodded and turned toward the door and started walking quickly. I had one more appointment to keep before getting back to work. I had to pick up some burglary tools.

~ ~ ~ ~ ~

"You know how to use these things?"

"That's about all I did, when I was in the joint. Lift weights and practice with burglary tools."

The tools were in a leatherette shaving kit that sat between us in the front seat of the taxi. The rain made the interior smell of cigarette smoke and dampness and perfume and aftershave and a few other odors I didn't especially want to identify.

Delia had picked me up after work. She gave me a careful, appraising look. She was scruffy and cute in a lost-kitten way. Delia was a bottle blonde with quick, intelligent brown eyes and a smile that a dentist needed to do some work on.

She heeled the horn with her hand and spat a few naughty words and then said, "I hate bus drivers."

Delia drove her taxi with great psychotic glee. She seemed to be under the impression that the founding fathers of our little Midwestern city had given her exclusive right-of-way on all streets and avenues twenty-four hours a day.

As she continued driving me back to work, she said, "I followed him, the way you wanted me to."

"I appreciate it. I'd get a car but—"

"Terms of your parole. Tell me about it. Last time Kip was out, he had the same thing." She tamped a cigarette from her pack of Camel filters. I gave her a light from the Ronson lighter my wife Sara had given me for our fifth anniversary. I didn't smoke anymore but I always carried the lighter as a reminder of her.

Kip was her husband, whom I'd met in prison. When I'd told him what I planned to do, he said, "My wife'll help you, kid, long as you keep your hands to yourself. She's true-blue."

She was too. I'd seen any number of guys come on to her, and she'd always raised her hand as if she were about to send them the Finger, then suddenly she'd point to the wedding ring on her left hand.

She also knew a hell of a lot about burglary and burglary tools.

"All right, you got the tools down pat, but how about security devices?" she said.

"Kip told me a lot about them."

"He's my man, Bob, and I'd never say anything bad about him, but Kip doesn't know squat about security devices. Once you figure out where you want to break in, you let me know. I'll scope it out for you."

"I appreciate that."

"My pleasure."

We rode the rest of the way in silence. Or I was silent, at any rate. Delia frequently took umbrage at the way drivers chose to drive and pedestrians chose to walk. There was a war going on and Delia was determined to win it.

As I looked out the window at the pedestrians hurrying to escape the rain, I thought of when I spent most of my time down here, in the loop area. The girls I'd taken to movies; the friends I'd hung out in record shops with; the small park where I sat and dreamed of a fine shiny adulthood that would see me with all the girls and all the friends and all the records a man could ever want. Well, that wasn't to be. For one thing, shopping malls squatted on three different edges of the city like invading armies and abducted all the retail business from downtown—and for another, women don't especially like to hear that you've spent your last few years rooming with guys named Lefty, the Skull, and Killer.

"So you'll be around at eight tonight?"

"Uh-huh. That's when he leaves the office?"

"Last three nights, he has."

"Hard working man," I said.

"You sure you want to do this, Bob? Thing like this goes wrong a lot of the time, and then you end up back in—"

"I'm sure I want to do it, Delia. Real sure. Nothing else's worked out for me. She told me something once, about MacDonald; and this shrink business may be just what I'm looking for."

Delia shook her head. "You ask me, it's the shrinks who're crazy."

"Could be."

"Last time Kip was out, they always made him go see this shrink and I always had to go with him, like I was his mom or something. The shrink was crazier than both of us put together. For one thing, he kept givin' me sexy eyes, you know what I mean? He even suggested that maybe I should come back alone sometime and see him."

"Sounds like a nice guy."

"Like I said, you ask me, shrinks're the ones who're nuts."

She pulled up to the curb of my ancient brick apartment house. Back in the thirties, when it was new, the upwardly mobile of their time had probably stood in line to get in here. Now the people who mowed the lawns and scrubbed the toilets of the upwardly mobile lived here.

"Maybe you can take a nap before I pick you up. Probably do you good."

"I don't think I should nap now. Too edgy."

She took my hand and gave it a squeeze. "You're one of the good ones, Bob. I just hope everything goes good for you tonight."

"Thanks, Delia."

~ ~ ~ ~ ~

I was wrong about not being able to take a nap. I went inside and took off the Stanley Blacker sport coat and slacks combination I'd worn today, and then went into the tiny bedroom and lay on the soft bed for ten minutes watching the lightning tear holes in the sky. Sometimes when the lightning struck, it lit up the framed photograph on my nightstand, giving Sara the same glow she'd had in life. I tried not to think about her, or how much I'd loved her, or how pointless her death had been. For seven years now I'd been trying to avenge her, but without any success at all. I had spent three work afternoons the last couple of weeks—the time off that so displeased my boss—trying to put together a few different plans. But none of them worked.

I slept. In the dream, I was back in prison, as I was most nights when I dreamt. But this time my cellmate was Ralph DeConcini, my parole officer, and he kept claiming that he couldn't get our TV set turned off. It was set on a religious channel and the minister was down on his knees, sobbing. He needed more money quick or his ministry would die. Then Ralph himself started crying and said, "The poor bastard."

Thunder awoke me, the thunder of some murderous prehistoric era, rolling down the time lines like the voice of some angry god we no longer believe in. The angry god rattled a lot of windows that night.

When I swung my legs off the bed and put my face in my hands, I had to smile. God, imagine if I did get caught breaking into the shrink's office tonight, and if I were sent back to prison, and if my cellmate were Ralph DeConcini.

Talk about cruel and unusual punishment.

~ ~ ~ ~ ~

"There are two types, basically," Delia said a couple of hours later, explaining to me the kind of security devices I'd likely find on a small office in a duplex like the shrink's. "The most modern kind is called a digital keypad system, which only people who know a lot about computers can defeat—you know hackers, creeps like that."

"And the other kind?"

We were nearing a suburban area of small, elegant shops and big, elegant aspirations. Perrier probably flowed from the taps. The night shone like a black diamond, the rain-washed streets throwing back the glow of traffic lights and neon signs. There was a curious beauty in this sort of bleakness. Wind whipped the still naked April trees and made the human heart—at least this human heart—pine for the warmth and glow of a fireplace and the solace of a good book. Or a nice lady, even better.

"Well, there are three other kinds, actually, but the first two aren't used much anymore. And anyway, if you run into them, you'll probably set off the alarm, first thing you do."

"Great."

"He probably uses something with an infrared motion detector."

"What's that?"

"It's very good at triggering alarms too, but there's a simple way to defeat it if you know what you're doing."

She then went on to explain that on the back door, cleverly hidden, would be a detector that noted any activity and would then pass this information along to the alarm system. This all sounded pretty discouraging, but then, being good old Delia, she explained how I could trick the detector. . .

~ ~ ~ ~ ~

Vertical wood siding gave the duplex a rustic look. It sat isolated and imperious on the shelf of a pine hill. Delia drove past, went halfway around the block, and then took the slanting gravel alley up to the duplex, cutting her headlights as she did so.

Delia was not only cute, she knew what she was doing.

"The one on the left," she said.

"You sure you want to wait for me? There's no sense in you getting involved."

"Hey, I help out all of my old man's friends. It's just my nature."

I smiled at her. "I appreciate it."

"Just remember what I told you about that beam. That could screw up everything. If there's any trouble out here, I'll honk—once if there's trouble, twice if it's all clear."

"I'll remember. And thanks again, Delia."

"Good luck, Bob."

I nodded, picked up the bag of tools and opened the door, wind and rain sprinkling across my face.

Then I went to try my luck again at the somewhat difficult art of burglary. Difficult for me, anyway.

The last time I'd tried something like this, I'd ended up in prison for four and a half years.

~ ~ ~ ~ ~

The detector setup was just as Delia had described it. Took me a few minutes to do what Delia had instructed me to do, but then I was inside, beyond the door my tools had helped open with little trouble, and standing in a darkness that smelled of slightly burned coffee and sweet furniture polish. In the pale light from outside, the waiting room could best be described as trendy-on-a-budget—a lot of dark, angular furnishings that looked awfully fragile. To the right of the receptionist's desk were three four-drawer filing cabinets, on top of which rested a half-dozen framed family portraits.

I started with the filing cabinets. I learned where the good Dr. Wyman bought his paper towels wholesale; the fact that he was thirty

days in arrears on his account at Bonanza Office Supply; and that he
paid $65 a month to his late-night answering service.

Not exactly what I was looking for. A few moments later, I stood
inside his personal domain, which was filled with just as much cheap
flashy furniture and just as many framed family photos as the waiting
room. There was a modern glass desk and spindly chair. And the inevitable Freudian couch complete with an ashtray on one arm and a
box of Kleenex—but from the arrangement of the leather armchairs, I
suspected that this was where most of his business was done.

For a long minute I just stood there, imagining all the people who
had been in here, all their woes and griefs—the faithless husband; the
wife who felt her life was too confining; the teenager already far gone
into drugs; the successful young man trying to make sense of the fact
that he was dying of AIDS.

Not exactly a job I'd want.

I set to work, occasionally glancing up the hill to where Delia's
cab sat, a dark figure against a darker night. By now the rain was little more than a mist. The good doctor hid his patients' records in two
filing cabinets tucked far back into a walk-in closet. I had to wind my
way through a couple of raincoats and trod on a pair of rubbers that
felt squishy as I passed over them.

Each cabinet was locked, but not very earnestly.

The good old burglary tools came in very handy.

I put the tiny flashlight into the corner of my mouth like a cigar
and proceeded to riffle through the patient files.

I tried not to notice the personal information of anybody whose
name didn't concern me. I figured I owed those folks at least that
much discretion. There was only one name that concerned me.

Delia honked.

I closed the cabinet drawer I'd been looking through. I clicked
off my flashlight.

I hadn't realized it till now, but I was coated with chill sweat; I
wasn't a natural-born thief. Burglary took both a physical and a mental toll on me.

I didn't know what else to do but stand there, breath coming in
short hot gasps, fingers trembling slightly. Prison images filled my
mind. Was I headed back there? At the thought, my stomach felt
tight, sick.

I don't know how much time passed—enough, anyway, for me to
go through a jury trial and a sentence hearing and to be assigned both
a cellblock and a cell.

I even heard the prison loudspeaker barking for "Lights out" on a steamy August night when you lay drowning in your own sweat.

A horn. Once. Twice. Delia.

All clear.

I went back to work.

I found the correct section—the M's—but I didn't find his name. A terrible thought: maybe he knew this shrink socially. Maybe they played golf together and he simply stopped in to see him sometimes and wasn't a patient at all.

I went through the next filing cabinet on the unlikely hope that somewhere else I'd find another M section.

I didn't find another M section.

There was no other M section.

I went back to the first filing cabinet, took several deep breaths, and forced myself to calm down.

He had to have a file in here somewhere. Had to.

I rolled the top drawer out on its oily wheels and started riffling through the tops of various file folders.

At last I came to one marked: NEW CLIENTS.

I took this one out, stuck the flashlight into the corner of my mouth and started looking through the material.

Whoever did the filing was a wee bit behind. Some of the "new" clients had visitation sheets that stretched back seven, and occasionally, eight months.

That's where I found him.

He'd been coming here seven months.

Tempting as it was, I didn't read the eight or nine sheets of scrawled notes that the good doctor had made about him.

There wasn't time.

I took the notes and went out to the front office and flipped on the Xerox machine.

The damned thing made a lot of noise in an empty office duplex like this one. Crisp electric fire outlined the lid of the copying machine. I hurried. My stomach was starting to act up again, probably in anticipation of prison food.

I made the copies, returned the originals to the file, closed up the cabinet, walked back over the squishy rubbers on the closet floor, and then went back to the front door and began to make my way out.

I crouched down so as not to set off the invisible beam. Less than a minute later I dropped myself into Delia's front seat and let her put a cigarette in my mouth.

It tasted a whole lot better than the flashlight had.

~ ~ ~ ~ ~

"I think it's great how much you loved her."

"Yeah. I suppose it is."

"Even after everything she did and all."

"That part I try not to think about."

"But we all do crazy things. That doesn't mean she was bad."

"That's how I look at it, Delia. That she just made a mistake, was all. Just one little mistake."

She was taking me home after we'd had a few cups of coffee, during which she explained that she'd honked when a teenage couple had pulled up the driveway, looking for a place to make out. Everything had gone well.

"You still think about her a lot, huh?"

"Yeah, I do, Delia."

"You get ready to meet a nice lady, you call me."

"Oh?"

She laughed. "Don't worry, Bob. Not me. I'm true-blue. It ain't easy all the time, with Kip in the joint and everything, but I do all right. I was thinkin' about my cousin."

"Your cousin?"

"Betsy. Wait till you see her in a bikini."

"Nice, huh?"

"Nice? Boy would I love to have *her* chest."

"Maybe when this's all over," I said.

"Probably better you wait for a while anyway. She's tryin' to break it off with this Angie guy, he's this biker, and the guy she tried to date, Angie smashed out all the windows in the guy's car."

"Guy ever call her again?"

"You kiddin'? But she didn't care anyway. She found the guy was married, can you believe it? She sneaks around and gets Angie all riled up, and then the bastard is married."

You didn't need country western radio stations when Delia was around.

"Yeah," I said, "I think I'll wait a little while on Betsy."

"I can tell you're a little worried about Angie, and I don't blame you. But he'll be back in detox another two, three months, the way I figure, so you 'n' Betsy will have clear sailin'."

"That's good to know."

My apartment house took shape inside deep, windblown shadows.

Tonight, when she pulled the cab over, I gave her a little kiss on the cheek and said, "I really appreciate all the help, Delia."

She nodded to the papers I had rolled up and stuck inside my blue windbreaker.

"I just hope you have somethin' in there you can use."

"So do I."

~ ~ ~ ~ ~

To caf or not to caf. That was the question.

Given all the pages I wanted to read through tonight, real caf coffee was probably what I needed to be alert. There were a lot of pages and I was tired from a long day's work at the store and I didn't want to miss some subtle message buried in the middle of the material I'd stolen from Dr. Wyman.

On the other hand, if I wrapped up early, I might find myself with caffeine jitters staring at a long, hard night of bad memories and those little flare-ups of useless anger that make dawn seem even more distant.

So I stood dumb, in all senses of that word, a jar of instant decaf in my left hand, a jar of instant caf in the other, weighing them as if they were jars of gold. Finally I decided to live a life of danger, and I filled the teakettle with water and set the kettle on the hot plate, which was about the only modern convenience in my wan little sleeping room, and then I spooned two heaping teaspoonsful of manly caf into a slightly cracked coffee cup.

And then I finally sat down and started reading about the life and times of one David George MacDonald.

~ ~ ~ ~ ~

During that long malaise of prison life, I became a serious reader, and some of the serious reading I did included Andre Malraux, whose *Man's Fate* contained a brief interview with a seventy-five-year-old priest. What have you learned, in your fifty years of hearing confessions? Malraux wanted to know. And the old priest replied, "That there's no such thing as an adult."

I knew what he was talking about as I read through the file on David George MacDonald.

Here you had the rich, handsome, forty-year-old son of a wealthy investment banker. We were talking Yale. We were talking a five-year tenure at Mellon Bank. We were talking a six-year span at one of his father's investment companies. And yet. . . David had been inexplicably drawn to the dark side of American business. Contractors who skimped on promises and whose housing developments became rat traps after only a few years. Refinancing deals for home owners that were little better than the juice loans you could get from the mob. Used car wholesaling where turning back the odometer was mandatory. Expensive furs that were certainly stolen. And on and on.

You could see in Dr. Wyman's notes that MacDonald tried to pass himself off as a simple, honest businessman, but I knew his real background. . .and in the notes it became obvious that Dr. Wyman had at least begun to *suspect* his real background.

Here were his women, and they were myriad; here were marriages, three in all, trouble with the law for beating all three of them; and here were the hookers he could never quite lose his taste for, the midnight cruise and the hasty hot reality of sex in a car seat with a woman who would please you any way you asked; and in passing once—just once—was a mention of my wife and how mad she'd made him because she'd tricked him into getting her pregnant.

At this point I set the material down, put my head against the back of the chair, closed my eyes.

I'd known she was pregnant, the autopsy had revealed that, but all along I'd assumed it was our child.

But now I knew better.

Their child.

One he hadn't even wanted.

It had died trapped inside her dead womb.

Really fucking peachy.

I spent the next fifteen minutes doing my self-pity aerobics—you probably do them yourself, at least sometimes. Has anybody ever been this betrayed before in all human history? Has such a bad hand ever been dealt to such an all-around wonderful human being as *moi* before? Has anybody ever deserved to feel such unashamed sorrow for his poor pitiful self before?

Fortunately, I got pretty sick of it all after a while and went down the hall to pee.

Sara hadn't been an ideal wife, but I hadn't been an ideal husband either. How about that cute little Nancy I'd spent one spring bopping in places as various as my office closet, the maintenance room in the basement, and the backseat of her ancient Buick warwagon? Or the college-senior waitress I'd met at Pizza Hut? Or the Chanel saleswoman I'd had several nooners with at a motel out on Forester Road?

No such thing as an adult.

It wasn't virtue I was trying to defend here—it was justice. Sara and I hadn't been all that morally superior to David MacDonald—but we hadn't murdered anybody.

David had murdered Sara.

And had gotten away with it, the police investigation dropped.

But faithless husband that I was, I wanted the killer of my faithless wife brought to trial.

My last best hope was that I'd find something useful in Dr. Wyman's notes. Nothing else had worked.

I had some more caf.

I even opened the window so the 43-degree wind would drive out any lurking sleepiness.

I started reading again.

Just before five and the first sharp cry of birds, I saw what I'd been looking for ever since I'd been released from prison. David George MacDonald had himself two very notable psychological anxieties. . .

I saw the way I was going to nail his gold-plated ass to the wall.

~ ~ ~ ~ ~

Next day on my lunch hour, Delia drove me over to the library, where I checked out six books, three of which applied to one subject, three to another.

"You're going to be busy tonight," she said.

"Yeah. I will be."

"You closin' in on MacDonald?"

"I hope so."

"I hope so, too."

~ ~ ~ ~ ~

The afternoon went slowly. A customer named Burgess came in, a customer I ordinarily enjoyed talking to, but today everything he said irritated me. I knew why. I didn't want to be here. I wanted to be home with my library books.

Burgess bought a blue blazer and a pair of gray slacks. He needed some additional clothes now that he'd given up smoking and put on fifteen pounds.

It felt as if I'd spent a couple of hours with him, but when he left I checked my watch. I saw that I still had three and a half hours to go.

I spent the rest of the afternoon considering some of the words

I'd found in Dr. Wyman's notes on David MacDonald: Anxiety dis-order Anxiolytic medicine Anticipatory anxiety Systematic Desensi-tization. I had a long night ahead of me, one I looked forward to.

~ ~ ~ ~ ~

Around ten that night, I called Delia and asked her if she could help me out.

"Sure. What do I do?"

I told her.

"That should be easy," she said.

"I'd really appreciate it, Delia."

"Say," she said, just as I was about to hang up. "Guess who I ran into."

"Who?"

"My cousin Betsy. You know, the one with the big—"

"She still having trouble with her biker?"

"No. In fact, she said that they're probably gonna get married. I mean, he's agreed to start using deodorant and everything."

"No wonder they're getting married."

"But I told her about you anyway—you know, just in case it don't turn out too good—and she said that if she ever dumps him, she'd really like to meet you."

"Well, I'll be wearing her name on my lips."

"Huh?"

"Nothing. Just being a smart-ass. Look, Delia, I really appreciate all the help you've been giving me."

"No sweat, Bob. I just wish it'd worked out between you and Betsy."

"Maybe when we're reincarnated."

"You saw that Oprah show too, huh?"

I smiled. "Not that one. But I've seen a lot of others." She was crazy, Delia was, but relentlessly sweet. "Good night, Delia."

" 'Night."

~ ~ ~ ~ ~

Three weeks went by before Delia was able to find any pattern in David MacDonald's work life.

He always parked his splashy new Lincoln in a lot directly be-hind the office building he'd inherited from his father.

But as for when he arrived at work and when he left—he was

usually erratic, no particular schedule being apparent to Delia.

Except for Thursday nights. Thursday nights, for some reason neither of us could figure out, he usually worked till around nine. A janitorial crew started cleaning the place up around three a.m.

Four different lunch hours, Delia drove me over to the office building so I could see what I needed to do. I'd been in here before, back when I used to go up to see Sara when she was working for MacDonald, but I'd never really studied the place.

It was a nice building built back at the turn of the century, defined by its curtain walls and its internal metal structure, then very fashionable. At least that's what the library book on local architecture had to say about it. And more: the soaring three-bay exterior is divided into three major sections: a two-story triple-arch base, an eight-story shaft of two tiers of projecting bay windows, and a crowning section marked by paired windows. Easy to imagine shiny black limousines pulling up here in the old days, and robber barons appearing in capes and squeaky black shoes.

The interior had been refurbished: pink marble and heavily rococo interior design. Your footsteps echoed on the marble floor, all the way over to and up the single elevator that ran up the very center of the building.

On my third visit to the place, an hour after work, I rode up to the ninth floor and went through a dry run of what I needed to do. I was in equal parts scared and excited. The run-through took twenty minutes. I managed to get through without anyone seeing me—that I was aware of, anyway.

Back in the car, Delia said, "You're a mess."

"Thank you."

She laughed. "You know what I mean."

"It's messy work."

"And scary work."

"A little bit, I guess."

"You guess? You couldn't get me to do that in a million years."

"I just hope it works."

"Yeah," Delia said, putting the car in gear and pulling away from the curb, "so do I."

~ ~ ~ ~ ~

The following week, driving me back to MacDonald's, Delia said, "You scared?"

"A little."

"I'd be a lot scared."

"Well, I think that's more accurate."

"That you're a lot scared?"

"Uh-huh."

"Maybe it won't go the way you want it to. Maybe he won't—"

"I know."

"You could get killed, you know."

"I know."

"You're a lot braver than I'd be."

"I'm not brave at all, Delia. I wish I were."

Her headlights swept the parking lot in back of the building, highlighting bumpers and fenders and license plates with cute personal statements such as: I'M CUTE. I doubted that anybody who had to brag about being cute actually was.

There was a cold mist and all the streetlights were haloed as I stepped from the car. We were getting winter in nickel-and-dime increments.

"I'll be saying prayers," Delia said.

"I'll need them."

"You'll be fine," she said in a way that suggested I probably wouldn't be fine at all.

"See ya," I said. I took my gym bag and left.

~ ~ ~ ~ ~

Some of the books I'd brought home from the library dealt not only with the structure of buildings but with the elevators they used. Starting in 1853, elevators of various kinds were introduced to the world. There had been steam elevators and hydraulic elevators and finally electric elevators. And it was on the electric elevator that I'd concentrated.

The dark front doors of the office building opened after I spent two hasty minutes working on them with a pick. The burglar alarm system had not been set yet. The janitorial service did that when they left in the middle of the night.

Once inside, I walked straight to the two elevators and rode all the way to the ninth floor. On the way up, I changed into the blue coveralls I'd stuffed inside the bag. I checked my watch. In the next fifteen minutes or so, if he was true to his usual schedule, David MacDonald would board this same elevator car on the floor beneath me.

I went to work. The first thing I did was hang an OUT OF OR-

DER sign on the second elevator and then rush back to the first car.

I punched the button to take the car to the eighth floor. On the way up, I opened the EMERGENCY phone box and ripped the two-inch receiver cord from its moorings. There'd be no calls from this elevator.

I left the car on the eighth floor. I found the metal door with the FIRE sign above it and took the stairs down to the seventh floor, where I took a crowbar from my bag.

Everything was ready. MacDonald would board the car on the eighth floor. I'd give him a few seconds to start descending, then open the seventh-floor elevator doors with a crowbar. The electric interlock would freeze the car right where it was—between floors — and I'd then run up to the ninth floor, where I'd again part the doors. Only this time I would step out onto the top of the elevator, which would be only a few inches below the ninth-floor elevator entrance.

I paced the seventh-floor hallway. The old building was filled with the ghosts of ancient plumbing and creaking floors. Every time one of them made a sound, I turned to the elevator. After several false alarms, I forced myself to calm down.

When he was finally there, one floor above me and putting his weight into the elevator car, I was daydreaming and didn't respond immediately. Then I had to hurry.

I pressed my ear to the elevator doors and listened for the eighth-floor doors to rumble closed. They did.

Then I waited to hear the whine of the machinery as the elevator began its descent. The car started to slowly descend.

I grabbed the crowbar and set to work.

In seconds I had the doors open. I heard the car stop. MacDonald shouted, "What the hell's going on here!"

I ran to the fire door and took the steps two at a time. After six years and two months, after a prison term and numerous failed plans to prove that MacDonald had killed Sara, I finally had my best last chance to force MacDonald to tell me exactly what had happened.

All those fancy terms I'd found about him in his shrink file—anticipatory anxiety and anxiety disorder—meant one thing: Mac-Donald's lifelong claustrophobia had most recently manifested itself as a terror of the elevator in his office building. Over and over again he'd told his shrink about his nightmares—of being trapped in the elevator and suffocating.

He took medication, he did all the mental exercises his shrink suggested (this was where the term "systematic desensitization" came in), and he even considered moving his offices to a one-story building.

But none of that mattered now.

He was trapped on a very small elevator car, and before he left it, he was going to confess to killing my wife. And I was going to record it all on the hand-sized cassette player I'd brought along.

~ ~ ~ ~ ~

By the time I reached the ninth floor, MacDonald was screaming and pounding on the interior doors.

I got the ninth-floor doors open and stepped out onto the top of the car, where I knelt down and wrenched the T-handle straight up. This opened the emergency hatch. I looked down into the car at MacDonald.

He was aware of me immediately. He recognized me immediately, too. "You sonofabitch, what d'you think you're doing?"

"The last time I broke into your office, MacDonald, you had me sent to prison. But I've learned a few thing since then." I stuck my recorder through the hatch and waggled it at him. "This time you're going to do all the work. And this time *you're* going to go to prison." I tapped the recorder. "You're going to tell me how you murdered my wife because after you were done with her you were afraid she'd turn you over to the district attorney for some of the scams she'd seen when she was your secretary."

"You think I'm going to listen to some dumb-ass ex-con?"

"You will or you'll never get off this elevator alive. You'll have a heart attack." I smiled. "You should've gotten on an exercise regimen a long time ago, MacDonald."

He was one of those men—you see them especially among male opera stars—who manage to carry an extra hundred pounds and still look handsome. There was a kind of baronial splendor to MacDonald, the long dark hair just now starting to show dramatic streaks of gray; the flowing dark suits meant to hide his girth and that somehow suggested a Victorian cape; and the masklike face, the cruel good looks of angry dark eyes and a petulant, crafty mouth. Sara had been pretty sensible. Or I'd thought so, anyway, until she got involved with MacDonald and his power games.

"You tore the fucking phone out, didn't you?"

"Guilty as charged."

"This time, asshole, you're going to go to the slammer and never get out."

I smiled. "I'd try to calm down, MacDonald. You're going to be in there for a long time."

"Maybe not," he said, and before I quite realized what he was doing, a blued .45 appeared in his hand and he started firing bullets into the ceiling of the car.

I dove from the top to the ninth floor. I let him fire, counting the shots as he did so. They echoed off the half-century silence.

He had one bullet left.

"It's not going to do you any good, MacDonald, that last shot," I said. "It's not going to get you out of that elevator."

~ ~ ~ ~ ~

The waiting started. According to the books on phobias I'd read, what I could expect next were several outward manifestations of panic—shouting, then screaming; pounding fists and then kicking as well; hurling himself to the floor and maybe even pounding his head against the wall. And pleading; earnest, savage pleading.

It sounded great.

Over the next forty-five minutes, at least according to the books, MacDonald had developed stomach cramps, lost his ability to stand up straight, probably wet his pants, had a difficult time swallowing, was terrified that he was about to smother to death, and could not focus his mind on any logical plan of escape.

That was when he began pounding the walls.

That was when he began shrieking.

That was when he began slamming at the doors with his fullback girth and his wounded-animal rage.

During this time, I snuck back to the top of the car, got my cassette player rolling again and shouted, "As soon as you tell me you killed Sara, MacDonald, I'll get you out of that car."

He couldn't help himself. He was too far gone. He'd planned to hold on to his last bullet until he really got a good chance to hit me—but he couldn't control his anger.

He fired his last shot up through the open hatch.

It ricocheted off the ceiling of the building, knocking loose some ancient dust, and then disappeared. I closed the hatch again.

I had some more waiting to do.

~ ~ ~ ~ ~

This time, roughly twenty minutes later, he started sobbing. That was the only word for it. Wild, hysterical crying, and slamming his fists into the walls of the elevator car. The car shifted and shimmied beneath me; I looked up the shaft at the cable. In the oily darkness, I felt the cable tremble from the terrible beating the car was taking. I opened the hatch. "You killed her, MacDonald, admit it and I'll let you out of here." He spit upward, his oyster getting me on the forehead. Without a whole hell of a lot of dignity, I withdrew my head from the emergency hatch. Another fifteen minutes.

~ ~ ~ ~ ~

He started praying. It was odd hearing a man like MacDonald say the Hail Mary and Our Father, but he spoke them with his usual harshness, so they came off more curse than prayer.

Then he said, "Fuck you up there! I ain't gonna admit shit!"

~ ~ ~ ~ ~

After another fifteen minutes, I leaned into the emergency hatch and said:

"You didn't need to kill her, MacDonald."

"I didn't kill her."

"You didn't know her. She never would've turned you in. She loved you too much." The words weren't easy for me to say, but they were the truth. She'd told me that herself. "I loved her, MacDonald, and I would've taken her back and we would've moved away and eventually she would've forgotten all about you. You didn't need to kill her."

And that's when I realized how badly my elevator-phobia plan was going. MacDonald wasn't crying over Sara; I was. This was turning into a kind of therapy session for me: I was saying all the flinty things I'd kept in my stony heart during prison.

They needed to be said for me, not for him, and I didn't even give a damn if he listened or not.

I must've talked another ten minutes.

~ ~ ~ ~ ~

After an hour and a half, with Delia sitting out in the parking lot surely sensing that yet another of my plans had gone wrong, I started to wonder if MacDonald wouldn't beat me at his own phobia.

He phased in and out of terror, never getting quite so bad that he gave in to me. Of course, then he'd erupt again, panic overtaking him, screaming, screeching, crying out for his mother, pounding and pounding and pounding the walls.

I needed one more thing that was one more thing too many—one more thing that—

I'd been crouching on top of the elevator, my recorder sitting on the edge of the emergency hatch.

My legs were dead from crouching so long. I needed to stand up.

And when I did—

Something fell, clanking from my pocket. And when I reached down to get it. . .

"You're dead, you fucker!" I shouted down through the open emergency hatch.

I was jubilant.

MacDonald was going to be confessing real soon now.

Real soon.

~ ~ ~ ~ ~

I didn't get out of the police station till much before dawn.

Delia was waiting for me in the freezing gray morning.

When I got in the car, she handed me an empty paper cup and poured some steaming coffee into it.

"So what did our fine friends the flatfoots make of the tape you played 'em?"

"They said that the DA wouldn't be happy that I got the confession that way, but that it would still be useful in prosecuting Mac-Donald."

"So they are going to prosecute him?"

I nodded. "The cops hate him as much as I do. They've wanted to nail him for years. Now they think they can get him on a first-degree murder rap. They're very happy."

She looked over at me, her wise eyes gentle. "How about you?"

"Me?"

"You happy, Bob?"

"I guess."

"You really loved her, didn't you?"

"Yeah," I said, "in my imperfect way."

"Your imperfect way, my ass. You're a good man, Bob, even if you won't admit it."

She put the taxi in gear and we pulled out of the lot. When we were streaking down the street, pulling into a Hardee's drive-through for breakfast, she said, "You know, I was startin' to think you weren't ever gonna get him to confess."

I smiled. "Yeah, so was I. Then that lighter Sara gave me for our anniversary fell out and. . . Well, as soon as I started lighting paper and dropping it into the elevator car. . . Well, MacDonald started talking right away. Claustrophobia and pyrophobia is a pretty deadly combination. Of course, he's really going to have claustrophobia in that little cell of his."

"You want cheese on your eggs this morning, Bob?" she said.

"Yeah," I said, feeling almost ridiculously good about everything all of a sudden, "cheese sounds great."

Even seeing my parole officer Ralph DeConcini a few hours from now sounded great.

Hell, *everything* sounded great.

RIFF

Just before dawn I wake up and listen to the hushed sounds from the room next to mine. When I hear these particular sounds at this particular time on a cancer floor in a hospital—three or four rushed whispering voices; faint squeaks of gurney wheels; and then elevator doors opening down the hall, eight floors down to the basement and the morgue—I know what's happened.

Charlie Grady died. I'd see him a couple times a day on my little walks up and down the hall. The nurses don't make me walk. I do it on my own.

I sort of knew Charlie wasn't going to hang on much longer. His wife was talking to a hospice woman but I figured Charlie wouldn't make it even that long. He was a nice old guy, real estate rich, never asking me the standard questions I get about my so-called fame. In fact, he said right out one day that he didn't care much for jazz. And he hoped that didn't offend me. His kind of money can give you that kind of confidence. He didn't give a damn if it offended me or not.

His wife is a weeper. She came twice a day to see him—his lung cancer and his eighty pounds overweight were shaping up to bring on one massive heart attack—and she never left but she was wailing. I sure don't blame her. She loves her man. But that doesn't make it any easier to take when you're in the room next door and trying to deal with your own problems. Health-wise, I mean. And every-other-wise, for that matter.

I have a 7:00 am visitor, right after the doc making his rounds leaves my room. Guy named Larry Donnelly. Kind of a fix-it guy for jazz folk. Very serious jazz cat, Larry is. Really got into it in the slam where he served ten years for torching a building with a janitor still in it. Larry had no idea, of course. I called Larry a couple of days ago, asked him to stop up. He hesitates in the doorway now. Some people get like that about cancer. Scared. Like it's a plague you can pick up. "C'mon in, Larry."

~ ~ ~ ~ ~

He's only there ten minutes. And is kind've junkie-twitchy all the time. Can probably feel the cancer working its way through his veins as he stands there trembling. Then he's gone.

I fall back asleep and wake up for a second time. This time it's the nurse with the rattling breakfast cart. They keep telling me to eat but my appetite has gone with all the rest of it. I'm in pretty much the same shape as Charlie Grady was. Except mine's in the pancreas. I'm hoping I'm as lucky as Charlie. A heart attack like that, you're one lucky man. And so are your loved ones. Quick and clean. Instead of hanging on.

Hanging on.

That's what I've done with my wife Karen the last five years. Met her in a jazz club in Chicago. She was a singer, then. Not much of one. But she had the Look. That slender body, that melancholy face, the dark eyes, the tumbling dark hair. She was from Omaha but she made you think international. Paris in spring, where I gigged with Brubeck. And London in autumn, where I gigged with Miles. Milan, baking in the summer while we were working on my live album. I dumped wife number four for her, just as I'd dumped all the old ones for new ones. I never said I was proud of myself. But you get on the road, you're six, seven months out from seeing the wife and the kiddies, you're just naturally going to fall in love with somebody else.

What I didn't know that night in Chicago was that it was payback time. I'm sitting in the back of this tiny, drafty club and people are coming up asking for my autograph and if she isn't singing they ask me did I dig playing with Brubeck, was Miles as much of a diva prick as people said, was my label ever going to do a box set of my music—and hey, that was one fine article in *Time*, "The Legend of The Saddest Sax in Jazz History: Mike Thorne." It was actually the usual thing, that *Time* piece, how I'd managed to survive and prosper in a music world dominated by rock and rap, and how I was the Chet Baker of my time—handsome, media friendly and probably the best sax man of the past two decades. Thank God, the article concluded, that I never got hooked on junk the way poor Chet had. You read about Chet, man, and you want to cut your wrists.

So I'm sitting there trying to be nice to the people who come up but I'm paying more and more serious attention to this singer Karen Miller. The clarity of her beauty is astonishing.

Between her sets, I ask her over to my table for a drink. I can see how flustered she is. Mike Thorne, fifty-three-year-old jazz legend, asking twenty-two-year-old nobody to have a drink with him.

I get to play the cool dude that night. I'm properly humble when she's flattering me, I'm properly appreciative when we talk about her own performance, and I'm properly matter-of-fact when I drop some big jazz names I'm meeting later that night for drinks. What I am really is so smitten I'm like I was at the tenth grade dance when I could never quite work up nerve enough to ask Marietta Courtney to dance slow with me.

But that wasn't what was really going on at all. Subtext they call it. You know, where it seems like you're really saying this but you're really saying that, just below the surface.

What I was really doing was setting myself up for payback. For every time I'd ever cheated on a woman, for every promise I'd broken to my three daughters, for every heartbreak I'd caused—old numero uno was about to get his. Maybe this Karen Miller from Omaha couldn't sing worth a damn. But she sure knew how to lie, cheat, steal, betray and humiliate you.

If there is a Green Beret unit of heartbreakers and ballbusters, Karen Leigh Miller of Omaha, Nebraska was Commander-in-Chief.

~ ~ ~ ~ ~

Thirty-eight years I play clubs. When I'm in my prime I'm hitting Letterman and Leno and guest playing on albums by big rock stars who want the cachet of having a jazz star on their CD. They don't know diddly about jazz but they think it sounds cool to the reviewers.

This is when I start collecting jazz memorabilia. I'm in places where Satchmo and Charlie Parker and Gerry Mulligan and people like that have played and so I start buying up things they left behind in the clubs and that the club owners might otherwise throw out in a box in the back.

This is also the time I get the critics on my back for playing Vegas. Just once, for God's sake. I don't have a right to make a fucking living? I can't take the scorn. A serious jazz musician playing Vegas as the opening act for some jiggle-titted TV star who thinks she can sing? Karen digs it, of course. Me being in Vegas. While I'm on stage, she's sitting at a table out front with Cameron Diaz and Bruce Willis, who are in town shooting a picture together. Your regular jazz clubs—the kind I usually play in—you don't get Cameron Diaz and Bruce Willis, let me tell you.

Sam Caine is with them, too. Sam is my agent and manager. I met him twenty years ago when he was just one of the many hungry young men you see running up and down the halls of William Morris in search of clients who might have stumbled and fallen and would appreciate the hungry young man who helped pick them up.

Sam was then the assistant to my agent. By the time I decide to do a lot of my own booking, Sam is a full-fledged agent who is just about to open up a small shop of his own. He wants clients, I'm sick of big agencies. I handle most of the small gigs, he books the big ones. He's a failed actor, our Sam. You always hear about how many beautiful failed wanna-be actresses there are in Hollywood. There are an equal number of beautiful failed wanna-be actors.

Sam has no interest in jazz. He's a club lizard. If you can't hustle chicks while it's being played, Sam doesn't want to hear it. But he's funny and shrewd and gets me bookings I couldn't get for myself.

The years go by, my CDs aren't selling the way they used to, Letterman and Leno's people don't return Sam's calls, and you know what? By now, I don't care. I'm married to Karen.

The fourth year of our marriage, I learn three things.

1) Karen has spent most of the nearly two million dollars that was for my retirement. You should see our house, our cars, her clothes. It sounds like a joke but two million isn't what it used to be. My accountant keeps saying you gotta do something about this, Mike. But I never do. I'm scared she'll leave me. That started the second year, the way she'd get whatever she wanted by saying, just kind of off-handed, "I've gotta be honest, Mike. Sometimes, I wonder if we did the right thing." And of course I'd give in and say, sure, baby, buy whatever you want. She went right straight through my money.

2) I find a note that she threw away in the tiny basket next to her dressing table—you could land a fighter jet on that table; an aircraft carrier should be so lucky to have that room—and right away I see what it says. And right away I recognize the handwriting. Now, I know she's had little nights when she's strayed. A couple of her boys got so hot for her they even broke the rules and called the house for her. I listened in on the extension. The first couple of times, I literally rush to the john and throw up. Now I know what I put all those women through. This time somebody else is holding the gun. But I don't confront her. It's the same with the money she spends. If I confront her, she'll leave me. But this time it's different. This time it's Sam and in the note he talks about how much they're in love. I do a lot of throwing up for several days running. And that's not so unheard of, you know. They say when Sinatra caught Ava Gardner cheating on him, he started puking around the clock, lost his voice, and ended up trying to kill himself.

3) I start losing weight. My skin color changes. Nothing drastic.

But there's a peculiar faint yellow tone. The maid—of course we have a maid—she's the first one to say anything. She says I should see a doctor right away. All I can think of though is Karen and Sam. It was only a week ago that I found the note. The maid is insistent; and then Karen starts in on me about how I'm looking all of a sudden. I go to the doctor, there are so many tests I lose count at twelve, and the diagnosis is pancreatic cancer. Now I'm in the hospital. I hear Karen and the lady from the hospital in the hall the other day. "A cancer like this," the hospice lady says, "it never takes long, Mrs. Thorne."

~ ~ ~ ~ ~

Karen says, "You really look good in those pajamas, Mike."

"Thanks for getting them for me, honey."

Night. You know how it is, night in a hospital. You can always tell the rooms where death has no dominion. There's laughter and maybe grandkids and a lot of plans about what's going to happen when the patient finally gets out of here. But the other rooms—there's a whispery quality and a tension and long terrible aching silences and both sides prepare themselves for the flap flap flap of houseslippers that come down the hall in the middle of the night. An elderly obscene gent who puts his gnarled papery hand in yours and leads you into a world you cannot fathom.

Sam says, "You sound a lot better than you did last night."

"Yeah, I thought I'd go dancing later."

Karen laughs, leans over and gives me a little kiss. They're on opposite sides of my bed. "Oh, honey, it's so good you've kept your sense of humor."

Sam looks at his watch. "Well, guess I'll push off, Mike. But I'll be back tomorrow."

They've been here fifteen minutes. Talk about strained conversations.

What he's going to do, of course, is go downstairs and wait for her. She'll stay another ten, maybe fifteen minutes and then leave.

I notice the strain on Sam's face. The strain isn't entirely because of the situation with Karen. He's lost his three biggest clients this year. The sniffling sounds he makes—nobody wants a coke head for an agent. Sam's deep in debt. Deep.

"Take care, Mike," he says and leaves the room.

"He's such a good friend to you," Karen says after he leaves.

"Loyal," I said. "Nobody more loyal than Sam."

I say that staring right into those elegant violet eyes of hers. She looks uncomfortable. "Yes, loyal."

The tone sounds. Visiting hours will be over in ten minutes.

As she bends over to me for her goodnight kiss, I see a moment of distaste in her eyes. I got a glimpse of myself this morning. I'm a lurid dirty yellow color. Even my eyes have a yellow tint to them. I've lost twenty-six pounds in just under seven weeks.

"You're all I think about, babe," she says.

"Yeah," I said. "You're all I think about, too."

"You're such a good husband," she says. And the tears come right on time. Fed Ex delivers them. You can order them in pints, quarters or gallons. "Such a good husband."

Fondling her hand. "And you're such a good wife."

The tone rings again and she says, "I'll see you tomorrow night. I thought I'd run up the coast tomorrow. See Shirley."

The good friend "Shirley" she's been talking about for three years. I've never met "Shirley" because she doesn't exist.

She gives me a peck on the cheek and then gives me another look at those pure glistening tears you order from Fed Ex. And then she goes.

~ ~ ~ ~ ~

Larry calls just after nine. He knows better than to say anything meaningful. He just says, "Just wanted to say it was good seeing you today, Mike. Guess I'll have me a beer and watch the news."

"Sure wish *I* could have a beer," I say. "Guess I'll just have to settle for the news."

It's the fifth story on the ten o'clock news. "The home of jazz legend Mike Thorne was destroyed by fire tonight. First estimate is that everything was destroyed, including his collection of jazz memorabilia said to be worth between two and three million dollars."

Good job, Larry.

Karen and Sam would've sold the memorabilia first. The collection would've brought more like four instead of the three the anchorman said. The house was worth another million-and-a-half by now, with all the improvements she put in it. Insurance money is sweet.

But I canceled the policy last week. No insurance on the house, no insurance on my memorabilia.

~ ~ ~ ~ ~

I wake up near dawn again. Sweet Ruth Andrews this time. Two doors down. Breast cancer. The gurney, the whispers, the elevator to the morgue downstairs.

I lie in darkness, waiting my turn.

TRADITION

At least the caller had the good grace to wait until Amy and I had finished making love. What with both of us working and two kids, the old days of spontaneous and frequent lovemaking were long gone. Now we made appointments and tonight we'd penciled in a frolic in our bedroom. I can't say it was a frolic as such but it was one of those times when lust and tenderness reminded me of how much I loved my wife of nine years and how nice it was afterward to lay with her sleeping on my chest.

We'd been a little late getting started because she'd gotten a call from Paula Crane, a fellow high school teacher. She'd wanted to know all about the English teacher who joined the faculty lately. Since Amy also taught English Paula assumed that she'd have lots of gossip about the man. Several of the female teachers had been at the house a few weeks back and all they'd talked about was this Bruce Peters. Apparently the women couldn't stop flirting with the handsome bachelor. As Amy hung up, she laughed and said, "Sorry, honey. If I didn't know better I'd swear Paula wasn't married. She talks like she's still single."

The clock radio said 11:24 as I reached to pick up the receiver. I had to roll to my right to reach it. I tried to do this without waking Amy up but my acrobatic skills failed. Her blonde head snapped up and she looked at me with the fuzzy confused gaze of a child. "What's wrong, honey?"

"The phone."

"Oh." Then, brushing hair from her face, alert now: "Oh, God."

I suppose that is a phrase common to many women married to law enforcement officers when their phone rings late at night. A mixture of irritation and vague fear.

She sat up and began running a slender hand across her face.

By now I could see Called ID. My father.

"Just got a call that David Neely is dead."

"Dead? How?"

"All I know is that he's lying on the river road straight down from the cliff behind his A-frame. Dink Hopkins was out on his motorcycle and found him about five minutes ago. Didn't call the shop. Phoned me at home."

"I'll meet you there in about ten minutes."

"Tell Amy I'm sorry about the late call."

Amy was up and hurrying out the bedroom door to check on the kids. Even though Sarah is seven and Brad is six she still checks on them three or four times a night, the way she did when they were smaller.

I grabbed socks, my L.L. Bean Bison Chukas, black sweater, jeans, the plastic loop that carries my official ID, dressing quickly in the Halloween shadows from the naked tree limbs on this cold October night. The last two items were my fedora— and I'm well aware of the vanity involved with wearing it—and the .38 I holster on my belt.

Amy was back in a rush, sliding her arms around me, holding me tight, letting smell the good clean scent of her hair and recently showered skin. "Did somebody die?"

"David Neely. Dink Hopkins found him on the river road a few minutes ago. That's all I know."

She leaned back. "Oh, God. I wonder if he was murdered—I wonder if it was one of his married women." Then: "Oh, listen to me." Her hands dropped from my sides. In the wan streetlight she looked like a sensual college girl, just skimpy red panties, nothing else. "Can you be any more of a bitch, Amy? I shouldn't have said that. The poor man's dead. It's just that he was—"

"An asshole."

"Yes. An asshole. He ruined my best friend's marriage."

"Well, Donna had a little something to do with it, too. He didn't exactly force her into that affair." I leaned in and kissed her. "I need to get going. I call you in your cell in awhile so it won't wake Cindy."

"Love you."

"Love you, too."

Alveron, population 4,680, is in northern Illinois fifty-three miles from Lake Michigan. At this time of night everything except a few taverns and convenience stores are closed and the houses, which tend to be small except for a handful of McMansions on the eastern edge of town, are hunkered down in dreams and darkness. There was no reason to use a siren. My father, the county sheriff, would already have dispatched an ambulance as a well as the county medical examiner, a capable middle-aged black doctor who had yet to find complete acceptance in the mostly white community. He fit into a quiet community with a murder rate that was the lowest per population in the state and had been for more than twenty-five years. Our previous ME had been something of a showboat.

I couldn't drive these streets without being at the mercy of memories good and bad. Being the son of the sheriff in a small town means you'll have lots of friends whether you want them or not. You enjoy something like celebrity. My folks are good and decent people. My father believes that physical force is always the last resort and he has fired more than a few men over the years who have taken their problems out on their prisoners. Last year he hired a young woman as his newest deputy. She and Dr. Thomas face about the same amount of resistance. A black doctor? A female officer? What the hell is going on here? That's Chicago foolishness and not at all for Alveron.

I was the detective in the five man sheriff's department, meaning that I had gone through the police academy in Chicago and taken four night school courses in criminology. At that I was lucky to be anything in the way of law enforcement. I had been the law-breaking son of the town cop. Drugs, reckless driving, more than a few fights and ten nights spent in one of my father's cells over a two-year period. Amy had been my salvation. We'd been high school lovers until she could no longer deal with my drinking. Four years after graduation, when my father had a serious cancer scare, he made me promise that I would give up drinking. Even though I promised it shouldn't have worked. Liquor trumps loyalty. But between giving my word and meeting Amy again after she'd worked in Chicago for a few years, I've managed to stay dry since the day I told the old man I'd keep my word.

The river was on my right. Pale full moon riding the far piney bend in the river; the silver-limned water cold and forbidding; and several cars lined behind the blue-flashing box of ambulance.

I could see my father talking to one of the paramedics. Like most of us males who bear the name Winters Con (for Conor), Winters is a tall man who gives the impression, and a true impression it is, of rangy prairie boy power. He has the red hair, now going to gray, and thoughtful, somewhat melancholy face of our tribe. His pride is that he is not a hayseed lawman. He is, like his own father who preceded him as county sheriff, a reader and a thinker and a man who weighs his words.

The limestone cliff loomed in the lights. I parked and started walking toward the ambulance. Behind me I could hear cars pulling up, parking. The vampires. No matter how late at night, no matter what the weather conditions, they come out. To stare at death. Maybe they think it will buy them some extra time of their own. Voodoo.

The paramedic saw me before my father did. "Here's Cam now," he said, watching me approach.

The night was cold enough for breath to run silver. Mike Sullivan was the paramedic's name. We played softball on the same team in the hot months.

My father said, "Neely's on the gurney over there."

"Looks like he won't be bed hopping much anymore," Sullivan said.

"Not anymore he won't." My father had disliked Neely from the first day the man had moved here six years ago. I remembered sitting in Millie's Café and my father saying, "He'll be trouble, you wait and see." Neely had been here all of two days then. His feelings had never changed. Even the mention of Neely had always brought a harshness into my father's blue gaze.

"Head caved on the left side from the fall," Sullivan said. His lean face brightened into a smirk. "I'm sure even Dr. Thomas'll be able to figure this one out." Sullivan was one of those who found it hard it believe that a black man could be a competent doctor.

"You think you and your crew will ever give him a break, Mike?" It came out harsh, the way I intended.

"You think you two could hold off the bullshit till we figure out what happened here?" my father said.

The children had been chastised.

I walked over to the gurney and pulled back the sheet. In the beam of my flashlight the left side of his head was a stew of blood and bone and brain. His carefully kept dark beard gleamed with soaked red highlights. Neely had been a commercial artist working from the A-frame he rented. But his real work had been in posing as a serious painter. He lectured at the local library frequently, spending most of his time talking about Van

Gogh and hinting that his own work, which even I could see wasn't very good, might someday compared to the man he called "his mentor." If he hadn't been a swaggerer and a pretty boy none of the married women he'd slept with would have paid any attention to him.

Sullivan came over and stood next to me. "I piss you off?"

"Yeah."

"I'm sorry I shot my mouth off."

"Doctor Thomas is a good man. I'm sick of you and everybody else in this town cutting him down."

"I'll watch it." He nodded to the body. "You can see bone sticking out of that arm."

"Yeah."

"Your dad found three of his imported beer bottles near the cliff. He must have been drunk on his ass. He drank all the time anyway. I saw him half in the bag plenty of times in the afternoon. I was surprised he could service so many women when he was like that." Neely had indeed had a problem with alcohol. Two DUIs and a pair of drunk and disorderlies.

Sullivan smiled. "I have a few too many and my little man goes right to sleep."

My father stood beside us now. "Doctor Thomas just pulled up, Sullivan. You heard what Cam here said."

"I hear you, Sheriff. I already apologized to Cam."

"You want to get to work, Cam? I'm assuming this is an accident but I won't settle on that until you tell me that that's what it is."

In the Academy I learned all about such modern crime scene techniques and tools as blood spatter and flight interpretation, Electro-Static Dustprint Lifter, Super glue fuming, portable lasers, and alternate light sources. The problem our little shop has is that these are way too expensive for our budget. On a homicide we have to get the state boys and girls involved.

One other thing I learned in the Academy is that most detectives approach crime scenes pretty much in their own way. They develop their own approach over the years. The two rules are to gather evidences scrupulously and to document everything to help the county attorney make the case when the time comes.

Josh Cummings, our night deputy, came here after helping the Highway Patrol with a two-car accident on the asphalt strip north of the town limits. Teenagers drag racing. Bad pile up, nobody killed. I tried to sound as angry about it as Josh did but since I'd done a lot of drag racing in my teenage years I suspect my words sounded hollow.

We stayed an hour inside the A-frame. At one point Josh came out grinning. He held a super-size box of super-size condoms. "No wonder the ladies liked him." That was the highlight of our search. No evidence of any foul play. Three dozen or more bad paintings laid against the wall of Neely's large office. No sign of any of the advertisements or brochures he produced. He apparently wanted to keep them secret even from himself.

When we got back outside my father was working the backyard with a flashlight big as a trapped sun. He had his pipe going, too. The cancer scare had had to do with throat cancer. My mother and I had badgered him into quitting for a few months but he started smoking down at the shop and gradually easing back into it at home. My mother told me that she lights a special votive candle once a week for him. But she'd quit arguing with him about it. My father reasoned, quite unreasonably, that all the bike riding he did kept him healthy. A bright, ordinarily realistic man kidding himself into an early grave.

Josh and I used our smaller flashlights to join in the search. The brown autumn grass gleamed with frost. I walked toward the pine trees that formed a windbreak on the far side of the A-frame, the scent of them sweet on the cold night. A narrow trail ran down the center of them. Long before the A-frame had been built up here kids my age had ridden their bikes up here much against their parents' will. The cliff, of course, was dangerous to play near. And in fact in the time of both my grandfather and father there had been three deaths of children who'd fallen from it, smashed on the road below. I walked right on the edge of it many times, one time, on a dare, blindfolded.

When the light found something red flashing in the grass I stopped and bent down to see what it was. A large reflector used on the rear fender of a bicycle. With a jagged crack down the middle.

"You find something?" Josh said as he walked toward me.

"Nah," I said, slipping the reflector into my pocket. "I dropped my keys and was just picking them up. You find anything?"

"Just a few beer cans. He sure liked his booze."

We drifted back to the A-frame where my father stood talking to Dr. Thomas. The doctor is a quiet, slender man who at forty-five is starting to lose his hair. His clothes of choice run to button-down long-sleeved shirts, dark neckties and dark slacks. He carries both a beeper and a Blackberry. In addition to being the county ME he also oversees our little clinic which he's improved considerably with meager funds the county has been able to give him. Our boys are on the same soccer team.

"Evening, Stephen."

"Evening, Cam. I was just telling your father that I should have something for him around breakfast time."

"That'll make for a long night. What's the rush?"

My father put his hand on Stephen's shoulder and said, "Cam doesn't understand how us old-timers like to get things done right away."

I smiled at Stephen. "Dad's sixty-three, in case you didn't know."

"Oh, that's all right. My kids think I'm an old-timer, too. I'm used to it. And I don't mind pulling an all-nighter. Have to earn my keep." He nodded to the A-frame. "Well, he didn't die the way I thought he would."

"Oh?" my father said.

"He's been a patient of mine for the last year. The alcohol was starting to do serious damage to his liver. I suggested him trying AA or even going to a rehab center somewhere. He wouldn't hear of it." He zipped up his blue windbreaker and said, "I'd better get going. 'Night everybody."

We said goodnight and watched him walk to his gray Saab.

"Good man," my father said. Then: "I guess that's about it for tonight. Thanks, Cam. Sorry I had to drag you out of bed." He pointed to Josh. "You may as well start making your rounds for the night."

"Right," Josh said. "See you two later."

As we were walking back to our cars, my father said, "You all right?"

"Tired I guess."

"You never could kid me, Cam. You seem tense. Everything all right at home?"

"Why wouldn't everything be all right at home?"

He stopped and looked at me. Studied me, actually. "You're wound pretty tight, Cam. I just asked a question. A harmless one. And you climbed on my ass. Now I'm asking you, is everything all right at home?"

He was wrong. I'd kidded him all my life and gotten away

with it. I kidded him now. "You're right, Dad. We just had a little argument tonight about that outboard motor I want to buy. You know how Amy is about staying on a budget." There'd been no argument of course. But in the chill and shadow and weariness of the moment it sounded true.

"I knew it," my father said. "I knew something was wrong. And I'm the same way Amy is about budgets. About staying on them. You've always been like your mother. Budgets are just something you write down and then throw away. I'd give that new outboard some more thought before you buy it. The one you've got now is fine."

"Good idea, Dad."

Then we said good night and got into our cars.

In the morning I drove over to the county seat. I had to testify in a trial in which a drunken driver I'd arrested had caused considerable damage to a house he'd rammed his car into. When I got back to the shop just before lunch time I stopped where my father's bike was padlocked to a steel pole. He rode the ten-speed back and forth to work. I saw what I was afraid I would find.

Millie's was crowded. Tuesday lunches are meat loaf and mashed potatoes. They're as good as the Wednesday spaghetti lunches are bad. There should be a federal investigation into what Millie can do to spaghetti.

My father was in the last booth with his newspaper. It was town etiquette that you did not bother the high sheriff when he was reading his newspaper. Sons were the exception to this rule.

"How'd it go in court?"

"No problem. Open and shut."

He yawned. "Late nights remind me that my retirement's coming up in another year or so."

"I'll believe it when I see it."

"Oh, you'll be seeing it all right. Even if I didn't want to turn in my badge, your mother would force me to. She watches those damned travel channels on cable all the time. She thinks we should spend the rest of our lives being tourists."

"Here you are, Cam."

Millie had gotten her hair tinted red again. The color clashed with her pink waitress uniform. Her dentures gleamed in one of her soft smiles. "Now tomorrow, young man, I want you tell me how good my spaghetti is."

I'd been coming in here since I was fourteen. I would always be "young man". "As long as I don't have to swear it on a Bible."

"I think you should arrest this boy of yours, Sheriff."

We laughed as we always laughed. It was a ritual, the dialogue, the smiles, the laughs.

I cleaned half my plate before I said anything. "I saw the autopsy on your desk."

"Accidental death just the way we figured."

"Drunk and walked too close to the edge."

"Forty-five foot drop. That'd kill anybody. Plus he landed on his head."

"Still."

He had his coffee cup halfway to his mouth when I said it. He looked at me straight and hard. And set his cup back down. "Still? Still what, Cam?"

"It's possible—just possible—that somebody gave him a little help falling off that cliff."

"You read the autopsy."

"Nothing wrong with the autopsy. But an autopsy doesn't give us any sense of whether he fell off or was pushed off."

The blue of the eyes were that special simmering color of my teens and twenties, the eyes that assessed me with anger and disappointment. "I'm halfway through finishing up my report. I'm listing it as an accidental death. Nobody who knew him would have any doubts about that." He made a show of smiling. "Except my son the detective."

I took it from my shirt pocket and laid it in the center of the formica-covered table.

"What's that?"

"Bike reflector."

"I can see that. But what's it supposed to tell me?" But the voice was tighter now and the gaze nervous.

Nothing special about the reflector. Round, red. One of those that ignites in the dark when light strikes it.

"There's one thing wrong with it. Notice the crack down the center."

"I've got eyes, Cam."

"Same as your bike reflector. Cracked in shipping. You took it because it was the last one they had."

He sat back in the booth. "All right. And this is amounting to what?"

"It's amounting to nothing, Dad. I found it near the pine

trees near the A-frame last night. Right about where the trail was. All I'm wondering is why you didn't tell me you were up there recently."

"I ride my bike all over this town. Up on Indian Cliff included. Not that it's any of your particular damn business. I lost that reflector several days ago—though I don't know why the hell I owe you an explanation about it."

"Look at the condition of it, Dad. That reflector hadn't been there very long. The adhesive on the back still works if it you press it against something hard enough. It rained yesterday morning and there was frost last night. The adhesive would have been ruined by either one of those if it had been there for more than a few hours."

He was out of the booth before I could say anything else. Out of the booth and out of Millie's front door.

Halloween came and went with the usual damage to a few gravestones and dirty words spray-painted on the high school. In a town this size it was easy to find the culprits and put them to work undoing their damage. Amy's migraines began to fade and Jenny insisted on wearing her Halloween Cinderella costume every night before bedtime. We had a light snow one night but it melted by noon. And the few downtown stores that had survived the outlet malls a few miles to the west started putting up Christmas decorations. Or Xmas decorations as a few of them insisted on.

I never mentioned the bicycle reflector again to my father. I'd even begun to wonder if he'd been telling the truth after all. Maybe the reflector had been in the grass for several days. The first few days after our talk at Millie's had been strained but one night he and my mother were sitting at our dinner table talking to a delighted Jenny. She much preferred them to Amy and me. They never gave her orders or scolded her. And they gave her a king's ransom in gifts.

After the meal we were father and son again. With icy rain coming down every other day we were busy with traffic accidents large and small. And it was because of one of the accidents that I found the photographs.

I was working late, alone in the office, working on the computer. Even with a Mac reporting on traffic accidents is tedious work. My father was bowling tonight and I told him file his work, too. I was grabbing his reports when I realized that I needed a requisition form for more supplies. The town council takes its work too seriously. We always joked that one day they'd make us requisition permission to take a piss. The requisition forms were in my father's middle drawer. There was a pile of them. I skimmed three off and was about to close the door when I saw the edge of a photograph sticking out from under the stack I'd dislodged.

Who can resist looking at a photograph? I tugged it free and held it up. A minute later I'd pulled four more photographs from under the requisition forms. I took them back to my desk and sat down and stared at them for a long time. They were the kind of thing a private detective takes for a client worried that his or her mate is cheating. They'd been taken with the digital camera my mother had bought my father for his last birthday.

I spent five minutes with them. Given that they showed David Neely and two different women from town entering one of those old-fashioned garden motels they didn't need to be pornographic to tell their story. In some ways they were worse than pornographic. The prurient mind, and I certainly have one, could paint any picture it wanted to.

The clock stood at nine. My father would still be bowling.

I had two beers while I sat in the café section of the bowling alley. I'd never taken to the game. I had too much cool kid arrogance left over from my youth to ever wear one of those shirts for one thing. And for another there was something suffocating about watching adults take it all so seriously, a certain desperation I guess. Amy always said that I was a snob and in many ways I supposed she was right.

My father came up a couple of times but I didn't mention the photographs. I wanted to be alone with him. The second time he stopped by I caught a look of concern in the blue eyes. He stared at me a bit too long but didn't say anything.

Outside in the parking lot, after all the interminable beery good nights among the two teams, my father started toward his car but I grabbed his arm. "I need to talk to you, Dad."

"Everything all right at home?"

"Fine."

He seemed confused. He had his pipe going. "Then it couldn't have waited till later?"

"I found the photographs, Dad. I was looking for a requisition form in your desk and I came across them."

"I don't know what the hell you're talking about."

"Sure you do."

He not only knew what I was talking about, he gaped nervously around to make sure that we were the only ones in this section of the parking lot.

"Maybe it's not what you think."

"Then again maybe it is."

He nodded to his car. "Get in. I don't want to talk out here."

He started the engine and turned on the heater. We sat next to each other but didn't talk for some time. His pipe smelled good. The wind was strong enough to rock the car. The lane shut off its lights. There was a prairie loneliness to the way it looked now, a pastel green icon alone on the fields.

"You followed him and then you killed him."

He angled himself so that he could face me. His yellow bowling shirt was gaudy inside his open brown suede jacket. "I'm going to tell you something and after I'm done you can decide what to do about it."

"I'm listening." Then: "I don't enjoy this, Dad. I'm pretty sure you killed him. Murdered him. This isn't easy for me."

"I know it's not, Cam. But at least listen to me."

I listened.

"When your grandfather was sheriff he had three murders in the first few years after he took office. One of them was a tavern fight and two of them were husbands killing wives for being unfaithful. The women had both slept with the same man, a car salesman named Blount. You grandfather didn't like that at all. Here were two women dead and two men in prison—one of them eventually got executed—and two entire families destroyed. And here was Blount still strutting around town looking for more women to land on. And he seemed to prefer married women, I suppose because there couldn't be any permanent attachments. Well, one day your grandfather saw this Blount coming on to the wife of your grandfather's best friend. The marriage was having some problems so he was afraid the woman might be vulnerable. He told me that after that day he wondered what life would be like here without Blount causing so much pain. But he didn't do anything about it until a woman who worked at the courthouse got into a shouting match with her husband over at Millie's. The story was that Blount had been sniffing around the lady and the husband was jealous. A couple of days later Blount drowned. It was all accidental of course."

"Grandfather killed him."

"Then another tomcat showed up a few years down the line. He was even worse than Blount. He was a rock musician. Nobody famous, mostly played little jobs up and down the lake here. But he flaunted it. He wanted people to know he was a lady killer. Your grandfather watched him ruin the lives of three different families and then he just couldn't put up with it anymore. This Boehner kid electrocuted himself with his guitar equipment one night."

"Grandfather again."

"There was a woman once, too. Came back here when her Chicago sugar daddy dumped her because she'd had the gall to turn thirty-five. Cindy McBain was her name. Damned good looking woman. And she cut a wide swathe. Caused three divorces the first year she was here. Died in a tragic fire."

"And now you're carrying on the tradition. That was what Neely was all about."

"You have any idea how much pain that man caused the people in this town? You ever see the faces of the little kids when their folks are going through a divorce? And here was some drunken so-called artist not giving a damn about any of it. I was pretty damned patient. I even warned him. I was careful not to make it a threat—not anything he could sure the town for—but he got the message and all he did was laugh at me. Said I was just jealous. I would've been mad but I figured that was just par for the course with somebody like him."

"You committed first degree murder."

He looked straight at me. "Yes, I did. And I don't regret it."

"You've just confessed a capital crime to me, Dad."

"Who the hell do you think you're talking to, Cam? I was sheriff while you were still riding a tricycle. I know damned good and well that I just confessed to a capital crime. But I'm not going to turn myself in for it. I'm going to leave that up to you."

He angled back so that he faced the steering wheel. "Now I need my sleep, Cam. I'm not as young as you in case you hadn't noticed. I'll see you in the morning."

He put the car in gear and waited for me to get out. He didn't have to wait long.

"Hey, you didn't eat any of that macho man breakfast I fixed you."

Soy bacon. Eggbeaters and wheat toast with soy margarine. I guessed that was what passed for breakfast macho these days when I was trying to keep weight off and avoid a heart attack before fifty.

"It's good, Dad," Cindy said. She pointed her fork at her empty plate. "I ate every bite."

The smile and the blue blue family eyes made me reach across the table and take her small hand. "I'll do my best."

"Unfortunately, Cindy, you've got to get ready," Amy said. "The bus'll be here in less than ten minutes. Scoot now. I'll help you with your backpack."

Leaving me alone with a breakfast I had to force myself to eat.

Cindy always went out the front door. She ducked into the kitchen, gave me a tiny wet kiss on the cheek and then charged through the house, Amy right behind her.

I managed to eat one piece of bacon and half the toast by the time Amy reappeared.

"If I had time I'd find out what's bothering you, honey. But that's always a long, involved process so I'll have to wait until tonight. I counted you getting up three times in the middle of the night and you were sitting down here staring into space when I came down for breakfast. I worry about you. But you know that."

This kiss was on my mouth. And it lingered. But as I was kissing her I had a thought that made me hate myself. Neely had certainly gotten around with married women. . .Amy had her nights out. I'd always taken her word that she was out with her female friends, usually shopping at the outlet malls and then getting a pizza afterward.

I brought her to me. Kiss her tenderly, ashamed of what I'd been thinking. Then, like Cindy, she was gone.

All the way to the shop I prepared myself for an awkward morning. I wondered if I'd even be able to look at my father. He murdered a man. And basically he was daring me to turn him in.

This morning was his turn to put in a court appearance so he didn't appear in the front door until after eleven o'clock. I was at my desk on the phone enduring my monthly call from an auxillary deputy who had a library full of ideas on how to turn our sheriff's department into the same kind of brave and fearless crime fighting he saw on cop shows every night.

My father remained in the doorway watching me as I watched him. After I hung up, he said, "Mason wants us to start carrying grenades?"

"Ground to air missiles."

"Sounds good to me."

He came in and poured himself some coffee and went over and sat down at his desk. His in front of mine. He swiveled his chair around. "It wasn't easy to tell you what I did last night."

"It wasn't easy for me to hear it."

Long lean fingers drew his pipe from his suit jacket pocket. "You ever think Amy might step out on you?"

The terrible thought I'd had at the breakfast table came back to me. "That's a hell of a thing to ask."

"Think of what would happen to little Cindy if you and Amy split up. If she'd stepped out."

"Well, she hasn't stepped out and she won't step out. Any more than I'd ever step out on her. We're not programmed that way."

"That's what your grandfather used to think. And I used to think it, too. But there's always somebody who comes to this town—usually a man but sometimes a woman—and they destroy people. I'm not naïve. They don't force people to sleep with them. Unfortunately the people want it. Want excitement, want something strange and new. But if that person hadn't come to town, hadn't offered them the opportunity—"

"You murdered a man."

"I'd murder him again. He was going to cause at least two families to come apart. Good people by and large. Friends of mine. People who belong in a town like this where they don't have Neelys prowling around like some rabid animal."

"You murdered a man."

He stuck the pipe in his mouth. "Then turn me in, Cam. Pick up that phone and turn me in."

He swiveled back to his desk and went to work.

I enjoyed a hearty meal at the Quick-Pick's microwave. Nothing more refreshing than standing in a convenience store that smells of disinfectant and gulping down a hamburger of questionable origin. But I didn't want to face my father at Millie's.

The manilla folder was on my desk when I got back. I sat down at my desk and opened it up. Inside were copies of three divorce notices from the local weekly. I knew two of the families very well. I'd gone to high school with the man and woman from one divorce and with the woman from the second divorce. The third couple were younger than me.

My father came in just as I was closing folder. "They missed you at Millie's."

"And the point of this is?" I said, jabbing my finger at the folder.

"The point of it is that when you count up all the children involved the number comes to nine. One of the fathers is now a useless drunk. One of the women is living on food stamps and can't get much medical care for her kids. And one of the kids who was a very bright student has now turned into a monster who may get kicked out of ninth grade. And Neely was involved in all of it."

"And you murdered him."

"And I murdered him because this is my town and the people I care about and because I owe to them to help them through life as well as I can. And given all the things you did when you were younger—and given the way the town forgave you—I'd say you owe it to them, too. And another thing—" The blue eyes blazed; the voice was fury. "You're so damned smug about this. Like I said last night, you're lucky Amy's never been unfaithful. I half-wished I could have told you that she was one of Neely's conquests. She wasn't but I know damned well how you would have reacted. So don't be so quick about judging me. Now give me that folder back and get it over with."

I was so caught up in his rage that I wasn't quite sure what he meant.

He cleared it up by reaching over to my phone and picking up the receiver. "You know the number of the county attorney. Tell him what I told you and tell him that he knows where he can find me and tell him that I won't be any trouble at all."

He shoved the receiver at me and then went to his desk and sat down, facing the door.

I don't how long I sat there with it in my hand. Long enough for the dial tone to change into a beeping sound. I wasn't even aware of hanging it up or going to the back near the four empty cells. In the bathroom I washed my face and stared into the mirror. He'd murdered a man. And my grandfather had murdered even more. And now he wanted me to carry on the tradition if I started to see the same pattern start happening again.

He was gone when I came up front. I spent the afternoon

working on several things, enjoying the luxury of temporary amnesia. He came back later. The temperature had dropped to the low thirties so his gaunted cheeks were red and the green woolen scarf he wore looked almost festive.

He stood at my desk once again. "You need to turn me in, Cam. For your own sake. I had no right to drag you into this thing and now I don't have any right to ask you to act the way your grandfather and I did. Just give me a little advance notice before you make the call. I'll need to prepare your mother." Then came the real surprise. He leaned over and put his hand on my shoulder and said: "I love you, son. You've turned into a hell of a good man. A lot better man than I've ever been."

My father never played on my sympathies. He was straight-forward. Nobody had ever called him a coward and he wasn't being a coward now.

"I told your mother I would pick up a pot roast for her over at Shop-Rite. I should be home in half an hour if you want to talk to me." He nodded goodbye and left.

Given all that had happened I'd almost forgotten about picking up Amy at school.

Alveron High came into existence ten years ago when three different small high schools consolidated into one. Better for the budget and for attracting more qualified teachers and expanding the curriculum. Amy had been there six years. She'd spent Cindy's first year at home but given my salary she had to go back to teaching.

The building was two stories and red brick. The windows were on fire with the dying sun. I pulled up out front. Twisted brown leaves scraped across the grounds, collecting around the silver flagpole. The students were long gone. Teachers began drifting out in twos and threes talking and laughing. Not that I paid much attention. I was thinking about my father and the copies of the divorce proceedings he'd shown me. And what he'd said about me being so smug. I hadn't suffered from any of it but now as I thought about it I remembered some of the domestic disturbances I'd covered. The rage and the pain pain pain. There is no equivalent to a domestic, seeing people at their rawest. The children are the heartbreakers, crouched in the corner, sobbing and pleading with their parents or so stunned and afraid that they are frozen in the moment, scalded in their misery, lucky even to have a heartbeat. And the Neelys of the world—

some of them married, some not—are often at the center of it all.

And what my father had done was try to relieve some of his people of some of their pain. I saw that now even though I still could not forget that in protecting his town, and I had no doubt that he thought that that was exactly what he was doing, he'd had to take a life.

And then Amy was coming out of the front door. Sight of her comforted me. I wanted to be home, sitting with Amy and Cindy on the couch. Being goofy the way we got so much of the time. A good dinner finished and a lazy night of watching some good tv shows.

Then he came out right behind her. He put a hand on her shoulder to slow her down. He was laughing and she was smiling. I had no doubt who I was seeing. The new English teacher. The one even Amy's married friend had a crush on.

He was tall and tanned with dark curly hair. In his white shirt and blue V-neck sweater and chinos he had a young preppy look about him. He was very handsome.

Amy stopped and he came up to her and slipped a piece of paper from one of his books and handed it to her. It was the way she stood hugging her books and staring up at him. A familiar sight from our own high school days. Except instead of him it had been me.

Then she said something and started walking toward my car.

I thought of my father and how he said I'd been spared the pain that had ripped apart so many other families.

I was going to have to keep a very close eye on Mr. Bruce Peters. And not only for myself but for all the good true people of our little town.

YESTERDAY AND THE DAY BEFORE

The rain didn't exactly help Elly Ward's mood.

She sat at her desk in her office at Sullivan & Kostik Advertising wondering how she was ever going to face him tonight. Neither ten months of seeing a shrink nor eleven months of taking every kind of anti-depressant imaginable had helped him much. He still went to the cemetery two days a week, and he still cried out for her in the middle of the night.

She watched the October rain streak the window here on the thirty-sixth floor. She felt confined, just as she had when she was a little girl and the rain made her stay indoors. She wanted to be outdoors, and she wanted the sun to be shining, and the wind to carry the scent of lilacs and the soft silent arc of butterflies.

A knock. She knew who it would be. She'd been dreading it all day.

"Yes?"

The door opened. Tom stuck his head in. "Hi."

"Hi."

"Busy?"

"Thinking, I guess."

"That's why you win all the awards. You think about what you write. Unlike some other people I could name."

Tom was an account executive. She'd won two Clios in the past three years and was the darling of the agency. Both the accounts she'd won the awards for were Tom's accounts.

"Just wondered if we could talk."

"Sure," she said. She just wanted to get it over with.

He came in, sat down in the leather chair facing her desk. He was handsome in a middle-aged sort of way. He'd been a professor before turning to advertising and college still clung to him. He wasn't quite as hard or cynical as the others, and seemed to have some occasional difficulty groveling before clients. Pride, she supposed, was the word she was looking for. Unlike most advertising people, Tom still had a little pride left.

He glanced only once at the framed photograph of the twelve-year-old girl, Danielle, on her desk, then looked quickly away.

"Is it all right to say," he said, "that I had a good time last night?"

She looked out the window, at the darkening sky, the slanting silver rain streaking the glass. Then, rumbling distant thunder. Easy to think it was actually gunfire of a distant war somewhere, people being killed, children. Especially children.

"I won't let it happen again," she said quietly.

"You deserve a life, too," Tom said earnestly. That was another thing she liked about him. He wasn't afraid of being earnest, even slightly foolish. Some of the men found Tom vaguely embarrassing. But she liked his foolishness. It was usually well-placed.

She turned and looked at him. "You seem to forget, Tom, I'm married. And I'm sorry but I feel like shit about last night. I've never committed adultery in my life, and I don't intend to ever again."

"God," he said, and smiled sadly. "We're really working at cross-purposes here, aren't we?"

"Oh?"

"Yeah," he said, the sad smile still on him. "I came in here to tell you that I've fallen in love with you."

~ ~ ~ ~ ~

David Ward told his secretary at the law office that he was leaving early because of a headache. She nodded knowingly, and not without sympathy. Ever since his daughter's death three-and-a-half years ago, Daniel had pretty much coasted through his job here at the law firm. He'd once been the firm's most aggressive lawyer. Now he just put his time in, and sometimes—as today—he didn't do even that. But it was an old-line firm—quiet as a church in its offices, its partners Presbyterian, Princeton, Republican—its one charitable inclination being that it took care of its own.

She smiled. "Going to get your costume ready?"

"Costume?" he said, throwing his topcoat over his arm.

"You know. For Halloween."

"Oh, yes. Halloween."

That was another thing since the accident. Half the time David was in some other world. Just didn't hear what you said.

The secretary looked out the window. "Well, at least the rain has stopped. The kids'll be out tonight, you know, trick or treating."

He nodded—she still wasn't sure he'd actually heard and understood what she'd just said—and then he was gone.

~ ~ ~ ~ ~

"It isn't a life, and you know it," Tom said, still being earnest. "It's just existing."

They were still in her office. The rain had stopped. The late afternoon rush traffic was just beginning. Up this high, Elly could see most of the freeways from here. Another twenty minutes, it would be bumper-to-bumper.

"Well, if you think it's bad for me," she said quietly, "think of what it's like for him. He's lost thirty pounds, he can't sleep, he has no interest in sex or work—he spends most of his time up in her room. He even sleeps in her bed half the time. And I can hear him in there talking to her." She paused. "And he scares me, the way he talks about the neighbourhood kids sometimes. What he'd like to do with them."

"The little bastards. It's too bad you can't do anything about them."

"Unfortunately, there's no law against cruelty." Tears glistened in her grey eyes. "The names they called her—the way they used to follow her around all the time—they'd write things on the front of her locker at school—and they'd stand out in front of our house and call her names till David would come out and chase them away. There wasn't anything she could do about her condition, how obese she was. It was her endocrine glands, they put too much of a hormone into her system. She just got bigger and bigger." She touched a fingertip to a lone tear silver on her cheek. "I really am afraid of what he might do to them. It was their fault, it really was—they were just so cruel, I'd never seen anything like it—it's just that I know there's nothing we can do." Then, "Maybe I'm being selfish."

"Selfish? How?"

"He's given himself to her. He won't let go of her. He's willing to lay down his whole life for her. Maybe I'm too selfish. Maybe I should be that way, too—instead of wanting to go on with my life." Tears choked her voice suddenly. "She was twelve years old."

Tom shook his head. "God, she was just twelve years old."

"Twelve," she repeated gently. How many times she'd whispered that lone word to herself. Twelve. All history, all suffering was in that word. Twelve. She'd come home and found her daughter dead. She'd overdosed on Tom's tranquillizers. Twelve years old.

"I've never heard of anybody that young doing—" He stopped himself before he said the actual words. The actual words would just make things worse, the way actual words often did.

"I hadn't, either," Elly said. "I hadn't, either. But the grief counselor we saw said that it happens more than most people realize. At that age, I mean."

After a time, when she was gone from him again staring out the window, he said, "I love you."

She looked at him, then, and said, "Oh, God, Tom. It's your divorce, can't you see that? Your wife left you and you need somebody and we see each other every day and so it's just very convenient. That's what last night was—not love, not love at all. We were just trying to comfort each other."

"You need somebody, Elly. You really do."

"I have somebody, Tom. My husband."

"But he isn't—" More actual words he didn't want to say. More actual words that would just hurt.

"I know what he isn't, Tom. But that doesn't mean that he's not still my husband and that doesn't mean I don't still love him. I do. And I'm going to tell him about what happened last night."

"Oh, God," Tom said. "I'm not sure I'd do that. I'm not sure that's a good idea at all."

She looked right at him and said, "It may not be a good idea, Tom. But I owe him the truth."

~ ~ ~ ~ ~

The smell of brownies reminded David of his childhood. Of his mom and winter days when he'd stay in and read his science fiction novels. She'd always bring two brownies and a glass of milk up the stairs to his room. The aroma was always rich, sweet, warm.

As it was now.

He'd spent the last hour making the brownies. He'd used a box of Pillsbury Brownie Mix. Even a non-cook like him had no trouble. These were special brownies. His special brownies. He'd added one extra ingredient.

As they cooled, he went into the living room. He wanted to make sure that the porch light worked fine. So all the neighbourhood kids would know he was home and ready to give them their Halloween treats. A beacon, that's what the porch light was. Summoning the neighbourhood kids. Summoning.

When the brownies were cool, he cut them neatly into squares and then put them on a large white serving tray. He covered the tray with aluminum foil. He wanted to keep the brownies nice and warm for the kids, the neighbourhood kids. He carried the tray into the living room and set it on a TV tray which he stood to the left of the front door.

Then he turned on a table lamp and waited. He would have preferred the darkness. But he wanted to make sure that they knew he was home.

He wanted to give them his very special brownies.

~ ~ ~ ~ ~

Elly got home an hour later.

She was late because every crosswalk she came to on her way home was filled with Dracula and Frankenstein and the glowing white mask of Jason from *Friday the 13th*. The littlest kids were the cutest, tiny bodies lost in vast costumes, booty bags almost as big.

Halloween. With a stab, she remembered they could never find costumes large enough for Danielle. Elly always made her costumes by hand. The neighbourhood kids were especially mean to Danielle on Halloween nights. Finally, Danielle just stayed in, hiding in her room as she did so often.

As she reached her own block and saw the kids who had tormented her daughter—she could recognize them even beneath their costumes—she felt some of the rage that David felt constantly. Here they were out and enjoying themselves. They'd forgotten Danielle utterly. Life was so unfair sometimes. She thought again of the idea she'd been discussing with David recently. Maybe they needed to move. New city. New lives.

Two Freddy Krugers were washed by her headlights as she pulled into the drive. They didn't move, just stood there boldly, glaring at her. She knew who they were, Ronnie Haskins and Bob Nolan, two of Danielle's most relentless tormentors. She had an impulse to floor the accelerator. She could almost feel them crumpling beneath her car. How satisfying that would feel. How terrible they had been to Danielle.

Finally, they moved on the walk leading to her front door. They were trick or treating.

She pulled up the drive and into the two-stall garage.

The kitchen smelled of brownies. Freshly baked. For a moment, she let the scent carry her back to her Minnesota childhood. Her mother had been a pretty bad cook—there were a lot of good-natured family jokes about that fact—but her older sister Doris was wonderful in the kitchen. These brownies smelled like something Doris would have made.

"David? David, are you here?" But of course he was here. His car was in the garage. But he didn't answer. For some reason, this made Elly uneasy. Even when he was at his most depressed, he answered her calls.

Elly walked over to the counter. It was a mess. Mixing bowl, Pillsbury brownie box on its side, half full quart of milk turning warm. And a small paperback book. She wondered what it was. The instructions for brownies would be right on the box.

She picked up the paperback, which had been flattened to pages 61-62. A sentence was underlined.

Swallowing or smelling a toxic dose of cyanide as a gas or salt sprinkles can cause immediate unconsciousness, convulsions, and death within one to fifteen minutes or longer.

Then she saw the small rumpled paper sack pushed far back on the counter. She looked inside and found the cyanide. It had been opened, used.

She knew what he'd done, then.

My God.

She ran into the living room. Empty. She ran up the stairs. Their bedroom, empty. The TV room, empty.

Danielle's room—that's where she found him.

He was lying on his back on her bed, hands folded across his sternum the way he'd be in his coffin, eyes staring straight up at the ceiling. The eyes were glassy, tear-stained. The room was a zoo of cuddly stuffed animals, red birds and blue monkeys and canary yellow dinosaurs. Danielle's best friends. How she'd loved them. The room was in darkness but for the miserly light of the quarter moon.

Before she could speak, he said, "I couldn't do it." He didn't look at her.

She came over and sat softly down next to him on the single bed with the festive pink spread. She lay down next to him, both of them fully dressed, not even their shoes off, lay on the bed together, husband and wife, best friends, brother and sister, so many, many different kinds of relationships in a good marriage.

"I've been planning this for months," he said, "and I couldn't do it. I'm too much of a coward."

He began sobbing, then, and she held him the way she'd held sobbing Danielle so many, many nights when simple existence became so overwhelming that it crushed them, and made them hate not their tormentors but themselves. Danielle had loathed herself. Nobody considered her more of a freak than she herself had.

"I owe it to her," he said, choking on his tears. "I owe it to her. They've got it coming—and I still can't do it. Even as much as I love her I can't do it."

Danielle used to cry herself asleep. Literally exhaust herself. David did this tonight. And it didn't take long, either. One moment, he was talking; the next, next to her, he was snoring softly.

The doorbell rang downstairs.

She didn't want to wake him.

He needed sleep. Then maybe he'd forget this terrible day.

~ ~ ~ ~ ~

She hurried downstairs before the doorbell rang again.

She was just about to reach for the doorknob when she saw the serving plate with the aluminum foil over it. The brownies. She touched the foil. Warm. Still very warm.

She opened the door and there in the grainy porch light of the damp October dusk stood the two Freddy Krugers. Ronnie Haskins and Bob Nolan. The neighbourhood kids.

The words came as from a far place, as from a puppeteer that had turned her into his handmaiden.

Instead of sending them away empty-handed, she put on the big fake smile that all adults use on Halloween night and said, "Treat 'r treat, I'll bet."

Both boys were technically a little old for trick 'r treating.

But she wasn't about to mention that now.

She filled their hands with brownies and said, "Right from the oven. Be sure and eat them while they're still warm."

They mumbled thank-yous and hurried down off the porch. Before they reached the next house, they'd flipped their masks up and were cramming the rich, chocolatey brownies into their mouths.

~ ~ ~ ~ ~

She went up and lay next to her sleeping husband. There would be no sleep for her.

She listened to the laughter and the sheer joyful shouting of the littlest ones as they went door to door. Nothing was more innocent than the sound of a child laughing.

She thought of Danielle and started to cry.

~ ~ ~ ~ ~

The ambulance—shrill siren, raucous red lights—raced into the neighbourhood twenty-three minutes later.

Ronnie Haskins was the first to die. He did not even make it to the hospital. At the hospital, Bob Nolan got the full treatment. They pumped his stomach and gave him an intravenous injection of sodium nitrite and sodium thiosulfate. But it did no good. He died nineteen minutes after reaching the hospital.

~ ~ ~ ~ ~

Elly did not answer any of the ringings of the bell or knockings on the door. Two were enough. Two settled the score.

But later there was a knock that sounded different—not a trick or treat knock—and she slipped away from her sleeping husband and went to the window and looked down.

A police car stood at the curb.

She thought of waking David, of telling him what she'd done. But, no, he deserved his sleep.

There would be plenty of time to tell him when he had to call the family lawyer and when the press came around to covet her with its cameras and put her—weepy and crazed-looking—on the six-o'clock news.

MOTHER DARKNESS

The man surprised her. He was black.

Alison had been watching the small filthy house for six mornings now and this was the first time she'd seen him. She hadn't been able to catch him at seven-thirty or even six-thirty. She'd had to try six o'clock. She brought her camera up and began snapping.

She took four pictures of him just to be sure.

Then she put the car in gear and went to get breakfast.

~ ~ ~ ~ ~

An hour-and-a-half later, in the restaurant where social workers often met, Peter said, "Oh, he's balling her all right."

"God," Alison Cage said. "Can't we talk about something else? Please."

"I know it upsets you. It upsets me. That's why I'm telling you about it."

"Can't you tell somebody else?"

"I've tried and nobody'll listen. Here's a forty-three year old man and he's screwing his seven-year-old daughter and nobody'll listen. Jesus."

Peter Forbes loved dramatic moments and incest was about as dramatic as you could get. Peter was a hold-over hippie. He wore defiantly wrinkled khaki shirts and defiantly torn Lee Jeans. He wore his brown hair in a ponytail. In his cubicle back at social services was a faded poster of Robert Kennedy. He still smoked a lot of dope. After six glasses of cheap wine at an office party, he'd once told Alison that he thought she was beautiful. He was forty-one years old and something of a joke and Alison both liked and disliked him.

"Talk to Coughlin," Alison said.

"I've talked to Coughlin."

"Then talk to Friedman."

"I've talked to Friedman, too."

"And what did they say?"

Peter sneered. "He reminded me about the Skeritt case."

"Oh."

"Said I got everybody in the department all bent out of shape about Richard Skeritt and then I couldn't prove anything about him and his little adopted son."

"Maybe Skeritt wasn't molesting him."

"Yeah. Right."

Alison sighed and looked out the winter window. A veil of steam covered most of the glass. Beyond it she could see the parking lot filled with men and women scraping their windows and giving each other pushes. A minor ice storm was in progress. It was seven thirty-five and people were hurrying to work. Everybody looked bundled up, like children trundling to school.

Inside the restaurant the air smelled of cooking grease and cigarettes. Cold wind gusted through the front door when somebody opened it, and people stamped snow from their feet as soon as they reached the tile floor. Because this was several blocks north of the black area, the juke box ran to Hank Williams, Jr. and The Judds. Alison despised country western music.

"So how's it going with you?" Peter said, daubs of egg yolk on his graying bandito mustache.

"Oh. You know." Blonde Alison shrugged. "Still trying to find a better apartment for less money. Still trying to lose five pounds. Still trying to convince myself that there's really a God."

"Sounds like you need a Valium."

The remark was so—Peter. Alison smiled. "You think Valium would do it, huh?"

"It picks me up when I get down where you are."

"When you get to be thirty-six and you're alone the way I am, Peter, I think you need more than Valium."

"I'm alone."

"But you're alone in your way. I'm alone in my way."

"What's the difference?"

Suddenly she was tired of him and tired of herself, too. "Oh, I don't know. No difference, I suppose. I was being silly I guess."

"You look tired."

"Haven't been sleeping well."

"That doctor from the medical examiner's office been keeping you out late?"

"Doctor?"

"Oh, come on," Peter said. Sometimes he got possessive in a strange way. Testy. "I know you've been seeing him."

"Doctor Connery, you mean?"

Peter smiled, the egg yolk still on his mustache. "The one with the blue blue eyes, yes."

"It was strictly business. He just wanted to find out about those infants."

"The ones who smothered last year?"

"Yes."

"What's the big deal? Crib death happens all the time."

"Yes, but it still needs to be studied."

Peter smiled his superior smile. "I suppose but—"

"Crib death means that the pathologist couldn't find anything. No reason that the infant should have stopped breathing—no malfunction or anything, I mean. They just die mysteriously. Doctors want to know why."

"So what did your new boyfriend have to say about these deaths? I mean, what's his theory?"

"I'm not going to let you sneak that in there," she said, laughing despite herself. "He's not my boyfriend."

"All right. Then why would he be interested in two deaths that happened a year ago?"

She shrugged and sipped the last of her coffee. "He's exchanging information with other medical data banks. Seeing if they can't find a trend in these deaths."

"Sounds like an excuse to me."

"An excuse for what?" Alison said.

"To take beautiful blondes out to dinner and have them fall under his sway." He bared yellow teeth a dentist could work on for hours. He made claws of his hands. "Dracula; Dracula. That's who Connery really is."

~ ~ ~ ~ ~

Alison got pregnant her junior year of college. She got an abortion of course but only after spending a month in the elegant home of her rich parents, "moping" as her father characterized that particular period of time. She did not go back to finish school. She went to California. This was in the late seventies just as discos were dying and AIDs was rising. She spent two celibate years working as a secretary in a record company. James Taylor, who'd stopped in to see a friend of his, asked Alison to go have coffee. She was quite silly during their half hour together, juvenile and giggly, and even years later her face would burn when she thought of how foolish she'd been that day. When she returned home, she lived with her parents, a fact that seemed to embarrass all her high school friends. They were busy and noisy with growing families of their own and here was beautiful quiet Alison inexplicably alone and, worse, celebrating her thirty-first birthday while still living at home.

There was so much sorrow in the world and she could tell no one about it. That's why so many handsome and eligible men floated in and out of her life. Because they didn't *understand*. They weren't worth knowing, let alone giving herself to in any respect.

She worked for a year-and-a-half in an art gallery. It was what passed for sophisticated in a Midwestern city of this size. Very rich but dull people crowded it constantly, and men both with and without wedding rings pressed her for an hour or two alone.

She would never have known about the income maintenance job if she hadn't been watching a local talk show one day. Here sat two earnest women about her own age, one white, one black, talking about how they acted as liaisons between poor people and the Social Services agency. Alison knew immediately that she would like a job like this. She'd spent her whole life so spoiled and pampered and useless. And the art gallery—minor traveling art shows and local ad agency artists puffing themselves up as artistes—was simply an extension of this life.

These women, Alison could tell, knew well the sorrow of the world and the sorrow in her heart.

She went down the next morning to the Social Services agency and applied. The black woman who took her application weighed at least three-hundred-and-fifty pounds which she'd packed into lime green stretch pants and a flowered polyester blouse with white sweat rings under the arms. She smoked Kool filters at a rate Alison hated to see. Hadn't this woman heard of lung cancer?

Four people interviewed Alison that day. The last was a prim but handsome white man in a shabby three-piece suit who had on the wall behind him a photo of himself and his wife and a small child who was in some obvious but undefined way retarded. Alison recognized two things about this man immediately: that here was a man who knew the same sorrow as she; and that here was a man painfully smitten with her already. It took him five-and-a-half months but the man eventually found her a job at the agency.

Not until her third week did she realize that maintenance workers were the lowest of the low in social work, looked down upon by bosses and clients alike. What you did was this: you went out to people—usually women—who received various kinds of assistance from various government agencies and you attempted to prove that they were liars and cheats and scoundrels. The more benefits you could deny the people who made up your case load, the more your bosses liked you. The people in the state house and the people in Washington, D.C. wanted you to allow your people as little as possible. That was the one and only way to keep tax-payers happy. Of course, your clients had a different version of all this. They needed help. And if you wouldn't give them help, or you tried to take away help you were already giving them, they became vocal. Income maintenance workers were frequently threatened and sometimes punched, stabbed, and shot, men and women alike. The curious thing was that not many of them quit. The pay was slightly better than you got in a factory and the job didn't require a college degree and you could pretty much set your own hours if you wanted to. So, even given the occasional violence, it was still a pretty good job.

Alison had been an income maintenance worker for nearly three years now.

She sincerely wanted to help.

~ ~ ~ ~ ~

An hour after leaving Peter in the restaurant, Alison pulled her gray Honda Civic up to the small house where earlier this morning she'd snapped photos of the black man. Her father kept trying to buy her a nicer car but she argued that her clients would just resent her nicer car and that she wouldn't blame them.

The name of this particular client was Doreen Hayden. Alison had been trying to do a profile of her but Doreen hadn't exactly co-operated. This was Alison's second appointment with the woman. She hoped it went better than the first.

After getting out of her car, Alison stood for a time in the middle of the cold, slushy street. Snow sometimes had a way of making even rundown things look beautiful. But somehow it only made this block of tiny, aged houses look worse. Brown frozen dog feces covered the sidewalk. Smashed front windows bore masking tape. Rusted-out cars squatted on small front lawns like obscene animals. And factory soot touched everything, everything. It was nineteen days before Christmas—Alison had just heard this on the radio this morning—but this was a neighborhood where Christmas never came.

Doreen answered the door. Through the screen drifted the oppressive odors of breakfast and cigarettes and dirty diapers. In her stained white sweater and tight red skirt, Doreen still showed signs of the attractive woman she'd been a few years ago until bad food and lack of exercise had added thirty pounds to her fine-boned frame.

The infant in her arms was perhaps four months old. She had a sweet little pink face. Her pink blanket was filthy.

"I got all the kids here," Doreen said. "You all comin' in? Gettin' cold with this door open."

All the kids, Alison thought. My God, Doreen was actually going to try that scam.

Inside, the hot odors of food and feces were even more oppressive. Alison sat on the edge of a discount-store couch and looked around the room. Not much had changed since her last visit. The old Zenith color TV set—now blaring Bugs Bunny cartoons—still needed some kind of tube. The floor was still an obstacle course of newspapers and empty Pepsi bottles and dirty baby clothes. There was a crucifix on one wall with a piece of faded, drooping palm stuck behind it. Next to it a photo of Bruce Springsteen had been taped to the soiled wallpaper.

"These kids was off visitin' last time you was here," Doreen said.

She referred to the two small boys standing to the right of the armchair where she sat holding her infant.

"Off visiting where?" Alison said, keeping her voice calm.

"Grandmother's."

"I see."

"They was stayin' there for awhile but now they're back with me so I'm goin' to need more money from the agency. You know."

"Maybe the man you have staying here could help you out." There. She'd said it quickly. With no malice. A plain simple fact.

"Ain't no man livin' here."

"I took a picture of him this morning."

"No way."

Alison sighed. "You know you can't get full payments if you have an adult male staying with you, Doreen."

"He musta been the garbage man or somethin'. No adult male stayin' here. None at all."

Alison had her clipboard out. She noted on the proper lines of the form that a man was staying here. She said, "You borrowed those two boys."

"What?"

"These two boys here, Doreen. You borrowed them. They're not yours."

"No way."

Alison looked at one of the ragged little boys and said, "Is Doreen your mother?"

The little boy, nervous, glanced over at Doreen and then put his head down.

Alison didn't want to embarrass or frighten him anymore.

"If I put these two boys down on the claim form and they send out an investigator, it'll be a lot worse for you, Doreen. They'll try and get you for fraud."

"God damn you."

"I'll write them down here if you want me to. But if they get you for fraud—"

"Shit," Doreen said. She shook her head and then she looked at the boys. "You two run on home now, all right?"

"Can we take some cookies, Aunt Doreen?"

She grinned at Alison. "They don't let their Aunt Doreen forget no promises, I'll tell you that." She nodded to the kitchen. "You boys go get your cookies and then go out the back door, all right? Oh, but first say goodbye to Alison here."

Both boys, cute and dear to Alison, smiled at her and then grinned at each other and then ran with heavy feet across the faded linoleum to the kitchen.

"I need more money," Doreen said. "This little one's breakin' me."

"I'm afraid I got you all I could, Doreen."

"You gonna tell them about Ernie?"

"Ernie's the man staying here?"

"Yeah."

"No. Not since you told me the truth."

"He's the father."

"Of your little girl?"

"Yeah."

"You think he'll actually marry you?"

She laughed her cigarette laugh. "Yeah, in about fifty or sixty years."

The house began to become even smaller to Alison then. This sometimes happened when she was interviewing people. She felt entombed in the anger and despair of the place.

She stared at Doreen and Doreen's beautiful little girl.

"Could I hold her?" Alison said.

"You serious?"

"Yes."

"She maybe needs a change. She poops a lot."

"I don't mind."

Doreen shrugged. "Be my guest."

She got up and brought the infant across to Alison.

Alison perched carefully on the very edge of the couch and received the infant like some sort of divine gift. After a moment the smells of the little girl drifted away and Alison was left holding a very beautiful little child.

Doreen went back and sat in the chair and looked at Alison. "You got any kids?"

"No."

"Wish you did though, huh?"

"Yes."

"You married?"

"Not so far."

"Hell, bet you got guys fallin' all over themselves for you. You're beautiful."

But Alison rarely listened to flattery. Instead she was watching the infant's sweet white face. "Have you ever looked at her eyes, Doreen?"

" 'Course I looked at her eyes. She's my daughter, ain't she?"

"No. I mean looked really deeply."

" 'Course I have."

"She's so sad."

Doreen sighed. "She's got a reason to be sad. Wouldn't you be sad growin' up in a place like this?"

Alison leaned down to the little girl's face and kissed her tenderly on the forehead. They were like sisters, the little girl and Alison. They knew how sad the world was. They knew how sad their hearts were.

When the time came, when the opportunity appeared, Alison would do the same favor for this little girl she'd done for the two other little girls.

Not even the handsome Doctor Connery had suspected anything. He'd just assumed that the other two girls had died from crib death.

On another visit, someday soon, Alison would make sure that she was alone with the little girl for a few minutes. Then it would be done and the little girl would not have to grow up and know the even greater sadness that awaited her.

"You really ain't gonna tell them about Ernie livin' here?"

"I've got a picture of him that I can turn in any time as evidence. But I'll tell you what, Doreen; you start taking better care of your daughter—changing her diapers more often and feeding her the menu I gave you—and I'll keep Ernie our secret."

"Can't afford to have no more money taken from me," Doreen said.

"Then you take better care of your daughter," Alison said, holding the infant out for Doreen to take now. "Because she's very sad, Doreen. Very very sad."

Alison kissed the little girl on the forehead once more and then gave her up to her mother.

Soon, little one, Alison thought; soon you won't be so sad. I promise.

MOM AND DAD AT HOME

Dad always called the night before he came home.

Sometimes he was in Kansas City, sometimes he was in Peoria, sometimes he was in St. Louis. He was a salesman, sold barber supplies, and sometimes he traveled as much as two weeks of the month. Usually, though, it was eight, nine days. He had a big territory because he was the owner and sole employee of his company. He said hiring salespeople was a pain. You always had to stand over them and make sure they were doing what they should. Plus they always wanted big monthly draws and full health insurance and a new car and insurance for the car and even then they were always griping about something the boss did or didn't do. So Sam worked alone and made out just fine.

Young Sam Culver never got much sleep the night before his daddy got home. Much as eleven-year-old Sam loved his mom, it was his father he adored. His dad was cool. And this wasn't just his opinion. All the kids in the Riverside Apartments said so, said they wished their dads were cool like Sam's. He was full of jokes, Sam Culver was, and he listened to a lot of the same rock and roll songs they did and when a kid used a dirty word he'd just grin and say, "You give me a buck, I won't tell your mom you said that." And then he'd wink at the kid and all the other kids would laugh. Cool.

Young Sam wasn't pure of heart, of course; nobody is. Another reason he couldn't sleep was he'd lie awake wondering what kind of gift his dad was going to bring him this time. Dad was great for gifts. A real nice one for Mom, a real nice one for Sam. He never forgot. The last few times, Sam had gotten a guitar, a CD player, a football helmet and new football, and a gift certificate to Blockbuster good for any five CDs Sam wanted.

He was usually sleepy, Sam, the day Daddy came home. Not that this slowed him down or dulled his excitement.

As now.

He came into the kitchen and Mom said, "You finish your comic book already?" She was at the sink, washing off dishes and putting them in the dishwasher. She wore tight jeans and an electric-blue blouse. She was pretty but she looked a lot older than Dad. Sam had heard her arguing with her sister once, Aunt Kathy, and Aunt Kathy said, "Good-looking man on the road all the time like that, you're just not looking at the facts, Mary Jo. I told you when you married him, a good-looking man twelve years younger than you, it's going to be trouble. But you know how you are about not looking at the facts."

Sam had never understood what "facts" Aunt Kathy was talking about. He just knew that after Aunt Kathy left that time, Mom collapsed on her bed and cried and cried and cried. Sam lay down next to her for a while and then she all of a sudden took him in her arms, her warm face against his neck, and he could smell her tears. It was so funny that tears had a *smell*.

"Yeah. I only had one comic anyways. 'Spawn.' "

"There aren't any cartoons on?"

"I tried to watch 'em. But I've seen 'em all already."

She looked down at him and smiled. It was kind of funny, how Mom's face was so wrinkled up and old already and Dad still looked so young and handsome. Sometimes he felt sorry for his mom and he'd go right up and hug her and he wouldn't even know why.

"Can you smell what I'm baking?"

He sniffed the air. "Great! Apple pie."

"With the crust crisscrossed on the top the way Dad likes it."

She put a soapy hand on his shoulder. "He'll be along, hon. He said when he called last night that it'd probably be around supper time. And that's not for another hour yet. So why don't you go play with some of your friends."

The Riverside Apartments was four large native stone buildings set up on a prairie hill on the west edge of the city. Almost all the couples who lived there had kids and all the women worked as well as the men and when they'd cook burgers on the outside grills, they'd sit around and drink beer and swat mosquitoes and talk about how nice it'd be when they could finally afford a house of their own. Every once in a while there'd be a fight between two of the men who'd had too much to drink, or between a man and his woman, the man usually accusing her of flirting with somebody. Dad always knew how to handle these situations. Everybody always said that nobody could calm people down like Dad. He just had the knack was all.

Sam went and played ball around the back of building four. It was a warm June and the late afternoon was sweet with a soft breeze and the smell of newly mown grass and the deep shifting shadows of oncoming dusk.

He told the kids that his dad was coming home and so what they wanted to know was what he figured his gift would be this time and he could see how envious they were. Birthdays and Christmas was when they got gifts. They didn't have dads who traveled and brought gifts home once a month.

He played until the mothers started coming home in their dusty cars. Even the new cars were dusty. The workday was so long there wasn't time for washing the car except once a month or so on Saturday mornings down at the do-it-yourself wash where the grit never quite got washed away. The mothers all took turns coming to the back of building four and calling for their kids. There was something melancholy about it, the sound of those female voices, something timeless, too, mothers calling their children home in the gathering dusk as they had for thousands and thousands of years. The girls were usually more obedient, and headed home right away. The boys stalled for a while. Sam was always curious about the young-looking mothers. Some of them still looked like they were in high school, still sweet and fresh. Sometimes for a week or two at a time, Sam would get a crush on one of these mothers. He always saved them from fires or burglars or dope addicts. He'd lie in bed and have these heroic daydreams and his crotch would feel funny and he would love these women so much and so truly at these moments that it was painful. Literally painful. The other mothers looked old, like his mom, old and wrinkled and worn, though you could see that they actually weren't all that much older than the young mothers. Time isn't always nice to some women, his mom had said one day.

Around six, Sam's mom was there, calling him in. He ran over to her and said, "Dad home?" Her smile gave her away.

He ran all the way to the back of their building and then up two steep flights of carpeted steps. The carpet still smelled kind of spicy from a recent shampooing.

He hit the door running. Dad sat inside on the edge of the couch. He had a beer in the hand that was resting on the arm of the couch. He wore a white shirt with the sleeves rolled up to the elbows and a pair of blue slacks. His sun-blond hair was movie-star long, curled slightly at the collar line. He had a smile that brought back a lot of Sam's loneliness and occasional resentment. And he smiled that smile now.

Sam ran over to him like a little kid. Dad stood up and got Sam under the shoulders and then started swinging him around. Sam giggled. "How's that boy of mine?"

"G-g-g-o-o-o-d!" Sam said, giggling so hard that the word was broken up.

"Don't swing him too hard," Mom said from the doorway. "We're going to eat in just a little while."

It was one of those things that moms said that didn't make any sense when you thought about it. What did swinging him too hard have to do with eating dinner? But that's the way moms were.

Dad put Sam on the couch next to him. "Bring this young man a martini, miss, and put it on my tab."

Sam giggled some more.

"I'll martini you two all right," Mom said, smiling as she went to check on the roast in the oven. That was Dad's favorite meal. Pot roast with potatoes and onions and carrots fixed in right with the meat. You put a piece of fresh apple pie with that and you had Dad's favorite meal. Mom fixed it just about every time Dad came home.

Dad had kind of a semiformal interrogation that he wove into his dinner conversation. He said to Sam:

"You been good to your mom?"

"Uh-huh."

"You make your bed every morning?"

"Uh-huh."

"You take out the garbage?"

"Uh-huh."

"You help your mom carry the groceries upstairs?"

"Uh-huh."

"You say your Our Father and Hail Mary and Glory Be every night before you go to sleep?"

"Uh-huh."

Then Dad would look slyly at Mom and say, "Well, honey, sounds like this is a boy who deserves a present."

Dad reached below the table to his lap and brought up a small gift-wrapped box and handed it to Sam.

Sam set a couple of world records getting the box open. Then he said, in order, "Oh, man!" followed by, "Fantastic, Dad!" And finally: "Cool!" Three new computer game CDs, three exclamations. Sam knew how expensive these CDs were. Once the word got out—and there is no faster form of communication than that of kids in an apartment complex—everybody would be stopping by the apartment and driving Mom crazy.

Mom got perfume and hand lotion. She threw her arms around her husband and held him tight. Sam looked at her hands behind Dad's neck. They were starting to wrinkle, too.

While they were having the apple pie, Dad said, "How about

helping me clean out my car tomorrow. Then we'll go wash it and stop by the ole DQ." That's how Dad always referred to the Dairy Queen. The ole DQ.

"Sure," Sam said. Dad always let him buy the most expensive stuff on the menu.

After dinner, Sam went immediately to the living room, where he rigged everything up so he could play one of his new computer games on the television. He chose "Space Harlots." The girls on it were cool.

Mom and Dad were in the bedroom with the door closed. She always gave him a back rub so he could go to sleep faster. After his trips, Dad would usually sack out about seven o'clock and sleep till eight, nine the next morning. He was a hard worker.

About an hour later Mom came out, closing the bedroom door very, very quietly, meaning that Dad was asleep.

"It's so good to have him home," she said, and yet she sounded somehow sad about it, too. Maybe you got that way, sad all the time, Sam reasoned, when you got older. Maybe your sadness defenses didn't work as well as when you were young. Sam was rarely sad.

She sat on the edge of the couch and watched him play. He had everything set up on the coffee table. A couple of times he said "Shit!" when he made a mistake but Mom didn't say anything.

After a while, she said, "You know what'd be nice?"

"What?"

"You could go down and clean Dad's car out now."

"Now?"

"Umm-hmm. So that when he goes down in the morning and sees his car, all the junk'll be hauled out of it."

He looked longingly at the computer in front of him. "Well—"

"C'mon, while you've still got some light left. Just take a plastic bag from under the sink and throw everything in there and just throw the plastic bag in the Dumpster when you're done."

Five minutes later, he was down in the parking lot. In the dusk he could see fireflies. And hear Jenny Akins. Jenny was his one true love. She was twelve and had no idea that he even existed. But someday she would. Someday he'd save her from a burning building or an alien attack and then she'd know he existed all right.

Dad was a self-described "muncher." Which was weird, because he never gained any weight. All the time he was driving and selling barber supplies, he was eating Baby Ruths and Almond Joys and Lay's salsa potato chips and Hostess pies (he was partial to blueberry) and Snickers. And drinking Diet Pepsi. Dad was a Diet Pepsi fiend. Cleaning out Dad's car meant gathering up all the candy wrappers that cluttered up the front and back seats and the floors as well. Dad was kind of an in-car litterbug. He had one of those cheap little plastic waste dealies you hung off the radio knob, but that was always full. So Dad just pitched things where they landed. There were magazines, too, mostly *Time* and *Newsweek* and *U.S. News & World Report*. Dad was a Republican. He liked to read articles that made the Democrats look bad. He'd always say, "Just listen to this one, honey." And then he'd read it out loud to Mom.

Sam spent maybe ten, twelve minutes cleaning out the car. He stuffed everything into the small plastic bag and carried the bag to the Dumpster. He hated opening the Dumpster lid. It smelled like a grave inside and there were always flies buzzing around it and he always wanted to wash his hands right away because he felt dirty all of a sudden.

He was in a hurry to get back to "Space Harlots." He was almost to the stairs when he felt Dad's car keys in his pocket bumping against his leg. He'd forgotten: Mom had asked him to bring up Dad's sample case from the trunk of the car. Dad always forgot to bring it up.

Sam went over to the car and opened up the trunk. The car was still new enough to smell new but now there was a different, sour scent, too. For some reason, he thought of the Dumpster and how it smelled like a grave.

The case was a black leather attaché case. It sat next to the spare tire and the jack. The trunk was very neat and organized. He lifted the case up—it wasn't heavy at all—and then he saw the newspapers. He wondered why Dad would have newspapers in the trunk.

He took the newspapers out to look at them in the starry dusk light of the dying day. There were four of them and they were all front sections of newspapers from the towns where Dad traveled.

There were smudges on the newspaper, too. Dark stains that looked faintly red in the dusk light. He thought of the time Jimmy Naylor had taken his pocketknife and stabbed a hamster in its bloated belly and how the blood had looked smeared on the newspaper in the bottom of the hamster cage. Smeared. Like this.

He looked at the headlines:

(St. Louis)
BEAUTICIAN SLAIN—INTENSE POLICE SEARCH

(Peoria)

POLICE HUNT KILLER OF XXX-DANCER

(Kansas City)
SUBURBAN HOUSEWIFE "BUTCHERED"

(Des Moines)
SPINSTER FOUND WITH THROAT SLASHED

And on each front page appeared the dark but somehow red stain. Holding these, he felt the way he did when he opened up the Dumpster. Dirty. Wanting to wash his hands.

He tried not to think about what it could mean. He'd seen a show once where this young boy was the only one who knew his older brother was a serial killer.

Sam shrugged. Dad probably had some good reason for saving the papers. He'd have to ask him, if he remembered to do it. With school out and "Space Harlot" on the screen, Sam would be likely to forget.

He went upstairs. Mom had an extra slice of apple pie waiting for him. He thought of how he'd come home from school sometimes and find her sitting at the kitchen table with tears in her eyes. He wondered if this was because of what Aunt Kathy had said about handsome younger men, or maybe because Mom knew about the stuff in the trunk.

"This is when I like it," she said, mussing his hair as he shoveled the pie into his mouth. "When it's late in the day and everybody's relaxed and I've got both of my men home with me."

She looked so tired now, even when she was smiling. So tired and so sad and it made him wonder if she knew about the newspapers and the blood in the trunk. He was trying hard not to think about these things but it was difficult. Very difficult.

After he finished his pie, he carried his dishes to the sink and then walked over to where his mom still sat at the kitchen table. He slid his arms around her and held her tight. He could *feel* the loose flesh in her neck. She loved Dad so much. So much.

Sam played "Space Harlots" until the ten o'clock news came on. Then he went in and brushed his teeth and kissed Mom good night and went into his own small bedroom and crawled into bed. He started thinking about the car trunk again but stopped himself. It was a lot better thinking about Jenny Akins. He loved her even more than he loved some of the young moms he had crushes on. He yawned. He was sleepy.

He fell asleep almost right away, even before he had time to save Jenny Akins from drowning or from being eaten by the escaped black bear. He always slept better for some reason when Dad was home.

RENDER UNTO CAESAR

I never paid much attention to their arguments until the night he hit her.

The summer I was twenty-one I worked construction upstate. This was 1963. The money was good enough to float my final year-and-a-half at college. If I didn't blow it the way some of the other kids working construction did, that is, on too many nights at the tavern, and too many weekends trying to impress city girls.

The crew was three weeks in Cedar Rapids and so I looked for an inexpensive sleeping room. The one I found was in a neighborhood my middle-class parents wouldn't have approved of but I wasn't going to be here long enough for them to know exactly where I was living.

The house was a faded frail Victorian. Upstairs lived an old man named Murchison. He'd worked forty years on the Crandic as a brakeman and was retired now to sunny days out at Ellis park watching the softball games, and nights on the front porch with his quarts of cheap Canadian Ace beer and the high sweet smell of his Prince Albert pipe tobacco and his memories of WWII. Oh, yes, and his cat Caesar. You never saw Murch without that hefty gray cat of his, usually sleeping in his lap when Murch sat in his front porch rocking chair.

And Murch's fondness for cats didn't stop there. But I'll tell you about that later.

Downstairs lived the Brineys. Peter Briney was in his early twenties, handsome in a roughneck kind of way. He sold new Mercurys for a living. He came home in a different car nearly every night, just at dusk, just at the time you could smell the dinner his wife Kelly had set out for him.

According to Murch, who seemed to know everything about them, Kelly had just turned nineteen and had already suffered two miscarriages. She was pretty in a sweet, already tired way. She seemed to spend most of her time cleaning the apartment and taking out the garbage and walking up to Dlask's grocery, two blocks away. One day a plump young woman came over to visit but this led to an argument later that night. Peter Briney did not want his wife to have friends. He seemed to feel that if Kelly had concentrated on her pregnancy, she would not have miscarried.

Briney did not look happy about me staying in the back room on the second floor. The usual tenants were retired men like Murch. I had a tan and was in good shape and while I wasn't handsome girls didn't find me repulsive, either. Murch laughed one day and said that Briney had come up and said, "How long is that guy going to be staying here, anyway?" Murch, who felt sorry for Kelly and liked Briney not at all, lied and said I'd probably be here a couple of years.

A few nights later Murch and I were on the front porch. All we had upstairs were two window fans that churned the ninety-three degree air without cooling it at all. So, after walking up to Dlask's for a couple of quarts of Canadian Ace and two packs of Pall Malls, I sat down on the front porch and prepared myself to be dazzled by Murch's tales of WW II in the Pacific Theater. (And Murch knew lots of good ones, at least a few of which I strongly suspected were true.)

Between stories we watched the street. Around nine, dusk dying, mothers called their children in. There's something about the sound of working class mothers gathering their children—their voices weary, almost melancholy, at the end of another grinding day, the girls they used to be still alive somewhere in their voices, all that early hope and vitality vanishing like the faint echoes of tender music.

And there were the punks in their hot rods picking up the meaty young teenage girls who lived on the block. And the sad factory drunks weaving their way home late from the taverns to cold meals and broken-hearted children. And the furtive lonely single men getting off the huge glowing insect of the city bus, and going upstairs to sleeping rooms and hot plates and lonesome letters from girlfriends in far and distant cities.

And in the midst of all this came a brand new red Mercury convertible, one far too resplendent for the neighborhood. And it was pulling up to the curb and—

The radio was booming "Surf City" with Jan and Dean—and—

Before the car even stopped, Kelly jerked open her door and jumped out, nearly stumbling in the process.

Briney slammed on the brakes, killed the headlights and then bolted from the car.

Before he reached the curb, he was running.

"You whore!" he screamed.

He was too fast for her. He tackled her even before she reached the sidewalk.

Tackled her and turned her over. And started smashing his fists into her face, holding her down on the ground with his knees on her slender arms, and smashing and smashing and smashing her face—

By then I was off the porch. I was next to him in moments. Given that his victim was a woman, I wasted no time on fair play. I kicked him hard twice in the ribs and then I slammed two punches into the side of his head. She screamed and cried and tried rolling left to escape his punches, and then tried rolling right. I didn't seem to have fazed him. I slammed two more punches into the side of his head. I could feel these punches working. He pitched sideways, momentarily unconscious, off his wife.

He slumped over on the sidewalk next to Kelly. I got her up right away and held her and let her sob and twist and moan and jerk in my arms. All I could think of were those times when I'd seen my otherwise respectable accountant father beat up my mother, and how I'd cry and run between them terrified and try to stop him with my own small and useless fists. . .

Murch saw to Briney. "Sonofabitch's alive, anyways," he said looking up at me from the sidewalk. "More than he deserves."

By that time, a small crowd stood on the sidewalk, gawkers in equal parts thrilled and sickened by what they'd just seen Briney do to Kelly. . .

I got her upstairs to Murch's apartment and started taking care of her cuts and bruises. . .

~ ~ ~ ~ ~

I mentioned that Murch's affection for cats wasn't limited to Caesar. I also mentioned that Murch was retired, which meant that he had plenty of time for his chosen calling.

The first Saturday I had off, a week before the incident with Peter and Kelly Briney, I sat on the front porch reading a John D. Mac-Donald paperback and drinking a Pepsi and smoking Pall Malls. I was glad for a respite from the baking, bone-cracking work of summer road construction.

Around three that afternoon, I saw Murch coming down the sidewalk carrying a shoebox. He walked toward the porch, nodded hello, then walked to the backyard. I wondered if something was wrong. He was a talker, Murch was, and to see him so quiet bothered me.

I put down my Pepsi and put down my book and followed him, a seventy-one year old man with a stooped back and liver-spotted hands and white hair that almost glowed in the sunlight and that ineluctable dignity that comes to people who've spent a life at hard honorable work others consider menial.

He went into the age-worn garage and came out with a garden spade. The wide backyard was burned stubby grass and a line of rusted silver garbage cans. The picket fence sagged with age and the walk was all busted and jagged. To the right of white flapping sheets drying on the clothesline was a small plot of earth that looked like a garden.

He set the shoebox down on the ground and went to work with the shovel. He was finished in three or four minutes. A nice fresh hole had been dug in the dark rich earth.

He bent down and took the lid from the shoebox. From inside he lifted something with great and reverent care. At first I couldn't see what it was. I moved closer. Lying across his palms was the dead body of a small calico cat. The blood on the scruffy white fur indicated that death had been violent, probably by car.

He knelt down and lowered the cat into the freshly dug earth. He remained kneeling and then closed his eyes and made the sign of the cross.

And then he scooped the earth in his hands and filled in the grave.

I walked over to him just as he was standing up.

"You're some guy, Murch," I said.

He looked startled. "Where the hell did you come from?"

"I was watching." I nodded to the ground. "The cat, I mean."

"They been damn good friends to me—cats have—figure it's the least I can do for them."

I felt I'd intruded; embarrassed him. He picked up the spade and started over to the garage.

"Nobody gives a damn about cats," he said. "A lot of people even hate 'em. That's why I walk around every few days with my shoebox and if I see a dead one, I pick it up and bring it back here and bury it. They're nice little animals." He grinned. "Especially Caesar. He's the only good friend I've made since my wife died ten years ago."

Murch put the shovel in the garage. When he came back out, he said, "You in any kind of mood for a game of checkers?"

I grinned. "I hate to pick on old farts like you."

He grinned back. "We'll see who's the old fart here."

~ ~ ~ ~ ~

When I got home the night following the incident with Kelly and Briney, several people along the block stopped to ask me about the beating. They'd heard this and they'd heard that but since I lived in the house, they figured I could set them right. I couldn't, or at least I said I couldn't, because I didn't like the quiet glee in their eyes, and the subtle thrill in their voices.

Murch was on the porch. I went up and sat down and he put Caesar in my lap the way he usually did. I petted the big fellow till he purred so hard he sounded like a plane about to take off. Too bad most humans weren't as appreciative of kindness as good old Caesar.

When I spoke, I sort of whispered. I didn't want the Brineys to hear.

"You don't have to whisper, Todd," Murch said, sucking on his pipe. "They're both gone. Don't know where he is, and don't care. She left about three this afternoon. Carrying a suitcase."

"You really think she's leaving him?"

"Way he treats her, I hope so. Nobody should be treated like that, especially a nice young woman like her." He reached over and petted Caesar who was sleeping in my lap. Then he sat back and drew on his pipe again and said, "I told her to go. Told her what happens to women who let their men beat them. It keeps on getting worse and worse until—" He shook his head. "The missus and I knew a woman whose husband beat her to death one night. Right in front of her two little girls."

"Briney isn't going to like it, you telling her to leave him."

"To hell with Briney. I'm not afraid of him." He smiled. "I've got Caesar here to protect me."

Briney didn't get home till late. By that time we were up off the porch and in our respective beds. Around nine a cool rain had started falling. I was getting some good sleep when I heard him down there.

The way he yelled and the way he smashed things, I knew he was drunk. He'd obviously discovered that his compliant little wife had left him. Then there was an abrupt and anxious silence. And then there was his crying. He wasn't any better at it than I was, didn't really know how, and so his tears came out in violent bursts that resembled throwing up. But even though I was tempted to feel sorry for him, he soon enough made me hate him again. Between bursts of tears he'd start calling his wife names, terrible names that should never have been put to a woman like Kelly.

I wasn't sure of the time when he finally gave it all up and went to bed. Late, with just the sounds of the trains rushing through the night in the hills, and the hoot of a barn owl lost somewhere in leafy midnight trees.

~ ~ ~ ~ ~

The next couple days I worked overtime. The road project had fallen behind. In the early weeks of the job there'd been an easy camaraderie on the work site. But that was gone for good now. The supervisors no longer took the time to joke, and looked you over skeptically every time you walked back to the wagon for a drink of water.

Kelly came back at dusk on Friday night. She stepped out of a brand new blue Mercury sedan, Pete Briney at the wheel. She carried a lone suitcase. When she reached the porch steps and saw Murch and me, she looked away and walked quickly toward the door. Briney was right behind her. Obviously he'd told her not to speak to us.

That night, Murch and I spoke in whispers, both of us naturally wondering what had happened. Briney had gone over to her mother's, where Murch had suggested she go, and somehow convinced Kelly to come back.

They kept the curtains closed, the TV low and if they spoke, it was so quietly we couldn't hear them.

I spent an hour with Caesar on my lap and Murch in my ear about politicians. He was a John Kennedy supporter and tried to convince me I should be, too.

For the next two days and nights, I didn't see or hear either of the Brineys. On Saturday afternoon, Murch returned from one of his patrols with his shoebox. He went in the back and buried a cat he'd found and then came out on the porch to smoke a pipe. "Poor little thing," he said. "Wasn't any bigger than this." With his hands, he indicated how tiny the kitten had been.

Kelly came out on the porch a few minutes later. She wore a white blouse and jeans and had her auburn hair swept back into a loose ponytail. She looked neat and clean. And nervous.

She muttered a hello and started down the stairs.

"Ain't you ever going to talk to us again, Kelly?" Murch said. There was no sarcasm in his voice, just an obvious sadness.

She stopped halfway toward the sidewalk. Her back was to us. For long moments she just stood there.

When she turned around and looked at us, she said, "Pete don't want me to talk to either of you." Then, gently, "I miss sitting out on the porch."

"He's your husband, honey. You shouldn't let him be your jailer," Murch said.

"He said he was sorry about the other night. About hitting me." She paused. "He came over to my mother's house and he told my whole family he was sorry. He even started crying."

Murch didn't say anything.

"I know you don't like him, Murch, but I'm his wife and like the priest said, I owe him another chance."

"You be careful of him, especially when he's drinking."

"He promised he wouldn't hit me no more, Murch. He gave his solemn word."

She looked first at him and then at me, and then was gone down the block to the grocery store. From a distance she looked fifteen years old.

He went two more nights, Briney did, before coming home drunk and loud.

I knew just how drunk he was because I was sitting on the porch around ten o'clock when a new pink Mercury came up and scraped the edge of its right bumper long and hard against the curbing.

The headlights died. Briney sat in the dark car smoking a cigarette. I could tell he was staring at us.

Murch just sat there with Caesar on his lap. I just sat there waiting for trouble. I could sense it coming and I wanted it over with.

Briney got out of the car and tried hard to walk straight up the walk to the porch. He wasn't a comic drunk, doing an alcoholic rhumba, but he certainly could not have passed a sobriety test.

He came upon the porch and stopped. His chest was heaving from anger. He smelled of whiskey and sweat and Old Spice.

"You think I don't fucking know the shit you're putting in my old lady's mind," he said to Murch. "Huh?"

Murch didn't say anything.

"I asked you a fucking question, old man."

Murch said, softly, "Why don't you go in and sleep it off, kid?"

"You're the god damned reason she went to her mother's last week. You told her to!"

And then he lunged at Murch and I was up out of my chair. He was too drunk to swing with any grace or precision but he caught me on the side of the head with the punch he'd intended for Murch, and for a dizzy moment I felt my knees go. He could hit. No doubt about that.

And then he was on me, having given up on Murch, and I had to take four or five more punches while I tried to gather myself and bring some focus to my fear and rage.

I finally got him in the ribs with a good hooking right, and I felt real exhilaration when I heard the air *whoof* out of him, and then I banged another one just to the right of his jaw and backed him up several inches and then—

Then Kelly was on the porch crying and screaming and putting herself between us, a child trying to separate two mindless mastodons from killing each other and—

"You promised you wouldn't drink no more!" she kept screaming over and over at Briney.

All he could do was stand head hung and shamed like some whipped giant there in the dirty porch light she'd turned on. "But honey. . ." he'd mumble. Or "But sweetheart. . ." Or "But Kelly, jeeze I. . ."

"Now you get inside there, and right now!" she said, no longer his wife but his mother. And she sternly pointed to the door. And he shambled toward it, not looking back at any of us, just shuffling and shambling, drunk and dazed and sweaty, depleted of rage and pride, and no longer fierce at all.

When he was inside, the apartment door closed, she said, "I'm real sorry, Todd. I heard everything from inside."

"It's all right."

"You hurt?"

"I'm fine."

"I'm real sorry."

"I know."

She went over to Murch and touched him tenderly on the shoulder. He was standing up, this tired and suddenly very old looking man, and he had good gray Caesar in his arms. Kelly leaned over and petted Caesar and said, "I wish I had a husband like you, Caesar."

She went back inside. The rest of our time on the porch, the Brineys spoke again in whispers.

Just before he went up to bed, Murch said, "He's going to kill her someday. You know that, don't you, Todd?"

~ ~ ~ ~ ~

This time I was ready for it. Six hours had gone by. I'd watched the late movie and then lay on the bed smoking a cigarette in the darkness and just staring at the play of street-light and tree shadow on the ceiling.

The first sound from below was very, very low and I wasn't even sure what it was. But I threw my legs off the bed and sat up, grabbing for my cigarettes as I did so.

When the sound came again, I recognized it immediately for what it was. A soft sobbing. Kelly.

Voices. Muffled. Bedsprings squeaking. A curse—Briney.

And then, sharp and unmistakable, a slap.

And then two, three slaps.

Kelly screaming. Furniture being shoved around.

I was up from the sweaty bed and into my jeans, not bothering with a shirt, and down the stairs two-at-a-time.

By now, Kelly's screams filled the entire house. Behind me, at the top of the stairs, I could hear Murch shouting down, "You gotta stop him, son! You gotta stop him!"

More slaps; the muffled thud of closed fists pounding into human flesh and bone.

I stood back from the door and raised my foot and kicked with the flat of my heel four times before shattering the wood into jagged splinters.

Briney had Kelly pinned on the floor as he had last week, and he was putting punches into her at will. Even at a glance, I could see that her nose was broken. Ominously, blood leaked from her ear.

I got him by the hair and yanked him to his feet. He still wasn't completely sober so he couldn't put up the resistance he might have at another time.

I meant to make him unconscious and that was exactly what I did. I dragged him over to the door. He kept swinging at me and oc-casionally landing hard punches to my ribs and kidney but at the moment I didn't care. He smelled of sweat and pure animal rage and Kelly's fresh blood. I got him to the door frame and held him high by this hair and then slammed his temple against the edge of the frame.

It only took once. He went straight down to the floor in an un-moving heap.

Murch came running through the door. "I called the cops!"

He went immediately to Kelly, knelt by her. She was over on her side, crying crazily and throwing up in gasps that shook her entire body. Her face was a mask of blood. He had ripped her nightgown and dug fierce raking fingers over her breasts. She just kept crying.

~ ~ ~ ~ ~

Even this late at night, the neighbors were up for a good show, maybe two dozen of them standing in the middle of the street as the whipping red lights of police cars and ambulance gave the crumbling neighborhood a nervous new life.

Kelly had slipped into unconsciousness and was brought out strapped to a stretcher.

Two uniformed cops questioned Briney on the porch. He kept pointing to me and Murch, who stood holding Caesar and stroking him gently.

There was an abrupt scuffle as Briney bolted and took a punch at one of the cops. He was a big man, this cop, and he brought Briney down with two punches. Then he cuffed him and took him to the car.

From inside the police vehicle, Briney glared at me and kept glaring until the car disappeared into the shadows at the end of the block.

~ ~ ~ ~ ~

Kelly was a week in the hospital. Murch and I visited her twice. In addition to a broken nose, she'd also suffered a broken rib and two broken teeth. She had a hard time talking. She just kept crying softly and shaking her head and patting the hands we both held out to her.

Her brother, a burly man in his twenties, came over to the house two days later with a big U-Haul and three friends and cleaned out the Briney apartment. Murch and I gave him a hand loading.

The newspaper said that Peter James Briney had posted a $2500 bond and had been released on bail. He obviously wasn't going to live downstairs. Kelly's brother hadn't left so much as a fork behind, and the landlord had already nailed a Day-Glo FOR RENT sign on one of the front porch pillars.

As for me, the crew was getting ready to move on. In two more days, we'd pack up and head up the highway toward Des Moines.

I tried to make my last two nights with Murch especially good. There was a pizza and beer restaurant over on Ellis Boulevard and on the second to last night, I took him there for dinner. I even coerced him into telling me some of those good old WW II stories of his.

~ ~ ~ ~ ~

The next night, the last night in Cedar Rapids, we had to work overtime again.

I got home after nine, when it was full and starry dark.

I was walking up the street when one of the neighbors came down from his porch and said, "They took him away."

I stopped. My body temperature dropped several degrees. I knew what was coming. "Took who off?"

"Murch. You know, that guy where you live."

"The cops?"

The man shook his head. "Ambulance. Murch had a heart attack."

I ran home. Up the stairs. Murch's place was locked. I had a key for his apartment in my room. I got it and opened the place up.

I got the lights on and went through each of the four small rooms. Murch was an orderly man. Though all the furnishings were old, from the ancient horsehair couch to the scarred chest of drawers, there was an obstinate if shabby dignity about them, much like Murch himself.

I found what I was looking for in the bathtub. Apparently the ambulance attendants hadn't had time to do anything more than rush Murch to the hospital.

Caesar, or what was left of him anyway, they'd left behind.

He lay in the center of the old claw-footed bathtub. He had been stabbed dozens of times. His gray fur was matted and stiff with his own blood. He'd died in the midst of human frenzy.

I didn't have to wonder who'd done this or what had given Murch his heart attack.

I went over to the phone and called both hospitals. Murch was at Mercy. The nurse I spoke with said that he had suffered a massive stroke and was unconscious. The prognosis was not good.

After I hung up, I went through the phone book looking for Brineys. It took me six calls to get the right one but finally I found Peter Briney's father. I convinced him that I was a good friend of Pete's and that I was just in town for the night and that I really wanted to see the old sonofagun. "Well," he said, "he hangs out at the Log Cabin a lot."

The Log Cabin was a tavern not far away. I was there within fifteen minutes.

The moment I stepped through the bar, into a working class atmosphere of clacking pool balls and whiney country western music, I saw him.

He was in a booth near the back, laughing about something with a girl with a beehive hair-do and a quick beery smile.

When he saw me, he got scared. He left the booth and ran toward the back door. By now, several people were watching. I didn't care.

I went out the back door after him. I stood beneath a window unit air-conditioner that sounded like a B-52 starting up and bled water like a wound. The air was hot and pasty and I slapped at two mosquitoes biting my neck.

Ahead of me was a gravel parking lot. The only light was spilling from the back windows of the tavern. The lot was about half full. Briney hadn't had time to get into that nice golden Mercury convertible at the end of the lot. He was hiding somewhere behind one of the cars.

I walked down the lot, my heels adjusting to the loose and wobbly feel of the gravel beneath.

He came lunging out from behind a pick-up truck. Because I'd been expecting him, I was able to duck without much problem.

I turned and faced him. He was crouched down, ready to jump at me.

"I'd still have a wife if it wasn't for you two bastards," he said.

"You're a pretty brave guy, Briney. You wait till Murch goes somewhere and then you sneak in and kill his cat. And then Murch comes home and finds Caesar dead and—"

But I was through talking.

I kicked him clean and sharp. I broke his nose. He gagged and screamed and started puking—he must have had way too much to drink that night—and sank to his knees and then I went over and kicked him several times in the ribs.

I kicked him until I heard the sharp brittle sound of bones breaking, and until he pitched forward, still screaming and crying, to the gravel. Then I went up and kicked him in the back of the head.

A couple of his friends from the tavern came out and started toward me but I was big enough and angry enough that they were wary.

"Personal dispute," I said. "Nothing to do with you boys at all."

Then they went over and tried to help their friend to his feet. It wasn't easy. He was a mess.

~ ~ ~ ~ ~

Murch died an hour and ten minutes after I got to the hospital. I went into his room and looked at all the alien tentacles stretching from beeping cold metal boxes to his warm but failing body. I stood next to his bed until a doctor came in and asked very softly and politely if I'd mind waiting in the hall while they did some work.

It was while the doctor was in there that Murch died. He had never regained consciousness and so we'd never even said proper goodbyes.

At the house, I went into Murch's apartment and found the shoebox and took it into the bathroom and gathered up the remains of poor Caesar.

I took the box down the stairs and out to the garage where I got the garden spade. Then I went over and in the starry prairie night, buried Caesar properly. I even blessed myself, though I wasn't a Catholic, and then knelt down and took the rich damp earth and covered Caesar's grave.

I didn't sleep that night. I just sat up in my little room with my last quart of Canadian Ace and my last pack of Pall Malls and thought about Kelly and thought about Caesar and especially I thought about Murch.

Just at dawn, it started to rain, a hot dirty city rain that would neither cool nor cleanse, and I packed my bags and left.

BLACK SHEEP

1

A good face is important, sure, as are good breasts, nice ankles and wrists, and a tight bottom. Not to mention good breath and not wearing anything flashy or trashy. But you also have to be able to talk to them. A lot of guys forget that. Because, frankly, a lot of guys just aren't as sensitive as Bill Avery. You have to be able to talk to them and they have to be able to talk to you. Especially when your life takes a terrible turn all of a sudden. If you can't talk to the girl you're seeing on the side, you may as well just pay for it and get yourself a hooker. . .

Today, Bill needs to talk. God, how Bill needs to talk.

The place for the conversation is Tiffany's bed in her apartment in the Windward Hills apartment complex. To Bill, who lives in a very nice new Tudor out in a very pricey new development, this place is sort of pathetic—toilets that won't flush the first time; water stains on the dining room walls; and not a single new car in the parking lot. But he's magnanimous about it. Tiffany is a small-town girl from Oskaloosa who came to Cedar Rapids and went to business school and then went to work for the law firm where Bill is about to become a full partner. He can identify with Tiffany because he came from the west side and went to all the wrong schools and instead of a degree from Yale or Princeton, which the senior partners always discuss proudly, he ended up at the U of Iowa. Nothing wrong with that, of course. A fine school. But still.

So they are in bed—this is after work and he's supposedly working late, that's the word he gave his wife anyway—and it's snowing in the dusk and in the apartment above them somebody is playing Nat "King" Cole Christmas songs and Bill Avery feels very, very sad. So sad, in fact, that he wasn't all that good in the sack tonight.

For which he apologizes for the tenth time.

"Oh, gosh, Bill, I don't expect a stud service."

"But I came and you didn't."

"Well, I remember a night when I came and you didn't."

"You do?"

"Yes. One night when you were drunk."

"Oh."

"So let's just say we're even."

"Really?"

"Sure," she says. "But you really want to talk about your brother, don't you?"

"My brother?"

"Sure. Are you surprised I remembered he was getting out?"

"Yeah. Yeah, he is. The Governor wanted to let a bunch of model prisoners out right before the year 2000. Good public relations and all that bullshit."

"You heard from him then?"

"No. But I can feel him here. You know that feeling? How you can feel somebody in the same town?"

"Oh, sure." She kisses him. She has warm, silken flesh. She is sweet in every sense.

"Who's really pissed is my wife."

"Well, gee, he served his time. And it was just a robbery. Nothing violent, I mean. He served his time and she should give him another chance."

"That's the bad part of marrying into a good family, I suppose."

"What is?"

"Oh, you have to be so concerned what everybody thinks. Sharon's afraid everybody at the firm and all her friends at the country club will find out that I have a younger brother who just got out of prison. That I have a younger brother who's been stealing stuff all his life."

"Oh, this wasn't the first time he stole stuff?"

"No, just the first time he went to prison."

"Oh."

"Kind of a career criminal, then, huh?" she says.

"No, not a career criminal. He just—takes stuff. I mean, it's not like armed robbery or anything." He thinks back. "When we were in grade school, he took twenty dollars from the desk drawer of this teacher. And when we were in high school, he stole a hundred dollars from this cash box at a school dance. And then a year later, he took a couple of real expensive watches from gym lockers at school." He sighed. "Then he took that necklace at Mrs. Parker's. And that's the one that put him in jail."

She holds him. Tightly. "God, you've had to go through so much with him. I mean, both your folks dying when you were only seventeen and you having to raise him and all. I just hope he appreciates it enough to stay out of trouble this time."

He nods. "God, so do I."

"I had a cousin who went to prison once."

"Really?"

"Uh-huh. He worked in a bank and embezzled. Over in Rock Island. It was funny."

"What was?"

"Oh, he was this real straight-arrow when he was in Iowa but as soon as he started living on the other side of the Mississippi—he changed; changed completely. That's when he embezzled, when he moved, I mean."

He smiles. "He just moved across the Mississippi and he changed?"

"I know it sounds weird but that's just what happened. Honest."

"You're nuts, you know that?"

She kisses him again. "Comes from not being very well educated." And laughs. She's much smarter than she seems to realize; and it always makes him feel bad for her, how she's always putting herself down all the time. She and Glen have the education thing in common. At least she went through high school and business college. Glen never even got through high school.

Suddenly, he feels claustrophobic. They're tangled up in covers, their body heat is searing him. He needs cool air. He needs to be alone. He disentangles himself and walks over to the window and looks down at the parking lot. All the clerks pulling in now, their cars heavy with snow on their roofs and trunks and hoods, big lumbering white bears in the cold Midwestern snow-blown darkness. That's who lives here, clerks. Shopping center folks. When Bill was growing up on the west side—God, was it really thirty years ago now?—wearing a tie to work was a big deal. You wore a tie to work you were somebody special. Today, you wear a tie to work it doesn't mean anything. Just ask of the clerks.

The lot is filling up. People are slipping cardboard windshield screens under the wipers. The swirling snow is getting heavy in the burning amber glow of the parking lot lights. All the clerks are hurrying to get inside. He isn't being very nice, thinking of them as clerks.

"You thinking about Glen?"

"Yeah."

"You nervous about seeing him?'

"Yeah."

"He loves you. Remember when you let me read those letters of his from prison that time? He really looks up to you."

"Yeah, he does, I guess."

"Talking about how your Dad would be so proud of you and all. God, I was really crying when I read that, remember?"

"Yeah, I remember."

"Maybe Sharon would like him if she gave him a chance." That always surprises him, the way Tiffany talks about Sharon as if she's a good friend they have in common.

"Not Sharon." That's the funny thing. He would have been much better off marrying somebody like Tiffany. Farm girl. No pretensions. Sweet. But what did marrying a Tiffany prove? Anybody could go out and marry himself a Tiffany. But marrying a Sharon. . .marrying a Sharon meant getting accepted into the best law firm in the city; marrying a Sharon meant inheriting a substantial amount of money and property when her father died; marrying a Sharon meant that most people at the club feared you a little. And he likes that. He doesn't exploit it—well not often, anyway—but he likes it, a west side boy like himself watching these major players pay him a bit of fearful deference. You don't get those kinds of benefits when you marry a Tiffany, no matter how sweet-natured she is.

He looks at his watch. "Well, I'd better be going."

"Oh, God."

"What?"

"Just the thought of you going." She holds her thin white arms out to him, entreating, the way one of his own little daughters would. He finds the gesture profoundly fetching, and oddly moving. She really wants him. Sharon and he are long shut of wanting each other; long shut.

They spend their last minutes just holding each other in the perfume-smell of her, the tenderness of her, that odd fetching little laugh of hers. At moments like these, he can disappear inside her, just vanish utterly, no will or ego or memory of his own, and tonight he needs badly to vanish.

2

It is an alien planet he finds waiting for him. The snow is coming down harder than ever. In the streets giant yellow creatures with wild burning amber eyes scrape the snow. Growling trucks drop sifting sand. Here and there cars are stuck, obstinate little animals trying to fight their way out of the grip of huge snow drifts they skidded into. There is beauty, too, of course, the moth-like way the large damp snowflakes flutter around the streetlights; the occasional pair of lovers, walking hand in hand in beatific harmony down the dark and snowy streets, their long scarves trailing behind them with perfect grace.

He keeps sliding around. He is not, in fact, an especially good driver and usually does the wrong thing in crisis situations. Such as slamming on the brakes when he's starting into a slide on an icy street. If he's not careful, he'll end up one of those cars buried in a snow drift.

He should go home. This is uppermost in his mind: should-go-home. He's been spending far too much time lately with Tiffany. But the way he goes home from her place, he always comes very near the neighborhood where he and Glen grew up. He usually resists the urge to drive past the old places, but tonight—God, of all nights, the roads being what they are—tonight, inexplicably, he can't resist.

Snow shrouds everything, lends beauty even where there is none, gives the rusting cars parked along the street an antique rather than junky look. The snow does the same for all the houses. During daylight hours, these places are scars of smashed windows and tilting front porches and falling down garages and neon APT. FOR RENT signs on weather-rotted front porch columns. But the snow softens all this for the eye, rounds all the edges, hides the cancer that daily devours wood and siding and paint and shingle and concrete. The snow even absorbs all the sounds that would normally be heard in this neighborhood— kids crying, couples arguing, mean hungry watchdogs barking—so that a curiously dignified silence befalls the streets and alleys.

Then he sees it. Little square box on the corner of 1st Street and 8th Avenue. Fuzzy neon glow of beer signs somewhat diminished in the snow. When you grew up in this neighborhood, this was the place you always dreamed of. The tavern where the really cool guys hung out. They had neat cars and neater women and they knew how to fight and how to play pool and Briney, the guy who owns the place, even gave them their beers on credit.

Even though Bill always wanted out of this neighborhood, Briney's tap was still a big deal for him. It was the place he bought his first legal beer. Drove back from Iowa City the night of his twenty-first birthday and went right to Briney's; and Briney, which he did for anybody who was celebrating a twenty-first birthday, Briney gave him a free pitcher of beer. You were somebody when Briney gave you that free pitcher of beer—somebody in the neighborhood anyway—and for all his success, Bill thinks back to his boyhood now, not with his usual resentment and distaste. . .but with true pleasure. Memory is a con-artist, of course, but for this moment he allows himself to be conned. . .he is twenty-one and on the hardscrabble streets again and inside Briney's everybody whispers about him. That kid's gonna make it; smarter'n a god damned whip; too bad his brother Glen didn't get any brains. Poor little guy's dumb as a post. Bill was one of the real stars of Briney's for a year or so back then, and he enjoyed it, he really did. . .

The cars in the lot all wear snow-skins. Their drunken drivers will have to spend several butt-freezing minutes scraping off their windshields. And then they'll wiggle and waggle home, having to be careful, you slide into a parked car or something with liquor on your breath and a cop makes you take one of those breath test deals. . .in this state you can kiss your license goodbye for two, three years, especially if you have some kind of prior. . .

Briney's: clack of pool balls, cries of country western jukebox, revolving Bud clocks in the gloom above the bar, smells of cigarettes, beer, whiskey, disinfectant, urine. He remembers a night when two guys got into it over pool and one kept banging the head of the other against the edge of the pool table until half the people in here thought he might be dead. What he notices most is the lack of young women: in the old days, so long ago now, it seems, and he's not yet forty, in the old days going to Briney's was as big a thing for the girls as it was the boys, and this meant the sexiest most stuck-up girls in the neighborhood, too. But not any more. The women are older now, sliding into middle-age, their bodies fighting the g-forces of the grave that make them so unrecognizable. In the old days, the girls in

Briney's had the faces of poetry; now they have the faces of bad, flat prose.

Briney himself is behind the bar, washing glasses. He watches Bill walk from the front door to the bar. A few other people start watching, too.

"Hey, Briney, how's it going?" Bill says. He's a little nervous, which he resents. It should be Briney who is nervous about seeing him. It's Bill who drives the BMW, it's Bill who belongs to the country club, it's Bill who went boating last summer with the mayor. But there's an obstinacy to the people in Briney's. A guy like Chucky O'Day, he starts making these tire gizmos in his home workshop, and pretty soon he's got his own business, the bank begging to loan him money, a nice house out where the yuppies are building on the far west side. . .Chucky O'Day tools in here in his new Firebird convertible, and he's still one of the boys. The clothes maybe more expensive, he may not get in parking lot puking contests the way he did back then, but he's still Chucky, and they're always glad to see him, happy for his success. Bill, it's another matter. Bill, he was always a little stand-offish, anyway. Bill, he isn't one of them now—if he ever was.

Briney says, "If you're looking for your brother, he ain't been in yet."

"I just thought I might have a drink."

"Slummin' tonight, huh?"

A couple of guys along the bar, with long ears, they pick up on Briney's sarcasm and snicker like second-graders. For Bill, life will always be like the second grade playground, where he learned that he didn't fit. Too cool for the nerds; too nerdy for the cool ones. He doesn't fit here and, truth be told, he doesn't fit with Sharon's friends at the country club, either.

"You know I like this place, Briney," Bill says, the sickening note of pleading still in his voice. How many of these people have ever even sat in a BMW, let alone owned one?

"Yeah, that's why you and your country club pals always come around."

More snickers from the guys at the bar. "Blue Christmas" by Elvis comes on the jukebox.

"You have Black & White Scotch? How about a shot and a glass of beer."

Shot-and-a-beer. The bona fides in a place like this.

Briney goes to get his shot. Bill starts to look around. A few grudging Christmas decorations here and there in the gloom. He can hear Briney: why put all that bullshit up when you have to take it right back down again?

Then he sees her and at first he doesn't think it's her, it's so dark in here. Then he knows it's her and then he knows that Glen's going to be in here tonight for sure.

Briney sets his drink down and says, "You seen her, huh? Susan Cramer. Sittin' over there."

"Yeah."

"She got in here a little before you did." He smirks. "Anybody woulda told me Susan Cramer ever woulda been sittin' in my place, I woulda laughed. Susan Cramer. She was always hangin' around the nuns. Surprised she didn't end up a nun herself."

And it's true, back when they were at Catholic school, and everybody was doing drugs and sleeping with each other and getting into various kinds of trouble. Back then, little Susan Cramer, who stood maybe five-two and didn't weigh more than ninety pounds, and who was very pretty in a quiet, melancholy way, Susan Cramer was one of the few kids who didn't join in. Mass every day, good grades, always helping the nuns deliver food baskets to the poor and things like that, and then home to her parents who were much older and sick. Never went out much. But had this humongous crush on Glen ever since they were in grade school. She was one of the few people who believed in him, one of the few people who tried to turn him away from this thing he had about stealing things. Bill hasn't heard— or thought of her—in years.

"Maybe I'll go over and say hi."

Briney smirks again. "Yeah, and be sure and tell her about your BMW and that big-ass mansion of yours."

The long ears are out again, the men along the bar snickering. Bill should be the one in charge here. It's a terrible thing to admit to—and Americans especially hate admitting to it—but there really is a social pecking order. Successful guy like Bill comes in, the other men should be intimidated by him. But that sure isn't the way it's working out.

"It isn't a mansion," Bill says. Why does he always sound so desperate? He's that way around his partners at the law firm; a little bit sweaty all the time.

Briney says, "It'll do till the real thing comes along."

And gets another laugh.

3

He remembers that she always looked spooked, scared, like somebody was about to hit her or something. That's how she looks when she sees him walking toward the booth she's sitting in.

"Hi. Remember me?" he says.

She nods.

"All right if I sit down?"

She nods again. She isn't exactly pretty but there's a wounded quality to the eyes and mouth that give her a vulnerability that some men—including himself—find erotic in a strange way. A child-woman, he supposes, that's her appeal. She never knew how to dress and she still doesn't, a rumpled brown sweater and blue eye shadow and blonde hair. She still doesn't weigh any more than she did in high school. Ninety pounds max.

He sits his beer-and-a-shot down and then follows it, sitting in the booth across from her.

"I shouldn't be drinking this," she says, and tilts her head to her beer.

He smiles. "I won't call the police. I promise."

She doesn't smile. "We have a lot of alcoholism in my family."

"Oh."

"My Dad and both his brothers."

"I'm sorry."

"So I get scared. Every time I have a beer, I mean."

"You have many beers?"

"This is my first in maybe a year."

He doesn't want to laugh and hurt her feelings. She's so sincere and ardent about everything. Has to be careful around her. She seems so skittish. 'Well, if all you drink is a beer a year, I don't think you have much to worry about."

"I hope not."

"You know who I was thinking about the other day?"

"Who?"

"Sister Mary Philomena. Remember her?"

"Yes."

"I was remembering how she took a swing at Charlie O'Donnell one day and hit the wall instead. And broke her hand?" He laughs. "God, Charlie never got tired of telling that story."

"I liked her."

"I sort of did, too. But it was funny. Her breaking her hand and all."

"I suppose. But she was the one who helped me get into the convent."

"Wow, I didn't know that. You were in the convent?"

She nods. "Three years."

"And you, what, dropped out?"

"Uh-huh. I decided I didn't have a true vocation."

"Well, good thing you didn't go all the way and take your vows and stuff, then."

"It was because I was writing Glen all the time. You know, your brother."

"Oh."

"That's why Mother Superior told me. Why I should drop out. Because of the letters."

"How did she know about the letters?"

"You have to tell them who you're writing."

"I see."

"She said that I was in love with him and that I should take it as a sign."

She'd followed Glen around since they were back in second grade. You saw Glen, Susan Cramer was never far behind.

"That I was in love with him, and that I didn't have a true vocation." Then, "But by the time I actually got back to town here, my Dad was real sick—he had throat cancer—and my Mom wasn't able to take care of him by herself, so I never really got to see Glen all that much. And then I started seeing this guy who lived next door. You remember Denny Walsh?"

"Sort of."

"Big comic book collector. That's a strange thing, you know, to say about somebody, I mean, when that's the first thing that comes to mind and all. But that was his life. He collected comic books. He's got this good job out at Rockwell but what he's really crazy about are his comic books. Anyway, I knew my Dad wanted to see me get married before he died, so when Denny asked me—I said yes." Then, "We got divorced a couple of months after my Dad died. The whole thing didn't last more than ten months. Denny caught me calling Glen one night and then I told him, I mean I should've been honest with him to begin with, told him that I was in love with Glen and that I probably would be in love with him the rest of my life. I know that sounds corny but that's the truth. And then he said what my Dad always said, that Glen was just a thief. And right after that, Glen got caught in that house, and they sent him to prison. You know how many letters I wrote him in prison?"

"How many?"

"I kept count. 162. 162 letters. One every three days. Can you imagine that? And I saw him twice a month on top of it."

"So now you're finally going to get together, you and Glen?"

"That's what I'm praying for. I pray for it every morning and every night. His last letter from prison, he wrote me that he loved me. He never said that before." She smiles and it is a sad and nervous smile. "I carry the letter right in my purse. Right with me all the time. You want to see it?"

"No, thanks. That's between you and Glen."

Something changes in her face, then. "There's just one thing I'd really like you to do for Glen."

"What's that?"

"Ask your wife to be nice to him when he comes to see his little nieces. He knows she hates him."

"She doesn't hate him," Bill says.

"Well, you know what I mean. A wealthy woman like that, she doesn't exactly like having an ex-convict for a brother-in-law." Then, "He loves you, Bill."

"I know. And I love him. Don't think I don't."

"That's why he went to prison for you."

For a moment, his heart stops. Literally. Terror seizes him. He can't believe what he's just heard. Assimilating, that's what he's doing. He's assimilating what she told him. Then—rage. Slams his fist hard on the table. "That's a goddamned lie!"

And even above the voices, even above the jukebox, even above the slamming of pool balls and the explosive flush of the toilet, even above all these things, they can hear his voice. And now they're looking at him, most of them, looking at him and wondering what he's so angry about. Who could be so angry with pathetic little Susan Cramer, she was a goddamned nun for c'rissake.

She says, very quietly, leaning forward so she can speak in whispers, "All those other times you stole stuff—that's why he always took the blame for you. Because he loves you. Your folks always expected you to be a success—Bill got the brains in the family, Glen always says—and he always looked up to you. He knew you couldn't help yourself, you know, about stealing stuff. So he took the blame every time you took something. Ever since you were little kids."

"If he told you that, he's lying." But the anger is gone now; there's just weariness. It's kind of funny, actually, little Susan Cramer—at this moment anyway—is in total control of the situation. What's even worse is that she's feeling sorry for him.

"Gee, Bill, calm down. I'm not going to tell anybody and neither is he. He loves you too much and I love him too much to do somethin' like that. He kind of lives through you—he's not the smartest guy in the world—you should hear him talk about you. That's why he had to make sure to return that diamond necklace you took from Mrs. Parker's when you were at her house for the party. He broke in the next night and was going to put the necklace under the couch. But they caught him."

He checks his watch. "I've got to get home."

She reaches out and touches his hand. "Bill, I pray for you every day. I really do. I pray you won't steal anything else so that you'll have a great life and so that Glen won't have to take the blame any more."

Gray, the way this neighborhood is gray; and worn beyond her years. The eroticism he once saw is gone now, at least in his eyes. Gray and worn is all she is. He shakes his head. "You don't know much about criminals, do you, Susan?"

"I know about Glen."

"Criminals always blame somebody else for their troubles. Glen is blaming me."

"He wouldn't lie to me, Bill. He really wouldn't."

"He wouldn't, huh?" He stands up. "I really do have to run."

"Bill. I really won't tell anybody. I really won't."

"Good," he says, throwing a twenty dollar bill on the table. "Good, because you shouldn't go around spreading lies."

As he passes the bar, Briney says, "Bring the wife around some time, Bill. I'm sure she'd like to meet us."

Another sure laugh with the gray and worn men along the bar.

4

The alien world again. But worse now. Cars stalled in snow-drifts all over the place. Even trucks spinning out of control on the icy snow-packed streets. He feels forlorn, isolated. He should've expected that someday Glen would tell somebody. Shouldn't be any big surprise. And certainly there was no threat in the way Susan spoke to him. God, she was understanding, if anything. Glen always wanted to please the folks. He knew they were counting on older brother Bill to be the one who made it. He had all the poise and polish and brains. Glen, to be brutally honest, just isn't all that smart. They lived long enough to see Bill become a successful lawyer—and long enough to see Glen go to prison. That's probably what killed them (they both died within a year of each other; heart attack for mom, cancer for dad). Now, Glen is out.

Then he's home. Spectacular Christmas lights on his street. His very prosperous street. A huge sleigh parked on one roof top, a beautiful Nativity scene taking up an entire, sprawling lawn. The neighborhood of a very successful man; the most prestigious area in all of Cedar Rapids.

Then he's turning into the long, winding drive that will take him to his Tudor-style house. Modest Christmas decorations here but the house looks gorgeous mantled with snow.

Needs to put Glen and Susan out of his mind. Enjoy himself. Everything is fine, under control. Next time he gets the urge to steal something—well, he'll just have to get the impulse under control, that's all.

He puts the car in the garage, next to Sharon's own BMW, and then walks up to the back door, snowflakes cold on his cheeks. He even opens his mouth, lets the snowflakes melt on his tongue the way he used to when he was a boy. But the air was cleaner back then. God only knows what kind of disease this snowflake is carrying.

He walks up into the kitchen. Sharon is lovely in a very nice, dark dress and a white apron. She is a very, very pretty lady.

"You look tired, honey," she says.

"Long day, I guess."

Then his two daughters burst into the kitchen. Three and four, they are, and even better looking than Sharon. "Daddy, Mommy said that Uncle Glen is a criminal. Is that true?"

"Yeah, is he a criminal like on TV, daddy?"

He gives Sharon an angry look.

She is standing there with a small cooking pan filled with sautéed onions. "I knew you wouldn't like me saying it, dear. But I wanted them to know the truth. I don't have anything against him—I'm a very open-minded person and I think you know that—but I just thought it would be a good thing if the girls knew the truth, was all."

The truth, he thinks all the time he's washing up for dinner.

The truth, he thinks all the time he's watching TV that night.

The truth, he thinks all the time he's lying there in the darkness tonight, unable to sleep. The truth.

BEAUTY

Most of us use code words. I suppose that sounds a bit melodramatic, but how else are you going to separate the wheat from the chaff? Or, more specifically, the real client from the undercover FBI agent who wants to bust your ass and send you away for a long, long time.

The lady called me while I was on the Stairmaster in my hotel room. She'd guaranteed a nice sum to fly to her city. I was nice and winded from my workout while she went through this nervous little introduction without once giving me that one word that could put us in business.

"Oh, damn," she said. "The—what do you call it?—the code word. You want that, don't you?"

"Be nice to hear it."

"Associates."

"There you go."

"So how do we proceed from here? I suppose you can tell I'm sort of nervous."

"Where are you?"

She told me. I mentioned a nice little Chinese place two blocks from her hotel.

~ ~ ~ ~ ~

During my brief tenure in the loving arms of the fine folk who run Joliet state pen—bank robbery gone wrong; nothing to do with my present occupation—I spent a lot of time reading psychology books. I figured that psychology would be useful no matter what kind of work I took up when they gave me back my cheap suit and the free bus ticket.

I had a friend in high school that had spent every possible minute tending to this cherry 1957 red Ford Thunderbird his wealthy father had bought him at the start of our senior year. Ken had once been a fun guy. No more. After he got the T-Bird, he lost interest in girls, smoking dope, cruising our hangouts, and even the XXX videos that had just become available to the general public.

The woman who slid into the booth across from me also had an obsession. Her obsession wasn't with a thing. It was with herself.

I don't keep up on all the things women can do to keep themselves beautiful if they have the money. I know about plastic surgery, of course, and facials and bikini waxes and things like that. But I'm sure there are at least a dozen devious little tricks most men know nothing about. With her, it was probably two dozen devious little tricks.

She was stunning more than beautiful. A lot of her appeal was in the important way she carried herself. She was fighting forty and winning.

The smile disarmed you. One of those ridiculously outsize Hollywood smiles that mere mortals can't muster. And what the smile couldn't accomplish, the blue blue eyes did. Now you were not only disarmed, but raising your arms in surrender. The elegant suit looked to be Armani, the enormous tooled earrings looked to be real gold, and the long, calculatedly tousled golden hair finished you off.

But she irritated me immediately. "What if I change my mind?"

"I'm told that's a woman's prerogative."

"Do you have a kill fee?" The smile was genuine. "Oh, God, I used to work at a magazine and that's what we called it when we canceled an article but wanted to give the writer something for his work. A kill fee. In this case, I guess it's a bad choice of words."

I smiled. "Nothing to worry about. And a kill fee is already taken care of."

"It is?"

I nodded. "Remember what I said on the phone. First half is payable right here, right now. If I don't have the second half in cash by the end of the day, I keep the first half whether I do the job or not."

"What if I called the police?"

"Again, your prerogative. But you'd be implicated in hiring me to kill someone. Conspiracy to commit murder probably wouldn't go over too well with your friends at the country club."

"How do you know I belong to a country club?"

"Please."

She frowned. "What you're saying is that I'm a cliché."

Never accuse a narcissist of anything. Their egos move in for the kill.

"You have a manila envelope. Let's get to it, shall we?"

"I resent your remark."

I started to slide out of the booth.

She held up her perfectly manicured hand. "Oh, forget it. I am very country club and I may as well admit it. It's just that common people are so snobby about country clubs. They don't know about all the fine people you meet at them."

Like ladies who hire hit men, I thought. Not to mention robber barons that cheat their employees out of their pensions, and then go home to sleep on thousand-dollar silk sheets in their ten-bedroom mansions.

She opened the 8 X 10 manila envelope and slid out a small package wrapped in brown paper, accompanied by a newspaper story that included a full-color photo with the caption: *Beauty of Beauties*. The rest of the text listed the names of the three runners-up and the beauty pageant winner. The runners-up tried desperately to look happy. The queen didn't have that problem, flashing a Hollywood smile that made you reach for your sunglasses.

"You won this beauty contest."

"State winner. I went on to Miss U.S.A. I was eighteen, just a sophomore in college." When she mentioned her age, melancholy hushed her voice to a whisper. I wondered if she'd cry. She wasn't putting me on. She was lamenting her lost youth. I suppose we all do that, though lamenting all the county jail time I'd put in wasn't a whole lot of my youth I even wanted to remember, let alone lament. "I didn't win Miss U.S.A. I was the second runner-up." She mentioned the name of a prominent male singer popular at that time in the mid-80s. "He was one of the judges. He knew I should have won and he wanted to help me get through it. He took me dancing and other things."

I knew better than to inquire about those "other things."

"Now my daughter is in a beauty contest and I don't want the same thing to happen to her."

"What 'same thing?'"

"To be cheated out of it. The word I'm getting is that the advertising agency man who runs this particular pageant is actually the father of one of the contestants. He got a girl pregnant when he was already married and now the daughter is in his show. I think the mother is blackmailing him. He won't have any choice but to figure out some way for his daughter to win. This could be a very important stepping stone for my daughter. I don't want some dirty old man to ruin it for her."

"When's the pageant?"

"Tomorrow night." She named a convention hall. "Eight o'clock. My daughter's all ready to go. She's not only the most beautiful, she's also the most talented."

"If you do say so yourself."

Another genuine smile. "If I do say so myself. I'm sorry if I sound egotistical. It's just that I want my daughter to win this."

"So I address my skills to the advertising man?"

"Oh, no. The man might be dead, but his illegitimate daughter would still be alive and ready to compete again. I hate to admit this, but she's a very good looking girl. And not bad in the talent department."

"So I direct my attention to her."

She leaned forward. "Yes, but not the full thing."

"The full thing?"

She nodded. "Right." Her voice dropped even lower. "I don't want her killed. I just want her disfigured. Permanently."

~ ~ ~ ~ ~

I spent the rest of the day deploying all the things I'd need for a perfect strike. Access would be the first problem. While the girl would be in her hotel room at various times, her floor would be shared by other contestants. A whole lot of problems there. She would be at a banquet tonight. I could get the security uniform I'd need, but again, the contestants would be everywhere. A clean getaway was dicey. My client had given me an itinerary that the girl followed every day. Up early for a quick jog around the hotel pool and then fifteen minutes of swimming before showering, eating a light breakfast, and then her singing and ballet lessons. A star in the making. The only problem was that this star seemed to always be accompanied by another woman, an older one, perhaps her mother or aunt or someone. It didn't matter to me; she was an inconvenience, nothing more.

I disguised myself for a quick tour of all the hotel sites that were possibilities for the attack. Late in the day, I went downstairs to where the maids and the bellboys check in and check out. Each had its own small locker room. I always carry a few elementary burglary tools with me. In one locker I found a bellhop uniform still in its dry-cleaning plastic. It wouldn't fit perfectly, but it would fit well enough.

Tonight, coming back from the banquet, the girl and her escort would probably walk back to her room via a wandering garden-like area that led directly to her entrance. My client said that this was the route they had followed the last three nights. She also said that the two never joined the other contestants in staying out a little longer.

They went right back to their room. They would be virtually alone on the garden walk. Neither one would be startled by seeing a bellhop.

~ ~ ~ ~ ~

I don't pretend to be Superman. I don't even pretend to be Jimmy Olson. Over the years, I've found that my job-related anxiety is at its worst two or three hours before the gig itself. I've tried antidepressants, a few shots of whiskey, even a joint or two of pot. But they all left me logy. Maybe the worst danger of all to a man in my profession.

Then I discovered the Stairmaster. I now insist on hotel rooms with Stairmasters. Pricey, yes, but invaluable. An hour of hard exercise and then a cold shower leaves me not only wide awake but focused entirely on the task ahead.

I'd just stepped out of the shower when the call came that I'd been expecting.

"I guess I'm backing out."

"Figures."

"You don't have to be sarcastic."

"I'm ready to go. Guess I'll have to find some other amusement for tonight."

"I was just thinking to myself *I'm not this kind of woman.* I'm a Junior Leaguer, for God's sake."

"All right. I've got the money and I'm hanging up now."

"I feel foolish. You must think I'm an airhead."

"A Junior League airhead? A contradiction in terms."

"There's that f-ing sarcasm again."

"Good night, Madam."

I was just adjusting the clip-on necktie that fitted the white shirt I wore under the uniform jacket when the second call came.

"I've changed my mind."

"Who is this?"

"You know damn well who this is. Now quit playing around."

"Oh, yes, the Junior League lady."

"I ought to hang up on you, you bastard."

"Go ahead. It's your turn."

"I want you to do it."

"I've already made other plans."

"You prick. You've got my money and I want satisfaction. And don't get cute with that last word."

I checked my Rolex. If I was going to do it, I had to move fast.

"One thing," I said.

"What?"

"I never want to hear your voice again."

I hung up, grabbed my stun gun, and drove over to the hotel.

~ ~ ~ ~ ~

The banquet ran late. A minor celebrity sang some songs and an even more minor celebrity gave a speech about why beauty pageants were the best expression ever of true American values. If there'd been a vomitorium nearby, I would have gladly bought my ticket.

Someday when I tell this story again to a few friends of mine, I'll fill it with a lot of intrigue and suspense. The whole stalking sequence you see in all those noir films. Close cuts of me hiding in the front of the garden area. The beautiful contestant coming out the door that leads to the garden, her mother holding her hand. Her innocently looking around. My hand tightening around my weapon of choice for this evening. Her walking briskly toward her entrance door. And then me coming up behind her, devilishly disguised, and saying in a safe, sensible voice, "Excuse me."

And her turning around and—

~ ~ ~ ~ ~

I'd just poured myself a drink when the phone rang in my hotel room. I picked up and said, "I thought I told you I never wanted to hear your voice again." Nobody else it could be. Nobody else knew where I was.

"I just wanted to thank you."

"I did my job."

"You did a fine job. Of course, I feel terrible about it. It's not the sort of thing I'd normally do but my daughter—" Then, "But this Tiny Tiara contest is real important to her." I could feel rather than hear her smile on the other end of the phone. "Call me the ultimate stage mother, I guess."

"I'm hanging up now."

"Well, that's nice. All I wanted to do was thank you. I mean it must've been weird for you throwing acid in the face of a little five-year-old girl. I'm just glad you could get through it."

I hung up.

The local news was all over it of course. A beauty contest for five- to seven-year- old girls. A barbaric act unheard of in the history of these pageants. Police searching for a dark-haired man dressed as a bellhop. So stealing the uniform and spending the time to get just the right wig had been worth the trouble.

Sleep didn't come easy but when it finally arrived I had an unwanted dream about screwing the woman who'd hired me. She was a lot better than I would've thought.

THE UGLY FILE

The cold rain didn't improve the looks of the housing development, one of those sprawling valleys of pastel-colored tract houses that had sprung from the loins of greedy contractors right at the end of WW II, fresh as flowers during that exultant time but now dead and faded.

I spent fifteen minutes trying to find the right address. Houses and streets formed a blinding maze of sameness.

I got lucky by taking what I feared was a wrong turn. A few minutes later I pulled my new station wagon up to the curb, got out, tugged my hat and raincoat on snugly, and then started unloading.

Usually, Merle, my assistant, is on most shoots. He unloads and sets up all the lighting, unloads and sets up all the photographic umbrellas, and unloads and sets up all the electric sensors that trip the strobe lights. But Merle went on this kind of shoot once before and he said never again, "not even if you fire my ass." He was too good an assistant to give up so now I did these particular jobs alone.

My name is Roy Hubbard. I picked up my profession of photography in Nam, where I was on the staff of a captain whose greatest thrill was taking photos of bloody and dismembered bodies. He didn't care if the bodies belonged to us or them just as long as they had been somehow disfigured or dismembered.

In an odd way, I suppose, being the captain's assistant prepared me for the client I was working for today, and had been working for, on and off, for the past two months. The best-paying client I've ever had, I should mention here. I don't want you to think that I take any special pleasure, or get any special kick, out of gigs like this. I don't. But when you've got a family to feed, and you live in a city with as many competing photography firms as this one has, you pretty much take what's offered you.

The air smelled of wet dark earth turning from winter to spring. Another four or five weeks and you'd see cardinals and jays sitting on the blooming green branches of trees.

The house was shabby even by the standards of the neighborhood, the brown grass littered with bright cheap forgotten plastic toys and empty Diet Pepsi cans and wild rain-sodden scraps of newspaper inserts. The small picture window to the right of the front door was taped lengthwise from some long ago crack, and the white siding ran with rust from the drain spouts. The front door was missing its top glass panel. Cardboard had been set in there.

I knocked, ducking beneath the slight overhang of the roof to escape the rain.

The woman who answered was probably no older than twenty-five but her eyes and the sag of her shoulders said that her age should not be measured by calendar years alone.

"Mrs. Cunningham?"

"Hi," she said, and her tiny white hands fluttered about like doves. "I didn't get to clean the place up very good."

"That's fine."

"And the two older kids have the flu so they're still in their pajamas and—"

"Everything'll be fine, Mrs. Cunningham." When you're a photographer who deals a lot with mothers and children, you have to learn a certain calm, doctorly manner.

She opened the door and I went inside.

The living room, and what I could see of the dining room, was basically a continuation of the front yard—a mine field of cheap toys scattered everywhere, and inexpensive furniture of the sort you buy by the room instead of the piece strewn with magazines and pieces of newspaper and the odd piece of children's clothing.

Over all was a sour smell, one part the rain-sodden wood of the exterior house, one part the lunch she had just fixed, one part the house cleaning this place hadn't had in a good long while.

The two kids with the flu, boy and girl respectively, were parked in a corner of the long, stained couch. Even from here I knew that one of them had diapers in need of changing. They showed no interest in me or my equipment. Out of dirty faces and dead blue eyes they watched one cartoon character beat another with a hammer on a TV whose sound dial was turned very near the top.

"Cindy's in her room," Mrs. Cunningham explained.

Her dark hair was in a pert little pony tail. The rest of her chunky self was packed into a faded blue sweat shirt and sweat pants. In high school she had probably been nice and trim. But high school was an eternity behind her now.

I carried my gear and followed her down a short hallway. We passed two messy bedrooms and a bathroom and finally we came to a door that was closed.

"Have you ever seen anybody like Cindy before?"

"I guess not, Mrs. Cunningham."

"Well, it's kind of shocking. Some people can't really look at her at all. They just sort of glance at her and look away real quick. You know?"

"I'll be fine."

"I mean, it doesn't offend me when people don't want to look at her. If she wasn't my daughter, I probably wouldn't want to look at her, either. Being perfectly honest, I mean."

"I'm ready, Mrs. Cunningham."

She watched me a moment and said, "You have kids?"

"Two little girls."

"And they're both fine?"

"We were lucky."

For a moment, I thought she might cry. "You don't know how lucky, Mr. Hubbard."

She opened the door and we went into the bedroom.

It was a small room, painted a fresh, lively pink. The furnishings in here—the bassinet, the bureau, the rocking horse in the corner—were more expensive than the stuff in the rest of the house. And the smell was better. Johnson's Baby Oil and Johnson's Baby Powder are always pleasant on the nose. There was a reverence in the appointments of this room, as if the Cunninghams had consciously decided to let the yard and the rest of the house go to hell. But this room—

Mrs. Cunningham led me over to the bassinet and then said, "Are you ready?"

"I'll be fine, Mrs. Cunningham. Really."

"Well," she said, "here you are then."

I went over and peered into the bassinet. The first look is always rough. But I didn't want to upset the lady so I smiled down at her baby as if Cindy looked just like every other baby girl I'd ever seen.

I even touched my finger to the baby's belly and tickled her a little. "Hi, Cindy."

After I had finished my first three or four assignments for this particular client, I went to the library one day and spent an hour or so reading about birth defects. The ones most of us are familiar with are clubfoots and cleft palates and harelips and things like that. The treatable problems, that is. From there you work up to spina bifida and cretinism. And from there—

What I didn't know until that day in the library is that there are literally hundreds of ways in which infants can be deformed, right up to and including the genetic curse of The Elephant Man. As soon as I started running into words such as achondroplastic dwarfism and supernumerary chromosomes, I quit reading. I had no idea what those words meant.

Nor did I have any idea of what exactly you would call Cindy's malformation. She had only one tiny arm and that was so short that her three fingers did not quite reach her rib cage. It put me in mind of a flipper on an otter. She had two legs but only one foot and only three digits on that. But her face was the most terrible part of it all, a tiny little slit of a mouth and virtually no nose and only one good eye. The other was almond-shaped and in the right position but the eyeball itself was the deep, startling color of blood.

"We been tryin' to keep her at home here," Mrs. Cunningham said, "but she can be a lot of trouble. The other two kids make fun of her all the time and my husband can't sleep right because he keeps havin' these dreams of her smotherin' because she don't have much of a nose. And the neighbor kids are always tryin' to sneak in and get a look at her."

All the time she talked, I kept staring down at poor Cindy. My reaction was always the same when I saw these children. I wanted to find out who was in charge of a universe that would permit something like this and then tear his fucking throat out.

"You ready to start now?"

"Ready," I said.

She was nice enough to help me get my equipment set up. The pictures went quickly. I shot Cindy from several angles, including several straight-on. For some reason, that's the one the client seems to like best. Straight-on. So you can see everything.

I used VPS large format professional film and a Pentax camera because what I was doing here was essentially making many portraits of Cindy, just the way I do when I make a portrait of an important community leader.

Half an hour later, I was packed up and moving through Mrs. Cunningham's front door.

"You tell that man—that Mr. Byerly who called—that we sure do appreciate that $2000 check he sent."

"I'll be sure to tell him," I said, walking out into the rain.

"You're gonna get wet."

"I'll be fine. Goodbye, Mrs. Cunningham."

~ ~ ~ ~ ~

Back at the shop, I asked Merle if there had been any calls and he said nothing important. Then, "How'd it go?"

"No problems," I said.

"Another addition to the ugly file, huh?" Then he nodded to the three filing cabinets I'd bought years back at a government auction. The top drawer of the center cabinet contained the photos and negatives of all the deformed children I'd been shooting for Byerly.

"I still don't think that's funny, Merle."

"'The ugly file?'" He'd been calling it that for a couple weeks now and I'd warned him that I wasn't amused. I have one of those tempers that it's not smart to push on too hard or too long.

"Uh-huh," I said.

"If you can't laugh about it then you have to cry about it."

"That's a cop-out. People always say that when they want to say something nasty and get away with it. I don't want you to call it that any more, you fucking understand me, Merle?"

I could feel the anger coming. I guess I've got more of it than I know what to do with, especially after I've been around some poor god damned kid like Cindy.

"Hey, boss, lighten up. Shit, man, I won't say it any more, OK?"

"I'm going to hold you to that."

I took the film of Cindy into the dark room. It took six hours to process it all through the chemicals and get the good, clear proofs I wanted.

At some point during the process, Merle knocked on the door and said, "I'm goin' home now, all right?"

"See you tomorrow," I said through the closed door.

"Hey, I'm sorry I pissed you off. You know, about those pictures."

"Forget about it, Merle. It's over. Everything's fine."

"Thanks. See you tomorrow."

"Right."

When I came out of the dark room, the windows were filled with night. I put the proofs in a manila envelope with my logo and return address on it and then went out the door and down the stairs to the parking lot and my station wagon.

The night was like October now, raw and windy. I drove over to the freeway and took it straight out to Mannion Springs, the wealthiest of all the wealthy local suburbs.

On sunny afternoons, Mary and I pack up the girls sometimes and drive through Mannion Springs and look at all the houses and daydream aloud of what it would be like to live in a place where you had honest-to-God maids and honest-to-God butlers the way some of these places do.

I thought of Mary now, and how much I loved her, more the longer we were married, and suddenly I felt this terrible, almost oppressive loneliness, and then I thought of little Cindy in that bassinet this afternoon and I just wanted to start crying and I couldn't even tell you why for sure.

The Byerly place is what they call a shingle Victorian. It has dormers of every kind and description—hipped, eyebrow and gabled. The place is huge but has far fewer windows than you'd expect to find in a house this size. You wonder if sunlight can ever get into it.

I'd called Byerly before leaving the office. He was expecting me.

I parked in the wide asphalt drive that swept around the grounds. By the time I reached the front porch, Byerly was in the arched doorway, dressed in a good dark suit.

I walked right up to him and handed him the envelope with the photos in it.

"Thank you," he said. "You'll send me a bill?"

"Sure," I said. I was going to add, "That's my favorite part of the job, sending out the bill," but he wasn't the kind of guy you joke with. And if you ever saw him, you'd know why.

Everything about him tells you he's one of those men who used to be called aristocratic. He's handsome, he's slim, he's athletic, and he seems to be very, very confident in everything he does—until you look at his eyes, at the sorrow and weariness of them, at the trapped gaze of a small and broken boy hiding in there.

Of course, on my last trip out here I learned why he looks this way. Byerly was out and the maid answered the door and we started talking and then she told me all about it, in whispers of course, because Byerly's wife was upstairs and would not have appreciated being discussed this way.

Four years ago, Mrs. Byerly gave birth to their only child, a son. The family physician said that he had never seen a deformity of this magnitude. The child had a head only slightly larger than an apple and no eyes and no arms whatsoever. And it made noises that sickened even the most doctorly of doctors. . .

The physician even hinted that the baby might be destroyed, for the sake of the entire family. . .

Mrs. Byerly had a nervous breakdown and went into a mental hospital for nearly a year. She refused to let her baby be taken to a state institution. Mr. Byerly and three shifts of nurses took care of the boy.

When Mrs. Byerly got out of the hospital everybody pretended that she was doing just fine and wasn't really crazy at all. But then Mrs. Byerly got her husband to hire me to take pictures of deformed babies for her. She seemed to draw courage from knowing that she and her son were not alone in their terrible grief. . .

All I could think of was those signals we send deep into outer space to see if some other species will hear them and let us know that we're not alone, that this isn't just some frigging joke, this nowhere planet spinning in the darkness. . .

When the maid told me all this, it broke my heart for Mrs. Byerly and then I didn't feel so awkward about taking the pictures any more. Her husband had his personal physician check out the area for the kind of babies we were looking for and Byerly would call the mother and offer to pay her a lot of money. . .and then I'd go over there and take the pictures of the kid. . .

Now, just as I was about to turn around and walk off the porch, Byerly said, "I understand that you spent some time here two weeks ago talking to one of the maids."

"Yes."

"I'd prefer that you never do that again. My wife is very uncomfortable about our personal affairs being made public."

He sounded as I had sounded with Merle earlier today. Right on the verge of being very angry. The thing was, I didn't blame him. I wouldn't want people whispering about me and my wife, either.

"I apologize, Mr. Byerly. I shouldn't have done that."

"My wife has suffered enough." The anger had left him. He sounded drained. "She's suffered way too much, in fact."

And with that, I heard a child cry out from upstairs.

A child—yet not a child—a strangled, mournful cry that shook me to hear.

"Good night," he said.

He shut the door very quickly, leaving me to the wind and rain and night.

After a while, I walked down the wide steps to my car and got inside and drove straight home.

As soon as I was inside, I kissed my wife and then took her by the hand and led her upstairs to the room our two little girls share.

We stood in the doorway, looking at Jenny and Sara. They were asleep.

Each was possessed of two eyes, two arms, two legs; and each was possessed of song and delight and wonderment and tenderness and glee.

And I held my wife tighter than I ever had, and felt an almost giddy gratitude for the health of our little family.

Not until much later, near midnight it was, my wife asleep next to me in the warmth of our bed—not until much later did I think again of Mrs. Byerly and her photos in the upstairs bedroom of that dark and shunned Victorian house, up there with her child trying to make frantic sense of the silent and eternal universe that makes no sense at all.

LAYOVER

In the darkness, the girl said, "Are you all right?"

"Huh?"

"I woke you up because you sounded so bad. You must have been having a nightmare."

"Oh. Yeah. Right." I tried to laugh but the sound just came out strangled and harsh.

Cold midnight. Deep midwest. A Greyhound bus filled with old folks and runaway kids and derelicts of every kind. Anybody can afford a Greyhound ticket these days, that's why you find so many geeks and freaks aboard. I was probably the only guy on the bus who had a real purpose in life. And if I needed a reminder of that purpose, all I had to do was shove my hand into the pocket of my P-coat and touch the chill blue metal of the .38. I had a purpose all right.

The girl had gotten on a day before, during a dinner stop. She wasn't what you'd call pretty but then neither was I. We talked of course, the way you do when you travel; dull grinding social chatter at first, but eventually you get more honest. She told me she'd just been dumped by a guy named Mike, a used car salesman at Belaski Motors in a little town named Burnside. She was headed to Chicago where she'd find a job and show Mike that she was capable of going on without him. Come to think of it, I guess Polly here had a goal, too, and in a certain way our goals were similar. We both wanted to pay people back for hurting us.

Sometime around ten, when the driver turned off the tiny overhead lights and people started falling asleep, I heard her start crying. It wasn't loud and it wasn't hard but it was genuine. There was a lot of pain there.

I don't know why—I'm not the type of guy to get involved—but I put my hand on her lap. She took it in both of her hands and held it tightly. "Thanks," she said and leaned over and kissed me with wet cheeks and a trembling hot little mouth.

"You're welcome," I said, and that's when I drifted off to sleep, the wheels of the Greyhound thrumming down the highway, the dark coffin inside filled with people snoring, coughing and whispering.

According to the luminous hands on my wrist watch, it was forty-five minutes later when Polly woke me up to tell me I'd been having a nightmare.

The lights were still off overhead. The only illumination was the soft silver of moonlight through the tinted window. We were in the back seat on the left hand side of the back aisle. The only thing behind us was the john, which almost nobody seemed to use. The seats across from us were empty.

After telling me about how sorry she felt for me having nightmares like that, she leaned over and whispered, "Who's Kenny?"

"Kenny?"

"That's the name you kept saying in your nightmare."

"Oh."

"You're not going to tell me, huh?"

"Doesn't matter. Really."

I leaned back and closed my eyes. There was just darkness and the turning of the wheels and the winter air whistling through the windows. You could smell the faint exhaust.

"You know what I keep thinking?" she said.

"No. What?" I didn't open my eyes.

"I keep thinking we're the only two people in the world, you and I, and we're on this fabulous boat and we're journeying to someplace beautiful."

I had to laugh at that. She sounded so naïve yet desperate too. "Someplace beautiful, huh?"

"Just the two of us."

And she gave my hand a little squeeze. "I'm sorry I'm so corny," she said.

And that's when it happened. I started to turn around in my seat and felt something fall out of my pocket and hit the floor, going *thunk*. I didn't have to wonder what it was.

Before I could reach it, she bent over, her long blonde hair silver in the moonlight, and got it for me.

She looked at it in her hand and said, "Why would you carry a gun?"

"Long story."

She looked as if she wanted to take the gun and throw it out the window. She shook her head. "You're going to do something with this, aren't you?"

I sighed and reached over and took the gun from her. "I'd like to try and catch a little nap if you don't mind."

"But—"

And I promptly turned over so that three-fourths of my body was pressed against the chill wall of the bus. I pretended to go to sleep, resting there and smelling diesel fuel and feeling the vibration of the motor.

The bus roared on into the night. It wouldn't be long before I'd be seeing Dawn and Kenny again. I touched the .38 in my pocket. No, not long at all.

~ ~ ~ ~ ~

If you've taken many Greyhounds, then you know about layovers. You spend an hour-and-a-half gulping down greasy food and going to the bathroom in a john that reeks like a city dump on a hot day and staring at people in the waiting area who seem to be deformed in some way. Or that's how they look at 2:26 A.M., anyway.

This layover was going to be different. At least for me. I had plans.

As the bus pulled into a small brick depot that looked as if it had been built back during the Depression, Polly said, "You're going to do it here, aren't you?"

"Do what?"

"Shoot somebody."

"Why would you say that?"

"I've just got a feeling is all. My mom always says I have ESP."

She started to say something else but then the driver lifted the microphone and gave us his spiel about how the layover would be a full hour and how there was good food to be had in the restaurant and how he'd enjoyed serving us. There'd be a new driver for the next six hours of our journey, he said.

There weren't many lights on in the depot. Passengers stood outside for a while stretching and letting the cold air wake them up.

I followed Polly off the bus and immediately started walking away. An hour wasn't a long time.

Before I got two steps, she snagged my arm. "I was hoping we could be friends. You know, I mean, we're a lot alike." In the shadowy light of the depot, she looked younger than ever. Young and well-scrubbed and sad. "I don't want you to get into trouble. Whatever it is, you've got your whole life ahead of you. It won't be worth it. Honest."

"Take care of yourself," I said, and leaned over and kissed her.

She grabbed me again and pulled me close and said, "I got in a little trouble once myself. It's no fun. Believe me."

I touched her cheek gently and then I set off walking quickly into the darkness.

Armstrong was a pretty typical midwestern town, four blocks of retail area, a fading brick grade school and junior high, a small public library with a white stone edifice, a court house, a Chevrolet dealership and many blocks of small white frame houses that all looked pretty much the same in the early morning gloom. You could see frost rimed on the windows and lonely gray smoke twisting up from the chimneys. As I walked, my heels crunched ice. Faint streetlight threw everything into deep shadow. My breath was silver.

A dog joined me for a few blocks and then fell away. Then I spotted a police cruiser moving slowly down the block. I jumped behind a huge oak tree, flattening myself against the rough bark so the cops couldn't see me. They drove right on past, not even glancing in my direction.

The address I wanted was a ranch house that sprawled over the west end of a cul-de-sac. A sweet little red BMW was parked in front of the two-stall garage and a huge satellite dish antenna was discreetly hidden behind some fir trees. No lights shone anywhere.

I went around back and worked on the door. It didn't take me long to figure out that Kenny had gotten himself one of those infra-red security devices. I tugged on my gloves, cut a fist-size hole in the back door window, reached in and unlocked the deadbolt, and then pushed the door open. I could see one of the small round infra-red sensors pointing down from the ceiling. Most fool burglars wouldn't even think to look for it and they'd pass right through the beam and the alarm would go off instantly.

I got down on my haunches and half-crawled until I was well past the eye of the infra-red. No alarm had sounded. I went up three steps and into the house.

The dark kitchen smelled of spices, paprika and cinnamon and thyme. Dawn had always been a good and careful cook.

The rest of the house was about what I'd expect. Nice but not expensive furnishing, lots of records and videotapes, and even a small bumper pool table in a spare room that doubled as a den. Nice, sure, but nothing that would attract attention. Nothing that would appear to have been financed by six hundred thousand dollars in bank robbery money.

And then the lights came on.

At first I didn't recognize the woman. She stood at the head of a dark narrow hallway wearing a loose cotton robe designed to conceal her weight.

The flowing dark hair is what misled me. Dawn had always been a blonde. But dye and a gain of maybe fifteen pounds had changed her appearance considerably. And so had time. It hadn't been a friend to her.

She said, "I knew you'd show up someday, Chet."

"Where's Kenny?"

"You want some coffee?"

"You didn't answer my question."

She smiled her slow, sly smile. "You didn't answer mine, either."

She led us into the kitchen where a pot of black stuff stayed warm in a Mr. Coffee. She poured two cups and handed me one of them.

"You came here to kill us, didn't you?" she said.

"You were my wife. And we were supposed to split everything three ways. But Kenny got everything—you and all the dough. And I did six years in the slam."

"You could have turned us in."

I shook my head, "I have my own way of settling things."

She stared at me. "You look great, Chet. Prison must have agreed with you."

"I just kept thinking of this night. Waiting."

Her mouth tightened and for the first time her blue eyes showed traces of fear. Softly, she said, "Why don't we go in the living room and talk about it."

I glanced at my wristwatch. "I want to see Kenny."

"You will. Come on now."

So I followed her into the living room. I had a lot ahead of me. I wanted to kill them and then get back on the bus. While I'd be eating up the miles on a Greyhound, the local cops would be looking for a local killer. If only my gun hadn't dropped out and Polly seen it. But I'd have to worry about that later.

We sat on the couch. I started to say something but then she took my cup from me and set it on the glass table and came into my arms.

She opened her mouth and kissed me dramatically.

But good sense overtook me. I held her away and said, "So while we're making out, Kenny walks in and shoots me. Is that it?"

"Don't worry about Kenny. Believe me."

And then we were kissing again. I was embracing ghosts, ancient words whispered in the back seats of cars when we were in high school, tender promises made just before I left for Nam. Loving this woman had always been punishment because you could never believe her, never trust her, but I'd loved her anyway.

I'd just started to pull away when I heard the floor creak behind me and I saw Kenny. Even given how much I hated this man—and how many long nights I'd laid on my prison bunk dreaming of vengeance—I had to feel embarrassed. If Kenny had been his old self, I would have relished the moment. But Kenny was different now. He was in a wheelchair and his entire body was twisted and crippled up like a cerebral palsy victim. A small plaid blanket was thrown across his legs.

He surprised me by smiling. "Don't worry, Chet. I've seen Dawn entertain a lot of men out here in the living room before."

"Spare him the details," she said. "And spare me, too, while you're at it."

"Bitch," he whispered loud enough for us to hear.

He wheeled himself into the living room. The chair's electric motor whirred faintly as he angled over to the fireplace. On his way, he said, "You didn't wait long, Chet. You've only been out two weeks. You never did have much patience."

You could see the pain in his face when he moved.

I tried to say something but I just kept staring at this man who was now a cripple. I didn't know what to say.

"Nice set-up, huh?" Kenny said as he struck a stick match on the stone of the fireplace. With his hands twisted and gimped the way they were, it wasn't easy. He got his smoke going and said, "She tell you what happened to me?"

I looked at Dawn. She dropped her gaze. "No," I said.

He snorted. The sound was bitter. "She was doin' it to me just the way she did it to you. Right, bitch?"

She sighed then lighted her own cigarette. "About six months after we ran out on you with all the money, I grabbed the strongbox and took off."

Kenny smirked. "She met a sailor. A fucking sailor, if you can believe it."

"His name was Fred," she said. "Anyway, me and Fred had all the bank robbery cash—there was still a couple hundred thousand left—when Kenny here came after us in that red Corvette he always wanted. He got right up behind us but it was pouring rain and he skidded out of control and slammed into a tree."

He finished the story for me. "There was just one problem, right, bitch? You had the strongbox but you didn't know what was inside. Her and the sailor were going to have somebody use tools on the lock I'd put on it. They saw me pile up my 'Vette but they kept on going. But later that night when they blew open the strongbox and found out that I'd stuffed it with old newspapers, the sailor beat her up and threw her out. So she came back to me 'cause she just couldn't stand to be away from 'our' money. And this is where she's been all the time you were in the slam. Right here waitin' for poor pitiful me to finally tell her where I hid the loot. Or die. They don't give me much longer. That's what keeps her here."

"Pretty pathetic story, huh?" she said. She got up and went over to the small wet bar. She poured three drinks of pure Jim Beam and brought them over to us. She gunned hers in a single gulp and went right back for another.

"So she invites half the town in so she can have her fun while I vegetate in my wheelchair." Now it was his turn to down his whiskey. He hurled the glass into the fireplace. A long, uneasy silence followed.

I tried to remember the easy friendship the three of us had enjoyed back when we were in high school, before Kenny and I'd been in Nam, and before the three of us had taken up bank robbery for a living. Hard to believe we'd ever liked each other at all.

Kenny's head dropped down then. At first I thought he might have passed out but then the choking sound of dry tears filled the room and I realized he was crying.

"You're such a wimp," she said.

And then it was her turn to smash her glass into the fireplace.

I'd never heard two people go at each other this way. It was degrading.

He looked up at me. "You stick around here long enough, Chet, she'll make a deal with you. She'll give you half the money if you beat me up and make me tell you where it is."

I looked over at her. I knew what he said was true.

"She doesn't look as good as she used to—she's kind of a used car now instead of a brand-new Caddy—but she's still got some miles left on her. You should hear her and some of her boyfriends out here on the couch when they get goin'."

She started to say something but then she heard me start to laugh.

"What the hell's so funny?"

I stood up and looked at my watch. I had only ten minutes left to get back to the depot.

Kenny glanced up from his wheelchair. "Yeah, Chet, what's so funny?"

I looked at them both and just shook my head. "It'll come to you. One of these days. Believe me."

And with that, I left.

She made a play for my arm and Kenny sat there glowering at me but I just kept on walking. I had to hurry.

The cold, clean air not only revived me, it seemed to purify me in some way. I felt good again, whole and happy now that I was outdoors.

~ ~ ~ ~ ~

The bus was dark and warm. Polly had brought a bag of popcorn along. "You almost didn't make it," she said as the bus pulled away from the depot.

In five minutes we were rolling into countryside again. In farmhouses lights were coming on. In another hour, it would be dawn.

"You took it, didn't you?" I said.

"Huh?"

"You took it. My gun."

"Oh. Yes. I guess I did. I didn't want you to do anything foolish."

Back there at Kenny's I'd reached into my jacket pocket for the .38 and found it gone. "How'd you do it? You were pretty slick."

"Remember I told you I'd gotten into a little trouble? Well, an uncle of mine taught me how to be a pickpocket and so for a few months I followed in his footsteps. Till Sheriff Baines arrested me one day."

"I'm glad you took it."

She looked over at me in the darkness of the bus and grinned. She looked like a kid. "You really didn't want to do it, did you?"

"No," I said, staring out the window at the midwestern night. I thought of them back there in the house, in a prison cell they wouldn't escape till death. No, I hadn't wanted to shoot anybody at all. And, as things had turned out, I hadn't had to either. Their punishment was each other.

"We're really lucky we met each other, Chet."

"Yeah," I said, thinking of Dawn and Kenny again. "You don't know how lucky we are."

MOONCHASERS

"There are men who can lust with parts of themselves. Only their brain or their hearts burn and then not completely. There are others, still more fortunate, who are like the filaments of an incandescent lamp. They burn fiercely, yet nothing is destroyed."

—Nathanael West, *The Day of the Locust*

For my son Joe from the old man with love and pride
And for Robert Mitchum

1

Yes, sir, it was just about the best sort of summer you could ask for, when you were fifteen, that is, and it was 1958 and you were living in Somerton, Iowa, which is forty miles due east of Waterloo, where just a month earlier I'd seen Buddy Holly, Little Richard and Gene Vincent and his Blue Caps all perform at the Electric Light Ballroom.

Of course, neither Barney nor I let on that it was a good summer because if there is one thing that Barney and I liked to do it was bitch about living our lives out in Somerton. Pop. 16,438. There were maybe five pretty girls our age, none of whom would have a damn thing to do with us, and one mean and muscular seventeen-year-old named Maynard whom Barney and I had in some way offended (if Maynard wanted to be pissed at anybody, it should have been his parents for giving him that name). Fortunately for us, Hamblin's Rexall had a good supply of science fiction magazines and Gold Medal suspense novels and Ace Double Books. And the Garden Theater likewise had the usual good supply of movies with monsters in them. And Robert Mitchum.

That was the big thing Barney and I had in common. Sure we liked *Amazing* and *Fantastic* with all those nifty Valigursky covers, and sure we liked all those teen monster movies with all those Southern California bikini girls, and sure we thought that Marlon Brando and Montgomery Clift and the late James Dean were really cool, but the coolest guy of all was Robert Mitchum. The Garden brought back *Thunder Road* for a week and Barney and I went four days running. And the same for when the Garden brought back *Night of the Hunter* and *Blood on the Moon.* We were there because Mitch was there.

Anyway, that's sort of the picture of how things were in our lives before that hot August night when Barney and I walked along the railroad tracks out on the east edge of town, smoking on a fresh contraband package of Lucky Strikes, and sipping at two ice-dripping eight-cent bottles of Pepsi.

We'd pretty much decided that this was going to be the night we broke into the abandoned warehouse and found out just what was in there. According to most of the little lads in Somerton, the warehouse was home to various kinds of spooks. Older kids, who didn't just have driver's ed learner permits like ours, took a different slant. They said that the migrant workers from the next town over snuck their daughters in there at night and ran a whorehouse that put all others to shame.

In the moonlight, the railroad tracks shone silver for a quarter of a mile. The air smelled of hot creosote from the railroad ties that had baked all day in the sun. Between tracks and warehouse was a winding creek, along the dark banks of which you could smell summer mud and hear throaty frogs and see the silhouette of the willow tree bent and weeping.

"We're gonna get our butts kicked," Barney said, "if they catch us."

Of course that's what Barney said before just about everything we ever did. Everything that was any fun, anyway.

But I didn't like to think uncharitable thoughts about Barney because he had it rough. His father had tried and failed in business several times. The family was pretty poor. And whenever his father quit going to his Alcoholics Anonymous meetings, he always got drunk for two or three days and beat up Barney's mom pretty bad.

A couple of times somebody had to call the chief of police and have him come over.

The warehouse was this big corrugated steel building with

loading docks on both the west and east sides. There was a large window on the north end revealing the shadowy space where the office had been.

The window had long ago been smashed out, of course, and most of the exterior warehouse walls bore the chalk scrawlings of various lads—*Class of '58, BG + FH, I Luv Judy!* The kind of stuff, I'm told by my army corporal and former Eagle Scout brother, Gerald, is proof positive of immature minds.

So there it sat like a big monument left behind by some alien species. When the warehouse was first closed down, back in '56, kids of every age trooped out there to smash windows and hurl rocks at the steel walls, which were pretty obliging about making neat sounds when the rocks struck. But then the kids got sort of bored with the place and quit coming. Now they mostly spent time at the abandoned grain elevator on the west edge of town. The elevator was more fun because it was more dangerous. One kid had already fallen off the interior ladder and broken a leg and an arm. It was only a matter of time till some poor overenthusiastic kid got killed in there and so the place had developed a certain dark aura that the warehouse could never match.

As we were climbing through the office window, Barney said, "You don't really think there are ghosts and stuff in here, do ya?"

I just shook my head. Barney just kept moving.

We spent the first ten minutes inside walking around the front of the place and stepping on crunchy little rat droppings. It was pretty neat, actually, sort of like in those movies where they drop the atomic bomb and the few survivors walk around inside empty grocery stores and places like that and take everything they want.

Of course, there wasn't much to take inside this warehouse.

I remember my dad, who owned the haberdashery in town, saying once that the two guys who built this warehouse had no head for business, which was why they went broke so fast. And their creditors must have cleaned them out because when we went through the door leading to the back, all we saw was this huge empty concrete floor with moonlight splashing through six dirty, broken windows.

"This is where I'm going to bring Janie Mills," Barney said, "and screw her brains out."

"Good idea," I said, "and I'll double with you and bring

Sharon Waggoner."

Barney had the grace to laugh. Janie Mills and Sharon Wag-goner were the two most stuck-up girls in our class. They wouldn't come out here with us if we had them at gunpoint.

The place smelled of dust and heat and rain-soaked wood and truck oil and a turd-clogged toilet somewhere that hadn't been flushed in a long time.

"Hey!" Barney shouted suddenly.

And then laughed his ass off when the word echoed back to us through the moonlight and shadows.

"Hey!" I shouted, too, and listened as my own sound like-wise began repeating itself.

This was another Somerton bust and we both knew it, which was why we'd both been shouting. Because there was nothing else to do. Because, as usual in Somerton, nothing was as it had been advertised. There were no spooks, no ghosts; and there were most definitely no voluptuous whores eager to free us from the prison of our virginity.

Barney took the Lucky Strike pack from the pocket of my short-sleeved shirt (we traded off the privilege of carrying the pack) and took a book of matches from his own shirt and lit up and that was when I saw the door move.

The door was way at the other end of the wide, empty ware-house floor, some kind of closet, I guessed. Barney's match had pointed my eye in that direction and that was how I came to no-tice the partially open door move a few inches closer to the frame.

Or I thought I had, anyway. Maybe, because I was so bored, I just wanted to think that something like that had happened.

"Let's go," Barney said. "We still got time to hit Rexall for a cherry Coke."

I nudged him in the ribs and nodded toward the end of the moonpainted floor.

"Huh?" he said out loud.

I whispered to him, "Somebody's in the closet up there."

He whispered back. "Bullshit."

"Bullshit yourself. I saw that door move."

Barney squinted his eyes and looked down the length of floor. He stared a long time and then whispered, "I didn't see it move."

"Somebody's in that closet."

And this time when he looked at me, I saw the beginnings

of fear in his eyes.

You're in a shadowy, empty building on the edge of no-where and you suddenly realize that not too far away is some-body or something lurking in a dark closet. Probably watching every move you make.

"Let's go," Barney whispered.

I shook my head. "I want to find out who's in there."

Barney gulped. "You're crazy."

"No, I'm just bored."

"You really gonna walk up there?"

I nodded and started walking.

At first it was sort of a lark. I could sense Barney behind me, watching with a kind of awe. That crazy sumbitch Tom was going to walk right up to that closet door, just the way Mitch would, and back here stood that A-1 chicken Barney. He would positively be ashamed of himself.

It was a great feeling, it really was. For the first twenty steps or so anyway.

Then I felt this sickening feeling in my stomach and bowels and a cold shudder went through me.

Hell, I wasn't brave. I was just some dumb-ass fifteen-year-old from Somerton, Iowa, and if I really believed that somebody was in that closet then I should turn around and get the hell out of here.

"I'll tell you, you're one ballsy guy and I mean that," Barney said. And then I knew I would go over and open that closet door because Barney's admiration was just too much to lose.

Besides, I was starting to convince myself that I had just imagined the door moving anyway.

We reached the metal door and I put my hand out and took the knob.

"God, Tom, you really gonna open it?"

For an answer, I yanked the door open.

And there, in the middle of the chill deep closet darkness, sitting with his back against the far wall, was a man holding in his left hand a big cop-style flashlight and in his right a big criminal-style pistol.

"God," Barney said.

"Anybody else with you?" the man said. And right away he looked sort of familiar but I wasn't sure why. He was a tall guy, a little on the beefy side, with a kind of handsome face and dark hair and the saddest eyes I'd ever seen on a man except for maybe my Uncle Pete when Doc Anderson told him that Aunt Clarice had only two months to live.

The guy was pointing the gun directly at me. Or so it seemed. "N-no, sir."

"How'd you boys find out about me?"

"We didn't find out about you, sir," I said. "I mean not till we got in the warehouse here."

He asked our names and we told him.

And then for the first time I saw him get all seized up and heard him give out with a hard little grunt, the way you do when somebody hits you in the stomach. Or when you're in an awful lot of pain.

He tried to sit up and still keep both his gun and his flash-light on us but he wasn't having an easy time of it. I knew right away it was because of the blood all over the side of his dirty white shirt, and the green pussy stuff that was all mixed up in it.

I'd seen enough gangster movies to know what was going on here, especially when I let my eyes wander over to the big canvas bag sitting maybe half a foot from him, just on the edge of the light.

"You going to kill us?" Barney said.

Which was just like something Barney would say.

The guy just looked at Barney and said, "You got any candy bars or anything like that on you?"

"No, sir."

"How about you?"

I shook my head.

The guy grimaced again. The pain must have been pretty bad. The smell sure was.

"Sir," Barney said. "I don't mean to be nosey or anything, but you look like you should see a doctor."

For the first time the guy smiled. And when he did, and just in the way he did, I realized who he looked like. "You know any doctors who'd be willing to come out here?"

"No, but we could help you into town to see Doctor Ander-son. He's real nice."

Barney was just jabbering, terrified.

"You boys know who I am?"

"I don't think so," I said.

"Danton's my name. Roy Danton. Yesterday in Des Moines there was a bank robbery. That was me and my brother. He set the whole thing up. We were careful not to hurt anybody but one of the guards there thought he saw a chance to stop us so he opened fire as we were leaving. He killed my brother and wounded me." The grimace again. "The whole state's looking for me by now." He let his eyes drift over to the money satchel. "Hell, I don't even know how much we got. And now I don't even care. With Mike dead, I mean."

There was this real long dusty silence in the closet with the guy just staring off and all and you could feel how sad he was about his brother.

"I'm sorry," Barney said. "About Mike, I mean. I've got a kid brother named Glenn and I'd sure feel bad if somebody shot him."

I didn't think it was the right time to point out that a lot of people in Somerton wanted the pleasure of shooting his obnoxious little brother, Glenn.

Danton looked us over again. You had the sense his mind was always working hard, always trying to figure things out. "You boys have probably never met anybody like me, have you?"

"No, sir," Barney said.

"Your folks are probably real respectable, aren't they?"

"Yessir," Barney said.

"And nobody in the family's ever been in any serious trouble, have they?"

"Except for my older brother Kenny," Barney said. "He got arrested for shooting off firecrackers the night before it was legal."

Danton laughed softly. "They give him the electric chair?"

"No, sir."

"I envy the hell out of you boys."

"Us?"

"That's right, Barney. You. It's summer and you don't have anything to think about except how you're going to spend all these long, lazy days, and what movie you're going to see downtown, and maybe what girl you hope you run into out at the swimming pool." His gaze was faraway now, as if what he was describing was more real than him being in this closet with a bullet in his side and a satchel of cash near his hand and two smalltown hayseeds standing in front of him.

"I never had that," he said. "But nobody's to blame for how I turned out except me. I don't hold with all the blame people put on each other. When you do something wrong, there's only one person to blame and that's yourself."

"Your folks still alive?" Barney said.

But Danton didn't say any more. He just grimaced once from the pain and then sat there and took a few deep shuddering breaths.

I could see how weak he was. The flashlight was shaking a little and the gun looked as if it was about to fall from his hand.

"How far from town are we?" Danton said.

"Mile and a half or so," I said.

"You boys interested in making a few dollars?"

Barney said, "Huh?"

"Getting me some things. A little food and a little medicine." Barney looked over at me and I looked over at him right back. Him being my best friend and all it was easy to tell that he was thinking the same thing I was. This guy had to be really crazy, letting us walk right out of here with the understanding that we'd get him some stuff and bring it back.

What we'd do, of course, was race back to town and run up the four wide steps of the one-story redbrick police station and tell McCorkindale, the night-duty desk cop, just where he could find himself a bank robber.

"Sure, we'd be glad to do that," I said. "And you wouldn't even have to pay us."

Danton laughed. "You must really think I'm dumb." We didn't say anything.

"I let you boys walk out of here and you go right to the cops. And then the cops come back here with shotguns and surround this place and then tomorrow morning, I find myself in jail. Where I'll be for the rest of my life probably."

Danton raised his eyes. "How old are you boys?"

"Fifteen and a half," Barney said. "I am, anyway. Tom is fifteen and a quarter."

"You two ever known anybody who killed himself?"

Barney gulped. "No, sir."

"How about you, Tom?"

"I guess not."

Danton stared at me with those sad eyes of his and all I could think of was Uncle Pete and how he came over late one night to tell Dad, who is his brother, about Aunt Clarice, and how he just sat in the recliner in the living room and cried like a baby.

"Well. I'm going to leave it up to you boys. How I'm going to handle things, I mean." He nodded to the bank satchel. "Barney, you come over here and dig out some money."

"Yessir."

Barney went over and knelt down. Being out of flashlight range, he worked mostly in the dark but a minute or so later he shoved his hand into the range of the flashlight. His tight fist was crammed full of green cash, bills sticking out every which way there were so many.

"That should do it," Danton said.

Barney stood up, real unsteady on his feet, and came back over next to me.

"You have a good memory, Tom?"

"Pretty good."

"See if you can remember this, then." And he sailed right into this long list of stuff like gauze and boric acid and bandages, things to take care of his wound, and food, a lot of stuff with sugar in it and then hot dogs because, he said, he could eat them cold. And at the end, he added, "And get me some kind of writing tablets and some envelopes." Pain tightened his face again. "I want to write my brother's, wife, Peg, a letter. They've got a six-month-old kid and I figure Peg could use some money." He nodded to the satchel.

"We'll take this money and get what you want and then come right back."

And then Danton laughed again and it was spooky, crazy laughter really, like the kind madmen always laugh in science fiction movies after they've created a monster or something, except in Danton's case it was real.

"Kid, I wish you could see how obvious you are. You just can't wait to get your ass out of here and go to the cops, can you?"

Barney gulped but didn't say anything.

"And you know what? I'd probably do the same thing if I was you. In fact, I'm sure I would." Then he quit smiling. "But you're going to have to make a real adult decision, both of you boys. I don't want to go to prison. I really don't. I'd never survive in there and I know it. I want to get up to Alaska where I've got a cousin and try living the way regular people do, the way I've never been able to before. That's why I need those medical supplies and that food. It'll at least get me going again."

He stopped talking. He just stared at us a long dusty sad

time and then he raised the gun and put the barrel of it right to his temple and said, "If you bring the cops back, I'll end it right here. And that isn't a bluff. And I'm sorry to put it on you like this but I don't have any choices left in my life. I'm leaving it up to you to decide."

Then there was just the dust and shadow and quiet of the closet and the sad (and I saw now) sort of crazy blue eyes of Roy Danton.

"You mean we can go?" Barney said.

"You can go."

"Just like that?"

"Just like that."

"Just walk right out of here?"

"Just walk right out of here."

"And you won't shoot us in the back?"

"And I won't shoot you in the back."

"Jeez," Barney said.

We turned around and left the closet and walked the moonlit length of warehouse floor, rat droppings crunching beneath our feet, without saying a word.

And then we started running like hell.

Five minutes later we were on the railroad ties and smoking Lucky Strikes and hurrying back to town. There was an owl in the night, and phantom clouds across the quarter moon, and a far rumbling train we could feel trembling in the tracks themselves.

"You think we'll get a reward?" Barney said.

"Probably."

"What'll you do with yours?"

"Save up for a car."

"You think Clarence will let you have your own car when you're sixteen?"

We always referred to our fathers by their first names. Clarence and George.

"Sure. Wouldn't George let you have one?"

"Not since Kenny knocked up his girlfriend in the backseat of that old Plymouth George bought him for his birthday."

"But Kenny and Donna are married."

"Now they're married. But they weren't then. And that's what George got so pissed about. Kenny was supposed to go on to college. But now he's working at the factory and he's got two lads and he isn't even twenty-one yet."

"Well, I'm pretty sure Clarence'll let me have a car."

We walked a little more, both of us tossing rocks still warm from sunlight down the silver beams of tracks.

"You know who he looks like?" Barney said.

"Who who looks like?"

"Roy Danton. Who he looks like?"

And then we stopped. We were just at the junction where the tracks swung eastward and went around Somerton.

By now my clothes were stuck to me because it was not only a hot summer, it was a humid summer.

"Yeah," I said. "I know."

"Robert Mitchum."

I nodded.

"That's the only thing that sort of bothers me about turning him in," Barney said. "It's kind of like turning in Mitch."

We just stared at each other for awhile, just a couple of smalltown teenagers, neither one of us wanting to say what we felt, and consequently not saying anything at all.

We left the tracks and walked into town. The houses started right away, neat little blocks of them, living rooms all aglow with black-and-white picture tubes, an occasional Elvis record on the air from an upstairs bedroom window, a few front porch swings squeaking in the darkness.

"You see the way he made those faces when the pain got him?" Barney said.

"Yeah."

"We're doing him a favor, turning him in."

By now we reached the town square. The shops and stores that surrounded it stayed open till nine because it was Friday night and night was about the only time farmers in the nearby towns could get in here.

The Dairy Queen was open, and so was Hamblin's Pharmacy, and Henry's Hawkeye Supermarket, and the big Shell station where they had four bays and where most of the drag-strip guys took their cars, and Seldon's International TV (he took a lot of kidding about that "International" bit believe me) and the Western Auto store and the Earle's Cigars and Billiards and four taverns so noisy they sounded like they were having jukebox wars inside or something.

People sat everywhere, on park benches and car hoods and curbsides, fanning themselves with paper fans of the sort that the funeral home gives you at wakes, with Jesus on one side and a message (plus the address and phone number) from the funeral parlor on the other.

The night smelled of cigar smoke and beer and heat and summer lightning and perfume. And there were old people and young people and pretty people and ugly people and rich people and poor people and people who loved each other and people who hated each other all caught up in those smells.

And Barney and I just stood on the corner across from the red brick building with the big Police sign over the double-wide front door. . .just stood and stared in through the front windows at the uniformed men on night duty.

"You really think he looks like Mitch?" Barney said.

"A little. Not a lot. But a little."

"We'd really get our butts kicked if we didn't turn him in."

"I know."

"You really think he'll kill himself if the cops come?"

"What am I, a swami? How would I know?"

But right away Barney got that patented hangdog look in his eyes, the one that makes you feel bad even when Barney's at fault, and I said, in a lot more friendly way, "I guess I'm afraid he would. Kill himself, I mean."

"Mitch would kill himself."

"You think so?"

"I know so. No prison bars for him. I think he said that in one of his movies."

"In several of his movies, actually."

"Mitch would definitely do it. Definitely."

I sighed. "I wish he'd killed somebody."

"Huh?"

"Roy Danton. I wish he'd killed somebody."

"Why?"

" 'Cause then it'd be easier to turn him in."

"Yeah?"

"Sure. Robbery's pretty bad but it's not like killing anybody."

"I never thought of it that way, I guess."

"So even though he's a bad guy he isn't a real bad guy. You know?"

Barney shook his head. "I don't want to turn him in either, Tom, but we gotta. We just gotta."

"I know."

"So let's get it over with."

The police station was real bright inside. And noisy. Phones were ringing and there was some kind of teletype deal in the corner and it was clacking away and three uniformed men were rushing around, their rubber heels squeaking on the tile floors the way nurse's shoes do in hospitals.

It was so cold from the air-conditioning that I nearly froze on the spot.

We walked up to the front desk where Sergeant McCorkindale normally sits only it wasn't Sergeant McCorkindale, it was the new recruit named Meeks who wore glasses and was pudgy and was already getting bald.

"Hi, boys."

"Hi," I said.

"Help you with something?"

"We need to talk to Sergeant McCorkindale."

"You don't look like fishes to me."

"Huh?" Barney said.

"Onliest people talking to Sergeant McCorkindale right about now would be the carp or the blue gill. He's up to Kahler's Lake fishing for two days."

And right then I saw Cushing coming out of his office down the hall.

"Well," he said, "look who's here. My two favorite little girls."

I suppose every town has a man like Cushing, a real slick operator that all the ladies think is cute, and the kind of cruel and cunning man that other men are always sucking up to out of plain undignified fear.

Clarence always said that he used to feel sorry for Cushing, the way Cushing's parents were both killed in that automobile accident when Cushing was just ten. But Clarence had long ago forgotten all about the accident and concentrated on what a jerk Cushing had grown up into.

Cushing was a decorated marine in Korea. He got home late from the war because of an injury to his leg and they had a parade just for him because not only was he a wounded war hero he'd also been the best high school quarterback this valley has ever seen.

He went six foot easy and if his gut was a little loose now and there was a little fleshy pad beneath the line of chin and jaw, he was still an impressive man, always dressed nattily in one of the many suits Bruce Harcourt over at Harcourt's Men

Shop gave him a discount on, and always cracking his chewing gum with a certain malicious delight. He had black black eyes that shone with a very strange light.

The summer previous Barney and I had broken into the deserted high school out near the highway. Assistant Police Chief (which generally meant the man who was in charge at night) Stephen B. Cushing happened to be cruising by at the very same time we were crawling in one of the windows.

And parked his car. And came in after us.

There are a lot of stories going around about what happened that night, some of them pretty juicy of course, but our version, and after all we were there, is pretty simple: he came in after us and we ran away. He called for us to stop but, given what we knew about Cushing we were afraid to stop, and so we climbed out of the building again and took off running.

Cushing hadn't been so lucky. He'd crawled out the window after us but instead of hitting the ground running, he'd simply hit the ground, falling one story to hard pavement and breaking his arm in the process.

I don't need to tell you how bad it looks for a cop to chase two punk teenagers and have those punk teenagers get away. But for a tough marine and former football hero to break his arm in the process—

My father, the respectable haberdasher, was not happy that his son had gotten into trouble with the law. I was grounded for two weeks, shorn of allowance, and ordered to leave the living room every time something good came on TV (I even had to miss the *Maverick* show where they made fun of *Gunsmoke*).

But even given his embarrassment about his son having to appear in juvenile court, my father at dinner one night broke into a grin and said, "You should see Cushing these days, dear. He won't look any of us merchants in the eye, and he's cut out his swaggering entirely. I'm not saying I think what Tom here did was right but maybe this was the only way to cut Cushing down a peg or two." Cushing used to come in all the stores and let it be known in various ways that as assistant police chief, he expected favors and discounts from the men he was sworn to protect. The merchants didn't like it but you didn't say anything against Cushing in this town. Not without Cushing getting even, anyway.

So now here we stood one year later and Cushing was still referring to us as "girls," which he did loudly whenever he saw us on the street. He couldn't get real mean with us, the way he got mean with that Negro who ended up in the hospital a few years back—I mean, haberdasher may not sound like much to you but in a town the size of Somerton, a haberdasher has some influence and Cushing had to be careful—but he could and did harass us whenever he got the chance.

Cushing watched us with his strange black eyes as Meeks said, "These boys were asking for Sergeant McCorkindale."

"They were?" Cushing grinned. "You girls come in to confess to something?"

Meeks looked uncomfortable when Cushing called us girls. He kind of wriggled and waggled around in his desk chair.

"They were real polite," he said. "I mean, they weren't causing any trouble or anything."

"That's the nice thing about little girls," Cushing said. "They're usually well-behaved."

He took out a pack of Cavaliers and tamped one down on the pack and then put it to his mouth and took out this really nice silver Zippo.

"So how can I help you two?" He apparently had other things to do. Now he sounded as if he just wanted to rush us out of here.

Barney's gaze strayed over to mine. We had the same thought. We couldn't tell Cushing about Roy Danton because if Danton didn't kill himself, Cushing would be glad to do it for him.

"He said he'd help us with this term paper we're gonna write next year," I said.

"Yeah, about the police."

Cushing grinned. He couldn't let an opportunity like this go by. "So you nice little girls are also A students, huh?"

A students? God, Barney and I together barely got passing grades. If they'd given courses in Ray Bradbury, Edgar Rice Burroughs and Robert Mitchum, we would have been hailed as geniuses. But unfortunately our school board was hopelessly square.

Cushing lit his cigarette. He was still looking us over. You got the impression that he'd have liked to start beating on us right then and there.

But all he said was, "Why don't you girls go on home? We're busy."

And with that, he turned around and went back to his office.

Meeks said, kind of sheepish, "He just gets in a bad mood sometimes."

And right then I liked the hell out of Meeks because he was the same kind of geek we were, fist fodder for all the Cushings in the world.

"Thanks, Meeks," I said.

"Yeah," Barney said. "Thanks."

When we were outside in the steaming night again, Barney said, "You know, if God gave me permission to kill three people you know who I'd name?"

"Cushing and who else?"

"Cushing, Cushing and Cushing."

I laughed. "Me, too."

Barney nodded to Hamblin's Pharmacy down the block. "We'd better hurry up if we're going to get Danton that stuff."

"I was thinking," I said.

"Yeah?"

"I'll bet if Danton didn't have that bullet in him, he could kick the living shit right out of Cushing."

"With one hand tied behind his back."

"And blindfolded."

"Let's go," Barney said, "and get that stuff."

"Yeah," I laughed. "Like good little girls."

Hamblin's was where I first read Ray Bradbury and Theodore Sturgeon and Robert Bloch and John D. MacDonald and Mickey Spillane so even given the fact that Mr. Hamblin, the shriveled-up little guy who owns it is something of a grouch, I'll always like the place. There's a soda fountain with twelve stools where one day Patty Lake accidentally leaned against my arm with one of her breasts and I fell in love with her for the whole school year; and the magazine stand where *Popular Photography* once had a nude shot of a very pretty young woman, and she wasn't even African; and the sacred wire paperback rack that kind of creaks when you turn it around; and the sandwich board where Ina makes the most incredible tuna salad sandwiches I've ever had, no offense Mom.

I was hoping Becky Martin would be working, Becky being not only the tallest girl in junior class but the most beautiful, too, reminding me a lot of Dana Wynter in *Invasion of the Body Snatchers*, who even two years later I still had a sort of crush on.

But Becky wasn't working, Hamblin himself was.

He was up on a stepladder putting boxes of storage away. I guess it was a sign of our growing maturity that neither Barney nor I smirked or poked each other when we saw it was boxes of Kotex he was putting away.

"Help you, boys?"

"Need some things, Mr. Hamblin," I said.

"Be right down."

A few minutes later he was behind the counter, this rabbity bald little guy who always reminded me of Andy Clyde who was Hopalong Cassidy's sidekick in the movies, and he got the first two items, bandages and gauze, and set them up but then he stopped all of a sudden, wiping his hands on his clean white apron and said, "Boric acid?"

"Yes, Mr. Hamblin."

"This for your folks?"

"Huh?" Barney said.

"Your folks. Is this stuff for your folks?"

"Yeah," I lied. "Yeah. My dad fell down and—"

"—broke his leg," Barney said.

Barney could sometimes be real dumb. My dad Clarence came into Hamblin's at least once a day. And when he wasn't sporting a broken leg—

"At least we think it's broken," I said. "You never can tell with a broken leg. One minute it's broken and the next it's—"

"And the next it's what?" Hamblin said.

"Huh?" Barney said.

By now Hamblin was watching us very carefully. "You're up to something, aren't you?"

"Huh?"

"Your pop don't have a broken leg any more than I do, does he?"

"Huh?"

"I ain't talkin' to you, Barney. I'm talkin' to Tom."

"No, sir," I said, "he doesn't have a broken leg. We're just getting this stuff so we can learn first aid."

"You two troublemakers learn first aid? For what? So you can patch up all the people you play jokes on?"

"We don't do that anymore, Mr. Hamblin."

"No, sir, we don't," Barney said.

"We want to join the Civil Air Patrol and one of the requirements is that you learn first aid."

"Civil Air Patrol, huh?"

"Yessir," I said. Actually, I had a cousin over in Cedar Rapids who was in the Civil Air Patrol, and he got up before dawn three mornings a week and went out to this little office on top of the broadcast booth at the football stadium and scanned the sky with his binoculars. He was supposed to be looking for Russian bombers that had somehow gotten through our radar but what he mostly saw was UFOs. According to him there were a lot more UFOs than most people realized.

"I'm going to give you boys this stuff but if I find out that you pulled any practical jokes on anybody tonight—"

"We don't do stuff like that anymore," I said. "We're in high school now."

We ordered six more items, all medical-type stuff, and Hamblin slammed each one down as he set it on the glass top of the display case.

He put it all in a paper bag and then without thinking I opened my fist, the one I had all the new green money inside of, and then the money all fluttered to the ground.

"God!" Barney said. And we were both on the floor picking it up.

I kept looking up at Hamblin. He kept staring at all the fifties and twenties in disbelief.

"Where'd you boys get money like that?"

"Huh?" Barney said.

"Savings," I said. "I've been saving my Christmas money for the past five years and here it is."

Which he didn't believe at all, of course. Not at all.

I took a twenty and paid him but he took it without looking at it, his eyes still fixed on all the other bills fanned out in my hand.

I stuffed the bills in my pocket and watched Hamblin go down to the cash register and punch the amounts up. The register bell dinged when the cash drawer opened. Barney started to say something but I shook my head.

Hamblin came back with my change, counted it out and handed over the bag.

"Your pop at home, Tom?"

"Yes, sir." And that was all he said. But of course he didn't have to say any more at all.

I picked up the bag and Barney and I walked out.

Barney said, "Old man Hamblin's gonna call Clarence."

"I know."

"And Clarence is gonna have a lot of questions for you when you get home tonight."

"I know."

"And then the cops are gonna find out about Roy."

"I know."

"Sonofabitch," Barney said, "I don't want to see the cops get Roy, do you?"

"I sure don't," I said. We went inside Henry's Hawkeye Supermarket and did the grocery shopping fast, getting stuff Roy could eat without cooking, cold cuts and Roman Meal bread and Hostess cupcakes and freezing Pepsis from the cooler and then Barney said, "You go ask the checkout girl to help you find something."

"Huh?" I said, sounding just like Barney.

"Go on."

So I did. She was the only employee I could see anywhere in the store. She helped me find paper lunch sacks, which I made a big fuss about needing desperately. I kept wondering what Barney was doing.

Then he was back and said, "Well, I'd better be going, Tom. George wants me home early tonight."

So we all went up to the lanes and she checked us out and Barney kept giving me this look I'd never seen before and without knowing quite why, I knew I wanted to get the hell out of there and fast.

On the street, Barney said, "I got 'em."

"Got what?"

"Cigarettes. Three packs. Chesterfields. I couldn't reach anything else. That's why I had you distract her."

There's this older kid, Lem, who usually buys cigarettes for Barney and me. He's real poor and sort of ugly and everybody laughs at him but he's actually a good guy and he has a six-year run of *Amazing Stories* and we pay him a dime every time he buys us a pack. But we didn't have time for Lem tonight.

We walked fast going back to the warehouse. And we walked a little scared.

The warehouse was just as dark as we'd left it. We climbed in through the window and went over to the closet. "Roy, Roy, we're back."

The door was still open but there was no answer from the darkness inside. No flashlight clicked on, and there wasn't any noise, either, that cramped pained noise Roy made every time he breathed.

"Roy?" Barney said.

No answer.

"Here," I said, handing Barney the sack of groceries.

"What're you gonna do?"

"Go in there. See what's wrong."

We both stared at the dark, dark closet.

I took two, three steps into the closet. I couldn't see anything.

The dust made me sneeze. What I didn't need now was an allergy attack.

And then I tripped over something and fell forward, putting my hands up flat against the back wall.

I stood there panting, sweating.

And then I heard him. It was real faint but I knew right away it was him because of the labored, reedy sound of his breathing.

"You OK?" Barney said.

"Get in here," I said.

By the time Barney made it into the closet, I was on the floor picking up the flashlight and getting it clicked on and shining the beam in Roy's face.

If he hadn't been breathing, I would have thought he was dead. One afternoon a few years back Barney and I snuck into the back of the Devlin Mortuary and peeked at two corpses old man Devlin had laid out on gurneys. It was pretty gross, the pasty fish-belly color of the flesh, that is, and the way they didn't move at all. But then I guess when you think about it, that's what being dead means, that you don't move. Never again.

"Hold this," I said to Barney and gave him the flashlight. He kept the beam on Roy. I grabbed one of the Pepsis and got it open and put the bottle to Roy's lips and forced a little into his mouth.

It took him maybe a full minute but his eyes finally came open.

And then it was maybe another twenty seconds before he showed any signs of recognizing us. His wound was starting to take its toll. He looked real pale and there was a kind of crust on his lips and his sweat was cold-looking and greasy and, to be honest, he kind of smelled pretty bad. That's one thing movies can't give you—smell. When John Dillinger and Pretty Boy

Floyd and Al Capone die up there on the screen, the audience doesn't have any idea of how bad they smell.

"Hey, slugger," Roy said to me.

"We got your stuff," Barney said.

Roy raised his eyes to Barney. Even that seemed to take a lot of effort. "Thanks, kid."

So we fed him. Barney propped the light up on top of the money sack and sat on one side of Roy and I sat on the other. We put the grocery sack between us and took turns feeding him, the way we once fed a hawk. We were out in the woods one bright fall morning and we heard this big booming gun go off and it was this hunter of course and then we heard something fall into the bushes beside us and it was this hawk. He was all covered with blood and his dark eyes were frantic and wild and we were scared for him and scared for us because we didn't know what to do. And so we just grabbed all these colorful autumn leaves and made him this little bed and he just sat there staring up at us and we tried feeding him grass and we tried feeding him leaves and Barney even dug up some nightcrawlers with his fingers but the hawk wouldn't eat any of them and so all we could do was pet him and say soft little things to him like the soft little things you say to sick kitties and we knew he was dying and he knew he was dying and then he started twitching and shuddering and making these tiny scared noises and so Barney picked him up and put him in his lap, not caring about the blood or anything, and sort of started rocking him, back and forth, back and forth, back and forth till I had to say, very softly, "Barney, I think he's dead," and Barney looked down at the unmoving bird and said, "You're a fucking liar, Tom, he isn't dead!" but he was dead, of course, the poor bastard, and so I took him from Barney's hands, lifted him real gentle, and all the time I did Barney just kept screaming at me "You're a fucking liar, Tom! That's what your fucking problem is, buddy-boy! You're a fucking liar!" And I took the hawk down to the river bank where the earth was softer and I scooped out this grave with my hands and I put him in it and even all the way down to the blue run of river, even above the jays and the owls and the ravens, I could hear Barney crying.

So it was sort of like that now, feeding Roy. I mean, because he was so weak he couldn't even hold a piece of cold meat in his fingers.

"It's so goddamned cold in here," he said.

On the bank Time and Temperature sign downtown about twenty minutes earlier the Temp had been 89.

Barney fed him the Twinkies and the Pepsi and I fed him the Oscar Mayer sliced bologna and dutch loaf. And then we both took turns feeding him the Cracker Jacks which Barney had said would be a good way to finish off the meal.

When he was finished eating, Roy said, "You boys bring the bandages and stuff?"

"Yessir," I said. "We sure wouldn't forget something like that."

And right then, just the way he gave me this almost imperceptible nod of thanks, he looked a whole lot like Mitch.

"You boys think you can clean a wound?"

"Sure," Barney said.

I looked over at him and frowned. What the hell did we know about cleaning a wound?

"You just take the hydrogen peroxide and let it soak into some of those cotton balls I told you to get and then you just kind of clean the wound," Roy said.

We cleaned the wound.

I'll tell you, it was unlikely either Barney or I were ever going to get scholarships to medical school, the way we poured too much peroxide on the cotton balls and spilled the stuff all over, and the way we grimaced when we had to tear the blood-soaked part of his shirt away from the wound.

"Oh, God," Barney said when we finally got a good look at the wound. So much for a quiet, steady manner.

I wanted to say oh, God, too, but I just bit down real hard on my lip and took one of the soaked cotton balls and put it up to the wound.

Where the bullet had gone in everything was kind of scabby and you could see green pus leaking from the hole.

"Yeah." Eyes still closed.

"Would you really have killed yourself if we'd brought the law back?"

Roy thought a long moment. "You want an honest answer?"

"Uh-huh."

"I don't know if I got the guts to kill myself. I've thought about it all my life off and on, and one night when I caught my girlfriend in bed with this guy, I put a gun in my mouth but I couldn't pull the trigger. I wanted to and I think in a strange way she wanted me to, too, but I couldn't. I just couldn't."

And then he made a little grunting sound again and he took the cigarette from his mouth and jabbed it out on the floor. And then he gave out with this deep sigh that made his chest shudder.

"I don't think I can talk anymore, boys. I need some sleep."

"We'll be back tomorrow night, Roy," I said. "We'll bring you better food, too."

We left him, left the warehouse, and went back to town.

"You think he's gonna die?" Barney said, just as we started down the tracks.

"I don't know."

"Maybe we should turn him in. Maybe that really would be doing him a favor."

"What if he killed himself?"

"You heard him. He said he didn't have the guts."

"No, he said maybe he didn't have the guts. There's a difference."

We came to Spring Street, my street.

"Night," Barney said.

"Night," I said, and started to walk away.

When I was out of the streetlight and walking in the shadows, I heard Barney say, "You really think he looks like Mitch?" and I called back, "Yeah, I think he looks a lot like Mitch," and then we were both lost to our respective blocks, just footsteps now in the summer night.

Our house has a lot of gables and gingerbreading which should make it a Victorian, I guess, but my mom says it's not really a Victorian, at least not a regular one anyway. She always says this whenever somebody visits us for the first time and says "I just love Victorian houses." Most of us in the family just close our ears when she starts in.

Mom and Dad were in the living room with my eight-year-old sister, Debbie, watching the Late News with Earle Rochester who my dad says is a) a Democrat and b) a funny-looking gink who can't keep his opinions to himself ("See how he sneers whenever he says the name Eisenhower?" he always says to my mom, by which you can guess that Clarence is a Republican).

Dad was sitting in the leather recliner, which is his sacred chair, and wearing his Purple Passion (as Mom calls them) Bermuda shorts and a sport shirt.

The first thing he said to me was, "How come you were buying hydrogen peroxide and boric acid and gauze and stuff like that at Hamblin's tonight?"

He kept staring right at the TV, as if he wasn't missing a word, but asking me his question and then waiting for an answer.

I was ready for him. On the walk home I'd thought up a good one. "Barney and I were going to fix up this tackling dummy like it got all beaten up and then hang a sign on it that said 'This is what happens to bullies, Maynard' but Barney got scared and chickened out."

"You're just begging Maynard to come after you again," Clarence said.

I said good night to everybody and went upstairs. Things had gone much easier than I thought they would with Dad, I thought, as I went in the bathroom and peed and brushed my teeth and washed my face.

Mom had turned the fan on in my bedroom so it was going to be pretty good for sleeping.

I got the light on and stripped down to my underwear and picked up a new issue of *Imagination*, which had a lead novel by one of my favorite writers, Dwight V. Swain. I started to lie down when the door eased open and Dad stuck his head in.

"All right if I come in and talk a minute?

"Sure." So it wasn't over. And I knew what was coming.

He sat on the edge of the bed and looked at me. He's not a very big guy but boy can he scowl.

"I'm going to ask you one question, one time only and if you ever told the truth in your life, it had better be this time. You understand?"

"I understand."

"Hamblin said you had a lot of money on you. Twenties and fifties. Is that true?"

"Yessir."

"Care to tell me just where the hell you found that kind of money?"

"Out by the old fairgrounds." I'd been ready for that one, too.

"The fairgrounds?"

"Down by the crick. In a paper bag. Nearly three hundred dollars."

"Is that the truth?" I didn't feel good about lying to Clarence but I didn't have any choice.

"That's the truth."

"That money should have been turned over to the police."

"We tried. We went to the police station and asked for Sergeant McCorkindale but he went fishing for a couple of days."

"There are other policemen there."

"Yeah but then Cushing came in and started calling us girls and insulting us the way he usually does."

"Cushing's a jerk. You shouldn't pay any attention to him."

I shrugged. "I get tired of being insulted."

"I'm going to speak to the chief about that. I'll tell him I want Cushing to keep his tongue off my son."

I shook my head. "That'll just make it worse, Dad. Cushing'll get me alone somewhere and then make fun of me for siccing you on the chief."

He nodded. "I suppose you're right." He glanced around the room. "Where's the rest of the money?"

"In my jeans pocket."

"How much did you spend?"

"Fourteen bucks."

"I'll take the rest of it over to the chief in the morning."

"Fine."

He thought a minute and said, "I wish I could tell you that the next time Cushing says something to you I'd clean his clock for him."

"I know, Dad."

"I'm just not very tough."

"Neither am I, Dad. I guess it runs in the family."

"But guys like that usually get theirs in the end. One way or another, they get it."

2

The next morning around ten, I met Barney by the water fountain in the town square. As usual, a lot of the old men who play checkers all day long had pulled their green park benches up so they could be closer to the fountain. I've never figured that out. All these old-timers must have had a bad drought when they were lads because they sure do treat the fountain like somebody was going to sneak up and take it away.

The first thing Barney asked, his red hair brilliant in the hot August sun, his blue-and-white striped polo shirt already showing little patches of sweat here and there, was "Clarence ask you about the money?"

"Uh-huh."

"You tell him what we talked about?"

"He was pretty cool about it, actually. I'm going to get a paper bag and stuff the rest of the money in it and give it to him. Roy won't need it. He's got plenty more."

"So old man Hamblin called him then?" Barney said.

"Sure. Did you think he wouldn't?"

"I wish we could go out there. To see Roy, I mean."

"So do I."

"I woke up in the middle of the night. I had this dream that Roy was dead."

"He's pretty tough. Did you read the newspaper this morning?" My dad subscribes to the *Des Moines Register*. Even though it's pretty much a "Democratic rag" as he frequently calls it, it's the only daily we can get in this part of the state.

"Yeah," Barney said. "He really is a tough guy."

Right there on the front page, in a big black blaring headline, it had said: *State Police Seek Fugitive* and just below this was a picture of Roy looking more like Mitch than ever. The story told of how Roy had been a war hero in Korea but that he'd drifted into crime with his older brother and how authorities suspected that they'd been responsible for at least ten bank robberies in the past six months.

"He's a pretty cool guy, no doubt about it," Barney said.

"Very cool guy," I said.

"What're we gonna do all day?"

"You wanna see a flick?"

"Which one?"

"*Blackboard Jungle* is back at the Rialto."

"And there's another one," Barney said.

"What's the other one?" In those days, the Rialto always played two and sometimes three movies. Of course, when they had three of them, you could bet that two of them were real dogs, usually something with Bing Crosby and a lot of nuns.

"It's a western with Rory Calhoun."

"I still say," I said, "that Rory is a fake name."

"You wanna go or not?"

I shrugged. "Guess there isn't much else to do."

So we killed two hours before going to the movies by riding our bikes all over town and seeing who was out and around. We saw Maynard the bully unloading peat moss at his uncle's hardware store and just as we were passing him, Barney said,

"I'll give you a buck if you give him the finger."

"I'll give you two bucks if you give him the finger."

But of course, wanting to live till sundown, neither one of us gave him the finger.

The Blackboard Jungle was still a pretty cool movie. The only problem was that I couldn't see myself as any of those kids. They were really kind of whiny and immature. I mean I'd much rather be Glenn Ford than any of the kids. (For one thing, Glenn had made two movies with Rita Hayworth, who I still think is the most beautiful and sexy and in some strange way saddest woman I've ever seen, her sadness being a part of her beauty.)

And Rory Calhoun was pitiful as usual. He looks like a decent guy and I'm sure he is a decent guy but he sure can't act. And when a fifteen-year-old kid from Somerton, Iowa, knows you can't act then you really can't act.

But it was air-conditioned and three rows ahead of us sat two really cute girls from Catholic school (Dad has never liked Catholics much but Mom says except for the Pope they're very fine people) and there were some especially neat coming attractions for two new monster movies. (Later on, I'd learn that coming attractions are a lot like life—the buildup is usually better than the payoff.)

When we got out, the sunlight was blinding and my body felt like some invisible demon had taken this huge paint roller and covered me with glue.

We got on our bikes and started down the block. We stopped at the corner for a red light and that was when the black Plymouth sedan pulled up to the curb. The window was rolled down on the passenger side. Cushing had to lean way over. "Afternoon, ladies." Neither of us said anything.

"I want you to ride those bikes of yours over to the square and wait for me there. I'll meet you by the drinking fountain."

Even Cushing was fixated on the drinking fountain. "You girls understand me?"

We didn't nod or anything but obviously we were going to do what he told us.

When he pulled away, Barney said, "I think we're in trouble."

"I think you're right."

"That jerk." We rode over to the square.

Since it was nearing suppertime, the square was pretty

quiet, except for a couple of squirrels running around the edges of the wading pool where I used to go when I was five or so. But one day I saw some little kid's turd floating in there and I got out of the water and I never got back in again. I mean never.

We sat on the bench next to the fountain. Cushing parked down by the railroad tracks so it took him a few minutes to get up there.

He had on a straw fedora and a baby blue-colored summer-weight suit and his usual big mean grin.

He went over to the fountain and had himself a drink and then flicked some water from his hand (everybody gets wet at that fountain) and then he took out this long pack of Viceroys and knocked one out on the edge of his fist and then he put it in his mouth and lit it and said, "Where'd you girls get all that money?"

"Huh?" Barney said.

"Last night at Hamblin's. Hamblin told me all about it."

"Found it," I said.

"Found it where?"

"Laying near the crick."

"What crick?"

"Out by the fairgrounds."

"It was just laying there?"

"In a sack."

"What kind of sack?"

"Paper sack."

"How much was in it?"

"About three hundred dollars."

"Where is it now?"

"At my house. My dad made me make up the money I spent from this savings account he keeps for me. He's gonna take it to the chief tonight."

"You could be in a lot of trouble."

"I know," I said. But I knew better than that and so did Cushing. The Chief and Dad are in Rotary and Lions and Odd Fellows and the Masons together and twice a year they go hunting and fishing and they're real good friends and so I'd practically have to kill somebody before the chief did anything to me. I guess that's what Roy meant when he said I was respectable.

Cushing dragged on his cigarette a few times and swatted flies with his big hand a few times and just kept staring at us.

"You know what I think?" he said.

"What?" I said.

"That there's more money somewhere and that you're just not telling your dad about it."

The shadows were getting longer and a yellow passenger train was just pulling into the depot, furious with August heat and oil and power, and the people sat in the windows looking out at our little town, city people most likely, wondering how folks could live in such a small place. Once in a while I'd see really pretty girls in those windows and I'd have dreams about them for long days after the train had pulled out.

Cushing looked at Barney now. "How about you?"

"Huh?"

"You gonna tell me?"

"Tell you what?"

"About the rest of the money."

"About the rest of what money?"

"About the rest of the money by the crick."

"He wasn't lying, Tom wasn't, Detective Cushing. We gave everything back except what we spent at Hamblin's."

"How about what you spent at Henry's supermarket?"

"How'd you know about that?" Barney said.

"When old man Hamblin told me about you being in there with all that crisp, green cash I just naturally got curious. I went to every store in town that was open last night and asked if you girls had been in there."

I guess that while he was one real big loud-mouthed show-boat, Cushing was also a pretty good detective.

"So how about it?" Cushing said.

He was back to looking at me.

"How about what?" I said.

"How about telling me where the rest of the money is."

I don't know why but something about the way he said that—the words he chose, I mean—seemed odd to me but right then I didn't have time to think about it. I just had time to say, "There isn't any rest of the money. There's nearly three hundred dollars in a sack at my house that my dad is taking over to the chief's tonight."

"So that's how it's gonna be, huh, girls?"

"Honest, Detective Cushing," Barney said, getting that kind of whiny tone in his voice. "Tom's telling the truth."

Cushing held his cigarette up high and then dropped it straight down to the wet ground around the drinking fountain.

Like he was dropping a bomb or something. And then he ground it out with the toe of his snappy black-and-white wing-tips.

And then he stared at us.

"This is gonna get real bad, girls. Real bad."

"What is?" Barney said.

"This whole thing. With the money."

"But—"

Cushing held up his hand. "The last time I had a run-in with you little girls, everything went your way. The chief wouldn't press charges and the juvenile officers didn't see your breaking into that place as any big deal. It's going to be different this time. And I think you know what I'm talking about."

And then he left. No more words. Just left.

When Cushing had vanished on the other side of the band-stand, Barney said, "You think he knows about Roy?"

"I don't know. But I think he thinks there's a lot more money and that we have it."

"You gonna tell Clarence about Cushing?"

"No, because if I tell Clarence he'll start asking me a lot more questions."

We sat quiet for quite a while, just watching the town at supper-time, merchants closing down, rolling up their striped awnings and turning out the display lights in the windows. Every summer seemed to get shorter the older I got, and at warm day's end there's a melancholy about everything, long purple shadows and mothers calling their lads in for dinner, and I felt this kind of sadness I can't explain, even though I was only fifteen I felt real old and I sensed that in just a few summers more all of us would be gone, I mean everybody I passed on the street young and old alike and all the people I loved including Mom and Dad and Gram and Debbie, all gone to ground and utterly forgotten with nobody to remember how beautiful the wine-colored dusk was on a snow-covered January night or how people laughed at Jack Benny on the radio or how neat it was to get a brand-new Ace Double Book or how the bonfire glowed on Homecoming night out at the football sta-dium or how lonely I felt the night Emmy Chambers told me that she liked Bobby Criker better than me or how much fun it was to chase fireflies with a jar on a July night with your aunt and uncle from Minneapolis sitting on the screened-in porch watching or how one spring night walking by the river I was so overwhelmed by the moonsilver water and the scent of apple blossoms and the friendly yips and yaps of neighborhood dogs that I knew absolutely positively that there was a God or how I sometimes had really corny dreams about saving some girl I loved from a burning house or how beautiful and neat and clean Main Street looked after a night rain— All those people and thoughts and memories would be dead. Mom and Dad would likely go first, and then all their friends and relatives, and then me and all my friends and relatives, and then Debbie and all her friends and relatives, generations born and generations dying until there was absolutely no trace of us left, almost as if we hadn't existed, absolutely nobody who could remember us at all, the people of Somerton with all their wishes and dreams and desires and fears would be at best a rotted skeleton or two to be dug up three thousand years hence and looked at and shrugged over and then forgotten utterly once again.

"You all right?"

Barney brought me back. "I'm fine," I said. But I wasn't. I never am when I start thinking of eternity that way.

"What time we going out to see Roy?"

"How about seven?"

"Meet you by the tracks?"

"Fine. But let's walk."

"OK by me."

"I'll stop by Henry's and pick up Roy's stuff and meet you then." I rode home. Douglas Edwards and the CBS News was on. Mom was serving the first sweet corn of the year along with broccoli and Jello. Usually Mom doesn't let us eat in front of the TV—she'd read a piece in *Parents* magazine about how the American family was going to hell in a handbasket largely because of TV and rock and roll—but the heat evidently changed her mind for tonight at least, the living room being a lot cooler than the family room.

I sat beside Debbie on the couch. We both had metal TV trays which were kind of wobbly. She said, "It's hard to eat this corn with that tooth gone, Mom."

Which was when I figured out why she'd looked so strange when I'd come in. One of her front teeth was missing. In case I forgot to mention it, she's eight.

"Just do your best, honey," which is what Mom usually said to stuff like that.

"Let's see," I said. Debbie put her little face with the big thick glasses she had to wear up for me to see. There was a hole in the top row. "You still have the tooth?"

"Upstairs."

"Be sure and put it under your pillow."

"How much do you think he'll leave this time?"

"Maybe fifty cents."

"Boy!" Last time she lost a tooth, Dad put a quarter under her pillow while she was asleep, then I went in my room and took a quarter from my Roy Rogers savings bank (I never got around to throwing things away, I guess) and then slipped it under her pillow, too.

We went back to eating. After Douglas Edwards the local news came on which of course set Dad off griping about how every single person in the news business was a Democrat if not a Communist. Dad had never forgiven the press for what they did—or what he said they did, anyway—to his idol Robert Taft. You know, when Ike "stole" the Republican nomination from him.

The phone rang. Mom, who was on her way to the kitchen, got it and said, "For you, Tom."

"Guess who's been cruising past my house?" Barney said.

"Who?"

"Who do you think? Cushing."

"Cushing? You sure?"

"Positive."

"When you leave, go out the back door. And then go down the alley. I'll meet you at our old clubhouse."

"Maybe he'll start cruising past your house, too."

"I'll see you in twenty minutes."

When I went back into the living room, a commercial was on so Dad was talking to everybody. "I took that money over to the chief and told him how you found it out by the crick and all. He wants you to stop in in the next couple days and talk to him."

"Is he mad?"

"Not mad but kinda disappointed, I think. That you didn't turn it in as soon as you found it. He said something I didn't even think about."

"Like what?"

"Like about that bank robber. The FBI thinks he's up in the northern part of the state but now the chief thinks maybe he's around here somewhere, the way you found that money and all.

Anyway, if you'd brought the money in right away, the chief could've put some men on looking for the robber. Now the guy's probably long gone."

I made a quick pit stop upstairs and in five minutes was ready to go. In the kitchen, I worked fast. I grabbed a paper sack from a drawer and dropped an apple in it, and then followed the apple with two slices of wheat bread, three slices of summer sausage, two bottles of Pepsi, a slice of Mom's chocolate cake with white frosting that I wrapped in wax paper, and some carrot sticks that Mom always kept in this plastic bowl. I didn't have to worry about them hearing me because the window air-conditioner sounded like a B-52 but I didn't want Mom to wander out in the kitchen and see me loading up and then start asking all these questions.

I went out the back way, down the three back porch steps, under the clotheslines, past the dog house, along the row of garbage cans next to the small white garage whose shingles smelled as if they'd melted some in the heat, and out into the narrow gravel chalk-dust alley where I used to be Roy Rogers, Gene Autry, Allan "Rocky" Lane and Lash LaRue, sometimes all on the same day.

It took me twenty minutes to get to the clubhouse, which was this long-abandoned garage on the downwind side of the city dump which, as you might think, did not smell exactly wonderful during a windless sundown of eighty-six degrees. I'd smoked my first cigarette in this garage, and then got so sick that I couldn't get out of bed for a day, and got my first glimpse of a *Playboy* foldout which Barney's sixteen-year-old cousin Stan had copped from his dad's bureau drawer.

The clubhouse resembled this old sagging weatherworn outhouse in this small field of burned grass and empty tin cans and jagged broken pop bottles.

Barney was inside, squatted over in a shadowy corner with a bottle of Pepsi and a Lucky Strike. The last of the dusty sunlight peeped through the spaces between the boards. I'd brought along my old Boy Scout flashlight, which is the color a baby shits when he's got the trots, and I shined it all over the dirt floor. About the only thing to see were a couple of squirming nightcrawlers who looked like my light had just woken them up.

"You see Cushing?" Barney said.

"Huh-uh."

"I didn't, either."

I asked him for a cigarette and when I got it going, I told him what the chief had said, about the found money maybe belonging to the bank robber.

"No wonder Cushing's following us," Barney said. "He probably thinks we can lead him to the robbery money."

"And to the robber. Wouldn't he get some kind of award?"

"Reward, Barney. You always say that. It's reward."

"Up yours."

"Spoken like a truly mature person."

Barney said, "How we gonna get to Roy without Cushing finding out?"

"We'll just have to be careful."

He poked the sack. "You swipe him some pretty good stuff?"

"He's probably so hungry he'd eat shoe leather."

"You wanna go?"

"Let's look for Cushing first."

One nice thing about the clubhouse, you've got spy holes all over the place.

I wish my house had a few spy holes, too. You never know when they'll come in handy.

Barney took one wall and I took the other. We both looked for any sign of Cushing's car. But there was just blanched prairie and the burning malodorous city dump and small frame houses on this particular edge of town.

So we went. We cut wide around the dump, Barney saying what he always said ("I'll bet there's a lot of valuable stuff in there if you just had the time to look through it all") and then saw the railroad tracks gleaming in the last few minutes of fiery sunlight.

All that separated us from the tracks was a wide area of dusty gravel. We were just walking over to it when Barney said, "Oh, God! Look!"

And there, maybe three hundred yards behind us, came Cushing's unmarked police car.

"What'll we do?" Barney said.

"Just calm down."

"Huh?"

"Just calm down, Barney, or he'll know something's wrong for sure. Just keep walking. But instead of turning up toward the tracks, we'll turn the other way to the crick."

Cushing's tires made a lot of slow crunching noise on the gravel.

He got alongside us, doing maybe five, six miles an hour, and said, "How're my little girl friends doing tonight?" He had on dark shades and he grinned like a killer.

We didn't say anything. We just kept walking toward the hill that would eventually slope down to the crick. There was a pussy willow tree there that gave a lot of shade during the day.

"You girls stop right there. I want to talk to you."

I heard him jerk on his emergency brake and then get out of the car. You could smell the gas and oil and heat of the motor.

He walked over in front of us. We'd stopped walking, just like he'd told us to.

"The sack. What's in it?"

"Nothing special," I said. Then, "We're going hiking tonight so we brought some food for a snack." I was getting so good at this lying business that I was starting to scare myself.

He took the sack, opened it and then shoved his hand way down inside it. I thought of the time Johnny Worchester did that with this old sack he'd found near the crick one day and this giant milk snake was coiled up inside. Legend has it that Johnny filled his pants right on the spot.

Cushing found the piece of chocolate cake. "Look here what I found." He grinned. "I always heard that your mom was a real fine cook, Tom."

"She is."

"Why don't I find out for myself and try this piece of cake?"

"That isn't yours, Cushing, it's mine."

"That's right, darling, it is your cake, isn't it?" At which point he took the cake and squeezed it in his fist, squishing and scrunching till there would be no way to separate the cake from the waxed paper. Now it was just this little brown ball.

He threw the cake back into the sack and then dropped the sack at my feet. "That story of yours is bullshit," he said.

"What story?" I said.

"About finding that money by the crick."

"That's where we found it," I said.

"You know where the rest of that money is, don't you?"

"Rest of what money?" Barney said.

"Rest of the bank robbery money, that's what money," Cushing said. "That's where you little girls are going tonight, isn't it? To get some more of that money?"

"We're going for a hike," Barney said.

"To Hampton Hill," I said.

"Watch the stars," Barney said.

"Have a little snack," I said.

We were pissing him off and it was great. He just stood there, this bully-boy cop with his bully-boy gun and his bully-boy Hollywood shades, and he knew we were lying to him and there wasn't a goddamn thing he could do about it.

"You girls have yourselves a real nice time tonight," he said. And right away I knew something was wrong, the sly way he said it.

"I'll see you later." And then he turned around and walked back to his car and got in and drove away.

I watched his tail lights flare as he turned the corner, then go out of sight behind the Solar Oil Company depot.

Gone. Cushing was gone. And he shouldn't have been. Not that fast anyway. Not without ragging us a lot more than he did.

"Pretty cool the way you stood up to him," Barney said. "Maybe he'll leave us alone now."

"Barney, he's up to something."

"Up to what?"

"I don't know and that's what scares me."

"Maybe he'll go talk to Clarence."

"Nah. He wouldn't do that. He's up to something else."

We walked and night lifted us up gently in the palm of its dark hand. The tracks thrummed again with the energy of distant trains and the jays and wrens and ravens sang their birdy asses off. It was cooler now, and so the night smelled not just of heat but of flowers and mown grass and fast chill creek water.

We crossed the tracks and jumped over the water and went up the slope to the warehouse that sat silent all in deep shadow and moonlight.

I felt nervous about everything but I couldn't exactly say why so I just kept walking to the warehouse, gripping the sack tighter.

We went in through the front window the way we had last night and then walked the length of the floor to the closet.

Roy wasn't there. I shined my Boy Scout flashlight all over the inside. There was no sign of him. Everything was gone except for two stubbed-out cigarette butts and dried red spots on the dirty, tiled floor. No doubt what the red spots were. Everything else he'd taken with him. Leaving no traces made sense, I thought. That way the cops would never know he'd even been here.

But it all bothered me. Roy hadn't looked too good last night, certainly not good enough to travel. Not very far anyway.

And then Barney said, "Listen."

I didn't hear it at first, not with all the electricity humming in the power lines above us and the frogs by the creek and an airplane somewhere up by the round golden moon.

But then I heard it.

Some faint noise at the front of the building. Barney wasn't quite inside the closet. Now he peeked his head out the door.

"See anything?" I whispered.

He shook his head.

We were getting spooked was all, I thought. Came in here and found Roy gone. No wonder we were getting spooked.

And then I heard it again. Some faint scuffing sound some-where at the front of the building.

"In here," I whispered, pulling him into the closet.

We waited in the darkness. Our breaths came in huge ragged gasps. We smelled of night and heat and sweat. Faintly, I could smell the food we'd brought Roy last night.

The scuffing sound came closer.

By now I knew what it was. Somebody walking across the floor, trying to be quiet.

Then somebody said, voice echoing in the darkness of the empty warehouse, "You girls having fun in there?"

"Shit," I said to myself.

Cushing had followed us.

We didn't make a big deal of it. I mean we didn't put our hands up or anything. We just walked out and stood in this little patch of moonlight with all the rat droppings crunching beneath our feet and then Cushing just came out of the shadows and said, "You girls are pretty easy to track. All I had to do was park my car on the other side of the oil depot and give you a few minutes and then start following you."

He pointed to the left cuff of his buff blue summer suit. The cuff was all muddy. "Except I took a wrong step when I got to the crick." He smiled. "I should send you little ladies the clean-ing bill."

"How come you followed us?" Barney said.

"No more of your bullshit, OK?" Cushing said. "I'm sick

and fucking tired of your bullshit. When I ask you a question this time, I want a straight fucking answer or there'll be hell to pay. You two little girls understand me?"

He'd just exploded like that, no warning at all. He was a scary guy, no doubt about it.

"Now," he said, "where's Roy Danton?"

"Who's Roy Danton?" I said.

He took one step forward and slapped me so hard I couldn't see for maybe a minute.

The whole side of my face felt hot and numb and I couldn't get rid of the stars flashing in my eyes.

"Where is Roy Danton?"

I wasn't sure I could do it but I wanted to try. I opened my mouth, eager to see what I'd say next. "I don't know any Roy Danton."

Before he could slap me again, Barney jumped in between us. "Leave him alone!"

This time he grabbed Barney and shoved him all the way back into the closet where he bounced off the back wall and dropped to the floor. Then he grabbed me and started slapping again. Two, three times, hard vicious slaps. I saw more stars. I tried hitting back and kicking back but he was too big and too skilled, like some mutant older brother.

"That's what this bag was for, wasn't it?" he said. "You were bringing Danton some food."

He'd let me go now and I started backing up to the closet.

Cushing took a flashlight from his jacket, a small silver one like Doc Anderson uses when he wants you to say Ahhh and looks at your tonsils, and then he pushed past me and went into the closet.

All I kept thinking of were the dried drops of blood on the floor.

Cushing looked up and down, his flashlight like a giant firefly in the darkness, and Barney just sat on the floor and watched him and rubbed the back of his head where it had collided with the wall.

I stood inside the door, to the right of Cushing, and that was how I saw the water drop from the ceiling to the top of Barney's head. Barney reached up and patted his head and then brought his finger away. There was a dark smear on the back of his fingers.

I looked up. It wasn't water dripping from the ceiling. It

was blood. And I had a pretty good idea whose blood it was, too.

A few seconds later, Cushing found the blood from yesterday. He kept his light pointed down to the floor, right on it.

He got down on his haunches for a closer look.

"How bad was his wound?" he said.

"Whose wound?" Barney said. For a moment, Cushing looked as if he was going to hit Barney again.

"Do you little girls have any idea how much trouble you're in?"

We didn't say anything. "This means Wayland, the juvenile detention home. You know the kind of boys you'll meet in that home? Did you hear about the stabbing they had there last year? Two kids just about your age stabbed to death in their sleep? And Wayland's just where you'll be going once I tell the chief that you've been helping that bank robber hide out."

And right then another drop of blood fell. I saw Barney's head jerk up and his eyes scan the ceiling and his hand go up and touch his scalp again.

Cushing had been watching me, not Barney.

"Your old man won't be able to help you out of this one, believe me," he said. "And neither will the chief, even if he wants to, which he probably won't."

Barney was staring at me and pointing to his head.

"You've only got one choice," Cushing droned on. "And that's to tell me the truth. Tell me everything that happened. And then tell me where he was going when he left here."

"Milwaukee," I said.

"Milwaukee?"

"He knows people there and when he left this morning, that's where he was headed."

"He left this morning?"

"Right."

"What time?"

"Just about dawn. That's what he said he'd do anyway." The lies were coming so good and so quick I was scaring myself again.

"If he left this morning, how come you came out here tonight?"

"He said he'd leave some money for us," Barney said. He was getting good at it, too.

"Did he?"

"No," Barney said, making himself look real dejected.

Cushing smiled. "That's where you girls are naive. Trusting a bank robber like that."

We were silent.

"Milwaukee," Cushing said again. "He say who he knew there?"

"Some name. I don't remember exactly," I said.

"Try."

"John," I said.

"I thought it was Don," Barney said.

"John or Don or something like that," I said.

"John or Don or something like that, huh?" Cushing said, and then backhanded me hard enough to push me all the way across the closet floor. I banged my head against the back wall just the way Barney had.

He turned off the light. "You little girls have yourselves a real nice hike."

And then he left.

He went out of the closet and back across the wide, moonlit floor and out the front window.

We just sat there, frozen, listening to his footsteps recede, listening to him become just one more faint noise in the night.

"Shit," Barney said.

I got my Boy Scout flashlight out and aimed it up at one of the ceiling tiles, which were very wide and very dark, which was why the dripping blood hadn't shown.

"Roy?"

"Yeah," he said. "Be careful. This may be a trick. He may be right outside. One of you boys go watch for him, all right?"

"I'll go watch," Barney said.

It took Roy several minutes to get down. He was dirty and sweaty and he looked even weaker than he had yesterday. He clutched his satchel of bank money tight against his wound. Some of his blood was smeared on the satchel.

In case you're wondering how he got up and down, he had a rope tied to a paint-splattered aluminum stepladder he'd found. After he used the ladder to climb up to the beams above the ceiling panels, he pulled the ladder up behind him.

"I wondered if you boys could keep our little secret so I thought I'd better get up there in case the law came looking for me," he said, as he started in on the food.

He didn't eat much and that's one way I knew he was worse

than he'd been last night. When you're real sick, you lose your appetite. He was in a lot of pain. Every few seconds a spasm would come and make him groan.

When he was done trying to eat, he took the pack of Chesterfields Barney had stolen and put one in his mouth.

He took out his Zippo. He got the lighter to his cigarette but when he tried to flick the spark up—

The lighter tumbled from his hands, a dim flash of metal in the weak dusty beam of my flashlight. The lighter made a metallic chinking sound when it hit the floor.

I picked it up right away and lit his Chesterfield for him.

"Thanks," he said, weakly.

Pretty soon, he was unconscious again and as I sat there staring at him in the beam of my flashlight, I saw that even when he was sleeping he looked a lot like Mitch.

I picked up the flashlight and moved the beam real close to his wound and got a good look at it. The pussy stuff covered the blood now like an oil slick. His whole body trembled. The smell was awful.

I knew what I was seeing, of course. I was seeing a man in the final stages of his life. I felt sorry as hell for him.

"Barney?" I said.

A moment later he was in the doorway.

"Look at him."

"God, he looks terrible."

"You know what we have to do?"

"Yeah. How long you think he's got?"

"I don't know," I said. "But not long if we don't get an ambulance and a doctor real soon."

We took a last look at Roy. He just sat there. His body was still twitching, his right leg especially. Even his eyelids, closed in sleep, twitched a little.

Then we got out of there.

We were going to get Roy some help and right then we didn't think of him having to stand trial or going to prison or anything. We just wanted him to live.

We were a few hundred yards from the warehouse when the two shots rang out somewhere behind us in the prairie night.

And then I was running, running faster than I ever had in my life, down to the creek and across the grassy flat to the warehouse, and then straight up to the warehouse window. Barney was right behind me.

By the time I reached the closet, my lungs were heaving so hard I thought I might throw up.

Then I knelt next to Roy and played the flashlight over his face and chest. Touched the artery on his neck. Touched the artery in his wrist.

"He's dead, isn't he?" Barney said.

"Yeah."

"Sonofabitch. Money's gone, too."

I looked. He was right. The money satchel was gone.

I brought the light down Roy's torso, to see where he'd been shot. The first wound had been in his side. This one was right in his chest. There was a tiny black hole right in the center of this huge blooming flower of blood.

I shone the light to the floor where his right hand lay turned up, his gun grasped in his fingers.

I thought of him being unconscious when we left, of him being so weak that he couldn't hold his lighter up.

There was no way he'd come to and grabbed his gun. Even a dumb teenager like me could figure out what had happened here.

"Cushing killed him in cold blood and then put that gun in Roy's hand," I said.

"And took the money."

"And took the money."

I guess until then the whole thing had been an adventure. When you grow up in a small town like Somerton, you keep hoping that something really remarkable will happen to you. And it sure did for us, finding Roy and all, and bringing him food and helping him hide out.

But now it was different. Now it was scary. One day outside one of the downtown taverns I saw two drunks get into it so viciously that one bit a piece of an ear off the other. Nobody could seem to get them apart. Finally, the tavern owner had to get out a hose and spray them down the way he would have two angry dogs. I remember thinking that for all the movie violence I'd seen, I really didn't know much about the real thing—the way men beat on each other with a frenzy and a relish that makes me sick inside.

The way Roy had been killed made me sick inside. The way Cushing made me sick inside.

"What're we gonna do?" Barney said.

"Tell the chief."

"Everything?"

"Everything."

Barney and I took one last look at Roy, bloody and waxen and dead, propped up sad and awkward against the wall. There was just this silence, a deeper silence than I'd ever heard before, and then I figured out what I was listening to—eternity. That's what I was hearing, something I'd always heard about but never heard for myself before. Eternity.

3

On the way in, Barney and I decided to tell our dads first—and let them tell the chief. It would be better that way, at least for us, even though telling Clarence and George wasn't going to be easy.

There was a fight on TV when I reached the front porch. Clarence was a boxing fanatic. He sat there in those purple Bermudas of his and whaled away at empty air just like he was Marciano whaling away at an opponent. He liked Negro boxers fine, especially if they reminded him in any way of Joe Louis, whom he inevitably called "poor Joe Louis," but for some reason he hated Mexican fighters. Maybe a Mexican beat him up once or something.

Anyway, that was the scene when I got home that night, Clarence alone in the living room in his purple Bermudas throwing lefts and rights and jumping up and down in his recliner and grunting and groaning loud enough to make the family cat look real spooked.

Mom and Debbie were long gone, of course. They knew better than to watch Clarence at the fights.

Anyway, Clarence in his purple Bermuda shorts and throwing punches with great and noisy abandon—he turned and looked at me and said—

"Somethin' wrong, son?"

"I need to talk to you, Dad."

"Son, there's a fight on."

"I know there's a fight on."

"It's Hurricane Jackson. He's getting ready to throw his bolo punch."

"Dad—"

His attention roamed back to the screen where two Negroes were pounding on each other. "Dad—"

Glancing over at me desperately: "Son, is it anything that can wait?"

"No, Dad, I'm sorry but it can't."

"Is this real serious or something?"

"Real serious, Dad."

"You want me to get your mom?"

"No, Dad. I just want to talk to you. Alone."

"Then let's go out to the kitchen. I need a beer." So we went out to the kitchen and sat down and—he had a beer and I had a Pepsi.

"So, son, what is it?" Clarence said as we sat in the kitchen where it was at least ten degrees hotter than the living room. The kitchen was great in the winter but in the summer it was a sweat box with only one tiny window for a breeze.

"You know that money I told you I found?" I said.

"Uh-huh."

"I didn't find it. Somebody gave it to me."

"Gave it to you? Who gave it to you?"

So I told him. Every single bit of it, right up to tonight where we left Roy dead in the warehouse.

"And Cushing killed him?"

"Yessir."

"And it wasn't self-defense, you don't think?"

"Nosir, Roy couldn't even hold up his lighter a few minutes earlier."

"So Cushing murdered him in cold blood?"

"Yessir."

"And then took the money?"

"Yessir."

"You don't have any doubt about that?"

"Nosir."

He pawed sweat from his face. "You're going to be in a lot of trouble, son."

"Yessir."

"Why the hell'd you help out a bank robber, anyway? And don't tell me it was because he looked like Robert Mitchum. That's the craziest goddamn thing I've ever heard of." He shook his head. "Jesus, Mary and Joseph, because he looked like fucking 'Mitch?' "

Until that very moment in my young life, I had never heard Clarence use the F word. And issuing from his lips, it sounded both more vile and more silly than it ever had before.

"Chief Pike'll probably bring charges against both you and Barney."

"I know."

"This is going to be pretty embarrassing at the Rotary."

"I'm sorry, Dad."

"A goddamn bank robber. Haven't I raised you better than that?"

"Yessir."

And then we heard the first sirens, loud and near on the hot dark night.

"They're probably going to get the body."

"Yessir."

He swigged more beer. "You let me go talk to Pike first. I'll tell him everything and then I'll call and have you come down."

"All right."

"He won't be happy when I tell him about Cushing. He's got a blind spot for that guy. Thinks he walks on water. I guess it's because his own son died in that tractor accident a while back and Cushing sort of fills the void. And Cushing's own folks died in that car accident when he was ten."

"Yessir."

He stood up. "I'm going to go get ready. Put on a clean shirt and all."

"Yessir."

"I'm also going to tell your mother."

I nodded.

He stood looking at me for a long time in silence then he shook his head and left the kitchen.

I went into the living room. I could feel this awful sadness come over me. I just kept thinking of Roy and how sad and frail he looked when he dropped the lighter because he'd been too sick to hold it up—

And right then I became aware of the lighter in my pocket. I dug it out and then turned on the floor lamp and held the lighter up to the round yellow bulb.

It was Roy's, the Zippo with the skull and crossbones designed into the silver surface. I must have stuck it in my pocket after I lit his cigarette. I shoved it back in my pocket. I wasn't going to mention it to anybody. It was something I intended to keep.

Clarence came down with Mom right behind him. They looked the way they usually do at funerals, grim in a very formal way. Clarence had on a short-sleeved white shirt and a dark pair of pants. He reeked of Old Spice. He walked over to me and said, "I'll call you in a little while."

I nodded.

Clarence went over and gave Mom a quick small peck on the cheek and then went out, the screen door banging behind him.

Mom went over and sat primly on the edge of the couch. I could tell she wanted to talk. I could also tell she didn't know what to say.

After a time, she cleared her throat and said, "You've hurt your father very deeply."

"I know."

"He has to maintain a certain reputation in this town."

"I know."

"And he's worried that you might—"

"I know what he's worried about, Mom. That I might have to go to reform school."

And then she broke into tears and in the light from the floor lamp she looked suddenly old and haggard and even more frail than Roy had there at the last, and so I went over to her and took her in my arms and held her and just let her cry the way Clarence would have in this circumstance. There really wasn't much else I could do.

Every few minutes while we waited, I'd touch the lighter and think of Roy dying and I'd get sad all over again. I'd never see him or hear him again. That's the strange part. How people just vanish from your life like that. Forever.

Just after eleven, the phone rang. Mom insisted on getting it. After she spoke a few words standing next to the stairway, I knew she was talking to Clarence.

She still looked pretty old, as if some kind of age transformation had taken place just in the last hour and a half.

Then she said, "Your father wants to speak with you," and held the phone out to me.

Clarence said, "You'd better get your butt over here fast. This isn't turning out the way I thought."

"I'm not sure what that means."

"I can't explain right now, son. But you get over here to the police station right now."

"How about Barney?"

"You let Barney's folks worry about Barney. Right now my

only concern is you."

"Yessir."

This late at night, the old town was pretty neat. Almost nothing moved, all the cars were parked, all the people were inside, and the streetlight shadows gave everything the texture and depth of a very gentle painting of a small town all asleep.

I rode my bike through the empty town square and down the block past all the storefronts where the mannequins watched me go. Only the taverns were open, big hot smoky machines grinding out chilly neon light and jukebox wisdom and hard desperate laughter. As I went by I smelled yeasty beer and dirty cigars.

There was a Channel 3 station wagon parked in the No Parking space in front of the police station. Up on the top of the steps stood Chief Pike and Detective Cushing being interviewed by a whole gaggle of reporters. Everything was a blaze of light and a click and clack of still cameras and motion picture cameras. The mayor was there and all the city council and maybe six local gendarmes in uniform and—

And Barney.

He stood right between Pike and Cushing.

And as I dropped my bike on the sidewalk and started walking toward the front of the station, Barney started talking into this microphone this reporter had put in his face.

"How does it feel to be a hero, Barney?"

A hero? What the hell was going on here? All I could think of was how strange Clarence had sounded on the telephone, how he'd said, "This isn't turning out the way I thought."

And then Chief Pike saw me and shouted, "Look! There's our other hero now!"

Fifty faces turned to look at me. Me—the most self-conscious guy I knew. Even walking up in front of a class to read a paper makes me sick to my stomach. All those eyes staring, staring—and right at me.

And the reporters deserted Pike and Cushing and Barney and came running down the stairs toward me.

I wasn't sure what to do. I wanted to run but I knew I'd better not do that.

"How does it feel to be a hero?" asked this guy in a bow tie and straw hat.

"I'm afraid I—" I started to say.

Flashbulbs went nova in my face. I was blinded.

"No need to be modest," another reporter said. "Detective

Cushing told us all about it. How you and Barney called him and told him where to find Roy Danton. You boys are heroes!"

"Too bad Detective Cushing didn't find the money, though," said a third reporter.

"Danton hid it somewhere around here, you can be sure of that," an auxiliary cop named Michaelson said. He was one of Cushing's friends, or liked to pretend he was anyway. But mostly he was a fat, pushy jerk.

My sight was starting to come back. I raised my eyes and looked up the stairs to Barney. He just shrugged, seeming just as confused about all this as I was.

"Even without the money, though," the reporter with the bow tie said, "you boys'll get some kind of reward. You just wait and see."

And then I felt an arm slide around my shoulder and when I turned my head I saw Clarence.

"How does that boy of yours make you feel?" asked a reporter.

"Proud. Darned proud."

"Let's get a picture of you two just like that," said a photographer.

Then they all started snapping pictures. And then somebody had the notion of me and Clarence going up the steps for a group shot. And after the group shot—

"How about you two boys standing over there on either side of Detective Cushing? We'll get a good shot of just you three."

It was all kind of like a movie, real and unreal at the same time, especially the part where Barney and I stood on the step beneath Cushing so he could put his hands on our shoulders.

"That's great! Just great!" cried the photographer. "Now if I could just get you boys to smile a little!"

Cushing dug his hands into our shoulders and leaned down and whispered, "I saved you two little assholes from going to reform school. So smile!"

So we smiled. Or tried to, anyway, but right now all I could think about was what a clever sonofabitch Cushing was, one hell of a lot cleverer than I ever would have thought.

And when the reporters were through with us they concentrated on Cushing alone. They sounded like high school girls cooing over Elvis.

"Were you scared going into that dark warehouse when you knew somebody like Roy Danton was in there?"

"Well, scared, sure, but that's what the folks in this community pay me to do."

"How'd you finally bag him, Detective Cushing?"

Another self-effacing shrug. "Just kind of snuck up on the closet where my two good friends Tom and Barney told me he'd be. Then I just told him that I was giving him twenty-five seconds to come out with his hands above his head or I'd be coming in."

"He say anything to that?"

Boyish grin. "Well, yes, he did say something to that but it sure isn't something I could repeat here."

"Then what happened?"

"Well, a policeman's only as good as his word. I'd warned him that I'd be coming in and that's just what I did. I kicked the door open and went in."

"Is that when he shot at you?"

He nodded. "One shot was all he had time to get off. That's when I killed him."

Barney and Clarence and I stood there and watched this Academy Award performance and I'm sure we were all thinking the same thing. Good ol' Cushing was going to have it every which way he wanted it. He'd killed a man in cold blood and he'd stolen nearly $50,000 in cash yet he was being treated as a hero.

And the only two people who could testify against him couldn't say a word because by now nobody would believe them. They were all running after Cushing like kids after a Fourth of July float.

I couldn't take any more. I just kept thinking of Roy and how eternity had talked back to me. I said to Clarence, "I'm going home."

I was about to say something else when people started turning their heads to the old white Buick ambulance slowly making its way around the far edge of the town square.

It was headed to the hospital. With Roy inside. If Cushing saw it, he didn't let on. He still stood at the top of the stairs, showing his gun to reporters and letting them get closeups of it. The chief just walked around shaking everybody's hand as if Cushing had given birth to a fifteen-pound baby or something. Just then Cushing did look up. He stared right at me. Ordinarily, what I saw in his eyes would have frightened me. But right now I didn't care. Right now all I could think about was Roy.

He held my gaze for a long time, giving me a full dose of his threatening look. Then he went back to a reporter who was snapping yet another picture.

More people kept coming. By now all the parking spaces around the square had been taken up. Some people didn't even seem to know what was going on. They'd just heard the noise and seen the lights and drifted over from their humid summer beds. It all reminded me of the scene in *Invasion of the Body Snatchers* where all the people in town come to the square so they can be made into pod people. I guess I was pissed off enough at that moment to think of Somerton that way—exulting in Detective Cushing's bravery without questioning it for a moment. Or wondering how it was that an already badly wounded man had needed to be shot to death. No, they didn't know these things but in their frenzy to have a hero, they wouldn't listen to them, either, even if I'd brought them up.

I went down to my bike and rode home.

Mom and Debbie were up in the living room. I went over and kissed them good night and started up the stairs. "Aren't you going to tell me what happened?" Mom asked.

"Dad'll tell you," I said. "I just really don't want to talk."

In my room, I turned off the lights and sat next to the window and smoked a Lucky. This way I could blow the smoke out the screen. Mom was less likely to notice the smell.

I used Roy's lighter to get my cigarette going and then I just sat there a long time, three or four cigarettes long, and thought of how much I hated Cushing. I could still see him smiling for the cameras. I could still see him pointing the gun dramatically for the reporters.

I Shot Jesse James. There was a film made with that tide once, a good film as I remembered it, and Cushing was just as much of a fink as Bob Ford—the man who shot Jesse in the back—had ever been.

Roy hadn't needed to die. Hell, he'd been unconscious. But if he'd lived, he would have been able to tell Chief Pike that Detective Cushing had stolen the money.

Finally, I went to bed. I tried to stop thinking about Cushing by thinking about the new girl everybody said was coming to school this fall. I'd always had this dream that this really elegant girl, like Audrey Hepburn say, would come to our school from some real sheltered background, a convent or something like that, and she wouldn't judge boys by the standards the other girls used—good looks or money or status or muscles—she'd just judge them by what was in their hearts. And so guess who the new girl, at least in my dreams, always fell madly in love with? Right.

I lay there a long time that night thinking about the new girl.

A long time later, the three of them came up and went to sleep. I waited until I thought it was safe and then I went into Debbie's room and put a silver dollar beneath her pillow. She snored in a cute little way and muttered something far below my ability to hear. I kissed her on the forehead and went back to my room, done with my job as Tooth Fairy.

When I got up in the morning, Clarence was there.

Usually, Clarence would have been at work by now but this morning he'd waited for me.

I had Wheaties and wheat toast and orange juice (or "OJ" as Debbie called it) and a vitamin and half a cup of coffee. I felt exhausted. Coffee helped sometimes.

"The governor's coming next Tuesday."

"The governor?" I said.

"The governor," Clarence said. "There's going to be a picnic for you and Barney and Cushing in the square and then the governor's going to give you each some kind of award."

"You know Cushing's got the money?"

"I know."

"And you know he killed Roy in cold blood?"

"I know."

"And you're not mad?"

"Son," he said, glancing up at Mom. "Son, your mother and I had a good long talk last night."

Whenever Clarence and Mom had a "good long talk" about anything, it always meant that I would have to do something I didn't want to.

"More Wheaties, hon?" Mom said.

I shook my head.

"We think you should go along with everything, Tom," Clarence said.

Mom came over and put her hands on my shoulders. "If Cushing had told the truth, you'd be in a lot of trouble, dear. A lot of trouble. This way—"

"This way, Cushing gets away with murder and gets to keep all the money!" I pushed back from the table and stood up, looking at them in disbelief and disgust.

"You aren't any better than Cushing! You're willing to go along with lies, too!"

"Tom, listen—" Clarence started to say.

But I was already on the far side of the banging screen door off the kitchen.

I got on my bike and rode over to Barney's. About halfway there I started feeling badly about yelling at my folks the way I had. They weren't perfect, true, but then I'd heard rumors to the effect that I wasn't perfect, either. Hard as that was to believe.

People always call Barney's area "the poor section" but I actually like it better than where we live. I guess it's the bluffs, all the woodsy hills that run right up to the backyards of most of the houses. Of course, the houses themselves aren't the best— old frame jobbies long in need of paint and roof shingles and uncracked window glass. But I would happily have traded our fancy new carport for just one of those bluffs.

Barney sat on the porch. He wasn't reading or eating. He was just staring.

When he saw me, he said, "You hear about the governor?"

"Yeah."

"God."

"Yeah."

"I'll bet Cushing buys a new suit."

"I'll bet he does, too."

I went up and sat next to him on the porch.

"You tell George the truth yet?" I said. Obviously, he hadn't told his father the truth last night.

"Not yet."

"When you going to?"

Barney didn't say anything for a long time. We just watched the traffic.

"I've been thinking," Barney said.

"About what?"

"About maybe not telling George the truth."

"What?"

He looked over at me. "Who'd believe us, anyway?"

"That's not the point."

"Sure it's the point. My mom says the governor's probably going to give us a reward or something. Wouldn't you like to get a reward?"

"Not this way. God, Barney, we owe it to Roy."

"I've also been thinking about Roy."

"What about him?"

"Now, don't go getting pissed."

"I'm going to sock you right in the mouth, Barney. You wait and see."

"All I mean is—"

"All you mean is that you're a chickenshit little bastard with no principles at all."

And then I hit him, and hard enough to bring forth some blood from his nose.

And right away I was sorry. And said so: "I'm sorry, Barney."

"Fuck yourself." He sat there dabbing at his nose with a finger. He looked like he wanted to cry.

"Maybe I'd better go," I said.

"Yeah. Maybe you'd better."

"You wanna go to a movie this afternoon?"

"No."

"You wanna—"

"I don't wanna anything, Tom. You're a spoiled prick is what you are. Maybe you don't need the reward but I do. I don't live in any fancy-ass house the way you do."

"Our house isn't fancy. It's plain."

"Plain hell."

Every time we got in a fight, no matter what it was about, it ended up about where I lived and where he lived. I tried to understand but I couldn't. Where I lived didn't make any difference to me; and I sure didn't care where Barney lived.

I went down the stairs and got on my bike. "I'm sorry I hit you."

"Yeah."

"I am."

"Just go, Tom. Just go."

"OK. And if you change your mind about going to the pool tonight—"

"I won't."

Everywhere I went that day, people kept stopping me on the street and congratulating me for helping brave Detective Cushing capture the notorious bank robber.

When I couldn't stand it anymore, I went home and sat on the screened-in porch reading *Double Star* and thinking about how Barney looked just after I'd slugged him.

A couple times I got up and went inside and called Barney

but his mom very carefully told me that he was out somewhere, which meant that he was hanging around the house but that he didn't want to talk to me.

After I finished Heinlein, I picked up a Rex Stout novel. I really liked Nero Wolfe, which is to say that like a lot of mystery readers I really hated Nero Wolfe. . .but I thanked Rex Stout for giving me so many opportunities to hate the fat man in such a pleasant way. I hoped I could be just like Archie when I grew up—acid-tongued and really successful with women.

The Stout novel gave me the idea for the letter. Nero Wolfe was looking into some poison pen letters and I started thinking. . .what if somebody left the governor an anonymous letter on the podium next Tuesday? And what if the letter told the truth, the whole truth and nothing but the truth about Roy Danton and how he'd come to be shot and where the money really was right now?

Wouldn't such a letter force the governor to look into the case more closely?

Around four that afternoon, the sunlight just starting to cool, I got up and mowed the lawn. Mom had been after Dad for two years to buy a power mower. Western Auto always has them on sale, she'd say. But Clarence could be real stubborn about some things and power mowers was one of them. I don't want to see any of Tom's fingers or toes getting ground up in those blades, he'd say. And when he put it that way, I wasn't sure I wanted a power mower, either.

That night I called Barney three times. He still wouldn't come to the phone. The next day I called him six times and the day after that I called him four—and he still wouldn't come to the phone. He was still mad at me for hitting him.

I spent most of Sunday cruising around on my bike and about two in the afternoon, I ended up at the Dairy Queen.

And who should be sitting on one of the benches, surrounded like two teenage rock-and-roll stars, but Barney and Cushing?

They each had tall twenty-five-cent cones and they each had their own little gaggle of admirers. Barney's were girls our age. . .and Cushing's were older women in their early twenties.

That's when I decided I wanted to punch Barney all over again. The way he was looking over at Cushing, it was easy to see they'd become friends.

Didn't Barney remember what Cushing had done to Roy?

Didn't Barney care anymore?

Monday, the day before Labor Day, I didn't do much. I didn't call Barney because I was afraid that if he did come on the phone I'd start yelling at him. I went down to the drugstore and bought a Lionel White Gold Medal novel called *Murder Takes the Bus* and went home and read it. At the time, I had just started reading Gold Medals and this one was very, very good. Not as good as Shell Scott, who managed to be tough and funny and sexy, but good nonetheless.

I guess I should tell you that people were still stopping me on the street and pumping my hand and saying how proud they were and wasn't it neat that the governor was coming—and what else could I say? I said I was glad they were proud and I pumped their hands right back and I said it was indeed neat that the governor was coming.

Monday night, I wrote the letter. Four times I wrote the letter. I knew it had to be short and to the point but I also knew that it had to shake him up when he read it.

Now all I had to do was figure out how I was going to get it up on the podium without anybody seeing me.

As I was sealing it, there was a tiny, soft knock on my door. I said come in and Debbie appeared. She wore her old faded WinkyDink T-shirt (remember the TV show where you drew on this plastic sheet you put over the TV screen?) and a pair of jeans and no shoes. Her hair was done in pigtails.

"I've been thinking," she said.

"About what?"

"The Tooth Fairy."

"What about him?"

"Well, on Christmas Eve Santa Claus gets around on a sleigh and on Halloween witches get around on brooms—but how does the Tooth Fairy get around?"

"He takes the bus."

She giggled.

"Really," I said. "He's got one of those twenty-trip passes you can buy for two bucks."

She giggled some more.

"I think you left that dollar under my pillow."

"Me? Nah. Where would I get a dollar?"

"I just wanted to thank you."

"Thank him. Not me."

"The Tooth Fairy? The one who rides the bus all the time?"

"That's the guy."

She smiled. And then she said it: "Mrs. Kelvin at the church is having me carry some flowers up and set them on the platform just before the governor gets there."

"God."

"What?"

"You suppose you could do me a favor?"

So I told her about the letter and how I needed to get it up there.

"You'd have to be fast."

"I will be," she said.

"And you'll have to be crafty."

"I will be," she said.

"And you could get in some trouble if you get caught."

"It'll be neat," she said.

So we went through it a couple of times, how she'd set the flowers down and then look around to see if anybody was watching her, and then how she'd set the letter down on the podium and get out of there, fast.

"You scared?"

"A little bit," she said.

"You won't tell Mom?"

"Huh-uh."

"Or Clarence?"

"Huh-uh."

"Promise?"

She held up her fingers in the Bluebird pledge. "I promise."

That night, I actually got some sleep. When I woke up, the letter was the first thing I thought of.

Today it was all going to come tumbling down for Cushing. I couldn't wait.

The event was right at noon. The only problem I had was passing the hours till that time came.

I rode over town and watched the city hall people put the final touches on the town square. There was so much red-white-and-blue it was almost blinding. The bandstand was draped in bunting and already a couple of chubby guys in red sportcoats from the Dixieland band were there sliding their trombones and walking around as if they were pretty hot stuff, butch wax on their hair and real loud heel clips on their shoes. I guess I don't like them because the time Clarence tried to get in with his clarinet they wouldn't take him. Clarence acted like it didn't bother him but I knew it did. Clarence is too nice a guy to get his feelings hurt like that. Anyway, they have a lousy band—every other song seems to be "Muskrat Ramble" and Clarence sure couldn't have made it any worse, even though, I have to admit, his clarinet playing is pretty lousy.

Then I heard somebody say, "Hey! Here comes the heroes!"

And when I turned to look over by the birdshit-speckled Civil War statue, there was Barney and his new best friend Detective Cushing.

Barney saw me but he pretended he didn't. He just kept walking right up to the bandstand with Cushing.

I went home and lay down on my bed.

Debbie came in wearing a white blouse and red shorts and blue Keds. "Red, white and blue. Get it?"

I nodded.

"Where's the letter?"

"On top of the desk."

"You OK?"

"Not really," I said. "But I'd rather not talk about it."

She went over and picked up the letter. "You ever going to tell me what it says?"

"Maybe someday."

"Boy, everybody sure is excited about the governor coming to town." She smiled. "Everybody except Pop."

Governor Hamling was a Democrat, a fact that Clarence wasn't exactly crazy about.

She came over and stood above me. "You ever going to be all right again?"

"Someday."

"It's been a long time."

"Just a couple days."

"Well, that's a long time, isn't it?"

"I guess."

"Come on."

"What?"

"You can walk me over to the square. It's about time, anyway." And so it was.

I went into the bathroom and got ready and then we went out to the garage and got my bike and Debbie got on the handlebars and we took off.

"Boy, look," Debbie said when we were two blocks from the square.

The highway runs right through town. Right now an entire block of traffic was crawling along with motorcycle cops at the front and back and this long black limousine right in the middle. Emergency lights—but no sirens—flashed. The motorcycle cops wore sunglasses and looked real mean.

I'd never seen—or felt—this kind of fervor before, not even for Little Richard.

Women stood on street corners waving handkerchiefs at the governor. Grumpy old men waved wrinkled old arms. And little kids jumped up and down and laughed and shouted and pointed.

And it was all for a lie, a damnable lie.

For the next half hour, people came to the square. They came from town and the small villages surrounding the town and they came from the farms and they came from places as distant as Des Moines. The Dixieland band was already whooping it up and a guy with a torpedo-like tank of oxygen sold red and yellow and green balloons and Harvey at his little white popcorn shack didn't have enough arms to keep up with all the business and up on the bandstand itself the mayor was showing off his familiar pot belly and his brand-new Panama hat. It was just like the county fair only there wasn't any cowshit smell floating on the breeze from the livestock barns.

I'd gotten there early enough to get a front row seat. I wanted to get a real good view of the governor opening that envelope, reading the letter and then announcing to everybody that he would have to call off the ceremonies— "And why?" he'd thunder. "Because this man"—and here he'd point like God with a lightning bolt shooting from his finger—"Because this man Cushing is a liar and a thief and a murderer!" And the crowd would ooooo and aaaaa and the chief would take out his gun and arrest Cushing and—

"You belong on the stage, son."

An older, male voice brought me out of my fantasy.

It was the mayor. "You hear me, Tom?"

"Uh, yeah, I guess."

The mayor led me up the steps to the stage of the bandstand. The Dixieland band—"The Hellcats" was what they called themselves though in the newspaper letters column one day, Mrs. J. D. Bing, who was always writing letters, suggested for the sake of propriety that they rename themselves the "Heck-cats"—the band was rolling out on "When the Saints Go Marching In." The noise was deafening. And I'm a guy who plays

"Summertime Blues" by Eddie Cochran so loud even our cats go down to the basement to hide.

Cushing and Barney sat to the right of the podium. The governor, who looked vaguely like the mayor with his big belly and his Panama hat, stood on the edge of the steps shaking hands and waggling his pudgy fingers at little babies and saying over and over and over what a fine lovely day it was for a festivity like this. That's what he called it. A "festivity."

The mayor led me to the front row. Cushing and Barney sat in folding chairs near the podium. Cushing was talking. Barney was laughing. The best of buddies. Didn't Barney remember Roy at all?

The mayor had me sit next to Barney. I started to object— but what was the use?

I could feel Barney and Cushing staring at me as I sat down. They'd quit talking and laughing. They just sat there now.

People came over and shook our hands and clapped us on the shoulders. A newspaper guy snapped several pictures. Aunts, uncles and cousins in the crowd out there would spot me and wave and I'd wave back, feeling self-conscious and awkward but not wanting them to think that being a "hero" had gone to my head, the way it had to my second cousin Larry's head the time he saved that dog from a burning building, and then had his friend in a country western band write a song about him. Larry had that damned thing recorded and pressed and four years later was still handing out copies of "Larry Baines, A Roy Rogers Kinda Guy." And his wife, at every single family gathering I'd attended ever since, always talked about Larry's "political plans" which he'd be announcing any day she always breathlessly confided. Larry pumped gas out at the Clark station on Highway 2.

Then the mayor brought the governor over to meet the three of us. The governor seemed like a real nice guy but shaking hands with him was like picking up a real fatty, greasy patty of sausage.

"This is a real thrill for me," he said to the three of us. "Our country needs more people like you."

I glared over at Cushing. Yeah, he was just what the country needed more of, all right.

And then I saw Debbie, half hidden behind this huge vase of yellow and blue and amber summer flowers. She brought them right up to the podium, setting them down on the railing of the bandstand.

Then she looked over at me and gave a little nod and then leaned up and set the white envelope down on the podium itself.

And then she was gone, half running, back down the steps and into the crowd.

I was starting to sit down again—you had to stand up to meet a governor, I guess—and that's when I saw him watching me. . .Cushing.

His eyes strayed over to the podium and then back to me. He'd obviously seen me watching Debbie and had gotten curious. . .and now he wanted to know about the envelope.

Just then the band, which had given us all a blessed break, sailed into the "Chattanooga Choo-Choo" and then there was just the confusion that results from nobody being able to hear anything. The band guys were puffing their cheeks out and bugging their eyes and spitting all over the place and making everybody on the bandstand silently plead for mercy.

Barney still wouldn't look at me but I saw him frown as soon as the music exploded. He hated Dixieland even more than I did. Then the mayor stepped over to the center of the bandstand. And then I saw Cushing get up and kind of edge over to the podium and I knew right away what he was going to do.

He was going to snatch the letter I'd written the governor and make sure that the governor never got to see it. I got up, too. I had to stop him.

Cushing did it the right way. He didn't make any bold play for the podium, he just eased his way over by shaking a few hands, patting a few backs, grinning a few grins. Even before becoming a "hero," he'd been a popular guy with many of the townspeople. War heroes never went out of fashion.

I got as close to him as I could without stepping on the backs of his shoes.

I knew now that I was going to have to take the envelope myself. I'd just hold on to it till I had the chance to slip it back up there.

Cushing was now maybe a foot from the podium. He was trying to inch his hand behind the broad back of the mayor, who was waving his hands at the band to wrap things up—inch it behind the mayor's back and pick off the white envelope Debbie had just set on the podium.

That was when I moved, moved so fast that I bumped into Cushing.

He looked down at me and scowled. He knew what I was trying to do. The same thing he was trying to do.

His eyes raised and settled on the envelope.

The bandstand was crowded. It was hard to move past all the bodies.

But he took a final step forward, put his hand out, his fingers started to close on the edge of the envelope.

I lunged—and snatched the letter from his fingers. I'd moved quickly enough that he hadn't been able to stop me.

But just as I turned to go back to my seat, he reached down and locked his hand around my wrist.

The odd thing was, the stage was so packed with people standing around gabbing that nobody could see how he was twisting my wrist. We stood in the middle of maybe twenty people. It was like smothering to death inside this tiny hot sweaty box.

Nobody had ever twisted my wrist like that.

"You little bastard," he whispered in my ear. I could hear him even above the band. "Give that to me."

His face was pure rage—but controlled rage—he couldn't afford to lose his poise in front of everybody.

He twisted my wrist harder.

And then the band stopped abruptly.

And the sweaty, important dignitaries made for their seats again.

And there we were, suddenly exposed so everybody could see us.

And Cushing let go immediately. What choice did he have? Here was this supposed hero and he was twisting the hell out of some poor kid's arm.

He let go.

And then I let go, too, my entire hand and wrist so numb from pain that I didn't feel the letter flutter from my grasp.

There it was on the floor—

And I was bending to pick it up—

And Cushing was bending to pick it up—

But before either of us got to it, the mayor stooped—no small feat, given his gut—and retrieved it from the floor.

He held it up and read aloud, "To the Governor."

Cushing glared at me and I glared right back.

"Your honor," the mayor said, "somebody wrote you a letter."

And the mayor of this fair city personally hand-delivered my letter to the governor for me.

"What's this?" the governor said.

But the mayor was already stepping to the podium and giving a little 1-2-3 test to the public address system.

Cushing stared at the letter in the governor's hand. For a second, I had the sense that he was going to jump the governor and rip the letter from him. Cushing looked highly pissed and at least a little bit crazy.

With the mayor already going into his introduction of the governor—"One of the favorite sons in this land of plenty of ours"—all Cushing and I could do was go back to our seats.

Which we did.

When I looked at the governor again, he was opening the envelope.

He took out the letter—

Unfolded it—scanned it quickly—

And just then the mayor said, "Ladies and Gentlemen, I give you our own beloved governor!"

The band played. And grown-ups applauded. And teenagers tried to make it look as if they were applauding. And babies cried because all the hoopla was scaring the hell out of them. And a cop turned on a siren. And several of the town dogs standing on the edge of the square started barking.

And the governor just kept reading and rereading the letter.

Just the way I'd wanted him to.

Everything died down, finally.

The governor stepped up to the podium, adjusted the microphone to his own height, the entire PA system ringing with the adjustment, and then he leaned forward and held the letter up for all the crowd to see and then he said—

"Over the years, I've noted that no matter what the occasion or what the event, there's always somebody who tries to spoil it. Out of envy or spite or plain mendacity, they want to ruin a splendid event that everybody else is enjoying. A few minutes ago somebody handed me this letter—and I'll tell you, I've never read such a pack of lies in my life. And if you don't mind, I'm going to take care of this matter right now."

And right then and right there, our own beloved governor of our own beloved state ripped the shit out of the letter I'd sent him.

White pieces of paper fluttered to the ground and our own

beloved governor said, "Now I want to thank you for inviting me here and letting me have the honor of handing out these awards to these fine citizens of yours."

To be honest, I didn't pay a lot of attention to the rest of the ceremony. I only knew that the few times I looked at Cushing, he was smirking.

And when the governor went to shake my hand, Cushing, who was right behind me, kicked me so hard in the ankle I could barely stand up.

4

Autumn came and with it all the pleasures of that season—the smoky air, the Indian summer sunlight, the ring of the school-bell in the crisp morning, the snap and crackle and glow of the bonfire on the prairie night at the Homecoming ceremony behind the stadium, and all the quick excited laughter of the little kids scurrying along the street on Halloween night, tripping on their too-long costumes and hoping that Mrs. Grundy was still giving out shiny new quarters, and shoving Tootsie Rolls and Clark bars and sticky sweet popcorn balls into their mouths—my favorite season.

The new girl came to school and she was almost painfully pretty and just as painfully stuck-up. I went up to her twice and tried to introduce myself but she saw me coming and then pretended to fall into deep conversation with the other stuck-up girl she was walking down the hall with. Stuck-up girls have this secret club they all belong to, and it runs coast-to-coast.

Then in the mornings on the way to school, you'd suddenly see skins of ice on the creek water, and the wraith of your breath as you spoke. Dad had his two best months ever at the store in September and October, Mom finally got the wall-to-wall carpeting she'd always wanted (a combined birthday-anniversary-Christmas gift, Dad explained) and Debbie got her first boyfriend, this very shy chunky kid who walked her home from school every night and then took off like an arrow whenever he saw me or Mom.

Somerton itself changed, too. The town square, for instance, had a naked and lonely look, shorn as it was of blooming trees and growing foliage. Litter skittered across the dead, brown grass and the bandstand took on the look of a home that had been mysteriously (and perhaps violently) abandoned. Even a little Dixieland music was preferable to this.

A few store-owners started putting up Christmas decorations in early November, with the expected number of old ladies complaining about it—"Show some proper respect. The Lord's birthday is in December, not November"—and there was the expected number of letters in the local paper about how crass Christmas had become.

Hunting season opened and while I could never kill an animal that way, I had to admit there was something thrilling about the stalking part of it, all dressed up in red-and-black checkered caps and jackets and armed with a long rifle and creeping through the fallen cornstalks and along the frozen creek and up the red clay hills, the air pure and fine and chill, and the chestnut roans beautiful as they ran on the pasture land nearby.

And you're no doubt wondering about Barney and Cushing.

As of November 10, Barney still hadn't spoken to me. We had several classes a day together, we had the same lunch period, we took the same route home, but Barney always managed to avoid me.

His friendship with Cushing ended right after the governor's appearance. At least I think it did. At any rate, you never saw him with Cushing anywhere. About the only person you ever did see Barney with was a country kid that everybody was always pretty cruel to, a cross-eyed boy who wore Big Mac bib overalls and who had a bad stutter. Jennings, his name was.

As for Cushing, he got himself a snazzy new aqua Plymouth two-door and gave the gossips some very good news by dating the town's only femme fatale, a very dramatic divorcee named Babe Holkup, who had once been the exclusive property of one R.K. "Buddy" Holkup, former high school football great and now resident of Ft. Madison Penitentiary because he kept taking home samples from the bank where he worked. Babe, whose real name was actually Elberta, divorced Buddy when he still had five years to go on his sentence. About this same time, at least according to the gossips I mentioned above, Elberta also started wearing falsies and hose without seams. And getting threatening letters from Buddy. It all sounded like one of those old George Raft movies they play on late-night TV. The times Cushing saw me, he just smirked a bit. He didn't call me a girl anymore and he didn't try to look scary. He just moved on. Apparently he didn't think I was any kind of threat to him.

And I guess I wasn't, not until I had the dream, the strangest dream of my life.

Here was Mitch and here was Roy and damned if they didn't look more alike than I'd even thought.

And Mitch said, "It's time you grow up, Tom. It's time you do right by Roy."

Well, first of all, I'd never had a movie star in my dreams before, so that part of it was startling enough, especially since it was Robert Mitchum himself.

And second of all, Roy looked kind of pissed off. Like maybe I really hadn't done right by him.

"I'm sorry, Roy."

And Roy said, "He's got the money."

"I know."

And then Mitch said, "You can get the money, Tom. You're a young man now. You're not a boy anymore."

And what was I going to do? Argue with Robert Mitchum, than whom there was no cooler guy in the entire known universe?

And then Roy said, "It's in his house somewhere. That's where you'll find it."

And then the dream was over and it was November 13 of a gray and frosty morning and I was just waking up and needing very badly to urinate and Mom was calling upstairs for breakfast and Debbie was in the bathroom gargling, which she always did very, very loudly.

—It's in his house somewhere, Tom.

—You're a young man now, Tom. You're not a boy anymore. In his house somewhere in his house somewhere in his house somewhere kept echoing through my mind the way it does in the movies sometimes.

And all the time I peed and all the time I showered and all the time I dressed and all the time I teased Debbie about her insistence on taking the first bowl of Sugar Frosted Flakes and all the time I walked along to school and all the time I played basketball in gym class during first period—

—all that time I just kept hearing it over and over and over and over again—

in his house somewhere in his house somewhere in his house somewhere

After school, I went home and got out my bike. Strictly speaking, it was a little late in the year for the old Schwinn. People were bundled up inside parkas already. And the Offenberger kids had already built their first snowman of the year—they built them so tall that sometimes the *Des Moines Register* put them in the paper—and the streets were so icy in spots they were dangerous. Cushing lived on the east edge of town where the houses grew much farther apart, and where the yards looked more like acreages because most of them had scrawny white chickens and grunting quick little hogs running around enclosed areas.

Cushing's place was an old two-story white clapboard house with a big red barn in the back. It sat on four acres of farmland which somebody down the road owned and farmed. There was a fat oak tree across from it, so I pulled in over there so I could look more closely at the house.

A screened-in porch covered the front. On the right side of the place was another door. The windows were all dark in the drab gray November afternoon. Smoke curled from the chimney. There was no garage nor a driveway as such but there were two strips of concrete that the tires of a car would fit. The strips ran along the left side of the house. A lost and lonely-looking stray mutt ran around in frantic circles in the winter-flat cornfield.

Unless Cushing had his car out back or something, nobody was home. His night shift would start in another twenty minutes, just at four. He was probably already at the station.

I wanted to walk over to that side door, jimmy it open, go in and find the cash and then carry it straight to the chief's office, drop it on his desk and then tell him where I got it.

Then I saw a black-and-white patrol car coming from a block and a half away so I quickly ran my bike down a slanting hill under a small bridge nearby. I waited there until I heard and felt the patrol car rumble over the ties overhead.

I didn't want a patrolman telling Cushing that he'd seen me standing across the street from Cushing's house.

It was completely dark and no more than twenty-five degrees when I left the house on foot that night.

It was a long walk to Cushing's. I smoked three cigarettes on the way.

With no nearby streetlight, and no cars washing their headlight beams over the place, Cushing's house was lost in shadow. There was only a quarter moon and a few stars bright above the flat fallen cornfield.

I went up to the front door. I had expected to find it securely locked and it was. I also expected to find the side door securely locked and, you guessed it, it was, too.

I went around back where against the left side of the small, enclosed back porch there was a latticework ensnarled with dead, spiky vines of some kind.

I was a good climber. At Scout camp I took merit badges in climbing—of course I also took merit badges, of the unofficial sort, in leading the most snipe hunts, using the most unique dirty words (a lot of which, to be honest, I more or less made up) and armpit farting, which is not necessarily something I'm proud of these days but I sure was at the time.

I went right up the latticework. I stood on the porch roof which was high enough so I could walk right over to the second-story window. I gave it a try. It was unlocked. I raised the bottom pane with no trouble at all.

One minute later, I stood in Cushing's bedroom.

It smelled of: gas, heat, sleep, cigarette smoke, minty aftershave, Wildroot hair oil and the same kind of bunion medicine Clarence used.

What I saw was: a well-made double bed, a large crucifix hanging above the headboard, a five-drawer bureau, two framed photographs of Cushing 1) in his marine uniform 2) in his Somerton police uniform. There was a shaggy throw rug on the floor, a tightly packed closet that smelled of mothballs, and a box filled with magazines and paperbacks, the former mostly Cavalier and the latter running to Gold Medals by people like David Goodis and Peter Rabe. It was tough to admit but Cushing and I liked the same kind of reading material.

I saw all these things in the narrow beam of my flashlight.

I spent twenty minutes in the room and found nothing spectacular except an extra handgun he kept in one drawer of the bureau and a can of lighter fluid and some underwear and socks and things in another. I then proceeded to go through the rest of the house.

I was there about an hour and a half. I learned that Cushing a) kept a tidy house b) was the proud owner of six fifths of Old Grandad bourbon c) used Trojans.

What I didn't learn was where he kept the money he'd stolen from Roy. I looked in all the obvious places—cupboards, closets, the bottom of his clothes hamper—and then in all the not-so-obvious places. . .behind the couch. . .and under the three throw rugs on the living-room floor (in the Hardy Boys books, there were always lots of trapdoors sitting around).

And—nothing.

I stood in his dark living room, my beam off. I'd been going at it hard enough to work up a sweat. My heart pounded.

I still had the dream of taking the money to the chief and throwing it on his desk and—

The phone rang and scared the hell out of me.

I stood there trembling and feeling foolish for jumping up the way I had. It was loud and alien-sounding in the darkness of somebody else's house. . .

It rang ten times and then was quiet. I decided now was the time to go. Maybe I hadn't found the money but I hadn't been caught, either.

I went back upstairs and out the window. Half a minute later, I stood on the porch roof looking at the barn out back. Talk about a perfect place to hide bank robbery loot.

Next time, I'd concentrate on the barn.

I climbed down the latticework and started around the side of the house and ran straight into Barney.

"What the hell're you doing here?" I said.

"I followed you."

"Followed me? For what?"

"I walk by your place just about every night after dinner but I'm always scared to come up to the door."

"I shouldn't have hit you that time, Barney. I'm sorry."

"No, you should've hit me. You should've beat the shit out of me. The way I let Roy down, I mean. I'm the one who should be sorry."

We didn't say anything then, just stood in shadow and moonlight and kind of slugged each other on the arm. Good old Barney. He was a pain in the ass sometimes but he was the only kid in town who knew who Ed Emsh the magazine cover artist was—so how could you turn your back on him?

I took out a cigarette and lit it and Barney looked at the lighter and said, "Roy's lighter, huh?"

He took it and held it up to the moonlight. "Pretty cool. Those little red jewels for eyes and all." He handed it back. "I spent my hundred bucks already. Did you?"

The governor had given us both one-hundred-dollar US savings bonds last summer.

"Nah. I gave mine to Debbie. I didn't feel right about spending it—" I knew this would make Barney feel bad and I wanted it to—then I thought about how poor his family was and how Barney always wore pretty old clothes and how Clarence always called Barney's father "luckless" and I said, "But I don't blame you for spending yours, Barney."

"You really don't?"

"No, Barney, I really don't." I socked him on the arm a few more times, like it was some kind of Olympic event I was training for, good old all-American armscolding, and then we left.

We took a back road home, one that ran along the tracks, one that wouldn't get us seen by any wandering cop cars, one that shone with frost.

"You didn't find the money, huh?" he said.

"Huh-uh."

"You going back?"

"Yeah. Tomorrow I'm gonna try the barn."

"You mind if I come?"

"I'll be pissed if you don't."

The next afternoon I got chewed out when the teacher found out that I had *Halo for Satan* by John Evans, which is a very good mystery, tucked down behind my history textbook.

Mrs. Morrissey, hoping to humiliate me, said, "And just what does Mr. Evans have to say about Napoleon?"

I just sat there and squirmed, the way she wanted me to.

"Or what does Mr. Evans have to say about Mozart?"

More squirming.

"Or Woodrow Wilson?"

You get the point. She threw out several more historical names and asked me what Mr. Evans had to say about each one of them and all I could do was sit there and take it, all the while wanting to tell her that he was actually a good writer and that she should try reading him sometime but of course you don't talk to teachers that way.

Finally the bell rang and when I went up to the door, she said, "Tom, come here, please, and bring that so-called book of yours."

That's what she always called paperbacks: so-called books.

I went over to her desk. Five years ago, I would have known what to do. Put my hands out, palms down, so she could beat them with a ruler. But we were both too old for that.

"This is the third time this semester I've caught you reading these so-called books in class. They're trash."

I knew I was getting red and hot, the way I do when I get

mad and can't do anything about it.

She grabbed the book from my hands and tore it in two and then dropped the two halves in her wastebasket. "Just where it belongs."

Last year, she'd taught us George Orwell's *1984*, and how the thought police worked. Mrs. Morrissey apparently didn't know that she'd become one of them.

I told Barney about this at lunch. Barney looked sort of depressed today, the way he usually does when something bad happened at home, usually meaning that George had quit going to his AA meetings and was drinking again.

On the way home, a gray and frozen afternoon, Barney said, "You scared?"

"About tonight?"

"Uh-huh."

"Huh-uh."

"Really?"

"Really. Just pissed."

"Because Cushing's getting away with it?"

"Uh-huh."

"You know those two days when he was taking me for rides and stuff?"

"Uh-huh."

"He wasn't that bad a guy."

"Yeah, he only killed Roy in cold blood and stole all that money."

"My mom says that's my problem."

"What is?"

"That I feel sorry for too many people."

"I feel sorry for a lot of people, too, Barney, but Cushing sure isn't one of them."

"When you watch him up close sometimes there's this kind of sadness about him. You know that book by Cain that I liked so much?" Barney couldn't ever remember titles.

"*Double Indemnity?*"

"Yeah. That's who Cushing reminds me of. The guy in that. He's real angry and tough but he's kind of sad, too, in a strange way. You know, how George gets when he gets drunk and cries sometimes about WWII and how his buddies died and all that stuff. You ever notice how there's something sad about real mean guys, even like Maynard? Like they get so pissed that they don't know what to do with themselves?"

And I had to admit that I had noticed that. When we got to the corner where he went east and I went west, I said, "I'll meet you here right at six-fifteen."

"OK." He looked at me then and said, "George went after Mom again last night."

"Beat her up?"

"Yeah."

"Bad?"

"Pretty bad. Black eye. Got a bruise on her cheek. Chipped tooth."

I could see he wanted to cry.

"I'm sorry, Barney."

"My little brother saw it and he really got scared."

"God, Barney."

"You know the worst thing?"

"What?"

"I feel sorry for him, too."

"For your old man?"

"Yeah."

I smiled bleakly and said, "Your mom's right, Barney, you feel sorry for too many people."

Barney called just as we were finishing dinner.

He was whispering and that usually meant only one thing. George was still drunk and on a rampage. I heard Barney's mom crying softly in the background. Barney sounded like he was crying, too. "I better not go out tonight, Tom. I better stay with my mom."

"She gonna be OK?"

"Long as I'm here to protect her," he said. Then, "I better go." I went up to my room and did my homework. A couple hours later I heard the phone ring and Mom called from downstairs and said it was for me.

Barney said, "Sorry I had to whisper when I called."

"Is everything all right?"

"He passed out. That's when everything gets back to normal. He sleeps it off for a day and then he's real sorry. You know how it goes."

"Did he hurt your mom?"

"He slapped her a couple of times is all."

That would sound funny to anybody who didn't know Barney and his family—how George had slapped her a couple of times "is all" but given the fact that he'd put her in the hospital a few times, "is all" was pretty modest.

"You up for tomorrow night?" Barney said.

"Yeah. Are you?"

"Can't wait. I need some excitement."

That was the only time Barney really liked to get into trouble, after a bout with George. It was like the only way Barney could forget it all was to lose it in doing something risky.

The next night, Barney was at the right corner at the right time. We took alleys and back roads out to Cushing's, not wanting anybody to see us, liking the idea that we were skulking even when we didn't necessarily have to.

We stood behind the oak tree across the street from Cushing's. All the windows were dark.

The wind in the chimney made a neat moaning sound.

"You ready?"

"Yeah," Barney said.

So we stepped out from behind the oak tree and started to cross the street and just then the car turned the corner several yards away, and shone its headlights on us.

"Just keep walking," I said.

And so we did. Across the street. Onto Cushing's lawn.

And then the car stopped even with us and somebody rolled down the passenger window—you could hear a radio play low and smell cigarette smoke—and then a voice said, "You boys up to anything in particular?"

I couldn't make out a face inside the car. "Who is it?"

"It's Michaelson, is who it is. And I'm curious what you boys are doing out here at this time of night."

And then he hit us right in the face with the spotlight he had mounted on his driver's door.

Michaelson was this fat slob who sold appliances during the day and was an auxiliary policeman on the side. Now everybody in Somerton knew that the most an auxiliary policeman ever did was direct traffic at the county fair and things like that. What they got was a uniform and a badge and a billy club. What they didn't get was a gun or a car or any respect. Michaelson had been on the steps of the police department the night Roy was killed—hanging around his supposed friend Cushing. Even Cushing didn't seem to like him all that much.

Of course, Michaelson pretended he was a pretty big deal strutting around the fair city of Somerton. He had a whip antenna on his '53 Ford fastback and he wore his uniform just to go buy a loaf of bread and the way he walked around with his gut hanging over his hand-tooled western belt, he gave the impression that he was one tough guy.

"You boys hear me?"

"Huh?" Barney said.

"I asked you what you was doing out here?"

I dug in my pocket and took out my Lucky pack and held it up in the beam of the spotlight.

"This is what we're doing out here. Smoking. We don't want our folks to find out."

"Oh," he said. Then, "You're too young to smoke."

"That's why we're sneaking around."

"I could run you two in."

Michaelson always said that. About running people in.

Then he did just what you'd expect somebody like Michaelson to do. He killed the spotlight, rolled up the passenger window, and then took off—laying a strip of rubber that must have run thirty feet.

"What a dink," I said.

We were in the dark again.

"I don't think we'd better go down to the barn tonight."

"Neither do I," I said.

"He's gonna tell Cushing he saw us out here sure as hell."

I agreed.

We walked back home.

On the way, he said, "Mom said she's gonna get a divorce."

"She always says that after something happens."

"He knocked her down and kicked her this time. Then I jumped him. This was the other night."

He sounded confused, and like he wanted to cry again. "I wish I was like Mitch. I wouldn't take shit from anybody. Not from anybody."

When we reached the corner where we always said goodbye, I said, "You're a good guy, Barney, you know that?"

"If I was a good guy, I'd help my mom better."

"You're doing all you can."

"Yeah but when I see her down there on the floor with blood all over her face—"

And this time he took off running, vanished in the darkness outside the small circle of streetlight, loping slapping footsteps in the winter gloom.

Because of Michaelson telling Cushing about us, we decided to wait for another week before going back out to the barn.

The night was somewhere in the low teens. Barney was in a better mood, anyway. George was deep into his penitent role now, begging his wife to forgive him and not toss him out. This was the only time the family really had any peace, when George was like this.

We got to Cushing's about 7:30. There was a frosty half moon and a sky low and bright with midwestern stars. No lights shone in the house. No car was parked in the driveway. We checked the corner. We didn't see Michaelson parked there waiting for us to make our move.

"Ready?"

"Yeah," Barney said.

We ran across the street and along the walk that paralleled the house and then Barney stopped.

"I'm freezing my ass off."

"You'll be fine. You got the whistle?"

"Yeah."

We'd agreed that Barney would scout—if he saw anything strange, he'd take this basketball whistle that belonged to my older brother, the right honorable Corporal Gerald, and blow the hell out of it.

"Hurry up," he said.

He was starting to irritate me, the way only somebody you really like can irritate you.

I took off running. The ground was winter-hard between house and barn.

I pushed the big sliding barn door back only far enough so I could slip in. The place smelled of hay and kerosene and sweet horseshit and winter. I got my flashlight on and moved the beam around the place.

It was pretty well empty, actually. From the ancient horse-collars on the walls and the hay rakes and manure shovels stuck in the corners, you could see that somebody had probably kept animals here at one time. Probably had farmed it, too. But that was long ago. Everything was now dusty and stiff and faded.

I'll skip over the next half hour. It was a bitch but it was also pretty boring. I must have covered every single inch of that barn, as well as the haymow. I had no idea what I was looking for, just something that looked like it would be a good hiding place. I remembered the tarpaulin sack Roy had had the money in. A guy could hide that without too much trouble.

I went up and down the haymow ladder twice, making sure that I hadn't overlooked anything up there. I went into each stall with the rake and cleared the floor of hay and looked for any kind of trapdoor. A lot of the older barns in this area had them. About halfway through all this, my flashlight started flickering on and off, which reminded me of a pretty neat way the Hardy Boys had sent signals in one of their books. At least it had seemed pretty neat to me when I was a little kid.

I found a lot of dead stuff, too: a cat, two rats, a sparrow and this really obese possum. Poor bastard probably ate himself to death.

And then I was walking straight down the center of the barn and I turned my ankle and I acted real mature about it—I stood right there, pain traveling up my ankle and calf and thigh like thunderbolts—and I must have strung somewhere between fifty and sixty swearwords together. I didn't know who to be pissed off at, but I was sure pissed off at somebody.

And then I tried to put pressure on my foot and ankle again and I realized that the reason I tripped was that below all the hay, there was a slight indentation in the ground.

I dropped to my knees and started digging up the hay like a dog searching for a lost bone.

I dug up hay and then I dug up earth with the help of the rake tines and then I felt a piece of cold unyielding wood below the level of dirt.

Among all the long-deserted gardening tools, I found a shovel and I went right to work. I was so excited I forgot all about my ankle.

I dug for about ten minutes. The hole grew wide, wide enough that I could reach down and feel the shape of a wooden box.

I set the shovel down. I started to bend over to raise the box from the hole when Barney said, "Tom."

I turned around.

Barney stood in the door of the barn.

"What're you doing in here?" I said.

And then a second silhouette stepped up behind Barney. "He didn't have any choice. Neither of you little girls have any choice now."

"Aw, shit," I said. "Aw, shit."

"Get in there," Cushing said to Barney and pushed him into

the barn.

"Michaelson cruised by and saw me, I guess. He musta gone and got Cushing," Barney said.

The three of us stood around the hole in the middle of the barn. Wind slammed the hay doors against the barn.

Cushing stepped into the light, such as it was, the flashlight lying on its side on the ground. He wore a nice new overcoat. He always looked spiffy. He also had a gun in his gloved hand.

"Get that box up from there," he said. "And hurry up."

"Why?"

He kicked me. There was no warning, there was no threat. He just kicked me. Right in the mouth, and so hard that my mouth filled up immediately with hot, thick blood.

"Leave him alone!" Barney said.

"You get down there and help him," Cushing said, and shoved Barney down next to me.

I didn't want to get kicked again, so I got to work. I worked fast and I worked good and in less than five minutes, I had the long, square box sitting up on the ground. There was a padlock on it the size of a catcher's mitt.

Cushing threw me a key. "Open it up, girls."

We got it open. Inside was the bag filled with cash.

"Take it out of there."

We took it out.

"Set it on the ground."

We set it on the ground.

"This time when I hide it, you little girls'll never find it. Believe me. Now stand up." We stood up. "Next time I see you little girls around here, you're really gonna get hurt. You understand me?"

I couldn't talk real well. I just sort of nodded. Barney just sort of nodded, too.

All I could think of was how much I hated Cushing, how smug and violent he was, and how he'd killed Roy when Roy had no chance of defending himself—

And that was when I remembered the lighter, Roy's lighter, in my pocket.

"Now you two little girls get the hell out of here and never set foot on my property again."

He waved his gun at us.

We got.

My ankle hurt and my mouth hurt and my head hurt. I felt

angry and humiliated and terrified.

We went maybe a quarter mile and I said, and it wasn't any too easy for me to speak, "I'm going back, Barney."

"Huh?"

"Back into his house."

"For what?"

I told him.

"You're crazy, Tom."

"Maybe so but I'm goin' back."

I turned around and started back in the darkness toward the house. Cushing wouldn't have had time to hide it yet.

A minute or two later Barney was right alongside of me.

"I know you'd be pissed if I didn't go along."

He was right.

Cushing's police car was parked along the side of his house. The kitchen light was on. I could see him, more shadow than substance, moving around in there.

We went to the back of the house and got on the latticework and went up real quiet. It wasn't difficult at all, not even with my ankle in the condition it was.

We got in his bedroom and then stood very still. All I could hear was our ragged breathing; all I could smell was our sweat.

I remembered right where it was, what drawer it was in, and where he kept the bullets, too.

Barney stood by the door watching and listening while I got Cushing's extra gun and loaded it up. My brother, Gerald, had taught me how to shoot, even if I didn't want to kill animals, which he said I'd "grow out of some day." Then I grabbed the small yellow can of Zippo lighter fluid, which Cushing kept in the drawer below.

When I got the gun all loaded up we crept down the hallway and then crept down the stairs and then crept across the darkened living room and crept out to the kitchen.

Cushing's back was to us. In the bright light, he sat at the table. He poured Old Grandad straight from the bottle into a small water glass. His gun was on the table. So was the bag of money.

"You make one move, Cushing, and I'm going to blow your fucking head off. You understand me?"

I thought I sounded pretty good for a guy with a mouthful of blood.

I moved into the kitchen fast, so that he could see that I held a gun on him.

Barney came in right behind me.

"Well," Cushing said, smirking, "if it isn't my two little girlfriends."

"Get the money, Barney, and put it over in the sink."

Mention of the money ended Cushing's smirk.

"What the hell do you think you're doing?"

He started to get up from his chair but I eased the hammer back on the pistol.

"I'm not real good with firearms, Cushing. I might just blow your head off by accident."

He saw the wisdom of that.

Barney took the sack over to the big white sink. He unzipped the top of the sack and started filling the sink with small bundles of cash.

"What the hell're you two doing?" Cushing said.

"Douse it, Barney," I said.

Barney took the can of Zippo lighter fluid I'd given him and squirted clear fluid all over the money.

"You crazy bastard," Cushing said to me, now that he'd figured out what we were going to do.

From my pocket I took Roy's lighter and held it up for Cushing to see.

And then I set the money on fire.

It went up in this huge whoof of flame and smoke.

Cushing jumped up and tried to get past me at the money.

But he was already too late. Barney had done a good job of soaking all the bills.

"You stupid little bastard," he said.

And that's when he made his lunge for his gun and that's when I shot him.

He screamed and dropped immediately to the floor, his gun falling away from his grasp.

I'd shot him somewhere in the shoulder, apparently in a place that was pretty painful judging by the way he kept rolling around and moaning.

"You little prick," he said when he saw me walk around the table and stand over him. "All that money—wasted."

"We better call somebody," Barney said.

I nodded, looked down with great disgust at Cushing and then remembered what Barney had said the other night—about feeling sorry for him.

And I did, too, just then because his face was different now—instead of rage and arrogance, there was this terrible sorrow.

I thought of the hawk that day, and how the hunters had brought him down.

"You had it coming, Cushing. You killed Roy."

I started to walk back to where Barney stood in the kitchen doorway, setting the gun down on the counter on my way.

I started to go call the chief but then Barney saw something behind me and shouted, "Watch out, Tom! He's got his gun!"

Cushing had inched his fingers to his gun and had tightened his hand around it.

I looked over to the gun I'd just set on the counter. And realized that I'd never be able to reach it before Cushing killed us.

"The chief's gonna know about you, Cushing," I said. "He's gonna know you killed us and know you killed Roy, too."

And then something pretty strange happened. Cushing tried to pull himself to an upright position, the way Roy had right before he died. . .and when he did this, just for a second, he looked just like Roy. And even a little bit like Mitch.

And then something even stranger happened.

Cushing raised his gun and started to point it straight at my heart but then stopped and pointed it right at—

He was—putting it—tight against his—forehead—and pulling the—trigger and—

And I heard Barney scream. And then I heard myself scream, too, and I heard the boom of the weapon discharging and heard the splat and splatter of his brains splash against the bottom of the wall like dishwater being emptied—

Then there was just this silence.

I'd only heard this silence one other time, those moments right after I realized Roy was dead and I was trying to call him back from eternity, shouting down this long dark endless corridor—

"God," Barney said. "God."

Because there really wasn't anything else to say. There really wasn't.

Here Roy hadn't had nerve enough to kill himself and was killed by Cushing who, in the end, did have nerve enough—

I tried not to think of how Cushing's folks had both been killed when Cushing was only ten. I didn't want to be like Barney. I didn't want to feel sorry for people I should hate. . .

5

Well, it took several long weeks to learn what the county attorney had in mind, but finally he told Clarence that he wasn't going to press any charges after all, and that given how it had all ended, we'd probably learned our lessons, Barney and I.

We were celebrities of sorts at school again. The new girl even asked if she could interview me for the school paper. Of course when I asked her if she'd like to stop at Hamblin's some time for a soda, she said (very politely) No Thank You.

In the spring, Barney's mom did finally divorce George, and then Barney and all of his family except George moved to Pennsylvania. For the first two months, he wrote every other week. Then I didn't hear much from him anymore until, eight years later, he was killed in fighting in Vietnam. His wife, a very nice woman named Deidre, called to tell me how much I'd meant to him and to say that she hoped we'd meet some day. Four years after that, Clarence died of liver cancer. Mom went to move in with Debbie, whose husband was a professor at the state university where Debbie was a junior. The professor had left his wife and two daughters for Debbie and Mom wasn't exactly what you called thrilled about it all.

I was the only one to stay in Somerton. I became Clarence's business partner in the haberdashery and when he died, I took over completely. I have one son who was born with spina bifida and another son who, I am happy to say, was born in perfect health. My wife, Myrna, is the sweetest, most gentle person I have ever known.

About every five or six years, whenever there's turnover at the local paper, some twenty-four-year-old reporter comes over to the store and says he'd like to talk to me about the Roy Danton incident. The folks of Somerton never seem to tire of hearing about it. I always agree. My sons, who always like to hear about it, too, would give me hell if I didn't.

On those occasions when I go to the cemetery to speak with my dead father and my dead friend Barney, I sometimes stop and look at the grave of Stephen B. Cushing. I'm not sure why. Perhaps because I've never quite been able to forget how Barney felt sorry for him—and how I, too, felt sorry for him right there at the very end—this man I so despised.

I see his desperate eyes right there at the last—and hear the lone gunshot. . .

It's a lot less trouble sometimes, when you just plain and simple hate somebody.

I still go for walks along the tracks sometimes, out where the warehouse is now a small manufacturing plant, and I think of that long-ago summer and it is like a dream somehow—lived out by somebody who was not exactly me, not the me in the mirror today anyway. . .

And I think of Roy, too, of course. But it's funny, you know. A few years ago I saw an old Robert Mitchum picture on the tube. . .and the truth is, Roy hadn't looked a damn thing like him. Not a damn thing like him at all. . .

PRISONERS

For Gail Cross

I am in my sister's small room with its posters of Madonna and Tiffany. Sis is fourteen. Already tall, already pretty. Dressed in jeans and a blue t-shirt. Boys call and come over constantly. She wants nothing to do with boys.

Her back is to me. She will not turn around. I sit on the edge of her bed, touching my hand to her shoulder. She smells warm, of sleep. I say, "Sis listen to me."

She says nothing. She almost always says nothing.

"He wants to see you Sis."

Nothing.

"When he called last weekend—you were all he talked about. He even started crying when you wouldn't come to the phone Sis. He really did."

Nothing.

"Please, Sis. Please put on some good clothes and get ready 'cause we've got to leave in ten minutes. We've got to get there on time and you know it." I lean over so I can see her face.

She tucks her face into her pillow.

She doesn't want me to see that she is crying.

"Now you go and get ready Sis. You go and get ready, all right?"

"I don't know who she thinks she is," Ma says when I go downstairs. "Too good to go and see her own father."

As she talks Ma is packing a big brown grocery sack. Into it go a cornucopia of goodies—three cartons of Lucky Strike filters, three packages of Hershey bars, two bottles of Ban roll-on deodorant, three Louis L'Amour paperbacks as well as all the stuff that's there already.

Ma looks up at me. I've seen pictures of her when she was a young woman. She was a beauty. But that was before she started putting on weight and her hair started thinning and she stopped caring about how she dressed and all. "She going to go with us?"

"She says not."

"Just who does she think she is?"

"Calm down Ma. If she doesn't want to go, we'll just go ahead without her."

"What do we tell your Dad?"

"Tell him she's got the flu?"

"The way she had the flu the last six times?"

"She's gone a few times."

"Yeah twice out of the whole year he's been there."

"Well."

"How do you think he feels? He gets all excited thinking he's going to see her and then she doesn't show up. How do you think he feels? She's his own flesh and blood."

I sigh. Ma's none too healthy and getting worked up this way doesn't do her any good. "I better go and call Riley."

"That's it. Go call Riley. Leave me here alone to worry about what we're going to tell your Dad."

"You know how Riley is. He appreciates a call."

"You don't care about me no more than your selfish sister does."

I go out to the living room where the phone sits on the end table I picked up at Goodwill last Christmastime. A lot of people don't like to shop at Goodwill, embarrassed about going in there and all. The only thing I don't like is the smell. All those old clothes hanging. Sometimes I wonder if you opened up a grave if it wouldn't smell like Goodwill.

I call K-Mart, which is where I work as a manager trainee while I'm finishing off my retail degree at the junior college. My girlfriend Karen works at K-Mart too. "Riley?"

"Hey, Tom."

"How're things going in my department?" A couple months ago Riley, who is the assistant manager over the whole store, put me in charge of the automotive department.

"Good, great."

"Good. I was worried." Karen always says she's proud 'cause I worry so much about my job. Karen says it proves I'm responsible. Karen says one of the reasons she loves me so much is 'cause I'm responsible. I guess I'd rather have her love me for my blue eyes or something but of course I don't say anything because Karen can get crabby about strange things sometimes.

"You go and see your old man today, huh?" Riley says.

"Yeah."

"Hell of a way to spend your day off."

"It's not so bad. You get used to it."

"Any word on when he gets out?"

"Be a year or so yet. Being his second time in and all."

"You're a hell of a kid, Tom. I ever tell you that before?"

"Yeah you did, Riley, and I appreciate it." Riley is a year older than me but sometimes he likes to pretend he's my uncle or something. But he means well and, like I told him, I appreciate it. Like when Dad's name was in the paper for the burglary and everything. The people at K-Mart all saw it and started treating me funny. But not Riley. He'd walk up and down the aisles with me and even put his arm on my shoulder like we were the best buddies in the whole world or something. In the coffee room this fat woman made a crack about it and Riley got mad and said, "Why don't you shut your fucking mouth, Shirley?" Nobody said anything more about my Dad after that. Of course poor Sis had it a lot worse than me at Catholic school. She had it real bad. Some of those kids really got vicious. A lot of nights I'd lay awake thinking of all the things I wanted to do to those kids. I'd do it with my hands too, wouldn't even use weapons.

"Well, say hi to your Mom."

"Thanks, Riley. I'll be sure to."

"She's a hell of a nice lady." Riley and his girl came over one night when Ma'd had about three beers and was in a really good mood. They got along really well. He had her laughing at his jokes all night. Riley knows a lot of jokes. A lot of them.

"I sure hope we make our goal today."

"You just relax, Tom, and forget about the store. OK?"

"I'll try."

"Don't try, Tom. Do it." He laughs, being my uncle again. "That's an order."

~ ~ ~ ~ ~

In the kitchen, done with packing her paper bag, Ma says, "I shouldn't have said that."

"Said what?" I say.

"About you being like your sister."

"Aw, Ma. I didn't take that seriously."

"We couldn't have afforded to stay in this house if you hadn't been promoted to assistant manager. Not many boys would turn over their whole paychecks to their Mas." She doesn't mention her sister who is married to a banker who is what bankers aren't supposed to be, generous. I help but he helps a lot.

She starts crying.

I take her to me, hold her. Ma needs to cry a lot. Like she fills up with tears and will drown if she can't get rid of them. When I hold her I always think of the pictures of her as a young woman, of all the terrible things that have cost her her beauty.

When she's settled down some I say, "I'll go talk to Sis."

But just as I say that I hear the old boards of the house creak and there in the doorway, dressed in a white blouse and a blue skirt and blue hose and the blue flats I bought her for her last birthday, is Sis.

Ma sees her too and starts crying all over again. "Oh God, hon, thanks so much for changing your mind."

Then Ma puts her arms out wide and she goes over to Sis and throws her arms around her and gets her locked inside this big hug.

I can see Sis' blue eyes staring at me over Ma's shoulder.

~ ~ ~ ~ ~

In the soft fog of the April morning I see watercolor brown cows on the curve of the green hills and red barns faint in the rain. I used to want to be a farmer till I took a two week job summer of junior year where I cleaned out dairy barns and it took me weeks to get the odor of wet hay and cowshit and hot pissy milk from my nostrils and then I didn't want to be a farmer ever again.

"You all right, hon?" Ma asks Sis.

But Sis doesn't answer. Just stares out the window at the watercolor brown cows.

"Ungrateful little brat," Ma says under her breath.

If Sis hears this she doesn't let on. She just stares out the window.

"Hon, slow down," May says to me. "This road's got a lot of curves in it."

And so it does.

Twenty-three curves—I've counted them many times—and you're on top of a hill looking down into a valley where the prison lies.

~ ~ ~ ~ ~

Curious, I once went to the library and read up on the prison. According to the historical society it's the oldest prison still standing in the Midwest, built of limestone dragged by prisoners from a nearby quarry. In 1948 the west wing had a fire that killed 18 blacks (they were segregated in those days) and in 1957 there was a riot that got a guard castrated with a busted pop bottle and two inmates shot dead in the back by other guards who were never brought to trial.

From the two-lane asphalt road that winds into the prison you see the steep limestone walls and the towers where uniformed guards toting riot guns look down at you as you sweep west to park in the visitor's parking lot.

~ ~ ~ ~ ~

As we walk through the rain to the prison, hurrying as the fat drops splatter on our heads, Ma says, "I forgot. Don't say anything about your cousin Bessie."

"Oh. Right."

"Stuff about cancer always makes your Dad depressed. You know it runs in his family a lot."

She glances over her shoulder at Sis shambling along. Sis had not worn a coat. The rain doesn't seem to bother her. She is staring out at something still as if her face was nothing more than a mask which hides her real self. "You hear me?" Ma asks Sis.

If Sis hears she doesn't say anything.

~ ~ ~ ~ ~

"How're you doing this morning, Jimmy?" Ma asks the fat guard who lets us into the waiting room.

His stomach wriggles beneath his threadbare uniform shirt like something troubled struggling to be born.

He grunts something none of us can understand. He obviously doesn't believe in being nice to Ma no matter how nice Ma is to him. Would break prison decorum apparently, the sonofabitch. But if you think he is cold to us—and most people in the prison are—you should see how they are to the families of queers or with men who did things to children.

The cold is in my bones already. Except for July and August prison is always cold to me. The bars are cold. The walls are cold. When you go into the bathroom and run the water your fingers tingle. The prisoners are always sneezing and coughing. Ma always brings Dad lots of Contac and Listerine even though I told her about this article that said Listerine isn't anything except a mouthwash.

In the waiting room—which is nothing more than the yellow-painted room with battered old wooden chairs—a turnkey named Stan comes in and leads you right up to the visiting room, the only problem being that separating you from the visiting room is a set of bars. Stan turns the key that raises these bars and then you get inside and he lowers the bars behind you. For a minute or so you're locked in between two walls and two sets of bars. You get a sense of what it's like to be in a cell. The first couple times this happened I got scared. My chest started heaving and I couldn't catch my breath, sort of like the nightmares I have sometimes.

Stan then raises the second set of bars and you're one room away from the visiting room or VR as the prisoners call it. In prison you always lower the first set of bars before you raise the next one. That way nobody escapes.

In this second room, not much bigger than a closet with a stand-up clumsy metal detector near the door leading to the VR, Stan asks Ma and Sis for their purses and me for my wallet. He asks if any of us have got any open packs of cigarettes and if so to hand them over. Prisoners and visitors alike can carry only full packs of cigarettes into the VR. Open packs are easy to hide stuff in.

You pass through the metal detector and straight into the VR room.

The first thing you notice is how all of the furniture is in color coded sets—loungers and vinyl molded chairs makes up a set—orange green blue or red. Like that. This is so Mona the guard in here can tell you where to sit just by saying a color such as "Blue" which means you go sit in the blue seat. Mona makes Stan look like a really friendly guy. She's fat with hair cut man short and a voice man deep. She wears her holster and gun with real obvious pleasure. One time Ma didn't understand what color she said and Mona's hand dropped to her service revolver like she was going to whip it out or something. Mona doesn't like to repeat herself. Mona is the one the black prisoner knocked unconscious a year ago. The black guy is married to this white girl which right away you can imagine Mona not liking at all so she's looking for any excuse to hassle him so the black guy one time gets down on his hands and knees to play with his little baby and Mona comes over and says you can only play with the kids in the Toy Room (TR) and he says can't you make an exception and Mona sly like bumps him hard on the shoulder and he just flashes the way prisoners sometimes do and jumps up from the floor and not caring that she's a woman or not just drops her with a right hand and the way the story is told now anyway by prisoners and their families, everybody in VR instead of rushing to help her break out into applause just like it's a movie or something. Standing ovation. The black guy was in the hole for six months but was quoted afterward as saying it was

356

worth it.

Most of the time it's not like that at all. Nothing exciting I mean. Most of the time it's just depressing.

Mostly it's women here to see husbands. They usually bring their kids so there's a lot of noise. Crying laughing chasing around. You can tell if there's trouble with a parole—the guy not getting out when he's supposed to—because that's when the arguments always start, the wife having built her hopes up and then the husband saying there's nothing he can do I'm sorry honey nothing I can do and sometimes the woman will really start crying or arguing, I even saw a woman slap her husband once, the worst being of course when some little kid starts crying and says, "Daddy I want you to come home!" That's usually when the prisoner himself starts crying.

As for touching or fondling, there's none of it. You can kiss your husband for thirty seconds and most guards will hassle you even before your time's up if you try it open mouth or anything. Mona in particular is a real bitch about something like this. Apparently Mona doesn't like the idea of men and women kissing.

Another story you hear a lot up here is how this one prisoner cut a hole in his pocket so he could stand by the Coke machine and have his wife put her hand down his pocket and jack him off while they just appeared to be innocently standing there, though that may be one of those stories the prisoners just like to tell.

The people who really have it worst are those who are in the hole or some other kind of solitary. On the west wall there's this long screen for them. They have to sit behind the screen the whole time. They can't touch their kids or anything. All they can do is look.

~ ~ ~ ~ ~

I can hear Ma's breath take up sharp when they bring Dad in.

He's still a handsome man—thin, dark curly hair with no gray, and more solid than ever since he works out in the prison weight room all the time. He always walks jaunty as if to say that wearing a gray uniform and living in an interlocking set of cages has not yet broken him. But you can see in his blue eyes that they broke him a long time ago.

"Hiya, everybody," he says trying to sound real happy.

Ma throws her arms around him and they hold each other. Sis and I sit down on the two chairs. I look at Sis. She stares at the floor.

Dad comes over then and says, "You two sure look great."

"So do you," I say. "You must be still lifting those weights."

"Bench pressed two-twenty-five this week."

"Man," I say and look at Sis again. I nudge her with my elbow. She won't look up.

Dad stares at her. You can see how sad he is about her not looking up. Soft he says, "It's all right."

Ma and Dad sit down then and we go through the usual stuff, how things are going at home and at my job and in junior college, and how things are going in prison. When he first got there, they put Dad in with this colored guy—he was Jamaican—but then they found out he had AIDs so they moved Dad out right away. Now he's with this guy who was in Viet Nam and got one side of his face burned. Dad says once you get used to looking at him he's a nice guy with two kids of his own and not queer in any way or into drugs at all. In prison the drugs get pretty bad.

We talk a half hour before Dad looks at Sis again. "So how's my little girl."

She still won't look up.

"Ellen," Ma says, "you talk to your Dad and right now."

Sis raises her head. She looks right at Dad but doesn't seem to see him at all. Ellen can do that. It's really spooky.

Dad puts his hand out and touches her.

Sis jerks her hand away. It's the most animated I've seen her in weeks.

"You give your Dad a hug and you give him a hug right now," Ma says to Sis.

Sis, still staring at Dad, shakes her head.

"It's all right," Dad says. "It's all right. She just doesn't like to come up here and I don't blame her at all. This isn't a nice place to visit at all." He smiles. "Believe me I wouldn't be here if they didn't make me."

Ma asks "Any word on your parole?"

"My lawyer says two years away. Maybe three, 'cause it's a second offense and all." Dad sighs and takes Ma's hand. "I know it's hard for you to believe hon—I mean practically every guy in here says the same thing—but I didn't break into that store that night. I really didn't. I was just walking along the river."

"I do believe you, hon," Ma says "and so does Tom and so does Sis. Right, kids?"

I nod. Sis has gone back to staring at the floor.

" 'Cause I served time before for breaking and entering the cops just automatically assumed it was me," Dad says. He shakes his head. The sadness is back in his eyes. "I don't have no idea how my billfold got on the floor of that place." He sounds miserable and now he doesn't look jaunty or young. He looks old and gray.

He looks back at Sis. "You still getting' straight A's hon?"

She looks up at him. But doesn't nod or anything.

"She sure is," Ma says. "Sister Rosemary says Ellen is the best student she's got. Imagine that."

Dad starts to reach out to Sis again but then takes his hand back.

Over in the red section this couple start arguing. The woman is crying and this little girl maybe six is holding real tight to her Dad who looks like he's going to start crying too. That bitch Mona has put on her mirror sunglasses again so you can't tell what she's thinking but you can see from the angle of her face that she's watching the three of them in the red section. Probably enjoying herself.

"Your lawyer sure it'll be two years?" Ma says.

"Or three."

"I sure do miss you, hon," Ma says.

"I sure do miss you too, hon."

"Don't know what I'd do without Tom to lean on." She makes a point of not mentioning Sis who she's obviously still mad at because Sis won't speak to Dad.

"He's sure a fine young man," Dad says. "Wish I woulda been that responsible when I was his age. Wouldn't be in here today if I'da been."

Sis gets up and leaves the room. Says nothing. Doesn't even look at anybody exactly. Just leaves. Mona directs her to the ladies room.

"I'm sorry she treats you this way, hon," Ma says. "She thinks she's too good to come see her Dad in prison."

"It's all right" Dad says looking sad again. He watches Sis leave the visiting room.

"I'm gonna have a good talk with her when we leave here, hon," Ma says.

"Oh don't be too hard on her. Tough for a proud girl her age to come up here."

"Not too hard for Tom."

"Tom's different. Tom's mature. Tom's responsible. When Ellen gets Tom's age I'm sure she'll be mature and responsible too."

Half hour goes by before Sis comes back. Almost time to leave. She walks over and sits down.

"You give your Dad a hug now," Ma says.

Sis looks at Dad. She stands up then and goes over and puts her arms out. Dad stands up grinning and takes her to him and hugs her tighter than I've ever seen him hug anybody. It's funny because right then and there he starts crying. Just holding Sis so tight. Crying.

"I love you, hon," Dad says to her. "I love you, hon, and I'm sorry for all the mistakes I've made and I'll never make them again I promise you."

Ma starts crying too.

Sis says nothing.

When Dad lets her go I look at her eyes. They're the same as they were before. She's staring right at him but she doesn't seem to see him somehow.

Mona picks up the microphone that blasts through the speakers hung from the ceiling. She doesn't need a speaker in a room this size but she obviously likes how loud it is and how it hurts your ears.

"Visiting hours are over. You've got fifteen seconds to say good-bye and then inmates have to start filing over to the door."

"I miss you so much, hon," Ma says and throws her arms around Dad.

He hugs Ma but over his shoulder he's looking at Sis. She is standing up. She has her head down again.

Dad looks so sad, so sad.

~ ~ ~ ~ ~

"I'd like to know just who the hell you think you are treatin' your own father that way," Ma says on the way back to town.

The rain and the fog are real bad now so I have to concentrate on my driving. On the opposite side of the road cars appear quickly in the fog and then vanish. It's almost unreal.

The wipers are slapping loud and everything smells damp—the rubber of the car and the vinyl seat covers and the ashtray from Ma's menthol cigarettes. Damp.

"You hear me, young lady?" Ma says.

Sis is in the back seat again alone. Staring out the window. At the fog I guess.

"Come on, Ma, she hugged him," I say.

"Yeah when I practically had to twist her arm to do it." Ma shakes her head. "Her own flesh and blood."

Sometimes I want to get really mad and let it out but I know it would just hurt Ma to remind her what Dad was doing to Ellen those years after he came out of prison the first time. I know for a fact he was doing it because I walked in on them one day. Little eleven-year-old Ellen there on the bed underneath my naked dad, staring off as he grunted and moved around inside her, staring off just the way she does now.

Staring off.

Ma knew about it all along of course but she wouldn't do anything about it. Wouldn't admit it probably not even to herself. In psychology, which I took last year at the junior college, that's called denial. I even brought it up a couple times but she just said I had a filthy mind and don't ever say nothing like that again.

Which is why I broke into that store that night and left Dad's billfold behind. Because I knew they'd arrest him and then he couldn't force Ellen into the bed anymore. Not that I blame Dad entirely. Prison makes you crazy no doubt about it and he was in there four years the first time. But even so I love Sis too much.

"Own flesh and blood," Ma says again lighting up one of her menthols and shaking her head.

I look into the rearview mirror at Sis's eyes. "Wish I could make you smile," I say to her. "Wish I could make you smile."

But she just stares out the window.

She hasn't smiled for a long time of course.

Not for a long time.

THE END OF IT ALL

For Nathaniel Gutman

> Sometimes the only thing worse than losing the woman is winning the woman.
>
> —French saying

> Embrace your fate.
>
> —French saying

I guess the first thing I should tell you about is the plastic surgery. I mean, I didn't always look this good. In fact, if you saw me in my college yearbook, you wouldn't even recognize me. I was thirty pounds heavier for one thing. And for another my hair had enough grease on it to irrigate a few acres of droughted farm land. And the glasses I wore could easily have substituted for the viewing instruments they use at Mt. Palomar. I wanted to lose my virginity back in second grade, on the very first day I ever saw Amy Towers. But I didn't lose my virginity until I was twenty-three years old and even then it was no easy task. She was a prostitute and just as I was guiding my sex into her she said, "I'm sorry, I must be coming down with the flu or something. I've got to puke." And puke she did.

This was how I lived my life until I was forty-two years old—as the kind of guy cruel people smirk at and decent people feel sorry for. I was the uncle nobody ever wanted to claim. I was the blind date women discussed for years after. I was the guy in the record shop the cute girl at the cash register always rolls her eyes at. But despite all that, I somehow managed to marry an attractive woman whose husband had been killed in Viet Nam, and I inherited a stepson who always whispered about me behind my back to his friends. They snickered mysteriously whenever they were around me. The marriage lasted eleven years, ending on a rainy Tuesday night several weeks after we'd moved into our elegant new Tudor in the city's most attractive yuppie enclave. After dinner, David up in his room smoking dope and listening to his Prince CDs, Annette said, "Would you take it personally if I told you I'd fallen in love with somebody?" Shortly thereafter we were divorced, and shortly after that I moved to Southern California where I supposed there was plenty of room for one more misfit. At least, more room than there had been in an Ohio city of 150,000.

By profession I was a stockbroker and at this particular time there were plenty of opportunities in California for somebody who'd managed his own shop as I had. Problem was, I was tired of trying to motivate eight other brokers into making their monthly goals. I found an old and prestigious firm in Beverly Hills and went to work there as a simple and un-hassled broker. It took me several months but I finally got over being dazzled by having movie stars as clients. It helped that most of them were jerks. It helped even more that several of them rarely bathed, and that several more were into sexual practices that made Jeffery Dahmer seem laid back and normal. Nothing like a little hard-core perversion to take somebody down a peg or two in your estimation.

I tried to improve my own sex life by touring all the singles bars that my better-looking friends recommended, and by circumspectly scanning many of the Personals columns in the numerous newspapers that infest LA. But I found nothing to my taste. None of the women who described themselves as straight and in good shape ever mentioned the word that interested me most—romance. They spoke of hiking and biking and surfing; they spoke of symphonies and movies and art galleries; they spoke of equality and empowerment and liberation. But never romance and it was romance I most devoutly desired. There were other options of course. But while I felt sorry for homosexuals and bi-sexuals and hated people who persecuted them, I didn't want to be one of them; and try as I might to be understanding of sado-masochism and cross-dressing and transexualism, there was about it something—for all its sadness—comic and incomprehensible. Fear of disease kept me from whores. The women I met in ordinary circumstances—at the office, supermarket, laundry facilities in my expensive apartment house—treated me as women usually did, with tireless sisterly kindness. I seemed to spend half my income on girlie magazines, even though they inspired in me a midwesternly shame when I went into the XXX stores to buy them. The alternative was subscribing, at which point the publisher would gleefully sell my name to hundreds of mail order companies that would besiege me with catalogs of films featuring men who liked to hump squirrels or glossy brochures depicting various sexual appliances, most of which looked not only obscene but vaguely painful. The word I want here is miserable. I had trekked 1900 miles, coiffed my thinning hair, taken to spending $1000 on suits—and my dates still mostly consisted of my right hand.

Then some crazy bastards had a gunfight on the San Diego freeway and my life changed utterly.

This was on a smoggy Friday afternoon. I was returning home from work, tired, facing a long lonely weekend when I suddenly saw two cars pull up on either side of me. They were, it seemed, exchanging gunfire. This was no doubt because of their deprived childhoods. They continued to fire at each other, not seeming to notice that I was caught in their crossfire. My windshield shattered. My two back tires blew out. I careened off the freeway and went halfway up a hill where I smashed into the base of a stout scrub pine. That was the last thing I remember about the episode.

~ ~ ~ ~ ~

My recuperation took five months. It would have been much shorter but one sunny day a plastic surgeon came into my room and explained what he'd need to do to put my face back to normal and I said, "I don't want it back to normal."

"Pardon me?"

"I don't want it back to normal. I want to be handsome. Moviestar handsome."

"Ah." He said this as if I'd just told him that I wanted to fly. "Perhaps we need to talk to Dr. Schlatter."

Dr. Schlatter too said "Ah" when I told him what I wanted but it was not quite the "Ah" of the original doctor. In Dr. Schlatter's "Ah" there was at least a little vague hope.

He told me everything in advance, Dr. Schlatter did, even making it interesting, how plastic surgery actually dated back to the ancient Egyptians, and Italians as early as the 1400s were performing quite impressive transformations. He showed me sketches of how he hoped I'd look, he acquainted me with some of the tools so I wouldn't be intimidated when I saw them—scalpel and retractor and chisel—and he told me how to prepare myself for my new face.

Sixteen days later, I looked at myself in the mirror and was happy to see that I no longer existed. Not the former me anyway. Surgery, diet, liposuction and hair dye had produced somebody who should appeal to a wide variety of women—not that I cared, of course. Only one woman mattered to me, only one woman had ever mattered to me, and during my time in the hospital she was all I thought about, all I planned for. I was not going to waste my physical beauty on dalliances. I was going to use it to win the hand and heart of Amy Towers Carson, the woman I'd loved since second grade.

~ ~ ~ ~ ~

It was five weeks before I saw her. I'd spent that time getting established in a brokerage firm, setting up some contacts and learning how to use a new live phone hook-up that gave me continuous stock analysis. Impressive, for a small Ohio city such as this one, the one where I'd grown up and first fallen in love with Amy.

I had some fun meeting former acquaintances. Most of them didn't believe me when I said I was Roger Daye. A few of them even laughed, implying that Roger Daye, no matter what had happened to him, could never look this good.

My parents living in Florida retirement, I had the old homestead—a nice white Colonial in an Ozzie and Harriet section of the city—to myself where I invited a few ladies to hone my skills. Amazing how much self-confidence the new me gave the old me. I just took it for granted that we'd end up in bed, and so we did, virtually every single time. One woman whispered that she'd even fallen in love with me. I wanted to ask her to repeat that on tape. Not even my wife had ever told me she loved me, not exactly anyway.

Amy came into my life again at a country club dance two nights before Thanksgiving. There were four country clubs in the city but this was the only one that mattered—old money and sound Eastern connections and even an occasional Jewish name to show how liberated all the old farts running the place had become. I wore a midnight blue dinner jacket and a black dress tie and a white shirt that shone like a winter moon and a smile that was a bit of a sneer, a smile I'd practiced in front of the mirror for several hours that afternoon.

I sat at a table watching couples of all ages box-step around the dance floor. Lots of evening gowns. Lots of tuxedos. And lots of saxophone music from the eight-piece band, the bandstand being the only light, everybody on the floor in intimate boozy shadow. She was still beautiful, Amy was, not as young looking, true, but with that regal obstinate beauty nonetheless and that small, trim body that had inspired ten—or twenty—thousand of my youthful melancholy erections. I felt that old giddy high school thrill that was in equal parts shyness, lust and a romantic love that only F. Scott Fitzgerald—my favorite writer—would ever have understood. In her arms I would find the purpose of my entire existence. I had felt this since I'd first walked home with her through the smoky autumn afternoons of third and fourth and fifth grade. I felt it still.

Randy was with her. There had long been rumors that they had a troubled marriage that would inevitably disintegrate. Randy, former Big Ten wide receiver and Rose Bowl star, had been one of the star entrepreneurs of the local eighties—building condos had been his specialty—but his success waned with the end of the decade and word was he'd taken up the harsh solace of whiskey and whores.

They still looked like everybody's dream of the perfect romantic couple and more than one person on the dance floor nodded to them as the band swung into a Bobby Vinton medley at which point Randy began dancing Amy around with Technicolor theatrics. Lots of on-looker grins and even a bit of applause. Amy and Randy would be the king and queen of every prom they ever attended. Their dentures might clack when they spoke, Randy's prostate might make him wince every thirty seconds, but by God the spotlight would always find its ineluctable way to them. And they'd be rich—Randy came from a long line of steel money and was one of the wealthiest men in the state.

When Randy went to the john—walking right meant the bar; walking left meant the john—I went over to her.

She sat alone at a table, pert and gorgeous and pre-occupied. She didn't notice me at first but when her eyes met mine, she smiled.

"Hi."

"Hi," I said.

"Are you a friend of Randy's?"

I shook my head. "No, I'm a friend of yours. From high school."

She looked baffled a moment and then said, "Oh, my God, Betty Anne said she saw you and—Oh, my God."

"Roger Daye."

She fled her seat and came to me and stood on her tiptoes and took my warm face in her cold hands and kissed me and said, "You're so handsome."

I smiled. "Quite a change, huh?"

"Well, you weren't that—"

"Of course I was—a dip, a dweeb—"

"But not a nerd."

"Of course a nerd."

"Well, not a complete nerd."

"At least 95%," I said.

"80% maybe but—" She exulted over me again, bare shoulders in her wine red evening gown shiny and sexy in the shadow. "The boy who used to walk me home—"

"All the way up to tenth grade when you met—"

"Randy."

"Right. Randy."

"He really is sorry about beating you up that time. Did your arm heal all right? I guess we sort of lost track of each other, didn't we?"

"My arm healed just fine. Would you care to dance?"

"Would I care to? God, I'd love to."

We danced. I tried not to think of all the times I'd dreamed about this moment, Amy in my arms so beautiful and—

"You're in great shape, too," she said.

"Thank you."

"Weights?"

"Weights and running and swimming."

"God, that's so great. You'll break every heart at our next class reunion."

I held her closer. Her breasts touched my chest. A stout and stern erection filled my pants. I was dizzy. I wanted to take her over into a corner and do it on the spot. She was the sweet smell of clean wonderful woman flesh; and the even sweeter sight of dazzling white smile against tanned taut cheeks.

"That bitch."

I'd been so far gone into my fantasies that I wasn't sure I'd heard her properly.

"Pardon?"

"Her. Over there. That bitch."

I saw Randy before I saw the woman. Hard to forget a guy who'd once broken your arm—he'd had considerable expertise with hammerlocks—right in front of the girl you loved.

Then I saw the woman and I forgot all about Randy.

I didn't think anybody could ever make Amy seem drab but the woman presently dancing with Randy did just that. There was a radiance about her that was more important than her good looks, a mixture of pluck and intelligence that made me vulnerable to her even from here. In her white strapless gown, she was so fetching that men simply stood and stared at her, the way they would at a low-flying UFO or some other extraordinary phenomenon.

Randy started to twirl her as he had Amy but this young woman—she couldn't have been much more than twenty—was a far better dancer. She was so smooth, in fact, I wondered if she'd had ballet training.

Randy kept her captive in his muscular embrace for the next three dances.

Because the girl so obviously upset Amy, I tried not to look at her—not even a stolen glance—but it wasn't easy.

"Bitch," Amy said.

And for the first time in my life, I felt sorry for her. She'd always been my goddess and here she was feeling something as ungoddess-like as jealousy.

"I need a drink."

"So do I."

"Would you be a darling and get us one then?"

"Of course," I said.

"Black and White, please. Straight up."

She was at her table smoking a cigarette when I brought the drinks back. She exhaled in long ragged plumes.

Randy and his princess were still on the dance floor.

"She thinks she's so god damned beautiful," Amy said.

"Who is she?"

But before Amy could tell me, Randy and the young woman deserted the floor and came over to the table.

Randy didn't look especially happy to see me. He glanced first at Amy and then at me and said, "I suppose there's a perfectly good reason for you to be sitting at our table."

Here he was flaunting his latest girlfriend in front of his wife, and he was angry that she had a friend sitting with her.

Amy smirked. "I didn't recognize him, either."

"Recognize who?" Randy snapped.

"Him. The handsome one."

By now, I wasn't looking at either of them. I was staring at the young woman. She was even more lovely up close. She seemed amused by us older folks.

"Remember a boy named Roger Daye?" Amy said.

"That candy-ass who used to walk you home?"

"Randy. Meet Roger Daye."

"No way," Randy said, "this is Roger Daye."

"Well, I'm sorry, but he is."

I knew better than to put my hand out. He wouldn't have shaken it.

"Where's a god damned waiter?" Randy said. Only now did I realize he was drunk.

He bellowed even above the din of the crowd.

He and the young woman sat down just as a waiter appeared.

"It's about god damned time," Randy said to the older man with the tray.

"Sorry, we're just very busy tonight, sir."

"Is that supposed to be my problem or something?"

"Please, Randy," Amy said.

"Yes, please, Dad," the gorgeous young woman said.

At first, I thought she might be joking, making a reference to Randy's age. But she didn't smile, nor did Roger, nor did Amy.

I guess I just kind of sat there and thought about why Randy would squire his own daughter around as if she were his new belle, and why Amy would be so jealous.

Six drinks and many tales of Southern California later— Midwesterners dote on Southern California tales, the way people will someday dote on tales of Jupiter and Pluto—Randy said, "Didn't I break your arm one time?" He was the only guy I'd ever met who could swagger while sitting down.

"I'm afraid you did."

"You had it coming. Sniffing around Amy that way."

"Randy," Amy said.

"Daddy," Kendra said.

"Well, it's true, right, Roger? You had the hots for Amy and you probably still god damned do."

"Randy," Amy said.

"Daddy," Kendra said.

But I didn't want him to stop. He was jealous of me and it made me feel great. Randy Carson, Rose Bowl star, was jealous of me.

"Would you like to dance, Mr. Daye?"

I'd tried hard not to pay any attention to her because I knew if I paid her a little I'd pay her a lot. Wouldn't be able to wrench my eyes or my heart away. She was pure meltdown, the young lady was.

"I'd love to," I said.

I was just standing up when Amy looked at Kendra and said, "He already promised me this one, dear."

And before I knew what to do, Amy took my hand and guided me to the floor.

Neither of us said anything for a long time. Just danced. The good old box step. Same as in seventh grade.

"I know you wanted to dance with her," Amy said.

"She's very attractive."

"Oh, Jesus. That's all I need."

"Did I say something wrong?"

"No—it's just that nobody notices me any more. I know that's a shitty thing to say about my own daughter but it's true."

"You're a very beautiful woman."

"For my age."

"Oh, come on now."

"But not vibrant, not fresh the way Kendra is."

"That's a great name. Kendra."

"I chose it."

"You chose well."

"I wish I would've called her Judy or Jake."

"Jake?"

She laughed. "Aren't I awful? Talking about my own daughter this way? That little bitch."

She slurred the last two words. She'd gunned her drinks—Black and White straight up—and now they were taking their toll.

We danced some more. She stepped on my foot a couple of times. Every once in a while, I'd find myself looking over at the table for a glimpse of Kendra. All my life I'd waited to dance like this with Amy Towers. And now it didn't seem to matter much.

"I've been a naughty girl, Roger."

"Oh?"

"I really have been. About Kendra, I mean."

"I suppose a little rivalry between mother and daughter isn't unheard of."

"It's more than that. I slept with her boyfriend last year."

"I see."

"You should see your face. Your very handsome face. You're embarrassed."

"Does she know?"

"About her boyfriend?"

"Uh-huh."

"Of course. I planned it so she'd walk in on us. I just wanted to show her—well, that even some of her own friends might find me attractive."

"You felt real bad about it, I suppose?"

"Oh, no. I felt real good. She naturally told Randy and he made a big thing over it—smashed up furniture and hit me in the face a few times—and it was really great. I felt young again, and desirable. Does that make sense?"

"Not really."

"But they got back at me."

"Oh?"

"Sure. Didn't you see them tonight on the dance floor?"

"Pretty harmless. I mean, she's his daughter."

"Well, then you haven't had a talk with good old Randy lately."

"Oh?"

"He read this article in *Penthouse* about how incest was actually a very natural drive and how it was actually perfectly all right to bop your family members if it was mutual consent and if you practiced safe sex."

"God."

"So now she walks around the house practically naked and he rubs her and pats her and gives her big long squeezes."

"And she doesn't mind?"

"That's the whole point. They're in on this together. To pay me back for sleeping with Bobby."

"Bobby being—"

"Her boyfriend. Well, ex-boyfriend I guess."

Kendra and Randy came back on the floor next dance. If any attention had been paid to Amy and I, it was now transferred to Kendra and Randy. But this time, instead of the theatrical, they embraced the intimate. I was waiting for Randy to start grinding his hips into Kendra dry-hump style, the way high school boys always do when the lights are turned down.

"God, they're sickening," Amy said.

And I pretty much agreed with her.

"She's going to try and seduce you, you know," Amy said.

"Oh, come on now."

"God, are you kidding? She'll want to make you a trophy a soon as she can."

"She's what? Twenty? Twenty-one?"

"Twenty-two. But that doesn't matter, anyway. You just wait and see."

At our table again, I had two more drinks. None of this was as planned. Handsome Roger would return to his hometown and beguile the former homecoming queen into his arms. Technicolor dreams. But this was different, dark and comic and sweaty, and not a little bit sinister. I could see Randy touching his nearly nude daughter all over her wonderful body; and I could see Amy—not a little bit pathetic— hurling herself at some strapping college student majoring in gonads.

Jesus, all I'd wanted to do was a little old-fashioned home wrecking. . .and look what I'd gotten myself into.

Kendra and Randy came back. Randy abused a couple more waiters and then said to me, "You having all that plastic surgery— surprised you didn't have them change you into a broad. You always were a little flitty. Nothing personal, you understand."

"Randy," Amy said.

"Daddy," Kendra said.

But for me this was the supreme compliment. Randy Big Ten Carson was jealous of me again.

I wasn't sure where Kendra was going when she stood up but then she was next to me and said, "Why don't we dance?"

"I'm sure Roger's tired, dear," Amy said.

Kendra smiled. "Oh, I think he's probably got a little bit of energy left, don't you, Mr. Daye?"

On the floor, in my arms, sexy, soft, sweet, gentle, cunning and altogether self-possessed, Kendra said, "She's going to try and seduce you, you know."

"Who is?"

"Amy. My mother."

"You may not have noticed but she's married."

"Like that would really make a difference."

"We're old friends. That's all."

"I've read some of your love letters."

"God, she kept them?"

"All of them. From all the boys who were in love with her. She's got them all up in the attic. In storage boxes. Alphabetized. Whenever she starts to feel old, she drags them out and reads them. When I was a little girl, she'd read them out loud to me."

"I imagine mine were very corny."

"Very sweet. That's how yours were."

Our gazes met, as they like to say in novels. But that wasn't all that met. The back of her hand somehow passed across the front of my trousers and an erection the goatiest of fifteen-year-olds would envy sprang to life. Then her hand returned to proper dancing position.

"You're really a great-looking man."

"Thank you. But did you ever see my Before picture?"

She smiled. "If you mean your high school yearbook photo, yes, I did. I guess I like the After photo a little better."

"You're very skilled at diplomacy."

"That's not all I'm skilled at, Mr. Daye."

'How about calling me Roger?"

"I'd like that."

I wish I had a big capper for the rest of the evening at the country club but I don't. By the time Kendra and I got back to the table, Amy and Randy were both resolutely drunk and even a bit incoherent. I excused myself to the john for a time and as I came back I saw Amy out on the veranda talking to a guy who looked not unlike a very successful gigolo, macho variety. Later, I'd learn that his name was Vic. Back at the table good old Randy insulted a few more waiters and threatened to punch me out if "I didn't keep my god damned paws" off his wife and his daughter but he was slurring his words so badly that the effect was sort of lost, especially when he started sloshing his drink around and the glass fell from his hand and smashed all over the table.

"Maybe this is a good time to leave," Kendra said, and began the difficult process of packing her parents up and getting them out to their new Mercedes which, fortunately, she happened to be driving.

Just as they were leaving, Kendra said, "I may see you later," leaving me to contemplate what, exactly, "later" meant.

After one shower, one night-cap, most of a David Letterman show and a slow fall into sleep, I found out what "later" meant.

She was at the door, behind a sharp knock in the windy night, adorned in a London Fog trench coat that was, I soon learned, all she wore.

She said nothing, just stood on tiptoes, wonderful lips puckered, waiting to be kissed. I obliged her, sliding an arm around her and leading her inside, feeling a little self-conscious in my pajamas and robe.

We didn't make it to the bedroom. She gently pushed me into a huge leather armchair before the guttering fireplace and eased herself gently atop me. That was when I found out she was naked beneath her London Fog. Her wise and lovely fingers quickly got me properly hard and then I was inside her and my gasp was exultant pleasure but it was also fear.

I imagine heroin addicts feel this way the first time they use— pleasure from the exquisite kick of it all but fear of becoming a total slave to something they can never again control.

I was going to fall disastrously in love with Kendra and I knew it that very first moment in the armchair when I tasted the soft sweet rush of her breath and felt the warm silken splendor of her sex.

When we were done for the first time, I built the fire again, and got us wine and cheese, and we lay beneath her trenchcoat staring into the flames crackling behind the glass.

"God, I can't believe it," she said.

"Believe what?"

"How good I feel with you. I really do."

I didn't say anything for a long time. "Kendra."

"I know what you want to ask."

"About your mother."

"I was right."

"If you slept with me only because—"

"—because she slept with Bobby Lane?"

"Right. Because she slept with Bobby Lane."

"Do you want me to be honest?"

I didn't really but what was I going to say? No, I want you to be dishonest. "Of course."

"That's what first put the thought in my mind, I guess. I mean coming over here and sleeping with you." She laughed. "My Mom is seriously smitten with you. I watched her face tonight. Wow. Anyway, I thought that would be a good way to pay her back. By sleeping with you, I mean. But by the end of the evening—God, this is really crazy, Roger, but I've got like this really incredible crush on you."

I wanted to say that I did, too. But I couldn't. I might be a new Roger on the outside but inside I was strictly the old model—shy, nervous and terrified that I was going to get my heart decimated.

By dawn, we'd made love three times, the last time in my large bed with a jay and a cardinal perched on the window watching us, and soft morning wind soughing the windbreak pines.

After we finished that last time, we lay in each others arms for maybe twenty minutes until she said, "I have to be unromantic."

"Be my guest."

"Goosebumps."

"Goosebumps?"

"And bladder."

"And bladder?"

"And morning breath."

"You're lost me."

"A, I'm freezing. B, I really have to pee. And C, may I use your toothbrush?"

In the following three weeks, she spent at least a dozen nights at my place, and on those nights when one or both of us had business to attend to, we had those lengthy phone conversations that new lovers always have. Makes no difference what you say as long as you get to hear her voice and she gets to hear yours. I had sent her dozens of flowers and dozens of notes, each signed "Love." Probably the truest measure of my condition was how my work suffered. Clients found me preoccupied and bosses singularly disinterested. And I didn't give one good damn. I even started dipping into the principal of my inheritance, something I swore I'd never do outside of a real emergency.

But somehow a shiny black sports car seemed in order, as did several new suits and jackets. Not to mention a diamond bracelet for Kendra's birthday.

Only occasionally did I pause and let the dread come over me like a drowning wave. I would lose her and be forever bereft afterward. I was suffused with her tastes and smells and sounds and textures—and yet someday all these things would be taken from me and I would be forever alone, and unutterably sad. But what the hell could I do? Walk away? Impossible. She was succor, and life source, and all I could do was cling till my fingers fell away and I was left floating on the vast dark ocean.

The 8th of December that year was one of those ridiculously sunny days that try and trick you into believing that spring is near. I spent two hours that afternoon cutting firewood in the back and then hauling it inside. Fuel for more trysts. On one of my trips inside, the doorbell rang. When I peeked out, I saw Amy. She looked very good—indeed much better than she had that night at the country club—except for her black eye.

I let her in and asked her if she wanted a cup of coffee, which she declined. She took the leather couch, I the leather armchair that Kendra and I still used on occasion.

"I need to talk to you, Roger." She wore a white turtleneck beneath a camel-hair car coat and designer jeans. There was a blue ribbon in her blonde hair and she looked very sexy in a suburban sort of way.

"All right."

"And I need you to be honest with me."

"If you'll be honest with me."

"The black eye?"

"The black eye."

"Who else? Randy. He came home drunk the other night and I wouldn't sleep with him so he hit me. He sleeps around so much I'm afraid he's going to pick up something." She shook her head with a solemnity I would never have thought her capable of.

"Does he do this often?"

"Sleep around?"

"And hit you."

She shrugged. "Pretty often. Both, I mean."

"Why don't you leave him?"

"Because he'd kill me."

"God, Amy, that's ridiculous. You can get an injunction."

"You think an injunction would stop Randy? Especially when

he's been drinking?" She sighed. "I don't know what to do anymore."

This was the woman I'd come back to steal but now I didn't want to steal her. I didn't even want to borrow her. I just felt sorry for her and the notion was disorienting.

"Now I want you to tell me about Kendra."

"I love her."

"Oh, just fucking great, Roger. Just fucking great."

"I know I'm a lot older than she is but—"

"Oh, for God's sake, Roger, it's not that."

"It isn't?"

"Of course it isn't. Come over here and sit down."

"Next to you?"

"That's the general idea."

I went over and sat down. Next to her. She smelled great. Same cologne Kendra wore.

She took my hand. "Roger, I want to sleep with you."

"I don't think that would be a good idea."

"All those years you were in love with me. It's not fair."

"What's not fair?"

"You should have gone on loving me. That's how it's supposed to work."

"What's supposed to work?"

"You know, lifelong romance. We're both romantics, Roger, you and I. Kendra is more like her father. Everything's sex."

"You slept with her boyfriend."

"Only because I was afraid and lonely. Randy had just beaten me up pretty badly. I felt so vulnerable. I just needed some kind of reassurance. You know, that I was a woman. That somebody would want me." She took both my hands and brought them to her lips and kissed them tenderly. I couldn't help it. She was starting to have the effect on me she wanted. "I want you to be in love with me again. I can help you forget Kendra. I really can."

"I don't want to forget Kendra."

"Deep down she's like Randy. A whore. She'll break your heart. She really will."

She put two of my fingers in her mouth and began sucking.

She was quite good in bed, maybe even better technically than Kendra. But she wasn't Kendra. There was the rub.

We lay in the last of the gray afternoon and the wind came up, a harsh and wintry wind suddenly, and she tried to get me up for a second time but it was no good. I wanted Kendra and she knew I wanted Kendra.

There was something very sad about it all. She was right. Romance—the kind of Technicolor romance I'd dreamed of—should last forever, despite any and all odds, the way it did in F. Scott Fitzgerald stories. And yet it hadn't. She was just another woman to me now, with more wrinkles than I had suspected, and a little tummy that was both sweet and comic, and veins like faded blue snakes against the pale flesh of her legs.

And then she started crying and all I could do was hold her and she tried in vain to get me up again and saw the failure not as mine but her own.

"I don't know how I ever got here," she said finally to the dusk that was rolling across the drab cold Midwestern land.

"My house you mean?"

"No. Here. Forty-two-god-damned-years old. With a daughter who steals the one man who truly loved me." A gaze icy as the winter moon, then, as she said, "But maybe things won't be quite as hunky-fucking-dory as she thinks they'll be."

Later on, I was to remember what she said vividly, the hunky-fucking-dory thing I mean.

Kendra appeared at nine that same night. I spent the first half hour making love to her and the second half trying to decide if I should tell her about her mother's visit.

Later, in front of the fireplace, a wonderful old film noir called *Odds Against Tomorrow* on cable, we made love a second time and then, lying in the sweet cool hollow of her arms, our juices and odors as one now, I said, "Amy was here today."

She stiffened. Her entire body. "Why?"

"It's not easy to explain."

"That bitch, I knew she'd do it."

"Come here, you mean?"

"Come here and put the shot on you. Which she did, right?"

"Right."

"But you didn't—"

I'd never had to lie to her before and it was far more difficult than I'd imagined it might be.

"Things get so crazy sometimes—"

"—oh shit."

"I mean you don't intend for things to happen but—"

"—oh shit," she said again. "You fucked her, didn't you?"

"—with all the best intentions, you—"

"Quit fucking babbling. Just say it. Say you fucked her."

"I fucked her."

"How could you do it?"

"I didn't want to."

"Right."

"And I could only do it once. No second time."

"How noble."

"And I regretted it immediately."

"Amy told me that when you were real geeky looking you were one of the sweetest people she ever knew."

She stood up, all beautiful brash nakedness, and stalked back toward the bedroom. "You should have kept your face ugly, Roger. Then your soul would still be beautiful."

I lay there thinking about what she said a moment and then I stalked back to the bedroom.

She was dressing in a frenzy. She didn't as yet have her bra on completely. Just one breast was cupped. The other looked lone and dear as anything I'd ever seen. I wanted to kiss it and coo baby talk to it.

Then I remember why I'd come in here. "That's bullshit, you know."

"What's bullshit?" she said, pulling up the second cup of her bra. She wore pantyhose but hadn't as yet put on her skirt.

"All that crap about keeping my face ugly so my soul would remain beautiful. If I hadn't had plastic surgery, neither you nor your mother would have given me a second glance."

"That's not true."

I smiled. "God, face it, Kendra, you're a beautiful woman. You're not going to go out with some geek."

"You make me sound as if I've really got a lot of depth."

"Oh, Kendra, this is stupid. I shouldn't have slept with Amy and I'm sorry."

"I'm just surprised she hasn't managed to tell me about it yet. She's probably waiting for the right dramatic moment. And in her version, I'm sure you threw her on the bed and raped her. That's what my father told her the night she caught us together. That I was the one who'd wanted to do it—"

"My God, you mean you—"

"Oh, not all the way. They had one of their country club parties and both Randy and I were pretty loaded and somehow we ended up on the bed wrestling around and she walked in and—well, I guess I tried very hard to give her the impression that we'd just been about to make it when she walked in and—"

"That's some great relationship you've got there."

"It's pretty sick and believe me, I know it."

I felt tired standing in the shadowy bedroom, the only light the December quarter-moon above the shaggy pines.

"Kendra—"

"Could we just lie down together?" She sounded tired, too.

"Of course."

"And not do anything, I mean?"

"I know what you mean. And I think that's a wonderful idea."

We must have lain there six, seven minutes before we started making love, and then it was the most violent love we'd ever made, her hurling herself at me, inflicting pleasure and pain in equal parts. It was a purgation I badly needed.

"She's always been like this."

"Your mother?"

"Uh-huh."

"Competitive you mean?"

"Uh-huh. Even when I was little. If somebody gave me a compliment, she'd get mad and say, 'Well, it's not hard for little girls to look good. The trick is to stay beautiful as you get older.'"

"Didn't your Dad ever notice?"

She laughed bitterly. "My father? Are you kidding? He'd usually come home late and then finished getting bombed and then climb in bed next to me and feel me up."

"God."

Bitter sigh. "But I don't give a shit. Not anymore. Fuck them. I come into my own inheritance in six months—from my paternal grandfather—and then I'm moving out of the manse and leaving them to all their silly fucking games."

"Is now a good time to tell you I love you?"

"You know the crazy god damned thing, Roger?"

"What's that?"

"I really love you, too. For the first time in my life, I actually love somebody."

~ ~ ~ ~ ~

On the night of 20 January, six weeks later, I went to bed early with a new Sue Grafton novel. Kendra had begged off our date because of a headcold. I'm enough of a hypochondriac that I wasn't unhappy about not seeing her.

I enjoyed twenty pages of Grafton and then I enjoyed the long leisurely fall into sleep. My last wakeful thoughts were of Kendra and of the marriage we'd begun to speak of in an awkward but eager way.

The call came just before two a.m., long after I was sleeping and just at the point where waking is difficult.

But get up I did and listen at length to Amy's wailing. It took me a long time to understand the exact message her sobs meant to convey.

~ ~ ~ ~ ~

The funeral took place on a grim snowy day when the harsh numbing winds rocked the pall bearers as they carried the gleaming silver coffin from hearse to grave site. The priest had the raw red nose of a rummy and the old man I stood next to, in between vast wet sobs, kept farting. A local TV anchorman, no brighter or more articulate than one would expect a local TV anchorman to be, made a few last claims about Randy's various virtues, and then turned things back to the priest who muttered and mumbled through some prayers that seemed to be neither quite Latin nor quite English. The land lay bleak as a tundra.

Later, in the country club where a luncheon was being served, an old high school friend came up and said, "I bet when they catch him he's a nigger."

"I guess it wouldn't surprise me."

"Oh, hell yes. Poor god damned guy is sleeping in his own bed when some jig comes in and blasts the hell out of him and then goes down the hall and shoots poor Kendra, too. They say she'll never be able to walk or talk again. Just sit in frigging wheelchair all the time. I used to be a liberal back in the sixties or seventies but I've had enough of their bullshit by now, I'll tell you that I've had their bullshit right up to here in fact."

Amy came late. In the old days, one might have accused her of doing so so she could make an entrance. But now she had a perfectly good reason. She walked with a cane, and walked slowly. The intruder who'd shot up the place that night, and stolen more than $75,000 in jewelry, had shot her in the shoulder and the leg, apparently leaving her for dead. Just as he'd left Kendra for dead.

Amy looked pretty damned good in her black dress and veil. The black gave her a mourning kind of sexiness.

A line formed. She spent the next hour receiving the members of that line just as she done at the mortuary the night before. There were tears, and laughter with tears, and curses with tears. The very old looked perplexed by it all—the world made no sense anymore; here you were a rich person and people still broke into your house and killed you right in your bed—and middle-aged people looked angry (those damned niggers) and the young looked bored (Randy being the drunk who'd always wobbled around pinching all the little girls on their bottoms—who cared he was dead, the pervert?).

I was the last person to go through the line and when she saw me, Amy shook her head and began sobbing. "Poor, poor Kendra," she said. "I know how much she means to you, Roger."

"I'd like to visit her tonight if I could. At the hospital."

Beneath her veil, she sniffled some more. "I'm not sure that's a good idea. The doctor says she really needs her rest. And Vic said she looked very tired this morning."

The bullet had entered her head just below her left temple. By rights, she should have died instantly. But the gods were playful and let her live—paralyzed.

"Vic? Who's Vic?"

"Our nurse. Oh, I forgot. I guess you've never met him, have you? He just started Sunday. He's really a dear. One of the surgeons recommended him. You'll meet him some time."

I met him four nights later at Kendra's bedside.

He was strapping arrogant was our blond Vic, born to a body and face that no amount of surgery or training could ever duplicate, a natural Tarzan to my own tricked-up one. He looked as if he wanted to tear off his dark and expensive suit and head directly back to the jungle to beat up a lion or two. He was also the proud owner of a sneer that was every bit as imposing as his body.

"Roger, this is Vic."

He made a point of crushing my hand. I made a point of not grimacing.

The three of us then stared down at Kendra in her bed, Amy leaning over and kissing Kendra tenderly on the forehead. "My poor baby. If only I could have saved her—"

That was the first time I ever saw Vic touch her and I knew instantly, from the proprietary way he did it, that something was wrong. He probably was a nurse, but to Amy he was also something far more special and intimate.

They must have sensed my curiosity because Vic dropped his hand from her shoulder and stood proper as an altar boy staring down at Kendra.

Amy shot me a quick smile, obviously trying to read my thoughts.

But I lost interest quickly. It was Kendra I wanted to see. I bent over the bed and took her hand and touched it to my lips. I was self-conscious at first, Amy and Vic watching me, but then I didn't give a damn. I loved her and I didn't give a damn at all. She was pale and her eyes were closed and there was a fine sheen of sweat on her fore-head. Her head was swathed in white bandages of the kind they al-ways used in Bogart movies, the same ones that Karloff also used as the Mummy. I kissed her lips and I froze there because the enormity of it struck me. Here was the woman I loved, nearly dead, indeed should have been dead given the nature of her wound, and behind me, paying only a kind of lip service to her grief, was Kendra's mother and a man eager to rest his hand on her the way a teenage boy rests his hand on the bottom of his girlfriend.

A doctor came in and told Amy about some tests that had been run today. Despite her coma, she seemed to be responding to certain stimuli that had had no effect on her even last week.

Amy started crying, presumably in a kind of gratitude, and then the doctor asked to be alone with Kendra, and so we went out into the hall to wait.

"Vic is moving in with us," Amy said. "He'll be there when Kendra gets home. She'll have help twenty-four hours a day. Won't that be wonderful?"

Vic watched me carefully. The sneer never left his face. He looked the way he might if he'd just noticed a piece of dog mess on the heel of his shoe. It was not easy being a big blond god. There were certain difficulties with staying humble.

"So you know Kendra's surgeon," I said to Vic.

"What?"

"Amy said the surgeon had recommended you to her."

They glanced at each other and then Vic said, "Oh, right, the sur-geon, yes." He gibbered like a Miss America contestant answering a question about patriotism.

"And you're moving in?"

He nodded with what he imagined was solemnity. If only he could do something about the sneer. "I want to help in any way I can."

"How sweet."

If he detected my sarcasm, he didn't let on.

The doctor came out and spoke in soft whispered sentences filled with jargon. Amy cried some more tears of gratitude.

"Well," I said, "I guess I'd better be going. Give you some qual-ity time with Kendra."

I kissed Amy on the cheek and shook Vic's proffered hand. He notched his grip down to mid-level. Even hulks have sentimental moments. He even tried a little acting, our Vic. "The trick will be to get her to leave before midnight."

"She stays late, eh?" I said.

Amy kept her eyes downcast, as befitted a saint who was being discussed.

"Late? She'd stay all night if they'd let her. You can't tear her away."

"Well, she and Kendra have a very special relationship."

Amy caught the sarcasm. Anger flashed in her eyes but then subsided. "I want to get back to her," she said. And Mother Theresa couldn't have said it any more believably.

I took the elevator down to the ground floor, then took the emergency stairs back up to the fourth floor. I waited in an alcove down the hall. I could see Kendra's door but if I was careful neither Amy nor Vic would be able to see me.

They left ten minutes after I did. Couldn't drag Amy away from her daughter's bedside, eh?

~ ~ ~ ~ ~

In the next six weeks, Kendra regained consciousness, learned how to manipulate a pencil haltingly with her right hand, and got tears in her eyes every time I came through the door. She still couldn't speak or move her lower body or left side but I didn't care. I loved her more than ever and in so doing proved to myself that I wasn't half as superficial as I'd always suspected myself of being. That's a good thing to know about yourself—that at age forty-four you have at least the potential for becoming an adult.

She came home in May, after three intense months of physical rehab and deep depression over her fate, a May of butterflies and cherry blossoms and the smells of steak on the grill on the sprawling grounds behind the vast English Tudor. The grounds ran four acres of prime land and the house, divided into three levels, included eight bedrooms, five full baths, three half-baths, a library and a solarium. There was also a long straight staircase directly off the main entrance. Amy had it outfitted with tracks so Kendra could get up and down in her wheelchair.

We became quite a cheery little foursome, Kendra and I, Amy and Vic. Four or five nights a week we cooked out and then went inside to watch a movie on the big-screen television set in the party room. Three nurses alternated eight-hour shifts so that whenever

Kendra—sitting silently in her wheelchair in one of her half-dozen pastel-colored quilted robes—needed anything, she had it. Amy made a cursory fuss over Kendra at least twice an evening, and Vic went to fetch something unimportant, apparently in an attempt to convince me he really was a working male nurse.

More and more I slipped out early from the brokerage, spending the last of the day with Kendra in her room. She did various kinds of physical therapy with the afternoon nurse but she never forgot to draw me something and then offer it up to me with the pride of a little girl pleasing her daddy. It always touched me, this gesture, and despite some early doubts that I'd be able to be her husband—I'd run away and find somebody strong and sound of limb; I hadn't had all that plastic surgery for nothing, had I?—I learned that I loved her more than ever. She brought out a tenderness in me that I rather liked. Once again, I felt there was at least some vague hope that I'd some-day become an adult. We watched TV or I read her interesting items from the newspaper (she liked the nostalgia pieces the papers some-times ran) or I just told her how much I loved her. "Not good for you" she wrote on her tablet one day and then pointed at her para-lyzed legs. And then broke into tears. I knelt at her feet for a full hour, till the shadows were long and purple, and thought how crazy it all was. I used to be afraid that she'd leave me—too young, too good-looking, too strong-willed, only using me to get back at her mother—and now she had to worry about some of the same things. In every way I could, I tried to assure her that I'd never leave her, that I loved her in ways that gave me meaning and dignity for the first time in my life.

Hot summer came, the grass scorching brown, night fires like the aftermath of bombing sorties in the dark hills behind the mansion. It was on one of these nights, extremely hot, Vic gone someplace, the easily-tired Kendra just put to bed, that I found Amy waiting for me in my car.

She wore a skimpy halter that barely contained her chewy-looking breasts, and startling white short-shorts. She sat on the pas-senger side. She had a martini in one hand and a cigarette in the other.

"Remember me, sailor?"

"Where's lover boy?"

"You don't like him, do you?"

"Not much."

"He thinks you're afraid of him."

"I'm afraid of rattlesnakes, too."

"How poetic." She inhaled her cigarette, exhaled a plume of blue against the moonlit sky. I'd parked at the far end of the pavement down by the three-stall garage. It was a cul-de-sac of sorts, protected from view by pines. "You don't like me any more, do you?"

"No."

"Why?"

"I really don't want to go into it, Amy."

"You know what I did this afternoon?"

"What?"

"Masturbated."

"I'm happy for you."

"And you know who I thought of?"

I said nothing.

"I thought about you. About that night we were together over at your house."

"I'm in love with your daughter, Amy."

"I know you don't think I'm worth a shit as a mother."

"Gee, whatever gave you that idea?"

"I love her in my way. I mean, maybe I'm not the perfect mother but I do love her."

"Is that why you won't put any make-up on her? She's in a fucking wheel-chair and you're still afraid she'll steal the limelight."

She surprised me. Rather than deny it, she laughed. "You're a perceptive bastard."

"Sometimes I wish I weren't."

She put her head back. Stared out the open window. "I wish they hadn't gone to the moon."

I didn't say anything.

"They spoiled the whole fucking thing. The moon used to be so romantic. There were so many myths about it and it was so much fun thinking about. Now it's just another fucking rock." She drained her drink. "I'm lonely, Roger. I'm lonely for you."

"I'm sure Vic wouldn't want to hear that."

"Vic's got other women."

I looked at her. I'd never seen her express real anguish before. I took a terrible delight in it. "After what you and Vic did, you two deserve each other."

She was quick about it, throwing her drink in my face, then getting out of the car and slamming the door shut. "You bastard! You think I don't know what you meant by that? You think I killed Randy, don't you?"

"Randy—and tried to kill Kendra. But she didn't die the way she was supposed to when Vic shot her."

"You bastard!"

"You're going to pay for it someday, Amy. I promise you that."

She still had the glass in her hand. She smashed it against my windshield. The safety glass spider-webbed. She stalked off, up past the pines, into invisibility.

~ ~ ~ ~ ~

I didn't bring it up. Kendra did. I'd hoped she'd never figure out who was really the intruder that night. She had a difficult enough time living. That kind of knowledge would only make it harder.

But figure it out she did. One cool day in August, the first hint of autumn on the air, she handed me what I assumed would be her daily love note.

VIC
CHECK
FIGHT
$

I looked at the note and then at her.

"I guess I don't understand. You want me to check something about Vic?"

Her darting blue eyes said no.

I thought a moment: Vic, check. All I could think of was checking Vic out. Then, "Oh, a check? Vic gets some kind of check?"

The darting blue eyes said yes.

"Vic was having an argument about a check?"

Yes.

"With your mother?"

Yes.

"About the amount of the check?"

Yes.

"About it not being enough?"

Yes.

And then she started crying. And I knew then that she knew. Who'd killed her father. And who'd tried to kill her.

I sat with her a long time that afternoon. At one point a fawn came to the edge of the pines. Kendra made a cooing sound when she saw it, tender and excited. Starry night came and through the open window we could hear a barn owl and later a dog that sounded almost

387

like a coyote. She slept sometimes, and sometimes I just told her the stories she liked to hear, Goldilocks and the Three Bears and Rapunzel, stories, she'd once confided, that neither her mother or father had ever told her. But this night I was distracted and I think she sensed it. I wanted her to understand how much I loved her. I wanted her to understand that even if there were no justice in the universe at large, at least there was justice in our little corner of it.

~ ~ ~ ~ ~

On a rainy Friday night in September, in an apartment Vic kept so he could rendezvous with a number of the young women Amy had mentioned, a tall and chunky man, described as black by two neighbors who got a glimpse of him, broke into Vic Bailey's place and shot him to death. Three bullets. Two directly to the brain. The thief then took more than $5,000 in cash and travelers checks (Vic having planned to leave for a European vacation in four days).

The police inquired of Amy, of course, as to how Vic had been acting lately. They weren't as yet quite convinced that his death had been the result of a simple burglary. The police are suspicious people but not, alas, suspicious enough. Just as they ultimately put Randy's death down to a robbery-and-murder, so they ultimately ruled that Vic had died at the hand of a burglar, too.

On the day Amy returned from the funeral, I had a little surprise for her, just to show her that things were going to be different from now on.

That morning I'd brought in a hair stylist and a make-up woman. They spent three hours with Kendra and when they were finished, she was as beautiful as she'd ever been.

We greeted Amy at the vaulted front door—dressing in black was becoming a habit with her—and when she saw Kendra, she looked at me and said, "She looks pathetic. I hope you know that." She went directly to the den where she spent most of the day drinking scotch and screaming at the servants.

Kendra spent an hour in her room, crying. She wrote the word "pathetic" several times on her paper. I held her hand and tried to assure her that she indeed looked beautiful, which she did.

That night, as I was leaving—we'd taken dinner in Kendra's room, neither of us wanting to see Amy any more than we needed to—she was waiting, in my car again, even drunker than she'd been the first time. She had her inevitable drink in her hand. She wore a dark turtleneck and white jeans with a wide, sash-like leather belt.

She looked a lot better than I wanted her to.

"You prick, you think I don't know what you did? I know your god-damned secret and don't think I don't."

"Welcome to the club. I know a lot of secrets."

"I happened to have fucking loved him."

"I'm tired, Amy. I want to go home."

In the pine-smelling night, a silver October moon looked as ancient and fierce as an Aztec icon.

"You killed Vic," she said.

"Sure, I did. And I also assassinated JFK."

"You killed Vic, you bastard."

"Vic shot Kendra."

"You can't prove that."

"Well, you can't prove that I shot Vic, either. So please remove your ass from my car."

"I really never though you'd have the balls. I always figured you for the faggot-type."

"Just get out, Amy."

"You think you've won this, Roger. But you haven't. You're fucking with the wrong person, believe me."

"Good night, Amy."

She got out of the car and then put her head back in the open window. "Well, at least there's one woman you can satisfy, anyway. I'm sure Kendra thinks you're a great lover. Now that she's paralyzed, anyway."

I couldn't help it. I got out of the car and walked over to her across the dewy grass. I ripped the drink from her hand and then said, "You leave Kendra and me alone, do you understand?"

"Big brave man," she said. "Big brave man."

I hurled her drink into the bushes and then walked back to the car.

~ ~ ~ ~ ~

In the morning, the idea was there waiting for me.

I called work and told them I wouldn't be in and then spent the next three hours making phone calls to various doctors and medical supply houses as to exactly what I'd need, and what I'd need to do. I even set up a temporary plan for private-duty nurses. I'd have to dig into my inheritance but this was certainly worth it. Then I drove downtown to the jeweler's, stopping by the travel agency on my way back.

I didn't phone. I wanted to surprise her.

The Australian groundsman was covering some tulips when I got there. Frost was predicted. "G'day," he said, smiling. If he wasn't over sixty with a pot belly and white hair, I would have suspected Amy of using him for her personal pleasure.

The maid let me in. I went out to the back terrace, where she said I'd find Kendra.

She liked to look at the rolling hills and the green green pines, remembering, I suppose, when she was young and had roamed this land, all bright and innocent and merry—merry as you could be with Amy and Randy as parents, anyway.

I tip-toed up behind her, flicked open the ring case and held it in front of her eyes. She made that exultant cooing sound in her throat and then I walked around in front of her and leaned over and gave her a gentle, tender kiss. "I love you," I said. "And I want to marry you right away and have you move in with me."

She was crying but then so was I. I knelt down beside her and put my head on her lap, on the cool surface of her pink quilted housecoat. I let it lie there for a long time as I watched a dark graceful bird ride the wind currents above, gliding down the long sunny autumn day. I even dozed off for a time.

At dinner time, I rolled Kendra to the front of the house, where Amy was entertaining one of the Ken-doll men she'd taken up with these days. She was already slurring her words. "We came up here to tell you that we're going to get married."

The doll-man, not understanding the human politics here, said in a Hollywood kind of way, "Well, congratulations to both of you. That's wonderful." He even toasted us with his martini glass.

Amy said, "He's actually in love with me."

Doll-man looked at me and then back at Amy and then down at Kendra.

I turned her chair sharply from the room and began pushing it quickly over the parquet floor toward the hallway.

"He's been in love with me since second grade and he's only marrying her because he knows he can't have me!"

And then she hurled her glass against the wall, smashing it, and I heard, in the ensuing silence, doll-man cough anxiously and say, "Maybe I'd better be going, Amy. Maybe another night would be better."

"You sit right where you fucking are," Amy said, "and don't fucking move."

I locked Kendra's door behind us on the unlikely chance that

Amy would come down to apologize.

We sat for three hours in the shadows of her room, watching the harvest moon and the silver jet trails glowing in the night sky. I told her that she'd soon be away from her mother and that we'd have our own life together, a better life than either of us had ever known before. And then I stretched her out on the bed and lay next to her and told her of Jack and the Beanstalk and The Three Bears. She liked the Bears especially because I tried different voices for Mama and Papa and Baby. And then we just lay there and I felt safer and saner and happier than I ever had before.

Around ten, she began to snore quietly. The nurse knocked softly on the door. "I need to get in there, sir. The missus is upstairs sleeping."

I leaned over and kissed Kendra tenderly on the mouth.

We set the date two weeks hence. I didn't ask Amy for any help at all. In fact, I avoided her as much as possible. She seemed similarly inclined. I was always let in and out by one of the servants.

Kendra grew more excited each day. We were going to be married in my living room by a minister I knew vaguely from the country club. I sent Amy a handwritten note inviting her but she didn't respond in any way.

I suppose I didn't qualify as closest kin. I suppose that's why I had to hear it on the radio that overcast morning as I drove to work.

It seemed that one of the city's most prominent families had been visited yet again by tragedy—first the father dying in a robbery attempt a year earlier, and now the wheelchair-confined daughter falling down the long staircase in the family mansion. Apparently she'd come too close to the top of the stairs and simply lost control. She'd broken her neck. The mother was said to be under heavy sedation.

~ ~ ~ ~ ~

I must have called Amy twenty times that day but she never took my calls. The Aussie gardener usually picked up. "Very sad here today, mate. She was certainly a lovely lass, she was. You have my condolences."

I cried till I could cry no more and then I took down a bottle of Black and White scotch and proceeded to do it considerable damage as I sat in the gray gloom of my den.

The liquor dragged me through a Wagnerian opera of moods—forlorn, melancholy, sentimental, enraged—and finally left me wrapped round my cold hard toilet bowl, vomiting. I was not exactly a world-class drinker.

She called just before midnight, as I stared dully at CNN. Nothing they said registered on my conscious mind.

"Now you know how I felt when you killed Vic."

"She was your own daughter."

"What kind of life would she have had in that wheelchair?"

"You put here there!" And then I was up, frantic crazed animal, walking in small tight circles, screaming names at her.

"Tomorrow, I'm going to the police," I said.

"You do that. Then I'll go there after you do and tell them about Vic."

"You can't prove a damned thing."

"Maybe not. But I can make them awfully suspicious. I'd remember that if I were you."

She hung up.

It was November then, and the radio was filled with tiny cynical messages of Christmas. I went to the cemetery once a day and talked to her and then I came home and put myself to sleep with Black and White and Valium. I knew it was Russian roulette, that particular combination, but I thought I might get lucky and lose.

The day after Thanksgiving, she called again. I hadn't heard from her since the funeral.

"I'm going away."

"So?"

"So. I just thought I'd tell you that in case you wanted to get hold of me."

"And why would I want to do that?'

"Because we're joined at the hip, darling, so to speak. You can put me in the electric chair and I can do the same for you."

"Maybe I don't give a damn."

"Now you're being dramatic. If you truly didn't give a damn, you would've gone to the police two months ago."

"You bitch."

"I'm going to bring you a little surprise when I come back from my trip. A Christmas gift, I guess you'd call it."

~ ~ ~ ~ ~

I tried working but I couldn't concentrate. I took an extended leave. The booze was becoming a problem. There was alcoholism on both sides of my family so my ever-increasing reliance on blackouts wasn't totally unexpected, I suppose. I stopped going out. I learned that virtually anything you needed would happily be brought to you if you had the money, everything from groceries to liquor. A cleaning woman came in one day a week and bulldozed her way through the mess. I watched old movies on cable, trying to lose myself especially in the triviality of the musicals. Kendra would have loved them. I found myself waking, many mornings, in the middle of the den, splayed on the floor, after apparently trying to make it to the door but failing. One morning I found that I'd wet myself. I didn't much care, actually. I tried not to think of Kendra, and yet she was all I *did* want to think about. I must have wept six or seven times a day. I dropped twelve pounds in two weeks.

I got sentimental about Christmas Eve, decided to try and stay reasonably sober and clean myself up a little bit. I told myself I was doing this in honor of Kendra. It would have been our first Christmas Eve together.

The cleaning lady was also a good cook and had left a fine roast beef with vegetable and potato fixings in the refrigerator. All I had to do was heat it up in the microwave.

I had just set my place at the dining room table—with an identical place setting to my right for Kendra—when the doorbell rang.

I answered it, opening the door and looking out into the snow-whipped darkness.

I know I made a loud and harsh sound, though if it was a scream exactly, I'm not sure.

I stepped back from the doorway and let her come in. She'd even changed her walk a little, to make it more like her daughter's. The clothes, too, the long double-breasted camel hair coat and the wine-colored beret, were more Kendra's style than her own. Beneath was a four-button empire dress that matched the color of the beret. . .the exact dress Kendra had often worn.

But the clothes were only props.

It was the face that possessed me.

The surgeon had done a damned good job, whoever he or she was, a damned good job. The nose was smaller and the chin was now heart-shaped and the cheekbones were more pronounced and perhaps a half-inch higher. And with her blue blue contacts—

Kendra. She was Kendra.

"You're properly impressed, Roger, and I'm grateful for that," she said, walking past me to the dry bar. "I mean, this was not without pain, believe me. But then you know that first-hand, don't you, being an old hand at plastic surgery yourself."

She dropped her coat in an armchair and fixed herself a drink.

"You bitch," I said, slapping the drink from her hand, hearing it shatter against the stone of the fireplace. "You're a goddamned ghoul."

"Maybe I'm Kendra reincarnated," she smiled. "Have you ever thought of that?"

"I want you out of here."

She stood on tiptoes, just as Kendra had once done, and touched my lips to hers. "I knew you'd be gruff the first time you saw me. But you'll come around. You'll get curious about me. If I taste any different, or feel any different. If I'm—Kendra."

I went over to the door, grabbing her coat as I did so. Then I yanked her by the wrist and spun her out into the snowy cold night, throwing her coat after her. I slammed the door.

Twenty minutes later, the knock came again. I opened the door, knowing just who it would be. There were drinks, hours of drinks, and then, quite before I knew what was happening and much against all I held sacred and dear, we were somehow in bed and as she slid her arms around me there in the darkness, she said, "You always knew I'd fall in love with you someday, didn't you, Roger?"

EYE OF THE BEHOLDER

1

All this started one spring when I couldn't find any women. The weather was so beautiful it just made me crazier. I'd lie on my bed in my little apartment, feeling the moon-breezes and would ache, absolutely effing ache, to be with a woman I cared about. I was in one of those periods when I needed to fall ridiculously in love. It wasn't just that sex would be better—everything would be better. Fifty times a day I'd spot women who seemed likely candidates—they'd be in supermarkets or video stores or walking along the river or getting into their cars. The first thing I did was inspect them quickly for wedding rings. A good number of them were unburdened. But still, meeting them was impossible. If you just walked up to them and introduced yourself, you'd probably look like a rapist. And if you told them how lonely you were, you might not look like a rapist but you'd sure seem pathetic. I tried all the usual places, the bars and the dance clubs and some of the splashier parties, but I didn't see it in their eyes. They were looking for quick sex or companionship while they tended broken hearts, or simply a warm body at their dinner tables when too many lonely Saturday nights became intolerable. But they weren't looking for the same thing I was, some kind of spiritual redemption. Not that I didn't settle some nights for quick sex and companionship, but next morning, I felt just as lonely and disconsolate. I couldn't settle very often. I wanted my ideal woman, this notion I've had in my mind since I was seven or eight years old, this ethereal Madonna I had longed for down the decades.

So of course the night I met Linda I wasn't even looking for anybody. I just walked into this little coffee shop over by the public library and there she was, sitting alone at the counter drinking coffee.

I wasn't sure she could rescue me, and I doubt she was sure I could rescue her, but at least the potential was there, so two nights later we started going to bed. Even though we were sort of awkward with each other, we kept trying till we got it right, and then we became pretty good lovers. The only thing that got me down was she was still pretty hung up on this football coach who'd dumped her recently. She kept telling me how it had only been for sex, and how he was an animal six, seven hours a night, which did not exactly fill me with self-confidence. I wasn't jealous of the guy but I didn't necessarily want to attend his testimonial dinner every night, either.

The only other thing that bothered me was her two teen-aged daughters. They were usually around the house while Linda and I were making love. Linda always laughed when I got uptight. "Hey, what do you think they do in their bedrooms when they bring their boyfriends over here?"

Linda was one of those modern parents. I'm not. My two kids, daughter and son, were raised pretty much the way I was: what your parents don't know won't hurt them. One boozy New Year's Eve I actually heard this teenage girl talking to her mother about how her tenth-grade boyfriend wasn't any good at oral sex. Linda wasn't that far gone but she was a lot more liberal with her daughters than I would've been. Even when my wife and I split up, we agreed that our kids would be raised properly, at least as we defined "properly."

I kept wanting Linda to go to my place to make love, but one night she laughed and said, "But your place is such a pit, Dwyer. I'm afraid I'd have cockroaches walking up my thigh."

Linda was three years divorced from a very prosperous insurance executive. She'd gotten the big house and the big car and the big monthly check. She only had to work part-time at a travel agency to make her monthly nut.

So we made love at her place, and even though we both figured out pretty quickly that we weren't going to rescue each other, the thing we had was better than nothing. So we kept it up, even though I had the sense that she was vaguely ashamed of herself for liking me. Her previous boyfriends had run to MD's and shrinks and business executives. Security guard was a long way down the ladder.

Then one night I went over and she was late getting home from work. And that was the night it happened, with her sixteen-year-old daughter Susan, I mean.

~ ~ ~ ~ ~

Started out with an argument in the kitchen between Susan and Molly.

I was sitting in the living room watching a boxing rerun on ESPN. Linda had just called and said she was running late.

First I hear screaming. Then I hear cursing. Then I hear a cup or a glass being smashed against the wall. Then screaming again.

I run out there and find sixteen-year-old Susan slapping fifteen-year-old Molly across the face.

You have to understand, they were both extremely good-looking girls. But Molly was even more than extremely good-looking. She was probably the single most beautiful person I had ever seen, a Madonna with just a hint of the erotic in her dark and brooding eyes. Her sister Susan had always been jealous of her, and now there was special trouble because Susan's boyfriend had developed this almost creepy fixation on Molly.

I got between them.

"Get the hell out of this kitchen," Susan said. "You don't even belong here."

"You shouldn't talk to him like that," Molly said.

"Why? Because our sweet mommy is fucking him?"

Molly shook her head, looked embarrassed, and left the kitchen. In moments, I heard her on the stairs, going up to the second floor.

Susan pushed past me and opened the refrigerator door. She took out a can of Bud, popped the tab and gunned some down.

"I'm sure you'll tell my mother I was drinking this." Before I could say anything, she said, "By the way, she's sleeping with this new guy Brad at the travel agency. That's why she's late. She's going to tell you all about it. But she doesn't want to hurt your feelings." She smiled at me. "On the other hand, I don't mind hurting your feelings at all."

"So your boyfriend dumped you, huh?" Hell, I was just as petty as she was.

For the first time, I felt sorry for her. The anger and arrogance were suddenly gone from her face. She just looked sad and lost and painfully young. She even lost some of her sexiness in that moment, tiny sad pink barrette turning her into a little girl again. She was all vulnerability now.

She went over to the breakfast nook and sat down in the booth.

"You want a beer, Dwyer?"

"You gonna tell your mom I took one?"

She laughed. "I actually like you."

"Yeah, I could tell."

"I'm sorry I told you about Mom's new boyfriend."

Women know all the secrets in the world. All the important ones, anyway. Men just know all that bullshit that doesn't matter in the long run.

"It was bound to happen," I said.

"You're not gonna be heartbroken?"

"For maybe a week. Or two. Probably more my pride than anything."

"He's sort of an asshole. I mean, I met him a couple of times. Real stuck on himself. But he's real cute."

"I'm happy for him. Maybe I'll take you up on that beer."

I felt betrayed, stunned, pissed, sad and slightly embarrassed. I was more of an interloper than ever in this house. Very soon now, I'd be back to roaming my apartment and talking to imaginary women again.

I got a beer and sat down.

"You ever been in love?" she said.

"Sure."

"Really in love?"

"Uh-huh."

"It's terrible, isn't it?"

"Sometimes."

"This is the third one."

"Third one?"

"Yeah, the third boyfriend I've had who's fallen in love with Molly. The first one was in sixth grade. His name was Rick. I loved him so much, I'd get the Neiman-Marcus catalog down and look at wedding gowns. Then one day I found a note he'd written her. It took me a year to get over it." She shrugged. "Or maybe I've never gotten over it."

"So it happened again."

"Yeah, Paul—you met him—he broke up with me six weeks ago and he's been calling her ever since. She doesn't encourage him—I mean, its not her fault—but he follows her around all the time. Takes pictures of her, too. He's the photographer for the high-school paper. Real good with a telephoto lens." She stared out the window. "He was like part of the family. Mom liked him, even. And she doesn't like many boys." She looked over at the sheepdog, Clarence, who was treated like the third child. Now he sprawled on the kitchen floor, watching her. "Clarence wouldn't bark at him or try to eat him or anything."

Reference to Clarence made her smile.

"If it isn't Molly's fault, why'd you hit her?"

She shrugged. "Because I hate her. At least a part of me does. If she wasn't so beautiful—" She looked at me. "She's even got one of her teachers in love with her."

"Really?"

"Yeah. One day I was afraid my boyfriend was writing her letters, and so I snuck into her room and started looking around and there was this letter from Mr. Meacham, her English teacher. He said he loved her and was willing to leave his wife and daughter for her."

"Molly ever encourage him?"

She shook her head. "Molly is the most virginal person I know. Sometimes I think she's retarded. I really do. She's still a little girl in a lot of ways. She gets these crushes on her teachers. This year it's Mr. Meacham. He's teaching her the Romantic poets and Molly keeps telling me how much she thinks he looks like Matt Dillon, who's her favorite movie star. To her, it's all very innocent. But not to Mr. Meacham." She hesitated. "I even think she's started seeing him at nights. Last week I was out at Warner Mall and saw them sitting together in the Orange Julius."

"Does your mother know about this?"

"I haven't told her. She's got problems of her own with Molly. Well, with Brad."

"The guy at the travel agency?"

"Uh-huh. He's been over here a few times and it's pretty obvious he's fallen in love with Molly."

"You said he was young. How young?"

"Twenty-one."

"Well, that's better than Mr. Meacham lately."

"He may be the one stalking her."

"Someone's stalking her?"

"Yeah. Grabbed her the other night in the breezeway. But she got away. And been sending her threatening notes." She sighed. "I want to be pissed off at her but I can't. She doesn't understand the effect she has on men. She really doesn't." Then: "I feel like shit. God, I can't believe I slapped her. I'd better go talk to her."

"Good idea. Tell your mom something came up and I had to go."

"Sorry I broke the news to you that way. I mean, about Brad."

"It's all right."

"Like Mom says, I can be a bitch on wheels when I want to be."

We stood up and she gave me a hard little hug and then I went away. For good.

2

So it was back to the streets for me the rest of the summer. I kept thinking about Molly and how beautiful she was and how otherwise sensible men, young and old alike, seemed to take leave of their senses when they were around her. While I wasn't looking for virginal fifteen-year-olds, I was looking for the same kind of explosive love affair those men were, one that blinds you to all else, the narcotic that no amount of drugs could ever equal. In a few years, I'd be fifty. There weren't many such love affairs left for me. I'd had three or four of them in my lifetime, and I wanted one more before the darkness. So I went back to the bars, I became infatuated ten times a day in grocery store and discount houses and even gas stations when I'd see the backside of a fetching lady bent slightly to put gas in her tank. But mostly my reality was my solitary bed and moon-shadow, white curtains whipping ghostly in the rain-smelling wind, my lips silent with a thousand vows of undying love.

The summer ground on. One of the investigators at Allied Security had to have a heart by-pass so they shifted me from security (which I like) to working divorce cases (which I hate). While I've committed my share of adultery, I can't say that it's ever pleasant to think about. Betrayal is not exactly a tribute to the human spirit. The men seemed to take a strange kind of pride in what they were doing. They didn't seem particularly concerned about being secretive, anyway. But the cheating women were all a little furtive and frantic and even sad, as if they were doing this against their will. Maybe they were paying back cheating husbands. Four weeks of this stuff before the investigator came back to Allied. My advertising daughter came to town just as August was starting to punish us. My son drove in from med-school in the east. Their mother had married again, third time a charm or so she said, a man with some means, apparently, whom they liked much better than husband number two, a bank vice-president with great country club aspirations.

"You've got to find yourself a woman," my daughter said right before she kissed me goodbye at the airport.

One night in late September, beautiful Indian Summer, I came home and found Linda sitting in my living room. "Your landlady let me in," she said. Then: "This is really a depressing place, Dwyer. You think we could go somewhere else?"

She didn't like any of the bars I recommended. Too downscale, presumably. We ended up in a place where businessmen yelled and whooped it up a lot about the Hawkeyes. The way they shouted and strutted around, you'd think they owned copper mines down in Brazil, where they could make people work for twenty-five cents an hour.

"Did you hear what happened to Molly? It was in the news about three weeks ago."

"I guess not."

"Somebody cut her up."

"Cut her up?"

"Slashed her cheeks. Do you remember a New York model that happened to a few years ago?"

"Yeah. She wasn't ever able to work again."

Linda's eyes glistened with tears. "The plastic surgeon said there's only so much he can do for Molly. She looks terrible."

"What're the police saying?"

She shook her head, sleek and sexy in a white linen suit, her dark hair recently cut short. "No leads."

"Molly didn't see her assailant?'

"It was dark. She'd parked her car in the garage and was just walking into the house—through the breezeway, you know—and he was waiting there. I guess this happened before—somebody in the breezeway I mean—but neither Molly nor Susan told me about it. Why should they tell me anything? I'm just their mother."

"She's sure it was a 'he'?"

"That's the assumption everybody's making. That it was a guy, I mean."

"She doesn't have any sense of who it might have been?"

Linda sighed. "Maybe."

"Maybe?"

She nodded. "I think she knows who it was but won't say."

"Why would she protect somebody?"

"I'm not sure." Pause. "I've been having terrible thoughts lately."

"Oh?"

"I've been thinking that Susan may have done this."

"Your daughter?"

"Yes." Pause. "She's very jealous of Molly. Molly—well, a few of Susan's boyfriends have fallen in love with Molly over the last year or so. About a month ago, Susan made up with this boy, Paul, the one who'd fallen in love with Molly. But then she came home one night and found Paul drunk in the living room putting the moves on Molly."

"You really think it's possible that Susan could do something like this?"

"She's been upstaged by Molly all her life. Even as a baby, Molly sort of unhinged people. I mean, she's the most beautiful girl I've ever seen. And I think I'm being objective about that."

"Anybody else who might have done it?"

"The police are talking to one of Molly's teachers, this Mr.

Meacham. That's another thing my girls didn't tell me until after this happened. It seems this Mr. Meacham offered to leave his wife and daughter for Molly. He's forty-three years old. My God."

"Anybody else you can think of?"

After another drink was set down in front of her, she said, "I have to tell you something. It's so ridiculous, it pisses me off to even repeat it."

I just waited for her to say it.

"Last night, my dear sweet daughter Susan accused me of slashing Molly's face."

Calmly as I could, I said, "Why would she say something like that?"

"I'm kind of embarrassed telling you the rest."

"Maybe it'll make you feel better."

"I trashed Molly's room."

"When?"

"Late August, I guess."

"Why?"

"Brad."

"The guy from the travel agency?"

"Uh-huh. He'd started phoning her—Molly, I mean—when I wasn't there. Then one night he came right out and asked me. I mean, I suspected something was wrong. He hadn't touched me in two weeks. Then this one night he said, 'Would it really piss you off if I asked Molly out?' I didn't want to let him know how pissed I was, so I just said that I didn't think that was such a great idea. But I said it in this real calm voice. I told him that technically she wouldn't reach the age of consent until October, and he said he'd wait. Then after he left—I sat in the den and got really drunk and then I went upstairs and started screaming at Molly. Then I started trashing her room."

She started crying. "My own daughter, and I treated her that way."

I changed the subject quickly. "You mentioned Susan's ex-boyfriend."

"Paul."

"Tell me about him."

"Right. He calls Molly four times a day. He says he doesn't care about her face being cut up. He loves her. His parents have called me, they're so worried about him. He went from A's to D's last semester. They want him to see a shrink. When Molly won't come to the phone, he gets furious."

"And you think Molly might know who did it?"

"I think so. Would you talk to her?"

"It'd probably be easier if you went through the agency. Ask them to assign me to you. I don't really have much time for any freelance on the side."

"Fine. I'll call them tomorrow. I really appreciate this, Jack." Then: "Oh God."

"What?"

"It's almost ten. I'm supposed to meet somebody at ten-fifteen way across town." She shrugged. "Met somebody new at the agency. He's a little older than Brad."

"Sixteen?"

She smiled. "Wise ass." Then: "I really am sorry. You know, about Brad and everything."

"I survived."

"I'd always be willing to see you again."

"I never take handouts except at Christmas time."

What the hell, it never hurts to sound dignified once in a while.

3

The next day, she led me up to the den on the second floor. "She sits in the dark. The blinds are drawn and everything, I mean. You'll get used to the shadows. She doesn't want anybody to see her. But I convinced her you only wanted to help her." Then she went away.

I knocked and a small voice said to come in and I went in and there she sat in a leather recliner by a TV set that was playing a soap opera. Just as I started to sit down in the chair facing her, a commercial came on, the bright colors flashing across the screen illuminating her face.

He'd done a damned good job. If it was a he. Long deep vertical gashes on both cheeks. The stitches were still on, and that just made her look worse. But even with the stitches gone, her beauty would be forever and profoundly marred.

"Remember me?"

She looked at me with solemn eyes and nodded.

"You think we could turn the TV down a bit?'

She picked up the remote and brought the volume down to a low number.

"Your mom wants me to make sure that you told the police everything, Molly. You understand that?"

Again she nodded. I had the unnerving sense that she'd also been struck mute.

"She told me what Susan said. About hearing somebody run away right after it happened. Is that true?"

Again, she nodded.

"I checked out your breezeway last night, Molly. That's where it happened, right?"

She said: "I wish I didn't have to go through this, Jack."

"I wish you didn't have to either, sweetheart."

"I mean your questions."

"Oh."

"My mom talked to the principal this morning. I'm going to finish my classes at home this year. So I don't have to see—anybody. You know, at school."

"You're going to sit in this room, huh?"

"Pretty much."

"With the blinds drawn."

"I like it when it's dark. When nobody can see me this way."

"Can I tell you about the breezeway, Molly?"

"The breezeway?"

"Uh-huh. I came out here last night and checked it out when everybody was asleep. You've got an alarm system that kicks on the yard lights whenever anybody approaches the house."

"I guess so."

"That means that when the person who did this to you ran off, you had a very good chance to see his face."

"Oh."

I waited for her to say more, and when she didn't, I watched her for a moment—she wore an aqua blouse and jeans and white socks— and then I said, "I think you know who did this to you. And I think that you're trying to protect him."

"You keep saying 'him,' Jack. Maybe it was a woman."

"Is that what you're telling me? That it was a woman?"

"No, but—"

"It'll come out eventually, Molly. One way or the other, the police are going to figure out who did this to you."

"I just want it to be over with. I've accepted it and I just want it to be over with."

"It was either Paul or Mr. Meacham, wasn't it?"

"I don't want to talk anymore, Jack."

"Your mother loves you, Molly."

"I know."

"And she's very worried about you."

"I know that, too."

"She doesn't like the idea that whoever did this is still out there running around free."

"It's over with, Jack. It happened. And I don't have any choice but to accept it. People accept things all the time. There was a girl in my class two years ago who lost her legs in a tractor accident. She was staying on her uncle's farm. She'll never be able to walk again. People accept things all the time."

"He should have to pay for doing this, Molly. I don't know what's going through your head, but nothing justifies somebody doing this to you. Nothing."

I stood up.

"Susan is worried about you, too."

She nodded. "I'd like to watch this show now, if you don't mind." But she smiled for the first time. Her scars were hideous in the flickering lights of the TV picture tube. "I appreciate you caring about me, Jack. You're a nice guy. You really are."

~ ~ ~ ~ ~

When I got downstairs, I found Susan and Clarence waiting for me. The big sheepdog lay next to the desk where Susan was working on her homework.

As always, the over-trained dog barked as I approached. I was going to get him some Thorazine for Christmas.

"Mom said to say goodbye. She had to run back to work." Then: "How'd it go with Molly?"

I told her about coming out there last night and testing the yard lights. "She had to've gotten a good look at the person who did this."

"You're sure?"

"Positive. Tell me one more time. You were sitting in here watching TV—"

"—and I heard her scream and then I ran out to the breezeway and I saw somebody at the edge of the yard running away. He went up over the white fence out there."

"You said 'he.' Male?"

"I think so."

"And Molly was—"

"Molly was in a heap on the breezeway floor. When I flipped on the light, all I could see was the blood. She was in pretty bad shape. Then Clarence came running out and he was barking like crazy." Then: "I think she knows. Who did it, I mean."

"So do I."

"But why would she protect him?"

"That's what I need to figure out. I'm going over to see our friend Paul."

"I'm trying to keep an open mind. The way he dumped me for Molly, I mean, I really hate him. But that doesn't mean he'd do something like this."

"No, I guess it doesn't," I said. I leaned over and gave her a kiss on the forehead. "Anybody ever tell you what a nice young woman you are?"

"Yeah," she said. "Paul used to tell me that all the time. Before he fell in love with Molly."

4

Paul lived in a large Colonial house on a wide suburban street filled with little kids doing stunts on skateboards.

As soon as his mother learned who I was, her polite smile vanished. "You don't have any right to ask him any questions."

I was still outside the front door. "The family has asked me to talk to him."

"He didn't do it," she said. "I'll admit that he's been pretty— involved with Molly lately. But he'd never hurt her. Ever. And that's just what we told the police."

She was a tall, slender woman in black slacks and a red button-down shirt. There was a kind of casual elegance to her movements, as if she might have long ago studied dance.

Behind her, a voice said: "It's all right, Mom. I'll talk to him."

Paul was taller than his mother but slender in the same graceful way. There was a snub-nosed boyishness to the face that the dark eyes belied. There was age and anger in the eyes, as if he'd lived through a bitter experience lately and was not the better for it.

"You sure?" she said to Paul.

"Finish fixing dinner, Mom. I'll talk to him."

He wore a Notre Dame football jersey and ragged Levi cut-offs. His feet were bare. There was an arrogance about him, a certain dismissiveness in the gaze.

His mother gave me a last enigmatic look and then vanished from the doorway.

"I don't have much time," he said.

"I just have two questions."

"The police had a lot more than two."

"Can you account for your time the night Molly was cut up?"

"If I have to."

"Meaning what?"

"Meaning I mostly drove around to the usual places."

"And 'the usual places' would be where exactly?"

"The mall and the parking lot next to the Hardee's out on First Avenue and then out to the mall again."

"And you can prove that?"

"Sure," he said. But for the first time his lie became obvious. His gaze evaded mine.

I said: "I saw her."

He didn't ask me who "her" was.

"When?"

"A few hours ago."

"Was she—"

"I didn't get a real good look at her. The room was pretty dark."

He surprised me, then, as human beings constantly do. His eyes got wet with tears. "The poor kid."

"She's a nice girl."

"She's a lot more than nice."

"Susan's nice, too."

"Yeah, she is. And I treated her like shit and I'm sorry about it." He cleared tears from his face. "I couldn't help—what I feel for Molly. It just kind of happened."

"Molly's mother thinks you're obsessed with her. In the clinical sense, I mean."

"I love her. If that's being obsessed." He sounded a lot older and a lot wearier than he had just a few minutes ago.

"Her mother also thinks you were the one who cut her."

He smiled bitterly. "That's funny. I've been thinking it was her mother who did it."

"Are you serious?"

He nodded. "Hell, yes, I'm serious. Her mother's got a real problem with Molly. She's very jealous of her. Molly told me how bitter she was when this Brad started coming after her. She pushed Molly down the stairs, bruised her up pretty bad."

"She show you the bruises?"

"Yeah."

"She wasn't exaggerating?"

"Not at all."

Somewhere inside, a telephone rang, was picked up on the second ring. His mother called: "Telephone, Paul."

"Maybe I'd better get that."

"You can prove where you were when Molly was being cut?"

He surprised me again. "No, I can't Mr. Dwyer. I can't. I was alone."

"How about the mall?"

He shrugged. "I just made it up."

"Then you were doing what?"

"Just driving around."

Mother: "Honey, somebody's waiting on the phone."

"Just driving around?"

"Thinking about her. Molly. I really have to go, Mr. Dwyer."

"Honey!" his mother called again.

5

This was the kind of neighborhood where college professors always lived in the movies of my youth, a couple blocks of brick Tudors set high up on well-landscaped hills. The cars in the driveways ran to Volvos and Saabs, and the music, when you heard it through the occasional open window, ran to Brahms and Mahler. At night, the professors would sit in front of the fireplace, a blanket across their legs, reading Eliot or Frost. Even if life here wasn't really like this, it was nice to think that even a small part of our world could still be so enviably civilized.

A knock and the door opened almost at once. A heavy woman in a green sweater and a pair of too-snug jeans stood there watching me with obvious displeasure. She wore too much makeup on her fleshy, bitter face. Women who lived in these houses were supposed to look dignified, not like aging dance club babes. "Yes?" she said. Her mouth was small and bitter. She'd sucked on a lot of lemons, at least figurative ones, in her time.

"I'd like to see Bob Meacham."

She did something odd, then. She smiled with a kind of nasty pleasure. "Oh, God, you're another cop, aren't you?"

"Sort of."

I showed her my license.

"Well, come in, Mr. Dwyer. Would you like some coffee?"

"No, thanks."

I couldn't figure out why she was so happy to see me suddenly. Why would the presence of a private detective bring her such pleasure?

She flung an arm to a leather wingback chair that sat, comfortably, near a fireplace. An identical chair sat just across the way.

"I'll be right back."

She didn't go far. The floor creaked a few times and then she said, "So it's all over, is it, you bastard? Well, guess who's here to see you? Another cop. Your little girlfriend must think you were the one who cut her up."

When he appeared, moments later, he kept looking over his shoulder at his wife, as if he was waiting for her to put a knife in his back.

He came over and said, "I'm Bob Meacham."

"Jack Dwyer. Nice to meet you."

We shook hands.

"What can I do for you, Mr. Dwyer?"

"I wanted to ask you some questions about Molly."

"Oh, I see."

His wife, who stood to the side of him, smirked at me. "When we first got married, Mr. Dwyer, I used to worry that my husband was secretly gay. I guess I should be happy he just has this nice heterosexual thing for underage girls."

Meacham obliged her by blushing.

Seeing that she'd scored a direct hit, she said, "I'll go back to my woman's work now, and leave you two to discussing the wages of sin."

"I know what you must think of her," Meacham said softly after his wife left. "But it's my fault, I mean, I've made her like this. I've—I've had a lot of affairs over the years. We should've gotten divorced a long time ago but—somehow it's just never happened."

He didn't fit the professorial mold, either. He was a little too beefy and a little too rough in the face. He'd probably played football at some point in his life. Or boxed. His nose and jaw had the look of heavy contact with violence. He wore a chambray shirt and jeans. His balding head didn't make him look any more professorial, either. It just added to the impression of middle-aged toughness. He didn't belong in a Tudor house with a Volvo in the drive and T.S. Eliot lying open on his knee.

"You said you've had some affairs."

"Yes."

"Were they with young girls?"

"Youngish."

"Meaning?"

"Always of consenting age, if that's what you're getting at."

"Molly isn't of age."

"Molly's the first. A fluke. Being that young, I mean."

"You realize that hustling her has opened you up to several legal charges if the cops want to press them."

"You may not believe this, Mr. Dwyer, but I wasn't hustling her. We haven't slept together. I don't plan to sleep with her till we're married. I know people laugh at me; I mean, I know I'm not much better than a dirty joke these days, but I don't give a damn about anything or anybody other than Molly."

He looked at me.

"You're smiling, Mr. Dwyer."

"Are you seeing a shrink?"

"No."

"You should be."

"I'm in love with her."

"She's fifteen."

"She's also the most spiritually beautiful creature I've ever known. That's why I say I'm not hustling her, Mr. Dwyer. That's why I say we won't make love till we're married."

"Or at least till he gets out of prison," Mrs. Meacham said, walking back into the room.

For the first time, I saw the sorrow Meacham had hinted at. Saw it in the slump of her shoulder, saw it behind the pain and anger in her gaze. She looked old and sad and slightly adrift.

"He's going to lose his teaching job—the school is already seeing to that—and then the district attorney will charge him with contributing. He brought her over here one day while I was gone and they drank wine together. Isn't that sweet?"

She hovered at the back of his chair. The smirk was back.

"He said he's going to leave me everything, when he runs away with her. Probably Tahiti, is what I'm thinking. He's always been obsessed with Gauguin. He even got sweet Molly interested in him."

She started wandering around the living room. We watched her with great glum interest.

"He's going to leave me everything, Mr. Dwyer. The mortgage. The car that has nearly 175,000 miles on it. The bank account that never gets above $2,000. And the cancer. I've had three cancer surgeries in the past four years, Mr. Dwyer. And I'll know in a few weeks if I need another one." This time there was no smirk, just grief in the eyes and mouth. "And you know the worst thing of all, Mr. Dwyer? I still love him. God, I'm just as sick as he is but I can't help it."

After a moment, Meacham said, "Why don't you go upstairs and lie down? You sound tired."

She looked at me. "I'm sorry for all this, Mr. Dwyer."

I didn't know what to say.

"That's why we don't have friends anymore. Nobody wants to come over here and hear all this terrible bullshit we put each other through."' Then: "Goodbye, Mr. Dwyer."

After she left, he said, "I suppose you're getting a bad impression of me."

I almost laughed. He was pursuing a fifteen-year-old, cheating on a wife with cancer, and thinking of running away and leaving that same wife with all the bills. Gee, why would that give me a bad impression of him?

"My opinion of you doesn't matter."

He stared at me a long time. "I'm a romantic, Mr. Dwyer. I believe in the ideals of art and beauty. That's why I was so drawn to Molly. She's beautiful in an idealistic way—perfectly untouched—a virgin of body and mind. That's why I want to take her away—to save her so that she doesn't become corrupted."

I thought of Brad dumping Linda for Molly; and Paul dumping Susan for Molly, and taking her picture all the time, and following her around obsessively; and I thought of how I'd been all summer, meeting perfectly fine women whom I rejected because they didn't fit my ideal. A dangerous thing, beauty. It brings out the best and worst in men. The trouble is, sometimes the best and the worst are there at the same time—Meacham here loving her in the pure way of a college boy dumbstruck by the beauty of art; and yet at the same time willing to hurt a wife who was sick and needed him. The best and the worst. Beauty has a way of making us even more selfish than money does.

"She said no."

"Who said no?"

"Molly."

"She told you that, Mr. Dwyer?"

"In so many words."

"So you think that because she was taking some time to think it over—"

I sighed. "Meacham, listen to me. She wasn't thinking it over. There was no way she was ever going to run off with you. Ever. But maybe deep down you really understood that. And maybe deep down that's why you cut her face."

"My God, you really think I could do that?"

"I think it's possible. You're so obsessive about her that—"

"'Obsessive.' That's a word my wife would use. A clinical word. There's nothing clinical in my feelings for Molly, believe me. They're pure passion. And I emphasize *pure* and *passion*. There's no way I could cut her up. She's the woman I've waited for all my life."

I wondered if I happened to be blushing at this point in the conversation. I thought again of all the women I'd stayed away from because they weren't my ideal. Good women. There's nothing like hearing your own sappy words put into the sappy mouth of someone else. Then you realize how inane your beliefs really are.

"Were you here the night it happened?"

"No, Mr. Dwyer, I wasn't. I was walking, actually."

"The entire night?"

"Most of it. You're wanting an alibi?"

"That would help."

"I don't have one—other than the fact that I'm a creator, Mr. Dwyer, not a destroyer. I have created something with Molly that is too beautiful for anybody to destroy. Even I couldn't destroy it if I wanted to."

I had to agree with his wife. I don't know why she stuck it out all these years, either.

"I'll be going now, Mr. Meacham."

A chill smile. "You don't like me much, do you, Mr. Dwyer?"

"Not much, " I said.

"You're like her," he said, and nodded upwards to where his wife lay in her solitary bed. "Very middle-class and judgmental without even understanding what you're judging."

"Maybe you're right," I said. "But I doubt it."

I left.

6

Clarence started barking at me the minute I pulled into the drive. He was in the breezeway, where he spent a lot of time on these unseasonably warm autumn evenings. Linda came out and calmed him down and then let me in.

"I guess we should be grateful he barks so much, as a watch dog and all, but sometimes he drives me crazy."

Then, apparently out of guilt for saying such a thing, she bent down and patted his head fondly, and said in baby talk, "You drive Mommy crazy, don't you, Clarence?"

Susan was in the kitchen setting out placemats on the breakfast nook table.

"We're doing Domino's tonight," Susan said. "Are you going to join us, Jack?"

I still couldn't imagine either of them doing it, cutting her up that way, daughter to one, sister to the other.

"Pepperoni and green pepper," Linda said.

"You convinced me."

Susan got beers for her mother and me and a Diet Pepsi for herself. Just as we were sitting down in the nook, Clarence exploded into barks again. The Domino's man had pulled into the drive.

"Maybe Clarence needs some tranquilizers," Susan said.

"I put a twenty on the counter there, hon," Linda said to her.

While Susan was out paying the pizza man, and calming Clarence, Linda said, "Did you talk to them?"

"Yes."

"Any impressions?"

"They're both good possibilities," I said. "Especially Meacham. I've been learning some things about him. He's a real creep. His wife has cancer and he's still running around on her. He thinks he's the last of the Romantic poets."

"Good for him. He's the one I'd bet on. For doing that to Molly, I mean."

Susan came back with the pizza and we ate.

Halfway through the feast, Linda said, "Tell him about Mark."

"Oh, Mom."

"Go on. Tell him."

Susan shot me a you-know-how-moms-are smile and said, "Mark Feldman asked me to the Homecoming dance."

"Great," I said.

"Honey, Dwyer doesn't know who Mark Feldman is. Tell him."

"He's a football player."

"Jeeze, honey, you're not helping Dwyer at all. Mark Feldman just happens to be the best quarterback who ever played in this state. He's also a very nice looking boy. Much better looking than that creep Paul. And he's really got the hots for my cute little daughter here."

"God, Mom. The 'hots.' That sounds like something you'd get from a toilet seat."

We all laughed.

"Congratulations," I said.

"And she was worried that nobody'd want to ask her out anymore, Dwyer. Pretty crazy, huh?"

A knock on the breezeway door.

Susan went out to the breezeway to see who was there. She came back in carrying two pans.

"Bobbi brought your cake pans back, Mom. She said the upside down cake was great and to thank you for the recipe, too."

"Thank Gold Medal flour," Linda said. "The recipe was on the back."

I guess it was the silence from the breezeway I noticed. Clarence tended to bark at strangers when they came up to the door and when they were leaving. But he hadn't barked at all with Bobbi.

"Why didn't Clarence bark just now?" I said.

"Oh, you mean with Bobbi?" Linda said.

"Right."

"He knows her real well. He doesn't bark with our best friends."

Then I remembered something that Susan had said to me back when I'd first met her.

I said, "He doesn't bark when Paul comes up, either, does he?"

"No," Susan said.

"The other night, when Molly was cut, you said you heard screams from the breezeway. But did you hear barking?"

Susan thought a moment. "No, I guess I didn't."

"Would Clarence have barked if Meacham had come up?"

"Absolutely," Linda said.

I tried not to make a big thing of it but they could see what I was thinking. I finished my three slices of pizza and my beer and then said I needed to go and do some work.

7

He wasn't too hard to find. I spent some time in the parking lot with some burglary tools I used on occasion, and then I went inside the mall looking for him.

He was hanging out with some other boys in front of a music store.

When he saw me, he started looking nervous. He whispered something to one of his friends.

Three good-sized boys stepped in front of him, like a shield, as I started approaching.

They were going to block me as he ran away.

"Molly wants to see you," I said over the shoulders of the boys.

He had just started to turn, ready to make his run, when he heard me and angled his face back toward mine.

"What?"

"She wants to see you. She sent me to get you."

"Bullshit," he said.

I shrugged. "All right. I'll tell her you didn't want to come."

The boy in the middle, who went two-twenty easy, decided to have a little fun with the old man. He stepped right up to me and said, "You want to rumble, Pops?"

The other kids laughed. Nothing kids love more than bad dialogue from fifties movies.

"Like I said, Paul, I'll tell her you didn't want to see her." I looked down at the tough one and said, "If that's all right with you, Sonny."

I hadn't kicked the shit out of anybody for a long time, but the tough one was giving me ideas.

"Fuck that 'Sonny' bullshit," the tough one said.

But Paul had a hand on his shoulder and was turning him back.

"She really wants to see me?"

"Yeah," I lied. "She does."

Paul looked at the tough one. "I better go, then, Michael."

"With this creep?" Michael said.

"Yeah."

Michael glowered at me. The others did, too, but Michael had done some graduate work in glowering, so he was the most impressive.

"Nice friends," I said, as we turned back toward one of the exits. I said it loud enough to get Michael all worked up again. "Especially the dumb one with the big mouth."

~ ~ ~ ~ ~

We sat in an Orange Julius.

"I thought we were going to Molly's."

"We are."

"When?"

"Soon as you explain this."

From my pocket, I took a stained paper sack. "Know what this is, Paul?"

"You sonofabitch."

"There's a hunting knife in there. A bloody one. I'll bet the blood is Molly's."

"You sonofabitch."

"You said that already."

"That's illegal."

"What is?"

"Getting into my trunk that way."

"Wanna go call the cops?"

"You sonofabitch."

"How about calling me a bastard for a while? Breaks the monotony."

"It isn't what you think."

"No? You ride around with a bloody knife in your trunk and you don't have an alibi for the other night and it isn't what I think? You're telling me you didn't cut her?"

He started crying then, sitting right there in Orange Julius. He put his face in his hands and wept. People watched us. Son and father, they probably figured, with the father being a prime asshole for making his son cry this way. I took out my clean handkerchief and handed it over to him. I felt sorry for him. I shouldn't have but I did.

Loving somebody can make you crazy. All the fine sane people in the mental health industry tell you that you shouldn't give into it so hard, but you can't help it. There was a poet named Charles Bukowski who said that the most dangerous time to know any man is when he's been spurned in love. And from my years as a cop dealing with domestic abuse cases, Bukowski was absolutely right. So I sat there hating him for what he'd done to poor poor Molly, and feeling sorry for him, too. He'd ended her life, now I was going to make sure that his life was ended, too. He'd be tried as an adult and serve a long, long sentence. The way all men who visit their rages on helpless women should be sentenced.

He started snuffling then and picked up my handkerchief and blew his nose and said, "You still don't understand, Dwyer."

"Understand what?"

"What really happened."

"Then tell me."

So he told me and I said, "Bullshit. I should beat your face in for even saying that."

"Let's go see Molly."

"Are you serious?"

"Absolutely."

I walked across to the pay phones, keeping my eye on him all the time. It was preposterous, what he'd said.

When Linda came on, I told her I was bringing Paul over and taking him up to the den to see Molly. I said I couldn't answer any of her questions. She did not sound happy about that.

~ ~ ~ ~ ~

Soft silvered shadows played in the darkness of the den. Molly wore a pair of jeans and white blouse and sat primly in the chair next to the dead TV. There was no question of turning on the lights. Molly had pretty much decided to live her life in darkness.

Paul and I sat on the edge of the narrow leather couch.

"He told me something crazy, Molly," I said. "I just wanted to give you the chance to tell me he's lying."

"I had to tell him, Molly," Paul said. "I'm sorry."

I told her what he'd said and she said, "Paul loves me."

"I guess I don't know what that means, Molly," I said gently. I was starting to get goosebumps because it appeared that Paul had told me the truth, after all.

"He loves me. That's why he did it."

"Why he cut you up that way?"

"Yes."

"You wanted him to cut you?"

"I asked him to. He didn't want to. But I kept after him till he did it. I just couldn't take the way people acted around me. My face. It's why I was having all this trouble with my mother and my sister and my friends. I didn't ask for my face, Mr. Dwyer. I'd be much happier if I was plain, because then I wouldn't have to have all these people after me—like I was some sort of prize or something." Then to Paul: "I finally made you understand, didn't I, Paul."

"Yes," Paul said.

"And he said he'd love me just as much if I didn't have my looks. And he does, don't you, Paul, even though I'll never be beautiful again?"

Even in moon-shadow, his young face looked set and grim. He nodded.

Then she started sobbing and Paul went over to her and knelt next to her and took her in his arms and held her with a tenderness that moved and shook me. This wasn't puppy love or lust. This was real and simple and profound, the way his young arms held her young body.

At that moment he was father and brother and friend and priest, and only coincidentally, lover. I let myself out of the den and went downstairs.

8

"I'm having one, too," Susan said, when her mother asked her to bring us beers.

She brought three and we sat in the breakfast nook and I told them what had happened.

Linda cried and Susan held her.

"You think we should go up there, Jack?" Susan said as her mother wept in her arms.

"I'd give them a few more minutes."

"Do you think she's sane?" Susan said.

I shrugged. "I think she probably needs to see a shrink."

Linda sat up suddenly. She was angry. "That little prick took advantage of her. That's why he cut her face that way. He figured if he made her ugly, nobody else would want her. He was just being selfish, that's why he did it."

She made a fist and muttered a curse beneath her breath.

"You think that's true, Jack?" Susan said.

"Maybe."

"Maybe he did it because he really loves her," Susan said.

"Maybe," I said.

"I'm not going to sit here and listen to this bullshit," Linda said. "I'm going up there."

And with that, she forced Susan out of the booth.

"Mother, maybe you'd better stay down here for a little while," Susan called.

"She's my god-damned *daughter*," Linda said, sounding hysterical. "My god-damned *daughter*."

She stormed off to the front of the house and the stairway.

Susan shook her head. "Maybe he really did do it because he loved her. Isn't that possible, Jack?"

She wanted to believe in love and romance, just the same way I wanted to believe in being redeemed by the right woman. There was a good chance we were foolish people. Maybe very foolish.

Then Linda was screaming and Molly was sobbing and a terrible rage and despair filled the house, like the scent of rain on a sudden chill black wind.

Susan said, "Could I hold your hand for a minute, Jack? For just a minute."

I did my best to smile but I don't think it was very good. Not very good at all.

"For just a minute," I said. "But not much longer."

Ed Gorman

Ed Gorman has written in practically every genre imaginable, from suspense and mysteries to science fiction and horror.

He has been dubbed the "Poet of Dark Suspense" and much of his work haunts that ill-defined land between horror and mystery where the emphasis is as much on fear and shock as it is on crime and detection.

Gorman has also been called "one of suspense fiction's best storytellers" by Ellery Queen, and "one of the most original voices in today's crime fiction" by *The San Diego Union*.

His work has appeared in magazines as various as *The New York Times*, *Redbook*, *Ellery Queen*, *The Magazine of Fantasy and Science Fiction*, and *Louis L'Amour's Western Magazine*.

His novel *The Poker Club* recently became a feature film.

RAMBLE HOUSE's

HARRY STEPHEN KEELER WEBWORK MYSTERIES

(RH) indicates the title is available ONLY in the RAMBLE HOUSE edition

The Ace of Spades Murder
The Affair of the Bottled Deuce (RH)
The Amazing Web
The Barking Clock
Behind That Mask
The Book with the Orange Leaves
The Bottle with the Green Wax Seal
The Box from Japan
The Case of the Canny Killer
The Case of the Crazy Corpse (RH)
The Case of the Flying Hands (RH)
The Case of the Ivory Arrow
The Case of the Jeweled Ragpicker
The Case of the Lavender Gripsack
The Case of the Mysterious Moll
The Case of the 16 Beans
The Case of the Transparent Nude (RH)
The Case of the Transposed Legs
The Case of the Two-Headed Idiot (RH)
The Case of the Two Strange Ladies
The Circus Stealers (RH)
Cleopatra's Tears
A Copy of Beowulf (RH)
The Crimson Cube (RH)
The Face of the Man From Saturn
Find the Clock
The Five Silver Buddhas
The 4th King
The Gallows Waits, My Lord! (RH)
The Green Jade Hand
Finger! Finger!
Hangman's Nights (RH)
I, Chameleon (RH)
I Killed Lincoln at 10:13! (RH)
The Iron Ring
The Man Who Changed His Skin (RH)
The Man with the Crimson Box
The Man with the Magic Eardrums
The Man with the Wooden Spectacles
The Marceau Case
The Matilda Hunter Murder
The Monocled Monster

The Murder of London Lew
The Murdered Mathematician
The Mysterious Card (RH)
The Mysterious Ivory Ball of Wong Shing Li (RH)
The Mystery of the Fiddling Cracksman
The Peacock Fan
The Photo of Lady X (RH)
The Portrait of Jirjohn Cobb
Report on Vanessa Hewstone (RH)
Riddle of the Travelling Skull
Riddle of the Wooden Parrakeet (RH)
The Scarlet Mummy (RH)
The Search for X-Y-Z
The Sharkskin Book
Sing Sing Nights
The Six From Nowhere (RH)
The Skull of the Waltzing Clown
The Spectacles of Mr. Cagliostro
Stand By—London Calling!
The Steeltown Strangler
The Stolen Gravestone (RH)
Strange Journey (RH)
The Strange Will
The Straw Hat Murders (RH)
The Street of 1000 Eyes (RH)
Thieves' Nights
Three Novellos (RH)
The Tiger Snake
The Trap (RH)
Vagabond Nights (Defrauded Yeggman)
Vagabond Nights 2 (10 Hours)
The Vanishing Gold Truck
The Voice of the Seven Sparrows
The Washington Square Enigma
When Thief Meets Thief
The White Circle (RH)
The Wonderful Scheme of Mr. Christopher Thorne
X. Jones—of Scotland Yard
Y. Cheung, Business Detective

Keeler Related Works

A To Izzard: A Harry Stephen Keeler Companion by Fender Tucker — Articles and stories about Harry, by Harry, and in his style. Included is a compleat bibliography.

Wild About Harry: Reviews of Keeler Novels — Edited by Richard Polt & Fender Tucker — 22 reviews of works by Harry Stephen Keeler from *Keeler News.* A perfect introduction to the author.

The Keeler Keyhole Collection: Annotated newsletter rants from Harry Stephen Keeler, edited by Francis M. Nevins. Over 400 pages of incredibly personal Keeleriana.

Fakealoo — Pastiches of the style of Harry Stephen Keeler by selected demented members of the HSK Society. Updated every year with the new winner.

RAMBLE HOUSE's OTHER LOONS

The End of It All and Other Stories — Ed Gorman's latest short story collection

Four Dancing Tuatara Press Books — *Beast or Man?* By Sean M'Guire; *The Whistling Ancestors* by Richard E. Goddard; *The Shadow on the House* and *Sorcerer's Chessmen* by Mark Hansom. With introductions by John Pelan

The Dumpling — Political murder from 1907 by Coulson Kernahan

Victims & Villains — Intriguing Sherlockiana from Derham Groves

Evidence in Blue — 1938 mystery by E. Charles Vivian

The Case of the Little Green Men — Mack Reynolds wrote this love song to sci-fi fans back in 1951 and it's now back in print.

Hell Fire — A new hard-boiled novel by Jack Moskovitz about an arsonist, an arson cop and a Nazi hooker. It isn't pretty.

Researching American-Made Toy Soldiers — A 276-page collection of a lifetime of articles by toy soldier expert Richard O'Brien

Strands of the Web: Short Stories of Harry Stephen Keeler — Edited and Introduced by Fred Cleaver

The Sam McCain Novels — Ed Gorman's terrific series includes *The Day the Music Died, Wake Up Little Susie* and *Will You Still Love Me Tomorrow?*

A Shot Rang Out — Three decades of reviews from Jon Breen

Mysterious Martin, the Master of Murder — Two versions of a strange 1912 novel by Tod Robbins about a man who writes books that can kill.

Dago Red — 22 tales of dark suspense by Bill Pronzini

The Night Remembers — A 1991 Jack Walsh mystery from Ed Gorman

Rough Cut & New, Improved Murder — Ed Gorman's first two novels

Hollywood Dreams — A novel of the Depression by Richard O'Brien

Seven Gelett Burgess Novels — *The Master of Mysteries, The White Cat, Two O'Clock Courage, Ladies in Boxes, Find the Woman, The Heart Line, The Picaroons*

The Organ Reader — A huge compilation of just about everything published in the 1971-1972 radical bay-area newspaper, *THE ORGAN*.

A Clear Path to Cross — Sharon Knowles short mystery stories by Ed Lynskey

Old Times' Sake — Short stories by James Reasoner from Mike Shayne Magazine

Freaks and Fantasies — Eerie tales by Tod Robbins, collaborator of Tod Browning on the film FREAKS.

Six Jim Harmon Double Novels — *Vixen Hollow/Celluloid Scandal, The Man Who Made Maniacs/Silent Siren, Ape Rape/Wanton Witch, Sex Burns Like Fire/Twist Session, Sudden Lust/Passion Strip, Sin Unlimited/Harlot Master, Twilight Girls/Sex Institution.* Written in the early 60s.

Marblehead: A Novel of H.P. Lovecraft — A long-lost masterpiece from Richard A. Lupoff. Published for the first time!

The Compleat Ova Hamlet — Parodies of SF authors by Richard A. Lupoff – A brand new edition with more stories and more illustrations by Trina Robbins.

The Secret Adventures of Sherlock Holmes — Three Sherlockian pastiches by the Brooklyn author/publisher, Gary Lovisi.

The Universal Holmes — Richard A. Lupoff's 2007 collection of five Holmesian pastiches and a recipe for giant rat stew.

Four Joel Townsley Rogers Novels — By the author of *The Red Right Hand: Once In a Red Moon, Lady With the Dice, The Stopped Clock, Never Leave My Bed*

Two Joel Townsley Rogers Story Collections — Night of Horror and Killing Time

Twenty Norman Berrow Novels — *The Bishop's Sword, Ghost House, Don't Go Out After Dark, Claws of the Cougar, The Smokers of Hashish, The Secret Dancer, Don't Jump Mr. Boland!, The Footprints of Satan, Fingers for Ransom, The Three Tiers of Fantasy, The Spaniard's Thumb, The Eleventh Plague, Words Have Wings, One Thrilling Night, The Lady's in Danger, It Howls at Night, The Terror in the Fog, Oil Under the Window, Murder in the Melody, The Singing Room*

The N. R. De Mexico Novels — Robert Bragg presents *Marijuana Girl, Madman on a Drum, Private Chauffeur* in one volume.

Four Chelsea Quinn Yarbro Novels featuring Charlie Moon — *Ogilvie, Tallant and Moon, Music When the Sweet Voice Dies, Poisonous Fruit* and *Dead Mice*

Five Walter S. Masterman Mysteries — *The Green Toad, The Flying Beast, The Yellow Mistletoe, The Wrong Verdict* and *The Perjured Alibi.* Fantastic impossible plots.

Two Hake Talbot Novels — *Rim of the Pit, The Hangman's Handyman.* Classic locked room mysteries.

Two Alexander Laing Novels — *The Motives of Nicholas Holtz* and *Dr. Scarlett,* stories of medical mayhem and intrigue from the 30s.

Four David Hume Novels — *Corpses Never Argue, Cemetery First Stop, Make Way for the Mourners, Eternity Here I Come*, and more to come.

Three Wade Wright Novels — *Echo of Fear, Death At Nostalgia Street* and *It Leads to Murder*, with more to come!

Eight Rupert Penny Novels — *Policeman's Holiday, Policeman's Evidence, Lucky Policeman, Policeman in Armour, Sealed Room Murder, Sweet Poison, The Talkative Policeman, She had to Have Gas* and *Cut and Run* (by Martin Tanner.)

Five Jack Mann Novels — Strange murder in the English countryside. *Gees' First Case, Nightmare Farm, Grey Shapes, The Ninth Life, The Glass Too Many.*

Seven Max Afford Novels — *Owl of Darkness, Death's Mannikins, Blood on His Hands, The Dead Are Blind, The Sheep and the Wolves, Sinners in Paradise* and *Two Locked Room Mysteries and a Ripping Yarn* by one of Australia's finest novelists.

Five Joseph Shallit Novels — *The Case of the Billion Dollar Body, Lady Don't Die on My Doorstep, Kiss the Killer, Yell Bloody Murder, Take Your Last Look.* One of America's best 50's authors.

Two Crimson Clown Novels — By Johnston McCulley, author of the Zorro novels, *The Crimson Clown* and *The Crimson Clown Again.*

The Best of 10-Story Book — edited by Chris Mikul, over 35 stories from the literary magazine Harry Stephen Keeler edited.

A Young Man's Heart — A forgotten early classic by Cornell Woolrich

The Anthony Boucher Chronicles — edited by Francis M. Nevins
Book reviews by Anthony Boucher written for the *San Francisco Chronicle,* 1942 – 1947. Essential and fascinating reading.

Muddled Mind: Complete Works of Ed Wood, Jr. — David Hayes and Hayden Davis deconstruct the life and works of a mad genius.

Gadsby — A lipogram (a novel without the letter E). Ernest Vincent Wright's last work, published in 1939 right before his death.

My First Time: The One Experience You Never Forget — Michael Birchwood — 64 true first-person narratives of how they lost it.

A Roland Daniel Double: The Signal and The Return of Wu Fang — Classic thrillers from the 30s

Murder in Shawnee — Two novels of the Alleghenies by John Douglas: *Shawnee Alley Fire* and *Haunts.*

Deep Space and other Stories — A collection of SF gems by Richard A. Lupoff

Blood Moon — The first of the Robert Payne series by Ed Gorman

The Time Armada — Fox B. Holden's 1953 SF gem.

Black River Falls — Suspense from the master, Ed Gorman

Sideslip — 1968 SF masterpiece by Ted White and Dave Van Arnam

The Triune Man — Mindscrambling science fiction from Richard A. Lupoff

Detective Duff Unravels It — Episodic mysteries by Harvey O'Higgins

Automaton — Brilliant treatise on robotics: 1928-style! By H. Stafford Hatfield

The Incredible Adventures of Rowland Hern — Rousing 1928 impossible crimes by Nicholas Olde.

Slammer Days — Two full-length prison memoirs: *Men into Beasts* (1952) by George Sylvester Viereck and *Home Away From Home* (1962) by Jack Woodford

Murder in Black and White — 1931 classic tennis whodunit by Evelyn Elder

Killer's Caress — Cary Moran's 1936 hardboiled thriller

The Golden Dagger — 1951 Scotland Yard yarn by E. R. Punshon

A Smell of Smoke — 1951 English countryside thriller by Miles Burton

Ruled By Radio — 1925 futuristic novel by Robert L. Hadfield & Frank E. Farncombe

Murder in Silk — A 1937 Yellow Peril novel of the silk trade by Ralph Trevor

The Case of the Withered Hand — 1936 potboiler by John G. Brandon

Finger-prints Never Lie — A 1939 classic detective novel by John G. Brandon

Inclination to Murder — 1966 thriller by New Zealand's Harriet Hunter

Invaders from the Dark — Classic werewolf tale from Greye La Spina

Fatal Accident — Murder by automobile, a 1936 mystery by Cecil M. Wills

The Devil Drives — A prison and lost treasure novel by Virgil Markham

Dr. Odin — Douglas Newton's 1933 potboiler comes back to life.

The Chinese Jar Mystery — Murder in the manor by John Stephen Strange, 1934

The Julius Caesar Murder Case — A classic 1935 re-telling of the assassination by Wallace Irwin that's much more fun than the Shakespeare version

West Texas War and Other Western Stories — by Gary Lovisi

The Contested Earth and Other SF Stories — A never-before published space opera and seven short stories by Jim Harmon.

Tales of the Macabre and Ordinary — Modern twisted horror by Chris Mikul, author of the *Bizarrism* series.

The Gold Star Line — Seaboard adventure from L.T. Reade and Robert Eustace.

The Werewolf vs the Vampire Woman — Hard to believe ultraviolence by either Arthur M. Scarm or Arthur M. Scram.

Black Hogan Strikes Again — Australia's Peter Renwick pens a tale of the outback.

Don Diablo: Book of a Lost Film — Two-volume treatment of a western by Paul Landres, with diagrams. Intro by Francis M. Nevins.

The Charlie Chaplin Murder Mystery — Movie hijinks by Wes D. Gehring

The Koky Comics — A collection of all of the 1978-1981 Sunday and daily comic strips by Richard O'Brien and Mort Gerberg, in two volumes.

Suzy — Another collection of comic strips from Richard O'Brien and Bob Vojtko

Dime Novels: Ramble House's 10-Cent Books — *Knife in the Dark* by Robert Leslie Bellem, *Hot Lead* and *Song of Death* by Ed Earl Repp, *A Hashish House in New York* by H.H. Kane, and five more.

Blood in a Snap — The *Finnegan's Wake* of the 21st century, by Jim Weiler

Stakeout on Millennium Drive — Award-winning Indianapolis Noir — Ian Woollen.

Dope Tales #1 — Two dope-riddled classics; *Dope Runners* by Gerald Grantham and *Death Takes the Joystick* by Phillip Condé.

Dope Tales #2 — Two more narco-classics; *The Invisible Hand* by Rex Dark and *The Smokers of Hashish* by Norman Berrow.

Dope Tales #3 — Two enchanting novels of opium by the master, Sax Rohmer. *Dope* and *The Yellow Claw*.

Tenebrae — Ernest G. Henham's 1898 horror tale brought back.

The Singular Problem of the Stygian House-Boat — Two classic tales by John Kendrick Bangs about the denizens of Hades.

Tiresias — Psychotic modern horror novel by Jonathan M. Sweet.

The One After Snelling — Kickass modern noir from Richard O'Brien.

The Sign of the Scorpion — 1935 Edmund Snell tale of oriental evil.

The House of the Vampire — 1907 poetic thriller by George S. Viereck.

An Angel in the Street — Modern hardboiled noir by Peter Genovese.

The Devil's Mistress — Scottish gothic tale by J. W. Brodie-Innes.

The Lord of Terror — 1925 mystery with master-criminal, Fantômas.

The Lady of the Terraces — 1925 adventure by E. Charles Vivian.

My Deadly Angel — 1955 Cold War drama by John Chelton

Prose Bowl — Futuristic satire — Bill Pronzini & Barry N. Malzberg .

Satan's Den Exposed — True crime in Truth or Consequences New Mexico — Award-winning journalism by the *Desert Journal*.

The Amorous Intrigues & Adventures of Aaron Burr — by Anonymous — Hot historical action.

I Stole $16,000,000 — A true story by cracksman Herbert E. Wilson.

The Black Dark Murders — Vintage 50s college murder yarn by Milt Ozaki, writing as Robert O. Saber.

Sex Slave — Potboiler of lust in the days of Cleopatra — Dion Leclerq.

You'll Die Laughing — Bruce Elliott's 1945 novel of murder at a practical joker's English countryside manor.

The Private Journal & Diary of John H. Surratt — The memoirs of the man who conspired to assassinate President Lincoln.

Dead Man Talks Too Much — Hollywood boozer by Weed Dickenson

Red Light — History of legal prostitution in Shreveport Louisiana by Eric Brock. Includes wonderful photos of the houses and the ladies.

A Snark Selection — Lewis Carroll's *The Hunting of the Snark* with two Snarkian chapters by Harry Stephen Keeler — Illustrated by Gavin L. O'Keefe.

Ripped from the Headlines! — The Jack the Ripper story as told in the newspaper articles in the *New York* and *London Times.*

Geronimo — S. M. Barrett's 1905 autobiography of a noble American.

The White Peril in the Far East — Sidney Lewis Gulick's 1905 indictment of the West and assurance that Japan would never attack the U.S.

The Compleat Calhoon — All of Fender Tucker's works: Includes *Totah Six-Pack, Weed, Women and Song* and *Tales from the Tower,* plus a CD of all of his songs.

Totah Six-Pack — Just Fender Tucker's six tales about Farmington in one sleek volume.

RAMBLE HOUSE

Fender Tucker, Prop.

www.ramblehouse.com   fender@ramblehouse.com

228-826-1783   10329 Sheephead Drive, Vancleave MS 39565